BACK IN BLACK

Black Knights Inc: Reloaded

JULIE ANN WALKER

To the original Black Knights Inc. fans…
You didn't think the ride was over, did you?

Nations do not die from invasion;
they die from internal rottenness.

—Jenkin Lloyd Jones

PROLOGUE

Arlington County, Virginia

H unter Jackson was happy for the AC.

The Mid-Atlantic states could be stifling in the relentless high summer heat, and he'd arrived at the meeting in full dress uniform. His medals weighed heavily upon his chest. His wool beret sat hotly upon his head. And the tailored jacket with its metal buttons made his movements stiff and awkward.

At least he wasn't alone in his discomfort. Arranged around the conference table were five guys, similarly attired. And even had they not been advertising their ranks, affiliations, and commendations on their sleeves and chests, he would've known them for what they were.

It was there in the way they carried themselves, so straight and sure and maybe just a bit cocky. There in the solid cant to their jaws.

There in the hard gleam in their eyes.

The men who'd arrive to the meeting had blood on their hands. Because anyone who followed orders ended up that way eventually. And each of them had considered consuming a lead diet at some point. Because everyone in their line of work, who had even an ounce of self-reflection, had seen and done enough bad shit that they recognized it was possible the world might be better off without them.

Stone-cold combatants.

Granite-hewn warriors.

Spec-ops soldiers.

Although, the giant seated across from Hunter wore the white uniform and the trident pin that identified him as a Navy SEAL. So technically, he was a spec-ops *sailor.*

They'd been shown into the windowless room in the bowels of the Pentagon by a balding man in a three-piece suit. But no introductions had been made. No explanations for why they'd been summoned had been offered. Which meant they'd sat in closed-mouth silence for the last five minutes.

One of the first things a man learns when it comes to all things covert and clandestine, Hunter thought as he unconsciously wound the antique watch strapped around his wrist, *is silence really is a virtue.*

Nothing graced the drab gray walls of the room except for a round, analog clock that kept the time and reminded him he'd been up well before the sun. The air was filled with the smells of fresh starch, shoe polish, and a mixture of aftershaves. Hushed and harried voices sounded beyond the closed door, making him take a deep breath in preparation for…well… whatever the hell this was.

He was used to being called into action in the middle of the night. Came with the territory for any Green Beret. But never had that call summoned him to the heart of the D.O.D.

"Sorry to keep you waiting. It's been one of those days." A tall man with broad shoulders and salt-and-pepper hair rushed into the room. He grabbed a seat at the head of the table and slapped down a stack of files.

Hunter noted his name graced the tab on the file second from the top and felt a frisson of foreboding skim down his spine. Whatever was about to happen in the drab, gray room, whatever was about to be discussed, was going to be life-changing.

Now…whether that change was going to be good or bad, he couldn't say.

"Although," the man went on after shooting his cuffs and adjusting the knot on his tie, "it's probably more appropriate to say it's been one of those six months. Ever since Madam President took office, it's been pedal to the metal."

"Holy shit!" The guy sitting cattycorner from Hunter and sporting the insignia for the 75th Ranger Regiment leaned forward in his chair. He had an amiable Midwestern accent that pegged him as having been raised in a place that grew two things: corn and evangelicals. "You're Leonard Meadows, chief of staff."

Hunter watched the older man incline his head and realized the ranger was right. He remembered seeing Meadows standing behind the president when she took her oath of office.

"And you're Sergeant Britt Rollins," Meadows replied. "The man who led the successful raid on Abu al-Bakr's compound in November 2020."

Hunter raised an eyebrow. That'd been a hell of a coup. A mission that'd earned the respect of every Special Forces operator who'd ever held the title.

In typical army fashion, Rollins shrugged self-deprecatingly and gave credit where credit was due. "Couldn't have done it without my team, sir. That job was a joint effort from start to finish."

The chief of staff narrowed his eyes consideringly. "Speaking of the job, Sergeant Rollins, do you enjoy it?"

The ranger's chin jerked back in surprise and Hunter found his own chin doing a little downward jig. It was rare to be asked that question, especially given the nature of the work they did. People didn't like the idea of someone actually *enjoying* being a soldier.

After a brief hesitation, Rollins answered honestly. "They pay me to do it, sir, not to enjoy it."

The man sitting next to Rollins, a handsome son of a gun sporting the Delta Force Airborne insignia, snorted in agreement while a small smile curled the corners of Meadow's stern-looking mouth.

It appeared the chief of staff was pleased by Rollins's response. That, or he'd been expecting something along those lines.

When he turned his piercing gaze on Hunter, training and habit had Hunter sitting straighter. "And what about you, Major Jackson?" Meadow's deep voice was tinged with curiosity. "When you think about your career so far, what do you envision for your future?"

Hunter could've prevaricated or given the standard response. *"I'm a military man through and through. I plan to keep on keepin' on climbing those ranks, sir."* But, like the ranger, he went with the unvarnished truth. "To be honest, I don't think much about yesterday *or* tomorrow. Yesterday is full of shit…" He winced. The military was known for cursory cursing. Sometimes he forgot to sensor himself around civilians.

"Sorry." He cleared his throat. "What I should've said is yesterday is full of things I'd just as soon forget. And tomorrow may never come, so there's no use wasting my time on it."

"Mmm." Meadows nodded and then continued around the table, asking each man a slightly different question, and getting back the same kind of response.

When he got to the end of the line, he sat back in his chair, steepling his fingers under his freshly shaved chin. "I have a proposition for you gentlemen." His tone made the hairs on Hunter's arms stand on end. In dread or anticipation, he couldn't say. "I hope each of you will seriously consider it."

Hunter listened intently to the chief of staff as he offered them a deal that seemed almost too good to be true. And when Meadows finished his pitch, silence cloaked the room. The only sound to break it was the *hum* of the air conditioner and the *thud* of Hunter's own racing heart.

Exhaling slowly, he practiced box-breathing and felt the beginnings of…maybe not excitement, but something a lot like it.

CHAPTER 1

Starke County, Indiana
Three and a half years later…

"**S**ome nights are so dark the dawn seems impossible."
The words Grace Beacham's father spoke to her that awful evening her husband filed for divorce came back to her as she used the outdoor spigot to wash the blood from her hands. Hands so shaky she could barely perform the task. Hands so pale the brightness shining from her lit cell phone screen made the skin appear translucent. She could see her veins snaking beneath her flesh like holding a leaf up to the sunlight.

Her father had been talking about the depths of her despair and the weight of her failure. But now she felt the simple truth of his words.

If she believed that text message, this moonless night may very well be her last.

Rubbing her wet hands on her thighs, she snatched her phone off the ground and forced herself to look at the screen again. Hoping the text had magically disappeared.

No such luck.

Who would think six little words could have terror weighing her down until her body felt like a bag of wet concrete?

Orpheus is hunting you. Run. Hide.

"Who's out there?"

When the porch light snapped on, she thumbed off her phone and crouched next to the bushes. They still had a few late summer blooms, and the smell from the flowers was sickeningly sweet.

She'd been sure no one was home. The house had been dark. There'd been no cars in the gravel drive. No bark of a dog on the lookout for trespassers.

"I heard the water running!" the raspy voice called again. "I know you're there. Show yourself!"

This command was followed by a sound Grace would recognize anywhere. For as long as she could remember, her father had carried a Glock 22. The weapon made a very specific metallic *shnick* when a round was chambered.

Damnit!

"FBI! Don't shoot!" She thrust her hands in the air at the same time she stood to her full height. When the yellow porch light beamed into her eyes, she squinted and scolded herself for stopping.

It'd take a full minute for her eyesight to adjust to the darkness after this. And on such a night, a minute could be the difference between life and death.

A ratty terry cloth robe covered the man who stepped through the open front door of the creaking old farmhouse that was nearly as bent and grizzled as he was. The few tufts of snow-white hair atop his liver-spotted head waved gently in the warm breeze.

The end of August in the upper Midwest was a capricious creature. Sometimes it held onto summer with tenacious fingers. Other times it slipped quickly and quietly into fall.

This August was shaping up to be one of the hottest on record.

As if on cue, a bead of sweat cut through the dust on the side of her face. The warm drop reminded her of the blood she'd washed into the man's flowerbed. How hot it'd been when she pressed her hands over the wound in Stewart's back. And then how quickly it'd turned cool and dried into a sticky crust that had stained her cuticles and coated the undersides of her fingernails. The iron-rich smell of it had made her retch anytime she'd breathed too deeply.

Hence, her giving in to the urge to use the outdoor spigot.

"FBI, eh?" The old coot stepped farther onto the porch. The wooden beams groaned under his slippered feet. "Got some ID to prove that, missy?"

"If you'll allow me to reach into—"

"Easy there." He waved his pistol in a fast circle. "One hand'll do 'er. Keep that other one sky-high if ya know what's good for ya."

She obliged. Partly because she didn't want to take a round center-mass. But mostly because the act of swinging the gun loosened the belt tied around the man's waist. She was beginning to suspect he was naked beneath that threadbare robe.

Wouldn't that be the cherry on top of this craptastic sundae? she thought a little hysterically. *Here it is, possibly my final night on earth, and one of my last visions will be of ancient, wrinkly wedding tackle.*

"You're the boss." She kept her right arm in the air and used her left to slowly pull her FBI credentials from the inside breast pocket of her jacket.

Unfortunately, he didn't lower his weapon even after she flashed her badge. "That real?" he asked instead.

"Why would a woman in a pantsuit be standing in your yard in the middle of the night with a fake FBI badge?" she countered, wincing when her impatience came through in her tone.

"You tell me." He hitched a narrow shoulder. "What were you doin' with my outdoor faucet, eh?"

"Getting a drink. It's a hot night."

"But what's an FBI agent doin' all the way out here?"

Running for her life, she thought, feeling the effects of the panic and desperation that'd been her dogged companions since she'd heard Stewart shout her name from the adjoining room. The thought of spending a few minutes rocking herself in a corner and indulging in a good old-fashioned pity party complete with teeth gnashing and hair pulling sounded really, *really* tempting.

Unfortunately, she didn't have the time.

"My partner and I are staying at the Moonlight Memories Motel down the road. We had a suspect escape and head in this direction. I gave chase on foot but lost the trail in the woods. When I stumbled on your house, I couldn't pass up the chance for water."

Lies. All lies.

They came to her easily, but that didn't mean they didn't sit on her tongue like poison pills. Having grown up a Beacham, she'd been taught being a straight shooter—both literally and figuratively—was the only thing that mattered.

"A suspect, eh?" The man lifted an eyebrow so bushy Grace imagined some of the hair from his head must've migrated down his face. "He the dangerous sort?"

"You should go inside and lock the door behind you. Better safe than sorry," she answered evasively.

The well-timed *ee-oo-ee* of a siren sounded in the distance. Usually she took comfort in the familiar hi-lo clammer. This time, and despite the stickiness of the night, she had to suppress a shiver.

"Those will be my colleagues." She was glad to give the codger at least one truth, even if it was only a *half* truth.

The sirens weren't crying out for some mysterious missing man. They were crying out for her. *She* was the suspect.

"Alrighty." To her relief, he lowered his sidearm and took a step back inside the door. "Happy hunting to ya, Miss FBI Agent. Hope ya catch the guy."

"Thanks." She offered him what she hoped passed for a smile and didn't wait around to see if he did as she instructed and locked the door behind him. Instead, she turned and sprinted for the cover of the woods.

The rubber lug soles of her sensible duty shoes seemed to find every twig and snap it in two. Spindly limbs made clattering noises as she brushed by because her night-blind eyes made them impossible to avoid. Her labored breathing sounded as loud as thunder as she bolted...where?

Where the hell am I going?

She had no idea.

Usually, when she was scared or in trouble, she ran home. Between her father, who was a sheriff, her two older brothers, who were both cops, and her kid sister, who was busy climbing the ranks of the U.S. Marshals, *one* of them would help her find a solution to her problem.

But she couldn't leave a trail back to Buncombe County. She didn't dare drag her family into this.

Whatever *this* was.

Skidding to a halt beside a fallen tree, she pressed a hand to the stitch in her side as she tried to catch her breath and think. *Think.* If she had any hope of making it through the night she needed her wits about her.

Something moved in the undergrowth to her left. Somewhere off in the distance an owl hooted. To her right? The snap of a twig broken by a footfall.

Instinct had her flattening herself beside the log. The rich smell of fertile soil and decaying plant matter tunneled up her nose. And she bit her lip to keep from crying out when another footfall landed on crunchy leaves.

Orpheus!

Her palms were so clammy she could barely grasp the butt of her service weapon as she slowly, ever so slowly, slipped her hand beneath her body to pull the semiauto from its leather holster.

How? *How* could Russia's most notorious assassin, a man whose very existence was hotly debated, have learned what she and her partner were up to?

Of course, as much as she might wish it weren't so, she knew how. It was just as she and Stewart had suspected.

Now the question became, since Orpheus *did* know, and since he'd been sicced on her by some mysterious player in this game of cat and mouse, how could she possibly survive him when so many before her had not?

Run. Hide, the text had read. But run to whom? Hide where?

The forest less than a mile from the motel wasn't exactly a world away from the scene of the crime. And this fallen log wasn't exactly a safe house.

She needed a place off the grid while she worked things out. She needed someone who could help her disappear into darkness so deep that not even the world's brightest spotlight could find her. She needed—

The crackle of another snapping stick had her squeezing her eyes shut. A poisonous brine of despair and terror swirled in her stomach. And muscles filled with adrenaline and twitching from inaction prompted her to leap up and run. Just escape into the night in heedless flight.

Before her lizard brain could take over and push her into foolhardy action, she heard a flurry of movement followed by the *clomp-clomp* of hoofbeats as something four-legged dashed off to the north. Straining her eyes against the darkness, she caught a brief flash of white through the trunks of the trees.

Not Orpheus. A whitetail deer foraging in the undergrowth. It'd spooked when it caught her scent.

"You won't last ten more minutes if you keep on like this," she admonished herself.

Before she could talk herself out of it, she re-holstered her Glock 19M and pulled her cell phone from her hip pocket.

Hiding the device inside her suit jacket—she didn't dare let the lit screen pinpoint her position—she thumbed it on. Her fingers trembled as she punched in her six-digit code and then immediately hit the phone icon.

She didn't need to scroll through her contacts. She could key in the telephone number by heart.

A thousand. That's how many times she'd stared at those digits since he'd plugged them into her cell. Nine-hundred-and-ninety-nine. That's how many times she'd been tempted to hit the "call" button so she could hear his voice. Nine-hundred-and-ninety-eight. That's how many times she'd refrained from doing exactly that.

There'd been that one time early on when she'd given into the urge. But she'd hit "end" before the first ring. Because an image of how his hazel eyes had held such sympathy, how his beautifully stern mouth had softened with compassion when he'd said, *"If you ever need anything, even if it's just a willing ear to listen, please call"* had popped into her head.

It'd been three years, but the sting of his pity still felt fresh.

Then and now, she hated that all he'd seen when he looked at her was a charity case. A spurned divorcee. A fragile woman who'd been rendered meek and mute when she'd come face-to-face with her ultimate failure in the middle of the Waldorf Astoria Hotel's ballroom.

She'd hoped that one day, if they ever bumped into each other in the real world, she'd be able to show him who she *truly* was. A strong woman. An independent woman. A woman capable of facing all comers.

And yet...here she was reaching out in desperation to the mysterious man who'd haunted her dreams. The enigmatic operator who'd entered her life in an instant, seemingly from out of nowhere, and then disappeared just as quickly.

Hunter Jackson.

His name was enough to make her mouth go dry.

CHAPTER 2

Black Knights Inc,
Goose Island, Chicago, Illinois

For those who knew how to listen to their senses—senses passed down through eons of ancestral memory—it was easy to detect an approaching threat.

Hunter knew how to listen.

His first warning someone snuck up behind him were the fine hairs lifting on the back of his neck. His second warning was the subtle, nearly imperceptible shift of the air around him.

When a hand landed on his shoulder, he instinctively ducked and spun. His arm flew out in a semi-arc as he used his momentum to aim the hard edge of his hand at his assailant's ribs. His attacker blocked his blow at the last second by chopping at his wrist.

Pain exploded in the joint. He barely noticed as his muscles coiled to take a second shot.

Of course, as soon as he saw it was only Samuel Harwood, he straightened from his fighting stance. "What the hell?" He plucked out his earbuds and pocketed them. AC/DC's "Back in Black" was replaced by the low *hum* of the overhead light and the quiet of the night. "You know better than to sneak up on a man programmed for extreme violence. I can't just shut that shit off."

Sam rolled his eyes. "Bruh, there's no one here but me, you, and Eliza. Who did you think would be coming at you sideways? This place"—Sam gestured around the cavernous space that used to be a menthol cigarette factory and now fronted as a custom chopper shop—"is Fort friggin' Knox."

"Sometimes muscle memory takes over," Hunter explained with a careless shrug. "Especially this late and when I'm low on sleep."

Sam shook his head. "You're gonna make a therapist very wealthy someday."

"You're one to talk."

"True," Sam agreed easily. "The difference between you and me, though, is that my way of coping with trauma is to employ a little gallows humor. Totally normal. Totally healthy. Your way is to go full-on hermit for days at a time. Ted Kaczynski ring a bell? Should I check your room for pipe bombs and triggering devices?"

Hunter hated how clearly Sam saw him. Not about being Unabomber 2.0, but about having to squirrel himself away in order to keep himself together.

Blame it on his youth. When things had gotten too chaotic, his only means of self-preservation had been to hide away in the abandoned cabin perched on the edge of town. There'd been no electricity. No running water. And the hole in the roof had let the rain and snow drift in. Still, he'd felt better there than he had anywhere else.

Cut to the present and he *still* only felt truly at ease when he was removed from the rest of the world. Somewhere quiet where he could listen to his own thoughts instead of other people's words. Somewhere hidden where he could be totally and completely *alone*.

Of course, he said none of that aloud. Aloud he told Sam, "Fuck you."

"Not even on your birthday," Sam deadpanned. "Besides, I wouldn't know what to do with your teeny, tiny Tic Tac testis and itty, bitty micro-peen. I mean, how *do* you manage to keep the ladies coming back for more? Do you always do it in the dark so they can't see what they're dealing with?"

The thing about men whose jobs required them to flirt with danger on the daily was that they tended to cut the tension by gleefully feeding each other heaping helpings of shit.

Hunter shook his head. "See, that would be funny except you know it's not true. You've seen what I'm packing. That time in Karachi?"

Sam shuddered. "Don't remind me. I dunno which was worse. That we had a deathstalker scorpion living under our bathroom sink? Or that when you found him, you ran out of there buck naked and screaming your head off? I still have nightmares."

"About the scorpion?"

"About your candy stick and giggleberries bouncing six inches from my face."

"Ah. I understand." Hunter nodded solemnly. "There's that old saying about comparison being the thief of joy, right?" He clapped a commiserating hand on Sam's shoulder. "I hate that I burst your bubble of self-delusion. But if you're really worried about it, I've heard there's some surgical options. A silicone implant? Maybe a fat transfer? Or you could even—"

"Well, look at you," Sam cut him off, "lowering yourself to aspersions about the size of my willy. What gives? When it comes to being a weapons-grade dingus, you usually leave that to me or Fisher."

Hunter snorted. *Weapons-grade dingus.* Sam had a rare gift for words. Which was probably why he liked Coen Brothers movies so much. They were filled with snappy, fast-fire dialogue.

"Blame it on us being left behind," Hunter admitted, taking a deep breath of air perfumed with the competing, and yet somehow complementary, scents of too-strong coffee and grease guns. "I hate having nothing to do. Makes my skin feel too tight for my body." To emphasize his point, he hitched his shoulder blades together.

"You and me both, brother." Sam nodded. "But I'm trying to focus on the bright side. We may hafta hold down the fort, but that's a thousand times better'n playing babysitter to some politician's spoiled spawn."

Black Knights Inc. had been the brainchild of President Thompson and the last administration. And even though the players had changed right along with the leadership when Madam President took over the seat at 1600 Pennsylvania Ave, the concept was still the same.

Some jobs were too clandestine or too pressing to leave to the usual suspects. Despite most of the people working for the CIA, FBI, and NSA being good at their jobs, their hands were often tied by red tape. Which meant threats against the U.S. slipped through the cracks as solutions and actions were debated by committee. Throw in posse comitatus and the international resistance to certain types of government-backed exercises, and the bad guys were allowed to escape scot-free more often than anyone would like to admit.

This frustration had prompted President Thompson to form his own *fast action response team*, for lack of a better phrase. He'd scoured military branches and government agencies for the best of the best when it came to spycraft and those gifted in reconnaissance, unconventional warfare tactics, and the ability to counter terrorism. Then he'd found a home for those highly trained individuals in the heart of Chicago. And when it'd been her turn in the hot seat, Madam President had done the same.

Behind the façade of a custom motorcycle shop worked the most elite, most covert group of spec-ops warriors the world had ever seen.

Warriors who didn't have to run their mission parameters up the chain of command. Warriors who could fly into action at a moment's notice and operate in complete secrecy without their actions being traced back to anyone inside the federal government. Warriors who sometimes got assigned bodyguarding jobs as a favor to Madam President herself.

Three days earlier, the Black Knights had received a request to ensure the secretary of defense's daughter didn't get kidnapped or killed on her end-of-summer trip to Venezuela. But the job had only called for four of the six current BKI operators since there were only four extra seats on the political debutante's private plane.

Hunter and Sam had drawn the short straws.

Or the long straws if one was to side with Sam that being stuck at home was better than playing bullet-catcher for a twenty-year-old kid who didn't know the difference between danger and dessert.

"I'm so bored I could eat a tire iron," Hunter lamented.

When he was on the job, his gray matter was occupied with how best to breach a position or take down a tango or rescue a hostage. And when he was in *self-imposed exile*, as Sam liked to call his trips north, he focused his mind on chopping wood or figuring out the best way to turn an old cattle trough into a raised garden.

But more and more often, and especially recently, when he found himself at loose ends, his brain filled up with thoughts about his future.

Or, more specifically, his *lack* thereof.

In the three and a half years since he'd come to work for BKI, he'd been watching the original crew, all the hardened operators who'd answered to the previous president and who'd left their mark behind on the world of international intrigue. To a man, the OG Black Knights had moved on with their lives. They'd gotten married and fathered children. They'd proved that even for guys like them, guys like *Hunter*, there was something to look forward to after service.

Except…it was different for Hunter, wasn't it? Not only did he not have the first clue how to build a family since he'd never been part of one, but he also lacked the basic means to begin even if he *had* known where to start.

The thought of never marrying, never becoming a dad, hadn't bothered him before. Mostly because he'd assumed it would be a miracle if he didn't end up running into a bullet with his name on it; *covert operator* was just a prettied-up description of a guy who grubbed for tin as a means of employment. But also because he'd had no clue what he was missing.

The men who'd come before him had had the unwitting audacity to show him everything he'd never thought was possible. Show him that even guys who'd witnessed so much brutality and bloodshed could still have the capacity to embrace domesticity. Show him just how sweet the flip side could be.

Now he was left wanting. *Wishing.*

Which pissed him off.

He hadn't wanted or wished since he'd been a kid and learned the hard way that life wasn't fair and that not everybody got their happily-ever-after.

"Well, you're better off twiddling your dick than messing with *that.*" Sam hitched his chin toward the motorcycle frame secured to the bike lift. "What the hell are you doing anyway?"

"I sanded off the powder coat on the engine mount so I can install the V Twin and the transmission," Hunter told him, happy to have his somber thoughts interrupted.

One of Sam's dark eyebrows arched so high it was nearly lost in his hairline. "Did Becky say you could do that?"

Becky Knight, née Reichert, was the wunderkind mechanic and motorcycle designer who made it possible for them to keep their covers intact.

Her creations were the faces Black Knights Inc. showed the world. Works of rolling, roaring art sought after by collectors from Texas to Taiwan. The ultra-wealthy stood in line to drop a quarter mil on something that only had two wheels. And professional athletes couldn't seem to pass up the flash and fury of a hand-designed and hand-built Harley.

Which was all to say, Becky was *super* picky about who she let touch her babies.

"She had no problem letting me do the last install." Hunter shrugged, figuring three and a half years of part-time apprenticeship meant he could mount an engine without Becky standing over his shoulder and supervising. "I thought it'd be a nice surprise when she comes into the shop in the morning. You know, one less thing."

Not to mention, he'd needed a distraction from the dream that'd had him waking up covered in sweat and throbbing with need.

For shit's sake, it's been three years! When are you going to forget her? It was four measly days and one little kiss.

Except, it *hadn't* been one little kiss, had it?

It was cliché, but he would swear the instant his lips touched hers, a piece of himself he hadn't known was missing locked into place. Just *click*.

It'd felt as if he'd...*come home.*

Which was ridiculous since he didn't *have* a home. Had *never* had one.

The dozens of crappy apartments his DNA suppliers had moved into and then been promptly kicked out of hadn't counted—he never thought of Bert and Susan Jackson as his *parents*; that title was reserved for people who actually protected and provided for their offspring. And the ten different foster families he'd been shuffled through after CPS intervened? None of those could carry the mantle of *home* either. At best they'd been temporary shelters where he'd gotten in out of the rain. At worst they'd been prisons manned by cruel adults whose sole incentive was to cash the government checks that'd come their way with each new kid they took in.

So what the hell was the matter with him? *Why* did he continue to dream two...three times a week of Grace Beacham and that kiss? Why, after all this time, did he continue to hold out hope she'd call him?

"Be sure to wake me up before you come downstairs in the morning," Sam said, and Hunter determinedly pushed all thoughts of Grace aside.

"Why?" He frowned.

"'Cause I wanna have time to pop some popcorn before the show."

"What show?"

"The one where Becky rips you two or three new assholes."

Hunter and Sam had grown up less than a hundred miles apart. But you'd never know it to hear them talk. Hunter had the quintessential Michigander accent, his vowels flat and his consonants staccato. But Sam? Sam's accent was pure Chicago Southsider.

Instead of *two or three*, when Sam said them, the words came out sounding like *two or tree*.

"Pfft." Hunter waved him off and then pointed to the chromed-out engine sitting on a nearby workbench.

He'd never been much of a motorcycle guy before coming to work for BKI. Now he couldn't get enough of the machines. When he wasn't on assignment or snugged away in his hidey hole, he could be found in the shop wielding a grinder or paint sprayer.

Maybe if things had been different, maybe if he'd been given a chance to decide what to do with his life instead of being forced to accept the only ticket out of town, he might've become a mechanic. A man who fixed things instead of destroying them.

"Help me lift this thing over the bike's rails so I don't scuff up the paint," he told Sam.

"Oh, no." Sam backed away. "My asshole is fine the way it is, thank you very much. And I'd prefer to keep it down to just the one."

Hunter rolled his eyes. "Becky is a hair over five feet and barely weighs a buck-ten. Don't tell me Sam the Supergun is afraid of her."

"What she lacks in physical presence she makes up for with a razor-sharp tongue. Besides, getting on her bad side is the shortest route to getting on Boss's bad side. And I don't know about you, but I've gone three and a half years without seeing that guy get angry. I'd like to keep it that way."

Boss, AKA Frank Knight, was Becky's husband. The retired Navy SEAL had been the original head honcho at BKI, but now his job title was CEO of the civilian side of their operation. He was part mentor, part benevolent landlord, and *all* dad all the time to his two little girls. But he had a habit of spinning a fixed-blade KA-BAR knife atop his desk when he was deep in thought that made Hunter think Sam was right. There was a scary side to Boss they didn't want to meet.

"Fine." He marched over to the workbench. "I'll do it myself."

"It's your funeral," Sam warned.

Before Hunter could wrap his arms around the heavy engine, his phone buzzed in his back pocket.

"It's two o'clock in the morning." Sam checked the time on his watch. "That's one thing and one thing only. Booty call."

Hunter wasn't what anyone would label a monk. Recently, however, he'd been whittling down the list of lovely ladies who occasionally phoned up to ask if he wanted company.

When he'd been in his twenties, having no strings attached and a willing woman in every port had been a dream come true. But he'd just celebrated his thirty-fifth birthday, and meaningless sex with partners who were simply passing through, or who couldn't be bothered to ask him more than his name, had lost its appeal. The hit-it-and-quit-it of it all had grown routine. Dull. *Hollow.*

He wanted more. He wanted…

What?

What was he looking for?

If he searched for the answer, he knew he'd find it. And he knew he wouldn't like it. So he pulled his cell from his back pocket and told himself he'd say yes to whichever woman was inviting him over. Told himself that the antidote to his boredom, and the best way to get over all his uncomfortable musings about what was missing in his life, was to get *under* a beautiful woman who wasn't asking him for anything more than a night of pleasure.

Except…he didn't recognize the number on his screen.

"Area code 202." He frowned at Sam. "That's D.C."

Sam nodded. "Which of your current paramours lives in the capitol?"

"Not a single one."

"Wrong number then?" Sam asked.

"Probably so." Hunter went to hit the button on the side of his phone. But at the last second, he hesitated. He didn't believe in the woo-woo magical alchemy of premonition or precognition, but something told him he should answer.

Something told him it was important.

Thumbing on the device, he held it to his ear. "Hello?"

"Hunter?"

He nearly shit his own heart. He would never forget the sound of her sultry voice, so sweet and smooth and hinting at her raising in the South. Whenever she spoke, he was reminded of tupelo honey.

"Grace?" By contrast, his voice came out strangled-sounding.

"I'm in trouble, Hunter. I need your help."

CHAPTER 3

Starke County, Indiana

The flutter of unseen wings matched the beat of Grace's heart.

Having grown up in the middle of the Appalachian Mountains, she was used to the sound of animals scurrying through the underbrush. Familiar with the deafening buzz of night insects calling for their mates. Accustomed to the cries of nocturnal creatures that'd been caught in the jaws of carnivorous beasts.

None of it had frightened her before.

Then again, *she* had never been the prey before.

She was the prey now.

The denizens of the forest grew quiet when the one who hunted her passed by. The warm wind shifted, and she caught a faint whiff of tobacco smoke. And there! She could just make out a dark shadow snaking around the trunks of the trees.

She was out of places to run.

And this was the only place she'd found to hide.

Clutching her sidearm close to her chest, she remained stock-still inside the oversized drainpipe running beneath the roadway. When fear tried to claw its way up the back of her throat, she did her best to swallow it down.

Her instincts told her to take aim and fire.

Logic and training kept her from listening.

It might not be Orpheus dogging her ever step. It could be one of her colleagues, an innocent FBI agent simply doing what they'd tasked him to do.

Besides, if Grace fired and missed—which, as good a shot as she was, was likely since the man was still deep inside the woods—she would give away her position. That was the dead last thing she wanted. This spot in the road, and more specifically the mile marker above her head, was where she'd told Hunter she'd meet him.

Even though she was a little hazy on which agency or branch of the government he worked for, she knew he called the Windy City home. Convenient since her latest assignment had brought her to Koontz Lake, Indiana. A wide spot in the road less than two hours from Chicago.

But it'd been dumb luck, or maybe simply good timing, he'd actually *been* home when she phoned. One of the few details he'd shared during their brief association had been that he spent more time out-conus—military speak for outside the continental U.S.—than he did in.

She wished she could check the time again on her phone. But after hanging up with him, she'd run a mile up the road and chucked the device over the side of an overpass.

Her cell was government-issued, encrypted, and difficult to trace. But there was a difference between difficult and impossible. Give her colleagues enough time and they *would* hack into her signal and pinpoint her location.

Plus, there was a golden rule when it came to going on the lam: lay down tracks in the opposite direction. Her phone was east of her position. And hopefully, once Hunter arrived, she'd be headed due west.

Once Hunter arrived…

If Hunter arrived.

How long has it been since I made that call?

Ninety minutes that felt like ninety hours.

Ninety minutes where she'd tried to sort out when and where and how her investigation had gone so wrong. Ninety minutes where she'd made herself stay still inside her hiding place even though her left leg was asleep and a beetle kept crawling back and forth across her lap. Ninety minutes of hoping and praying Hunter would believe her when no one else seemed to.

Headlights rounded the bend and hope swelled in her heart. It deflated like a popped balloon when the car passed the mile marker without slowing, its tires creating a hollow-sounding roar above her head that reminded her of the High Falls in Dupont State Forest where her father had taken her and her siblings camping during fall breaks.

What she wouldn't give to be back there now. Safe in the arms of family. Happy in a place where the only bad thing to ever happen was her oldest brother's twisted ankle.

The man in the woods ran headlong into a line of bramble bushes. She knew it was a line of bramble bushes because she'd stumbled through them herself.

She'd silently cursed even as she'd charged toward the safety of the quiet country road and the hollow steel drain running beneath it. Her pursuer wasn't so circumspect. He let loose with two words that made her mouth fall open in a soundless scream.

She didn't speak Russian. She had no idea what *zalupa konskaya* meant. But there was no longer any question who was out there.

It *was* Orpheus.

Whoever sent her that text had been telling the truth.

Terror fueled her movements as she carefully slipped her pointer finger from the trigger guard and curled it around the cool metal of the trigger itself. When her head buzzed, she raked in a slow, steadying lungful of air that smelled of damp concrete mixed with the cloying aroma of decaying flesh.

Something dead lay in a puddle of rainwater at the other end of the storm drain. She hoped like hell she wouldn't be joining its ranks anytime soon.

Concentrating on the sound of the assassin's approach, her brain absently noted that a mockingbird called from the trees. A bullfrog croaked from the tall grass near the side of the road. And off in the distance came the low rumble of thunder.

No. Not thunder. An engine.

A *big* engine.

Like the kind in a muscle car and—

Once again, headlights.

She chewed her bottom lip and didn't allow herself to take her eyes off the trees. If the headlights spotlighted the Russian, she would take her shot.

Her father's slow, Appalachian drawl sounded in her head. *"Fix your weapon on the target, Grace. Gently pull the trigger. Don't yank it."*

She'd been twelve years old the first time he'd put a gun in her hands. She realized how ridiculous that would sound to most people. But to the Beachams, mountain folks since King George II took over what would later become North Carolina from the lord proprietors and generated a land bonanza, learning to shoot, learning to handle a gun, was a rite of passage. A step into adulthood.

Her mother had taught her to shuck corn and make a quilt from fabric scraps, and her father had taught her to kill what she aimed at and to only aim at what she planned to kill.

Grace was a true-blue product of the hill country. A Blue Ridge Mountain girl through and through. And even though she would do things differently with her own kids—if she ever had any; her divorce had certainly thrown a wrench in *those* works—she couldn't find any fault in the way her folks had raised her.

Their parenting style might not have been conventional, but they'd given her the skills and the confidence to stand on her own two feet. And for that, she was forever grateful.

Wish I was sitting at Momma's table now, she thought longingly, *having buckwheat cakes and listening to Daddy talk about the Tourists' season.*

Her father enjoyed keeping up with the local minor league baseball club, the Asheville Tourists. And her mother loved to gift him with season tickets when they had the extra cash.

The noise from the approaching car grew obscenely loud and Grace grimaced. Then, to her relief, the big engine cycled down. When she heard a second vehicle shut off, she assumed Hunter had brought along backup.

In the next instant, however, her blood ran cold when her follow-up thought was that it was possible it wasn't Hunter on the road above. Maybe the Russian didn't work alone. Maybe Orpheus was the code name given to a group of—

"Grace?" Hunter's deep voice echoed into the night and she hiccupped on a sob she hadn't realized was sitting at the back of her throat.

"Hunter!" she screamed, bolting from the relative safety of the drainpipe and scrambling up the side of the embankment. Her motions were jerky;

she couldn't feel her left foot, only the pins-and-needles sensation of the blood rushing back into it. "I'm here! I'm coming!"

She could feel the Kremlin's assassin aiming at the invisible target on her back. Any second she expected a round to slam into her spine. Expected to feel the shock of the impact. The burst of agony.

But she topped the rise without any extra holes being drilled through her body. And the sight that met her eyes had her blinking in surprise.

It wasn't a pair of muscle cars parked in the middle of the roadway but a pair of motorcycles that appeared as mean as they were strangely beautiful. Two men in helmets and dark leather jackets sat astride the metal beasts.

Despite the darkness that was broken only by the white-hot glare of the bikes' headlights, she instantly knew which man was Hunter. The breadth of his shoulders and the casual way his gloved hand splayed across his denim-clad thigh was unmistakable. Even after three years.

"Start the engines!" she wailed, never breaking stride as her feet left the dirt of the shoulder and hit the pavement. "He's right behind me!"

Hunter didn't need to be told twice. He cranked over the bike's big engine and the night was once again filled with the throaty roar of a well-tuned piece of machinery. The second man followed suit. And by the time she made it to them, they'd swung the motorcycles around in the road.

She didn't wait to be invited before throwing her leg over the leather seat behind Hunter. Wrapping one arm around his waist, she screamed, "Go!" Then she turned to aim into the line of trees behind them.

Her desperate eyes searched for a tiny blackhole since the end of a weapon absorbed all light. But no matter how hard she looked...*nothing*.

No faint glint of matte-black metal caught in the glow of the taillights. No flash of orange because the shooter had taken his shot.

Hunter laid on the throttle and the bike's massive rear end fishtailed as its back tire fought for purchase on the pavement.

She was caught off guard. The only thing that saved her from being thrown off the bike and taking a face full of asphalt was Hunter. He reached around with one arm and pulled her tight against his back.

It was like being caught in a reverse bear hug.

Big, bulky guys might be able to throw their weight around. But guys who were lean and mean, with muscles made for stamina and staying power? *They* were the true strong men of the world.

And Hunter Jackson could be counted among them.

From one second to the next, they'd gone from a standstill to eating up the asphalt. The bikes' taillights cast the forest behind them in an eerie red wash. But that wasn't what made her shiver despite the warmth of the night.

It was the figure climbing the embankment.

The man made his way to the middle of the lonely, deserted road, but he didn't raise a weapon. He didn't shout or give chase. He just stood there, mouth pursed like he was blowing her a kiss.

No, she thought. *Not blowing me a kiss. He's whistling.*

She couldn't hear the tune over the rumble of the motorcycles. But something told her, had she heard it, she'd want to scrub her eardrums with bleach.

Pulling a lighter from his hip pocket, the Russian slowly lit a cigarette.

She shivered again when the yellow glow of the flame briefly lit his face. His features were made indistinct by the growing distance, but she was still close enough to catch the look in his eyes.

His casual curiosity seemed to scream his unconcern. It seemed to say he didn't doubt his ability to track her down and finish what he'd started.

It was an understatement to say she felt relief when they turned a corner and she could no longer see her pursuer. The sigh that shuddered out of her was long and windy.

She realized her hands were shaking when she tried to stow her gun and couldn't place the nose of her Glock inside its holster. It kept hitting the edge of the leather and sliding down the side.

Her third attempt was successful. And after snapping the strap over the butt of the weapon, she grabbed hold of Hunter with both hands.

The move was a relief in more ways than one. Not only was it nice to have something—some*one*—to hang onto when she felt so shaky she thought it a wonder her teeth weren't rattling around inside her mouth. But also, they were screaming down the road at sixty miles per hour and she was well aware of her precarious position perched on the back of the bike.

The wind buffeted her cheeks and yanked at her hair, caught the sides of her suit jacket and had it flapping behind her like a drunken bat. Hunter's reflected gaze in one of the rearview mirrors caught her attention. He tapped his helmet and then gestured toward the back of the bike.

Frowning, she turned to discover a helmet strapped to the U-shaped bar of the backrest.

Right, she thought. *Wouldn't it be ironic to escape Orpheus's clutches only to end up x-ed out from a head injury if I'm thrown off the motorcycle?*

The helmet was a little big and she struggled to secure the chin strap. But once she managed it, she snaked her arms back around Hunter's waist and yelled, "Thank you!"

He didn't so much as twitch. The noise of the booming engines and the wailing of the wind made it impossible for him to hear.

Just as well. Her heart was in her throat and beating hard enough to make talking, much less shouting, feel like someone was running a bottle brush across her tonsils.

Or maybe her sore throat could be blamed on her having held back frustrated screams for hours now.

Her operation was a bust, her partner was dead—*Jesus! Poor Stewart!*—a Russian assassin, not to mention her very own agency, was after her. And she had no idea where to begin to sort out any of it.

To make matters worse, she had to pee.

Her desperation to get far away from Koontz Lake, Indiana, was the only thing that kept her from poking Hunter on the shoulder and gesturing for him to pull over. Well, that and the last thing she wanted was for him to watch her run into the bushes and drop trou five minutes after racing to her rescue.

She needed to take her mind off her discomfort.

Fortunately, she was snuggled up behind the ultimate distraction.

Closing her eyes, she dragged the smell of Hunter into her lungs. A smell that was mixed with the aroma of the open road and the sweetness of the summer night.

For three years she'd dreamed of the complementary scents of spicy aftershave and leather oil. And she'd assumed that second note had to do with the antique watch he wore around his thick wrist. The one with the leather band. The one she'd noticed he wound when he was deep in thought.

Now, however, she realized he might smell of leather oil because he *wore* leather. Because he was some sort of spy/soldier/*biker*?

Didn't have quite the same ring as *Tinker, Tailor, Soldier, Spy* but it was close.

Who are you, Hunter Jackson?

The thought leaked out of her head when his gloved hand closed over the fingers she'd laced together at his waist. He gave her a pat before returning his grip to the handlebar.

It was a gesture of reassurance. Of comfort. And that small act of *noblesse oblige* had sudden tears burning the back of her throat.

Hunter was basically a stranger. One she hadn't seen or heard from in years. And yet, when she'd needed him, he'd come.

Without question.

Without hesitation.

She might not know who he worked for or who he really was. But one thing she knew for sure.

Tonight, he's my savior.

CHAPTER 4

"**S**he got away."

"What do you mean she got away?" The voice on the other end of the call sounded exasperated. Then again, to Pavel Siderov's ears, the American known as Bishop *always* sounded exasperated. It was his harried tone. His clipped words that even the voice changer could not disguise. "Did the FBI find her before you did?"

"*Nyet.*" Pavel shook his head and took another drag on his cigarette. "Two men on motorcycles took her just as I was closing in."

There was a brief pause. "Motorcycles? Did you catch the plates?"

"Illinois plates." Pavel was quick to scurry down the embankment when he heard a car approaching.

He took the car's measure as it sped by. SUV. Dark color. Factory-standard rims.

FBI, no doubt. Hunting for Agent Beacham.

Like always, they were one step behind.

His strategy to take out the male agent and frame the female agent for the murder had gone exactly to plan. Having studied human anatomy, he'd known just where to place the small blade so that death was inevitable. But the one thing he had *not* counted on? For Agent Beacham to run.

Why? he wondered.

In his experience, innocent people didn't run. They naively assumed the truth would set them free.

But the buxom blond agent had ducked out so fast no one had seen her leave. No one save for Pavel himself. And after spending a good thirty seconds blinking in surprise at her quickly retreating form, he'd given chase.

Unfortunately, having left his night-vision goggles in his rented car, he'd lost her in the darkness of the dense woods.

"The FBI just passed by," he told Bishop as he hopped back onto the road. "Probably tracking her phone. I suspect she tossed it."

"They won't find her. Not before you do."

Pavel was happy to hear the certainty in Bishop's voice.

Then again, why wouldn't the man be certain? After all, how many targets had Pavel neutralized for Bishop? A dozen? Two dozen? More?

When Bishop called, Pavel answered. Not only did Bishop pay well, but his ambitions closely aligned with Pavel's.

Bishop was after total societal collapse. The ruination of the American Dream. The spectacular downfall of that *shining city on the hill*, as Ronald Reagan had so often called the United States of America.

Pavel snorted at the audacity. *Imagine believing your country is such a beacon of hope for the world that you would refer to it in biblical terms.*

Things had changed in the decades since The Gipper occupied the oval office, and some of those things could be laid directly at the feet of the man himself. The seedy underbelly of American society had been exposed. All the corruption. All the bigotry, hate, racism and greed.

Pavel was happy to say he had not only watched the unmasking but had also played a part in it. Continued to play his part by irradicating any threats to people like Bishop.

Grace Beacham was a threat. One they'd hoped to easily nullify by making her look like a murderer. But the instant she'd run from the authorities, all bets were off. Her life was now forfeit.

Foolish woman.

"Give me the numbers for the plates," Bishop instructed. "I'll run them through the system. We need to find out who we're dealing with. Although, I think I already know."

"Do you?" Pavel's tone brightened with interest. "Who?"

"Trouble," Bishop said cryptically.

After Pavel rattled off the letters and numbers, he took one final drag on his cigarette. Tossing the butt onto the pavement, he crushed the smoldering tip with his bootheel and cut a sharp left, back into the trees. Back to the spot where he'd parked the rented car.

"What would you have me do now?" he asked as he opened the driver's side door and slid inside the vehicle.

"Cross your fingers I'm wrong about who has her. But head west toward Chicago all the same."

For the first time ever, Pavel detected a hint of apprehension in Bishop's altered voice. He was quick to reassure the man. "Trouble comes with the territory, yes? The plan has changed. But the outcome will be the same."

"If she's with who I think she's with? Things could get far more... *complicated*."

"I live for complications," he boasted. "They are the spice of life."

He disconnected the call without signing off. After pocketing the phone, he whistled his favorite tune.

Hunting humans always put a song in his heart and a skip in his step.

CHAPTER 5

Black Knights Inc.

H unter had assumed Grace's rattled nerves were the reason she'd spent the entire ninety-minute ride from Indiana to Chicago squirming around on the back of his bike.

As soon as they pulled up to the giant iron gates that kept the city of Chicago and all its inhabitants out of the BKI compound, however, he realized her nerves had nothing to do with her backseat boogie.

"Oh, thank god," she breathed when he cut the engine. "Ten more minutes and I might've pulled a Harry to your Lloyd."

"Huh?"

He'd like to blame his inarticulate response on lack of sleep. He'd only gotten a couple hours before the dream of her had wrenched him awake. And it was now going on six o'clock in the morning. But he knew the real reason he went all tongue-tied and ineloquent was because the instant he'd turned to look at her, he'd been struck by her eyes.

Those brown eyes that'd held him in their thrall since the first moment he'd seen them. Eyes that sparked with intelligence and wit. Eyes that could look soft and sad one minute, fierce and fiery the next.

Eyes that held a million mysteries.

Eyes he wanted to stare into until he'd solved each and every one.

"You know." She made a face as the morning sun peeked through the skyscrapers to the east, turning the sky overhead pink and gold. "*Dumb and Dumber*? The motor scooter scene? Come on, you must've seen it. It's a cult classic."

His mind latched onto a vague memory of the movie and the scene in question. He felt one corner of his mouth quirk. "Is this your not-so-subtle way of telling me you need to pee?"

Her delicious-looking mouth formed a moue. "Pee is an understatement. What I need to do will give Niagara Falls a run for its money."

There was the Grace Beacham he remembered. Funny. Forthright. And completely unconscious of just how damned adorable she was.

"Rafer!" He called to the giant ginger manning the guardhouse. "Open sesame, man! We got a woman who desperately needs to hit the head!"

Along with his three brothers, Rafer Connelly was BKI's first line of defense against anyone trying to gain access to the grounds that consisted of the old factory building, various outbuildings, and the little foreman's cottage. For years, the burly Chicago Irishmen had taken round-the-clock shifts guarding the gates. And it was only recently Hunter had learned to tell them apart.

They all stood at nearly six-and-a-half feet tall, sported orangey-red hair, were covered in freckles, and had thick Chicago accents that put Sam's Southside drawl to shame. But he'd learned Manus had a mole beside his nose. Geralt had a scar running across his cheek. Toran was always chewing gum. And Rafer? Well, Rafer had a habit of blasting yacht rock at deafening decibels.

Christopher Cross's "Sailing" crooned from the guardhouse when Rafer slid open the little window.

"Everything copacetic?" He hit the switch that had the iron gates clanging open. His eyes raked over Grace's form with equal parts curiosity and concern.

The Connelly brothers took their jobs seriously. And they *hated* admitting strangers into the Black Knights' lair.

"It's all gravy, man." Hunter shot him a salute before cranking over Canteen Green's engine.

Becky had built choppers for each new Knight during their first year of employment. And as was the case with all her custom bikes, each machine received a name.

Hunter had dubbed his ride in honor of his great-grandfather. A man he'd heard stories about but had never met. A man whose timepiece, called a "canteen watch," he'd worn with pride every day since he'd saved it from being pawned by his DNA donors.

Walter Jackson had been a WWII veteran. A member of the Underwater Demolitions Team tasked with clearing harbors of obstructions and ordinances. And a hero.

The *only* hero in Hunter's long line of lackluster ancestors and—

He realized he hadn't laid on the throttle fast enough when Grace pinched his thigh.

"Is there a switch I can flip for emergency speed?" she yelled above his bike's engine noise.

Stifling a grin, he hit the gas.

In an instant they were through the gates, across the paved grounds, and idling in front of one of the two large garage doors that opened to the shop floor. With the push of a button on the key fob in his jacket pocket, the door curled up on its rollers.

He didn't wait until it folded back completely. He held on long enough to make sure he didn't lop off their heads before he gave Canteen Green another hit of fuel and they rolled inside the old factory building.

The lights blazing in the shop and the pungent smell of freshly brewed coffee told him Eliza, BKI's secretary, hash-slinger, and all-around Girl Friday, was already up and at 'em. And the scent of bacon frying in the kitchen had his stomach growling with interest.

Grace was off the bike before he could cut the engine. Her mouth slung open as she stared up at the soaring ceiling and then around at the line of sparkling motorcycles before she blinked and shook her head.

"Who *are* you?" she asked once he'd switched off the bike and toed out the kickstand.

He couldn't pass up the opportunity. "I'm Batman."

Her mouth flattened. "Never mind." She yanked off her helmet and tossed it to him. "First things first. Bathroom?"

He pointed to the hallway past the metal stairs. "Second door on your right. If you hit the kitchen, you've gone too far."

"If I hit the kitchen, I might have to use the kitchen sink because I don't think I'll have time to turn around." With that, she took off like the hounds of hell were baying at her heels.

He hadn't imagined it three years ago. There *was* something there between them. A spark or a chemical connection or…like recognizing like. Whatever it was, it felt good to experience it again.

Sam rolled to a stop beside him and cut his motorcycle's engine. "What am I seeing?" Sam pulled off his helmet. "Is that…? Are you *smiling?*"

Hunter was quick to wipe his expression clean. "Nah. Just some sort of facial spasm."

Sam snorted. "Call it what you want. But that look in your eye?" Hunter found himself staring at the blunt tip of Sam's pointer finger. "It's lust. Pure, unfiltered, and high-octane."

Hunter made sure Grace had disappeared down the hallway before he frowned at Sam. "That obvious, huh?"

"If you were a dog, you'd be panting."

He pulled off his helmet and ran a hand through his hair in a futile attempt to mitigate helmet-head. "And here I thought I was being subtle."

Despite Grace's wiggling, or maybe *because* of it, he'd spent the entire ride from Indiana to Chicago supremely aware of her breasts pressed against his back. Of her feminine warmth curling around him. Of her fingers locked together a mere inch above the part of him the dream of her had rendered hard and hungry.

Sam swung off his ride and hooked his helmet over a handlebar. "She's not your usual type."

Hunter hitched a leg over Canteen Green's leather seat before stowing his helmet and resecuring the extra dome to the bike's sissy bar. "I have a type?" He was genuinely intrigued. He'd never thought of himself as having a type.

Unless female *and* willing *count as a type*, he thought.

"Yeah, man. Sexy. Sultry. A little superficial. The kind of woman more prone to carrying designer handbags than handguns."

Hunter frowned. He supposed Sam was right.

When he went on the prowl for…er…*companionship*, he *did* tend toward a particular brand of woman. The kind who cared more about the casts of reality TV shows than she did about climate change. The kind who didn't waste time digging beneath his surface because the surface of things was all she cared about. The kind who'd never tempted him with anything beyond a night of frivolous—and sweaty—fun.

Grace, with her clunky shoes, face free of makeup, mind like a steel trap, and depths so deep a man would need a submersible to explore all of her was the yin to his usual one-night stand's yang.

Maybe that's why he found her so fascinating. That her preferred personal currency was the contents of her gray matter and not the cut of her clothes or color of her latest manicure.

Grace Beacham was just so…authentic. A breath of fresh air to a man who'd realized the stuff he'd been sucking into his lungs was stale and uninteresting.

Before he could respond to Sam's observation, she reappeared at the end of the hallway, relief plastered all over her face.

"That was a close one," she said with a shiver.

Her golden hair was matted to her brow with sweat, but the ends were wild and windblown. Her boxy, dove-gray suit was covered in mud. And there was a smudge of dirt, or maybe it was grease, on her right cheek.

But as she marched across the shop floor, purpose in every step, he decided he'd never seen anyone more beautiful.

Grace didn't have the wildly arching eyebrows or the exaggerated lips that had become the fashion. Her eyebrows were a medium brown and straight, which made them that much more fascinating when she drew them together in a scowl or arched one high in intrigue. Her mouth was wide, prone to pursing, and upside down—her top lip being slightly fuller than the bottom. And her nose wasn't small and pert; it was long and straight.

In short, Grace's features were animated and interesting and real. The kind of beauty that didn't hit a guy in the face, but instead grew on him the longer he looked at her.

Then there was her body.

Hot damn.

In the four days they'd worked together on that assignment in Michigan, it'd become clear she was built like the proverbial brick shithouse. Her untailored suit jackets couldn't hide the heft of her breasts—but he'd been charmed by the way she pulled the front of her shirts away from her body in an attempt to do exactly that. Nor could her terribly functional slacks disguise the flare of her hips. And when, at the end of their mission together, he'd seen her in a red sequined cocktail dress? Not to put too fine a point on it, but he'd nearly swallowed his own tongue.

He could remember thinking, *Stand aside, Kat Dennings. Grace Beacham is in the house.*

When she stopped in front of him, looking expectantly toward Sam, he had to shake away the thoughts of the past so he could focus on the present.

"Right." He nodded and gestured toward his partner. "Grace Beacham, let me introduce Samuel Harwood."

Grace and Sam exchanged a handshake and the usual "good to meet yous" before Grace turned back to Hunter. She opened her mouth and he thought for sure she was going to circle back around to the whole *who are you* question. So he was happy when Eliza appeared at the mouth of the hall, interrupting whatever Grace had been poised to ask by saying, "I thought I heard the shop door roll open." She rubbed her flour-covered hands on her apron.

Eliza Meadows had a BA in political science, a master's degree in economics, and a doctorate in public policy. She was the daughter of the current chief of staff and was probably destined to someday run the country.

But her true passion? Cooking.

When she wasn't managing their missions, keeping the president apprised of their progress, or researching situations that required BKI's intervention, she could be found in the kitchen, whipping up something that tasted even better than it looked.

And her creations always *looked* fantastic. Like something one might see at a Michelin Star restaurant.

"Eliza." He gestured toward Grace. "Let me introduce Agent Beacham. I helped Grace with that operation in Michigan a few years back. You remember the one? My cousin and the Michigan Militia?" When Eliza nodded, he continued, "Grace, meet Eliza Meadows. Eliza is the brains behind all the brawn in this place."

The women exchanged pleasantries from afar. Then Eliza pointed to the mud caking the knees of Grace's suit pants. "You look like you've had a bad night."

"That's putting it mildly." Grace grimaced and Hunter felt his heart turn over.

She was putting on a brave face, but there was no hiding the fear in her dark eyes. The hammer of her too-fast pulse in her neck. Or the way she nervously twisted her fingers together.

He was tempted to take her in his arms and reassure her everything would be fine. Tell her she'd come to the right place. Whisper he'd do whatever it took to get her out of the trouble she was in.

Of course, those were all ridiculous notions since they barely knew each other.

Just because he'd spent the last three years conjuring up scenarios where they'd become *much* better acquainted, that didn't mean she'd done the same.

"Let's go upstairs and you can tell us what's going on and who that man was who followed you onto the road." He indicated she should precede him up the metal staircase.

Her cheeks, chapped by the warm wind, instantly paled. "Okay, but I should warn you. You're not going to like the answers."

"Since it took you three years to call me, and since the first words out of your mouth once you did were, 'I'm in trouble,' I pretty much figured that'd be the case."

Her expression turned apologetic. "I'm sorry. I didn't know who else to turn to."

"I'm glad you finally made good use of my number."

He decided too much of what he was feeling was showing on his face when her expressive eyes searched his.

"Come on." He lifted an arm to herd her upstairs.

"I'll bring up fresh coffee," Eliza announced. "I've also got a quiche in the oven. Anybody hungry?"

"When are any of us *not* hungry?" Sam blinked at her in confusion.

"True," Eliza chuckled. "What was I thinking?" She turned back toward the kitchen.

Hunter made himself concentrate on the small tear in the back of Grace's suit jacket to keep from ogling the tick-tocking sway of her sweet, heart-shaped butt as she made her way upstairs.

The old factory building was comprised of three floors. The lower level, a soaring space, housed the kitchen, the fabrication shop, and all the tools, machines, bells, and whistles that came part and parcel with building custom motorcycles.

The second floor was the beating heart of BKI's covert operations. Even though Boss and Becky had offices on that level—and ran the motorcycle design business out of them—the main square footage was taken up by what Hunter and his team called "the war room." It was a large space opened on one side to the shop floor below. It was filled with computer screens, a bank of servers, a conference table, and a cupboard full of high-tech gadgetry that would make James Bond weak in the knees.

The third floor was home to the Knights' living quarters. A TV room with a ping-pong table and pool table opened at the top of the stairs. And multiple bedrooms, each with en suite bathrooms, lined the hallway.

None of the original Knights still lived onsite. The old factory building, with its cache of state-of-the-art electronics, not to mention its shed full of all things that went *boom*, wasn't exactly the best environment for raising kids. Which meant Hunter and the others on his team had the run of the place.

Pulling out one of the rolling chairs pushed beneath the conference table, he gestured for Grace to sit. She sank into the cushioned seat and sent him a smile that made his jaw clench. The look was meant to express her gratitude, but there was no mistaking the desperation that tightened the skin across her cheeks.

He was beginning to suspect the kind of trouble she was in started with a capital T and ended with her kicking her oxygen habit and becoming worm dirt.

Not if I have anything to do with it, he thought resolutely as he snagged the chair next to her.

Sam plopped down in the seat directly across from them and steepled his hands on the table as he regarded Grace expectantly. She didn't notice his expression. She was too busy craning her neck around, gawking at the war room.

Hunter had to admit, it was impressive. Like NORAD. Or maybe a scaled-down version of NASA's Mission Control.

"Seriously." Her brows pinched together. "Who *are* you people?"

"I'm Batman," Sam said. "This"—he gestured to Hunter—"is Robin."

Hunter scoffed. "If anyone's the sidekick, it's you."

"Whatever you gotta tell yourself to be able to sleep at night." Sam's shrug displayed the height of unconcern.

"You realize your attempts at evasion don't work when you both give the same *Batman*"—Grace made finger quotes—"response, right?"

When neither man answered, she sighed. "So I'm just to assume you're… what? Part of a biker gang that sidelines as independent government defense contractors or something?"

"Hot on the independent government defense contractor part." Sam touched the side of his nose. It was as close to the truth as any of them dared get. "Cold on the biker gang part. Black Knights Incorporated is a world-renowned custom motorcycle shop. The leather jackets and the biker boots"—Sam gestured toward his own—"are simply a fashion statement."

"So between missions doing lord knows what, I'm supposed to believe you build motorcycles?" The timbre of her voice thickened with doubt.

"The civilian side of our operation does most of the heavy lifting on that front," Sam explained. "Although Hunter here fancies himself a budding motorcycle designer. When we're on site, he's usually down in the shop with a socket wrench in hand."

"Not a designer," Hunter disagreed. "I don't have the vision. I'm just your average, everyday grease monkey."

"And you were called on to help me with that assignment in Michigan how?" Grace pinned him with a sharp look. "How does an independent government contractor suddenly get hooked up with a little FBI investigation in Nowhere, Michigan?"

"Let's just say we work for people who keep their finger on the pulse of things. And when they heard you were trying to find an *in* with someone in the Michigan Militia, they sent for me."

Three years prior, the FBI had received a tip that the group of militiamen were plotting to poison the water in the office building of a local mayor, a man who'd been cracking down on some of their more illegal activities. When Grace and her team hadn't found a way to confirm or deny the allegations—the Michigan Militia was a close-knit group not known for letting things slip through the cracks—Hunter had been tapped because his cousin, Chuck, was part of the organization.

It'd been easy enough to introduce Grace to Chuck. And then Hunter had stayed on a few more days to make sure she'd been able to wrangle the information she was looking for out of his relative.

In that short amount of time, he'd gotten some of her story. North Carolina native. Family full of law enforcement officers. Recently divorced and nursing a broken heart.

Their acquaintance might have ended there. It probably *would* have ended there except, after she'd found out he was headed back to Chicago, she'd asked him to accompany her to an event in the city.

"It's a fundraiser sponsored by the bureau. My ex will be attending with his new fiancée," she'd said with a grimace followed by an imploring glance. *"I don't want to show up alone."*

The red sequined cocktail dress had followed as well as the kiss. *The* kiss. And the rest, as they say, is history.

He'd spent three years alternating between dreaming of seeing her again and telling himself he'd built her up in his mind. Assuring himself she wasn't as witty and wonderful and intoxicating as he remembered.

He'd been dead wrong.

She was *exactly* as witty and wonderful and intoxicating as he remembered. Looking at her now made him feel a little drunk. His head buzzed. His heart raced. And the only way he could stop himself from rubbing a soothing finger over the smudge on her cheek was to shove his hands deep into his jacket pockets.

"At least now I know why you don't have an online footprint." She narrowed her eyes. "As an independent defense contractor, it's not like you can go around posting on social media. But you should know, the fact I couldn't find *anything* on you? Not even a picture of some drunken high school shenanigans preserved on MySpace or a dumbass Vine Video showing you and your teenage friends skateboarding into a city park pond? That's creepy. In this day and age, not being Google-able is the equivalent of sporting a porn stache while wearing a trench coat and walking around a playground."

Hunter's identity had been scrubbed from the internet the minute he'd agreed to join the Black Knights. It was the same for all of them. Madam President preferred her fast-action response team to be populated by ghosts.

Of course, he couldn't admit as much. Instead, he said, "You looked me up?" Why did that idea make him want to grin like an idiot?

"Tried and *failed* to look you up," she corrected. "As I said."

"It's best for guys in our line of work to be…uh…untraceable," Sam supplied. And then quickly changed the subject. "So now you're up to speed on us. How's about you catch us up on what's going on with you?"

When Grace didn't immediately launch into an explanation, Sam cleared his throat and lifted an eyebrow at Hunter.

"Just…" Grace pointed at Sam's expression. "Give me a second, okay? I'm not purposefully evading your question. I'm trying to arrange my thoughts into some sort of order. There's been a lot that's happened in the past twenty-four hours."

"When the shit hits the fan, it usually doesn't waste any time," Hunter agreed.

After a heavy sigh, she began hesitantly, "Okay, so…I'm sure you're both aware that for a handful of years now we've seen a dramatic rise in disinformation campaigns targeting Americans, and that the aim of these campaigns is to drive the populace apart."

"Sure." Hunter nodded. "It's no secret foreign trolls have flooded social media and are infiltrating the feeds of those most likely to swallow their wild conspiracy theories, hate speech, and lies."

"Exactly." She pushed a lock of long, blond hair behind her ear. She'd had one of those sleek bobs when they'd first met. It'd suited her. But he liked her hair better this way. Long and messy and falling past her shoulders.

It made a no-nonsense FBI agent look…soft. Touchable.

He'd never wanted to touch a woman more, so he clenched his hands into fists inside his pockets.

"But despite being made aware of the threat," Grace continued, "people are still baited into following, liking, and sharing these posts. The bureau has discovered thousands of Facebook groups that *look* legitimate but are actually run by Russians who overtly and covertly foment discord."

"Like what happened in 2016 with that Islamic center in Houston," Hunter offered.

"Exactly." She nodded. "Which just goes to show online disinformation leads to real world actions that have the potential to become violent."

"Wait." Sam frowned. "Refresh my memory. What happened in Houston?"

"Back in May of that year, the Islamic Da'wah Center became the site of two dueling protests," she explained. "On the one side was a group named Heart of Texas. They were rallying against the Islamization of Texas."

Sam snorted. "Is that even a thing in the land of open carry and longhorn cattle?"

"This group was made to believe it was." She made a face. "Anyway, the counter-protesters were a group called the United Muslims of America. They were there to advocate for the study and teaching of Islamic knowledge within their community."

Her eyebrows pulled together. "The people on both sides were real Americans. Folks who fundamentally believed in their causes. But the entire scene was instigated and organized by the Kremlin. The Facebook groups were started and run by the Russians, and they used these groups to pit citizen against citizen and to organize an event that would end in violence. Or so they hoped."

"Right." Sam nodded. "I remember reading something 'bout that now."

Grace sighed heavily. "Luckily, that protest and counter-protest didn't devolve into anarchy. But since then there have been plenty of instances of disinformation causing divide that *have* resulted in bloodshed."

"But it's not like this sort of disinformation is anything new," Eliza observed as she topped the stairs. She'd shed her apron and in her arms was a tray filled with all manner of things that smelled delicious. Despite her grace and aplomb, Sam was quick to jump up and take the tray from her.

"What a gentleman." Eliza's tone was heavy with sarcasm. "But where was your chivalry that day I forgot my key and you left me standing in the rain for twenty minutes?"

"I didn't hear you knocking!" Sam declared defensively, setting the tray on the table.

"And when I called you?" Eliza's eyes narrowed to slits.

"I've told you one thousand times, my cell was charging in the other room and I didn't hear it ring."

"Hmph." After Eliza took a seat, she began pouring coffee from the French press into the coffee mugs she took from the tray. "So you say. But I have my doubts. Especially because you seemed to take such joy in showing everyone the security footage of me looking like a drowned rat and beating at the front door like a lunatic."

Sam laughed. "Can you blame me? You're always so"—he gestured toward Eliza's tidy bun and tailored, button-down shirt—"put together that seeing you wet and wild and running around with your arms flapping was sort of like seeing a fish walk on dry land. I couldn't keep that to myself. It was comic gold."

"You could've *tried*," Eliza declared with a fierce scowl. "And I don't recall a single arm flap. You made that part up."

Sam opened his mouth to continue arguing a point they'd been arguing for the past two years, but he was interrupted when Grace suddenly let out an *umph* followed by a squawk.

BKI's mascot had hopped into her lap.

"Uhhh." Grace blinked down at the giant tomcat who looked like he'd gone two rounds with a woodchipper and lost. His gray fur was patchy in spots. One ear was notched. And his tail took a sharp turn to the right about midway down its length.

"Well, hello there." A genuine smile softened Grace's features and made Hunter's heart go mushy. Seriously, the organ was suddenly so limp he was surprised it could still beat. "And who are you?" she crooned to the cat.

"That's Peanut," Sam informed her. "He came with the place. And just so you know, there are two things he loves most in life. Fancy Feast and women. Dump him off if you don't want him making biscuits on your thighs."

"No." Grace lifted a hand to pet Peanut, who eagerly butted his huge, round head against her palm. "I don't mind. Peanut, huh? Is that a joke? Like calling a big guy Tiny?"

"Apparently when the original crew set up shop here, he was just a scrawny thing. A little scrap of a kitten who was all skin and bones and battle scars from fighting off alley cats three times his size," Sam explained.

"The original crew?" Grace's dark gaze sharpened.

Eliza was quick to intervene. "Do you take cream or sugar in your coffee, Grace?"

"Black is good," Grace told her and gratefully accepted the mug Eliza slid her way.

Within seconds, steaming cups of fresh brew sat in front of Sam and Hunter. Eliza began cutting into the crusty, golden quiche she'd brought with her.

"Back to the subject at hand," she said, dishing up massive slices of the breakfast pie and passing them around. "Disinformation campaigns are nothing new. During the Cold War, Russia was known for peddling conspiracy theories right and left. They were the ones who first pushed the idea the CIA was involved in JFK's assassination. And weren't they the ones who claimed the AIDS virus was created by the U.S. military? They've been sowing distrust in our government and our governmental institutions for decades."

"True." Grace nodded, wincing slightly when Peanut began kneading her thighs and purring so loudly he drowned out the hum of the industrial size air-conditioning units. "But social media has made it *so* much easier to spread these false narratives. They go viral on a scale previously unimaginable. During the 2020 election alone, Twitter estimated Russia used 50,000 automated *bots*"—she made finger quotes—"to tweet out disinformation about the candidates and the electoral process. And that was just on Twitter. When you add Facebook, Pinterest, Instagram, and TikTok, the amount of what-the-fuckery circulating as fact is mindboggling."

Hunter was already halfway through his slice of quiche when he ventured, "So what does all that have to do with you calling me to come pick you up on the side of a deserted Indiana roadway in the middle of the night?"

She blew out a windy breath and obediently fed Peanut a piece of her quiche when he meowed at her demandingly.

"Three weeks ago, I got a tip from one of my CI's," she explained. "Remember when I said these social media posts and groups were becoming more sophisticated and difficult to spot as having originated from a foreign government? Well, according to this informant, that's because they aren't being created and pushed by Russia anymore. They're being created and pushed by Americans *working* for Russia."

"Otherwise known as traitors," Sam grumbled.

"But only if they *know* they're employed by the Kremlin and working against our democracy, right?"

Sam frowned. "What do you mean?"

"Look, it's not the first time our fellow citizens have taken jobs pushing wild conspiracy theories. Hell, there are entire special-interest groups that employee hundreds, if not thousands, of people to do exactly that." Another morsel of quiche went into Peanut's mouth, and the cat thanked her by rubbing the top of his head under her chin. "So my initial thought was there was a troll farm employing Americans and having them put out this disinformation without them knowing the content or their paychecks originated in Russia. I figured these people thought they were working for some group of like-minded radicals, but that they were under the impression it was at least an *American* group of radicals."

She took a bite of quiche and Hunter got distracted watching the fork disappear between her succulent lips.

Lips he knew were warm and soft. Lips that'd moved against his in an eager caress he'd relived a thousand times over.

"My partner and I set out to investigate," she went on, and Hunter forced his gaze away from her mouth by focusing on crushing the crumbs of crust on his plate with the tines of his fork. "It didn't take long for us to realize this troll farm, located in an old strip mall near Koontz Lake, was a much bigger threat than we could've imagined."

"Stewart and I…" She stopped and explained, "That's my partner. Or… *was* my partner." Her chin wobbled. Her eyes grew overly bright. And before Hunter could stop himself, he reached for her hand.

Her smile was wan and grateful when he squeezed her fingers, and something expanded in his chest when she briefly turned her hand over so that she could thread her fingers through his. But then Peanut caught sight of their clasped hands and let loose with a hiss that could've come from Satan himself.

Hunter was tempted to hiss back at the furry little fuck. The cat was too big for his britches.

Literally.

Peanut weighed in at a rotund seventeen pounds. And no matter how much Becky spent on diet cat food, the tom couldn't seem to drop the extra el-bees.

Probably because he had a way of begging for food that was impossible to ignore.

But instead of devolving into a pissing match with a foul-tempered feline, Hunter simply moved his hand back to his own lap when Grace released his fingers. Peanut expressed his satisfaction with this turn of events by once again butting the top of his head under her chin, all the while giving Hunter the evil eye.

Oblivious to the cat's Machiavellian machinations, she gave his big, furry butt a scratch above his crooked tail. And just like that, Peanut's motor was back to running.

"Am I to assume your partner is…" Sam let his sentence dangle.

"Dead." Grace swallowed convulsively. "Murdered."

Then she dropped the biggest bomb yet.

"And everyone thinks I did it."

CHAPTER 6

Grace's fingers tingled from Hunter's touch, and she forced herself to concentrate on that instead of the horror of her partner's death. Because if she focused on the horror of her partner's death, she might finally give in to corner-rocking, teeth-gnashing, hair-pulling breakdown that'd been threatening ever since she'd stumbled into Stewart's adjoining motel room.

So...Hunter. The ultimate distraction. Capable of staving off even a well-deserved panic attack.

She wouldn't have thought it possible, but he was even more handsome than she remembered.

His short brown hair seemed darker, more the color of mink. His sexy five-o'clock shadow was toeing over the line into beard territory. And the gold rimming the pupils of his hazel eyes appeared brighter, reminding her of a jungle cat staring out at her from deep inside the shadows of dense foliage.

Also...is he taller?

The notion was ridiculous, of course. A man in his thirties was well past growth spurts. It had to be the thick soles on his steel-toed biker boots. But still...

Yowza.

The first time she'd laid eyes on him, a word had sprung to life inside her head in all capital letters. MAN. It was there in the broadness of his palms, the jut of his Adam's apple, the dark, crinkly hair she'd glimpsed poking above the collar of his T-shirt.

He was one of those guys who oozed testosterone. Not in a toxically masculine way that was all about arrogance and aggression. But in the way he seemed so confident and comfortable in his own skin. In the way he came off as strong and capable, and yet was sensitive enough to take one look at her and know what she needed from him.

Her mind drifted back to that ballroom. To him turning to frame her face. To the feel of his hot mouth claiming her own.

Was she a fool for having spent the last three years dreaming of that kiss?

Yes, the little voice in her head declared. *Because it wasn't a real kiss. It was a pity kiss.*

"And *did* you kill your partner?" Sam dragged her from her thoughts which...*boo, hiss*. Her past—at least the part involving Hunter—was far preferable to her present.

"If you believe wishes can turn into stab wounds, then yeah." When Sam only blinked, she sighed. "Look, Stewart and I had only been partnered up for two months. But in that time, we'd managed to ruffle each other's feathers. I expected him to fall in line and follow my lead. And he was your typical frat-boy misogynist raised to believe he was the king of the world. He hated that I, a *woman*," she stressed, "who was two years younger than him, was the senior agent."

She screwed up her lips. "Of course, his lack of promotion probably stemmed from him being unable to find his ass with a map and a microscope. And I've been in forests less shady. He flashed his credentials every chance he got, hoping it'd get him free coffee, free dinner, the waitress's phone number, etcetera."

She shuddered thinking of what a worthless excuse for a partner Stewart had been. She'd run into plenty of people in her life whom she'd disliked. But Stewart? Him she'd *loathed*.

Even still, he hadn't deserved...

She shuddered at the memory of his last moments. At the fear and desperation in his eyes. And then...at the very end...at the look of understanding and resignation that'd crossed his face.

As much as she had despised him, she'd give just about anything to go back in time and save him from his fate. Go back and hide her pocketknife. Go back and take him up on his offer to order some Chinese food and watch reruns of *The Office*.

See? He wasn't all bad. At least he had good taste in television.

Of course, she suspected his favorite part of the show was Michael's obsession with *that's what she said* jokes. But that was beside the point.

The point was, despite all his faults, she'd have never wished on him such a violent and painful death.

Hell, she wouldn't wish that kind of death on anyone.

"Last week I emailed a request to have him transferred." She winced. "I think my exact words to the director were, 'Pair him with someone else or I'll wind up killing him.' Which, yeah, probably wasn't the best choice of words given how things turned out."

Hunter ran a hand over the stubble on his cheek. It made a delicious *scritching* sound that reminded her it'd been years since she'd had beard burn. Since she'd pressed her cheek up against a man's and experienced the thrill of soft skin meeting rough.

After her divorce, she'd been a classic case of *once bitten, twice shy*. And except for those four brief days she'd spent with Hunter in Michigan, that's the way she'd stayed.

But now…

Oh, now her hibernating libido was waking up after a long, hard winter. And wouldn't you know it? It was *ravenous*.

I want to jump in his lap and lick him until my tongue gets tired, she thought with no small amount of self-recrimination because…seriously? *Now is not the time, Grace!*

Besides, even if it were the time, she wasn't his type.

She knew this because she'd met his type at the fundraiser. A woman with long, inky hair, the perfect heart-shaped face, and lips like Emilia Clarke had walked up to him. No. The woman hadn't walked, she'd *sashayed*. Her hips had swung seductively back and forth and then she'd slipped a provocative, red-tipped finger around his collar while purring, *"I didn't know you were back in town, Hunter. Why didn't you call me?"*

Hunter, ever the attentive and polite date, had been quick to introduce Grace to Kiki, making it clear he'd attended the event with Grace. But that hadn't deterred the dark-haired vixen.

Barely sparing Grace a glance, Kiki had pursed her perfect lips, gone up on tiptoe, and whispered in Hunter's ear loud enough for Grace to hear, *"Well, you have my number. Don't forget to use it."*

After the woman had strutted away, Hunter had rubbed a hand through his hair. It'd been the first time Grace had ever seen him look uncomfortable. *"Sorry about that,"* he'd said.

To which she'd replied, *"There's no shame in the game."* And her stomach had fluttered with awareness when his lips had pulled back in an elusive smile.

Hunter was stingy with his smiles. Which meant she'd hoarded the image of *that* smile away like a dragon hoarded gold.

"I mean, sure, it looks bad," Sam said now, once again dragging her mind back to the subject at hand. "But surely your colleagues aren't fingering you for this based solely on that email. I mean, who *hasn't* threatened to kill someone they didn't like? It's a turn of phrase."

"Well, there's that. But also it was my knife that stabbed Stewart in the back. And then to add insult to injury, when the police arrived, I had his blood all over my hands," she told Sam.

He lifted one eyebrow. Eliza cleared her throat. But Hunter? Hunter just wound his watch and eyed her curiously.

"Ummm." Sam made a circular motion with one hand. "We're gonna need you to expand on those last two details."

She quickly recounted how she'd heard Stewart's bloodcurdling scream from the adjoining motel room. How she'd run to see what was wrong only to find her partner on his side on the floor, the Swiss Army knife her father had given her after she'd completed her training at the academy lying beside him.

And the blood…

Lord, there'd been so much blood. A stomach-churning amount of the stuff, all slick and dark.

"Help me, Grace," Stewart had rasped, tears leaking from his bloodshot eyes and spit trailing from the side of his mouth. *"Please, help me!"*

She'd immediately dialed 911. Then she'd fallen to her knees beside him as she gave the emergency dispatcher the address and the room number.

"What happened?" she'd asked Stewart, her heart racing in time with

the million-and-one questions swirling through her head. *"Who did this to you?"*

"D-didn't see," he'd panted, his pale lips pulled back in misery. *"P-please help me, Grace. I-I think I'm dying.."*

Lifting the back of his shirt, she'd nearly screamed at the blood pumping from his body. There'd been streams of it. Rivers of it. Far too much of it.

Everything that happened after that was disjointed and jumbled in her mind, like an old-time movie reel skipping frames.

She remembered putting pressure on the wound only to discover there was no amount of pressure in the world capable of stopping his hot blood from bubbling up between her fingers. She recalled the sound of the last breath that rattled out of him at the exact moment sirens blared in the distance. And there was no forgetting how the cops had peppered her with questions for nearly two hours before three FBI agents from the Chicago office had arrived to take over the interrogation.

"We've had an email from the director," one of the agents had said.

"We understand you didn't like your partner too much, Agent Beacham," the other had added. *"Even went so far as to say you'd kill him."*

It'd quickly become clear her colleagues considered her the prime suspect. And why not? All signs pointed to her being the one with the motive and the will and the weapon. Had the roles been reversed, *she* would've assumed she was the culprit.

During a lull in the interrogation, the text had come in. *The* text. The one she could still see if she closed her eyes because it was burned onto the backs of her eyelids.

The instant she'd read those six words, she'd known she was in far more trouble than just being a suspected homicidal maniac.

She'd told the agents she needed to use the facilities. But two seconds after she'd closed the motel's bathroom door behind her, she'd scrambled through the little window above the toilet and disappeared into the night.

"Wait." Sam raised a hand. "Orpheus is *real?* I thought he was nothing but rumor. Hearsay. A boogeyman conjured up by governments to explain away the more mysterious deaths of their agents and operators."

"You and me both." Grace swallowed convulsively. "But the man hunting me through the woods spoke Russian. So…" She lifted her hands and let them fall, trying to act nonchalant even though mentioning the assassin's name was enough to have the lone bite of quiche she'd managed to choke down threatening to make an explosive, Technicolor return.

"Who sent the text?" Sam asked.

"Your guess is as good as mine." She shook her head. "The number was blocked."

Sam ran a hand over his beard, making no bones about his growing impatience.

She was right there with him. She hated question marks that ran into conundrums that led to dead ends.

"Okay. Let's circle back 'round." His dark eyes skewered her in place and she got the distinct impression there was a keen mind underneath all that facial hair. "What happened with the troll farm? You said it was a bigger threat than you and your partner coulda imagined."

It occurred to Grace it was Sam asking all the questions while Hunter sat quietly beside her like the marble statue of a Grecian god—all square jaw and heavy brow and perfectly straight nose.

It'd been clear from the beginning Hunter wasn't much of a talker. He seemed content to listen. To monitor and observe. And even though she'd only known him for four short days, she'd feel comfortable telling anyone who asked that he was the type to speak only when spoken to or only when what he had to say would add to the conversation. Which was a pleasant change after she'd spent two months with Stewart, a man who'd loved the sound of his own voice.

It's not nice to think ill of the dead, the little voice that lived in her head reminded her, and she sent up a silent entreaty that if there was such a thing as an afterlife, then Stewart was in the good place.

He'd been an asshole. But he hadn't been a big enough asshole to warrant eternal torture.

"A little digging revealed every employee working at the troll farm knew they were spreading Russian propaganda," she told them wearily. Struggling to wrap her head around the idea that so many Americans, seemingly good and sensible folks, were not just willing but *wanting* to spread to their fellow citizens the lies of a foreign power.

What is happening to our country?

But she knew. From the time of slavery through the Jim Crow era and moving forward to present day, the United States had always had a political polarization problem. Instead of a nation of people coming together to tackle economic or social issues for the greater good, Americans preferred to split themselves into categories. *Us* versus *them*.

And never the two shall meet.

Unfortunately, with the rise of social media and the abolishment of the FCC fairness doctrine, which had forced news outlets to present "just the facts, ma'am" and steer clear of prejudice and slant, the divide between factions continued to grow as partisan politics was fueled by radical opinion journalism hiding behind the banner of "news."

Instead of listening to and evaluating all sides of an issue, most folks preferred to live and breathe in echo chambers. They surrounded themselves with people who looked like them, talked like them, believed like them, and consumed the same media as them. And then they vilified anyone they considered *other*.

Grace had been hoping that by exposing the troll farm to the world, it might open the nation's eyes to the danger this sort of polarization and propaganda posed to democracy.

But people don't want to see.

That thought was so depressing, she couldn't allow her mind to focus on it for long or she might be tempted to walk out into the street and wait for Orpheus to find her.

"These people received the memes, posts, videos, and Facebook Group information straight from the Kremlin," she continued. "And then they manipulated the individual postings, putting in new words or phrases or images, so it all looked more authentically American. The repetitious buzzword-filled lines the Russians have been using for years had become the telltale sign of a Moscow troll, and people were starting to catch on. Even heavily indoctrinated folks were beginning to recognize and look askance at some of this monotonous messaging. This troll farm in Indiana helps the Kremlin's posts appear less rote and robotic."

"So like I said"—Sam's face was full of derision—"everyone working at the farm are traitors. All of them."

"Yes," Grace agreed. "All two hundred of them."

"Fuck a duck," Hunter wheezed and Grace felt her tight lips soften. She remembered him using that phrase a few times in Michigan. Now, just as back then, it struck her as funny coming out of the mouth of such a serious man. "That's a lot of Americans who've become Russian agents."

"Yes." She widened her eyes. "Arresting and exposing them was going to be the biggest news story we've seen since 9/11. But then we started following the money and things got *really* interesting."

"More interesting than two hundred US citizens actively working with Russia and against America interests?" Eliza's expression was incredulous.

"Yes." Grace nodded. "The money funding these people's pay went through various shell companies and offshore banks, but it eventually landed in the account of a lone American before it was disbursed."

"Who was the American?" Sam lifted a dark eyebrow.

"That's the thing." Grace swallowed. "We could never find a name. Every subpoena for access to the account was denied. Every string we pulled frayed in our hands before we could follow it to its origins. It was almost like…"

She hated to even say the next part out loud. It was too outlandish. Too terrifying to consider.

"It was almost like whoever this person was, they were one step ahead of us and knowledgeable enough to stay the hands of federal judges."

"You think you've stumbled on a double agent in a position of power?" Hunter's voice was always deep and resounding, but never more so than when he'd gone all grim and glowering.

Not for the first time she imagined the terror his enemies must have felt when they met him across a battlefield. And she was *convinced* there'd been battlefields in his past. He'd never said as much, but she'd bet her bottom dollar he'd been a military man before he'd become an independent defense contractor.

There was no mistaking the way he sometimes lapsed into a fifty-yard stare. No ignoring the fact that he used phrases like *copy that* and *jocked up*. No denying the way he moved, with an economy of motion that only came from years of humping eighty pounds of flak jacket, Kevlar helmet, water, rations, weapons, and hundreds of rounds of ammunition over rough terrain.

"Yes," she admitted grimly. "Maybe someone in the Department of Justice? Or someone in the Cabinet? I mean, who else could wield that much influence? Stewart and I went to Indiana to see if anyone working at the troll farm knew the name of the person cutting their checks. And I think the big, bad double agent, whoever they are, sent Orpheus in to stop us."

Again, the sound of the assassin's name rolling off her tongue was enough to make her stomach churn. She took a sip of coffee and was surprised to find it was as thick as motor oil. And tasted just as bad.

She tried to hide her disgust behind a cough. But her expression must've given her away because Eliza grimaced. "Yeah. Sorry. I should've warned you. They"—she waved a hand between Sam and Hunter—"like their coffee strong enough to float a horseshoe. You sure you don't want cream or sugar? It helps make it palatable to those of us not born with iron stomachs."

"I think I'll take you up on that." Grace nodded as she reached for the little carafe of cream sitting on the tray because she *needed* the caffeine. With the letdown of adrenaline, she could feel herself fading fast, and she had too much to do to give in to the hours of sleep her body craved.

She was amazed how much cream she had to pour into her mug before the black liquid finally turned the color of chocolate milk.

Note to self, she thought, *avoid the coffee next time.*

If there *was* a next time. She still wasn't convinced she was going to survive *this* time.

"But how did the double agent find out what you were up to?" Sam asked.

She shook her head. "The only person who knew what Stewart and I were investigating was Director Morgan. I haven't the foggiest idea who *he* was sharing *his* information with, though. Something tells me if I can find that person, I'll find the traitor."

"Who's to say the director isn't the double agent?" Hunter's question had Grace's lungs collapsing in on themselves as if all the air had been sucked out of the room.

"I don't want to believe that," she admitted hoarsely. "I've known Director Morgan since I was a student at the academy. But it was something Stewart and I had considered."

"So then Director Morgan is the first person we need to start looking at," Eliza mused, screwing up her mouth in consideration.

"*We?*" Grace's chin jerked back. She shook her head. "No. I don't expect y'all to get yourselves embroiled in this. It's *my* mess. I just needed a ride out of Indiana and maybe a safe place to catch my breath. I'll be out of your hair and—"

"Why use your Swiss Army blade if the intent was to off you before you had a chance to expose him? Or her. Or *them*?" Hunter asked.

Grace looked over and found his dark eyebrows dipped into a V. "Sorry to interrupt." He lifted an apologetic hand. "It's just bugging me. That little knife. If the goal was to get rid of you and Stewart, it would've been easier to put one right between your eyes with a sniper rifle. Guaranteed lights out." He snapped his fingers and the sound echoed around the huge space.

A chill raced down Grace's spine. In the hours since Stewart's death, and even though she hadn't figured out any of the rest of it, she was pretty sure she'd come up with the answer to this question. "Two dead agents would've had people asking about our latest assignment and probably would've given credence to everything we've found, right? Better to make it look like one agent flipped their lid and killed the other. Not only would I be in jail for murder, but anything I said about the troll farm could be brushed off as the ravings of a murderous lunatic."

For a while after that, no one said a word. Then, Hunter ventured, "So just like Eliza said, what we need to do is to look into Morgan's communications and figure out who he was sharing his information with."

There's that we *again*, Grace thought, feeling a little panicky. She hadn't expected Hunter to shoulder the burden of her problem. And she *certainly* hadn't expected his friends and coworkers to join him in the effort.

It went against the grain to allow anyone to help her clean up a mess *she* had made.

"Right," Sam answered with a downward jerk of his chin before Grace had a chance to open her mouth. "But first thing's first. We gotta get Grace hell and gone off the premises."

"Why? BKI headquarters is the safest civilian space I know." Eliza waved an arm around the second floor room, drawing Grace's eye to the schematics lit up on one of the computer screens.

The computer-aided drawing was of a fantastical motorcycle with those tall, arching handlebars.

What kind of private government defense contractors work out of a custom motorcycle shop? she couldn't help wondering. *And, more importantly, why would they work out of a motorcycle shop?*

Instead of feeling like she had a clearer picture of Hunter Jackson after seeing his place of employment, she felt like she was even more in the dark.

"'Cause I'm assuming Grace called Hunter on her cell phone," Sam explained, looking to Grace for confirmation.

"I did." She nodded.

"Our phones might be encrypted, rerouted, and our numbers unlisted," he explained, "but that won't slow the Feds for long. Eventually, they'll track Grace's call here, and she needs to be out the door before they come knocking."

Just like with Hunter the first time she met him, she got the distinct impression there was more to Samuel Harwood than met the eye. Something that would explain the gruesome scar across his neck.

It looked like someone had tried to decapitate him.

"I thought about that before I made the call," she was quick to tell them. "But I planned to be long gone from here before they showed up."

"And where did you plan to go?" This from Eliza. "With your own agency hot on your heels, not to mention Orpheus hunting you, how will you start investigating Morgan and his contacts?"

In truth, Grace hadn't gotten that far. Her first step had simply been to slip through the assassin's clutches. "Not sure," she admitted with an upward tilt of her chin. "But I'm nothing if not resourceful. I'll find a safe place to hide and—"

"And what?" Hunter interrupted again, which was unusual for him. She couldn't tell if he was impatient with the whole scenario or just anxious to implement a plan. "You know how to hack into Director Morgan's accounts? You got a way to trace his calls without using FBI resources that'll pinpoint your location?"

A hard stone settled in the pit of her stomach. She hated to admit it, but... "No." She shook her head.

"Lucky for you"—there was one of his elusive smiles—"we do."

"Hang on," Eliza spoke up. "Ozzie and Samantha are on vacation for the next two weeks."

"Who are Ozzie and Samantha?" Grace managed to ask even though her head whirling at the speed with which she seemed to be losing control over the situation.

"Ozzie is an eighties hairband aficionado, Star Trek geek, and all-around tech wizard," Sam answered easily. "There isn't a code he can't crack or a firewall he can't dig under. He'd be able to shake the virtual tree until Morgan and his possible poisoned connection falls out. And Samantha is his wife."

"What about Becky?" Eliza asked. "Ozzie's taught her a ton about online spycraft over the years."

"Becky's already behind on her latest build." Hunter shook his head. "And the baby's teething, which means she's not getting much sleep at night. I don't think she'd thank us for dropping this in her lap too. Besides, the last time we asked her to help us, she ended up missing her deadline for delivery on the bike to that ancient German billionaire and he made her cut twenty Gs off the cost."

"I know someone who could help us," Sam offered. "She's the one I called when we were down in Pana—" He stopped suddenly. "Uh, she was the one who saved our bacon on that Central American job."

Hunter's eyes brightened with interest. "I've always wondered who you convinced to—" He stopped himself too, and Grace's natural curiosity gained ten pounds.

Private government defense contractors were certainly known for keeping zipped lips. The key to securing future jobs, after all, was to never talk about past ones.

"You think she'll do it?" Hunter asked.

"Yeah." Sam nodded. "I mean, as long as it doesn't interfere with what's she's got going at work." He further explained to Grace, "She's employed by the DOD's Cyber Crimes Division."

"Call her," Hunter instructed with a firm dip of his chin.

"Shouldn't we talk about where to stash Grace first?"

"Thought that was obvious." Hunter quirked an eyebrow and Grace watched Sam's eyes go wide.

"No." Sam shook his head. "Are you for real? The cabin?"

"Where else?" Hunter shrugged. "It's off the grid. It's owned by an LLC that's backed by a private trust, so it's not in my name."

When Grace's confusion showed on her face, he explained, "In our line of work, it's best to avoid putting our names on public records. The kind of jobs we do can make us some pretty nasty enemies. Anyway, the point is, there's no way the Feds could trace it to me even when they trace *you*"—he inclined his head toward her—"to me."

"He must really like you," Sam said. "He's never let anyone in his cabin. Hell, he's never even told any of us where it *is* exactly. Somewhere in the northern part of Michigan is all we know."

Despite her the whirlwind of conversation and characters going on around her, Grace was able to latch on to one irrefutable fact. "I can't just go stick my head in a hole while the rest of you push forward with my investigation," she insisted resolutely.

"Sure you can," Hunter said at the same time Sam declared, "Don't see how you got much choice in the matter."

She opened her mouth to continue the argument but was interrupted by the sound of a buzz followed by a beep. Following the other's glances over the second-floor guardrail, she saw the big door open. A slim woman with a long, blond ponytail walked in. She wore hot pink coveralls, carried a Starbucks cup, and had what appeared to be a sucker stick poking out of her mouth.

She'd barely made it halfway across the shop floor before she stopped in her tracks, tilted her head at something down in the workspace, and then jerked her gaze toward the second floor.

"Okay!" she yelled up at them, the sucker stick wiggling precariously. "Which one of you mother fuckers touched my bike?"

Sam pointed at Hunter. "Told you, bruh. You're a dead man."

When Hunter's cheeks paled, Grace was hit by the irony that he appeared to have zero concerns about the giant pile of shit she'd inadvertently dumped in his lap. But he was clearly afraid of a diminutive blond woman who could probably pass for Malibu Barbie.

CHAPTER 7

728 West Addison Street,
Apartment 2B

Hannah Blue was not a morning person.

I mean, what's good about mornings? Brain fog? Bad breath? Eye boogers?

"You know," Cesar said as he neatly flipped an omelet in a pan, "you can get away with sleeping in your makeup at twenty-nine. But at forty-nine it's going to come back and bite you in the ass. I bought you that skin care gift pack for a reason, darling."

Speaking of morning people… Hannah's best friend and roommate was the epitome of the phrase. His tan skin looked dewy. His black hair was freshly washed and neatly combed. And he hummed as he went about chopping fresh parsley on a cutting board.

Side note: it was parsley he'd grown himself in a window box.

Grrr. She hated him and his rosy cheeks and his jaunty chopping.

Okay, not really. In truth, she loved the man to pieces. But his sunshiny disposition every morning made her want to chew thumb drives.

"That skin care gift pack has nine bottles in it." She was hunched over her steaming cup of coffee like an ogre. *Or is it ogrette since I'm female? Ogress? Hmm. Something to google later.* "Four bottles for first thing in the morning and five bottles that are supposed to be used before bed. Who has time for that? Plus, I looked at the labels and one of them is some kind of acid. *Acid*, Cesar. Why would anyone put acid on their face?"

When he pointed at his flawless complexion, she was forced to concede. "Fine. You're right. The proof is in the pudding. But I'd rather take a bath with a toaster than spend twenty minutes rubbing goop on my mug before I can fall into my nightly coma."

She was a nocturnal type who did her best cyberpunk junk after the sun went down. It wasn't unusual for her to bang out her eight hours of labor for "the man" from six PM to two AM, and then come home to fall face-first into bed—her brain fried from staring at lines of code.

"What if I whittled it down to three bottles in the morning and four at night?" Cesar offered, tightening the belt on his silk kimono. "But the hyaluronic acid stays, darling. It works wonders."

"What if instead you whittled it down to one each?" she countered.

He narrowed his eyes until his sooty lashes cast shadows on his cheeks. "Two apiece and that's my final offer."

"Deal." She thrust her hand over the kitchen island before he could reconsider and try to negotiate her higher.

After they shook, he dutifully went back to humming and chopping. A handful of seconds later, the tune registered in her sluggish brain.

"'Sign of the Times.'" She pointed to his nose. "You got lucky last night." She glanced around their apartment, then leaned over the island and lowered her voice to a whisper. "Is he still here?"

Cesar tutted and dished up the perfect omelet before sprinkling parsley on top of it.

"Harry Styles is a man for *all* occasions, darling. Not just for"—he made a face of derision—"*getting lucky* as you so crassly put it. Also, are people still using *getting lucky*? Surely there are more modern euphemisms to choose from."

"Sure. Which do you prefer? Adding some ranch to the hidden valley? Locking legs and swapping gravy? Glazing the doughn—"

"Just stop." He held up his hand.

"So?" She lifted an eyebrow. "Is he still here?"

Instead of answering, he waved dismissively. "You know, instead of spending your time memorizing vulgarisms or reading that alien smut, you should think about getting dolled up and going out on the town with me to find a handsome, eligible bachelor for yourself." He slid the omelet in front of her. "How long has it been since you had a date?"

She glanced down at the paperback romance novel beside the plate and the buff blue alien printed on the cover. "I'm well past my club rat days. And this isn't smut." She tapped the book. "It's fun and sexy and incredibly well-written."

"But it's given you unrealistic expectations when it comes to...*getting lucky*," Cesar insisted. "I mean, how is a real man supposed to compete with your romance heroes who have tentacles that can pleasure a woman in ten different spots at the same time?"

"I have never heard anyone say so many wrong things in a row," she declared with a staunch dip of her chin. "I don't have unrealistic expectations when it comes to sex. I have woefully *realistic* expectations that guys will do anything to get into my pants before ghosting me. It's like sport fishing. Men my age are all about the catch and release."

She picked up the book and shook it at him. "Also, these guys don't have tentacles. They have penises that vibrate and saliva that's basically the alien equivalent of molly."

Cesar rolled his eyes. "You've just made my point for me. No *real* men can compare."

"No *real* men *try*," she clapped back.

He opened his mouth but was stopped by the tall, blond god who walked into the kitchen in a pair of boxer briefs and a lime-green T-shirt that read: Calm down, Karen.

The god dropped a kiss on Cesar's cheek before turning to Hannah. "You must be Hannah." She shook the hand he offered. "I've heard so much about you. I'm Pete."

"It's lovely to meet you." She cut her gaze over to Cesar, making sure her expression said, *Aha! I knew it!*

Cesar rolled his eyes again and told Pete to have a seat next to Hannah. "Do you like your omelets plain or would you prefer some veggies tossed in?" he asked.

"Veggies." Pete the Golden God said. "I'll help you chop."

As Pete grabbed a knife from the block, Hannah pointed to him and announced to Cesar, "It's not my alien romances that have ruined me for dating. It's *you*, bringing home the likes of Pete who's all polite and charming and too pretty to look at head-on. It's not that real men don't compare. It's that *straight* men don't compare."

"Aw." Pete winked at her. "Aren't you sweet? You're just as sweet as Cesar said you were."

"I *never* called her sweet," Cesar contradicted with a twist of his lips. "I said she was smart and funny and sometimes a serious pain in my balls. But sweet?" He shook his head. "Never. Well"—he screwed up his mouth in consideration—"sweet like cyanide maybe. But back to the lamentable subject of your straightness." He pointed the tip of the knife at Hannah. "You know if it were up to me I'd wave my magic wand and turn you into a femboy. *Poof!* Oh! And then the fun we'd have!"

"No." She shook her head. "Femboys have nine-step skincare routines. I'd want to be a bear. All burly and charismatic with a big, booming voice."

He stopped chopping to study her. "You'd never make it as a bear. There's just not enough of you. Maybe you could be an otter or—"

Her phone blared Lizzo's "About Damn Time." "Who in their right mind would be calling me before eight AM?" she snarled. Then she saw the number on the screen and nearly fell off the barstool. "Cockwaffle." The three syllables wheezed out of her.

"What is it?" Cesar was instantly serious. "*Who* is it?"

"S-Sam," she rasped. Saying his name had blood rushing into her cheeks until they felt like they were on fire.

"As in *the* Sam? Samuel Harwood?"

"Who's Samuel Harwood?" Pete asked from the side of his mouth. "And what's a cockwaffle?"

"Sam was Hannah's older sister's high school boyfriend," Cesar explained. "Hannah's been in love with him since she was in braces. And a cockwaffle is her favorite expletive when—"

"Shut up. Shut up!" She flapped her hand as she stared down at the number glowing on her screen. "I need to think."

She remembered the first time she'd seen those ten digits. It'd been six months earlier and she'd been in the middle of scrounging through the refrigerator for her last tub of strawberry yogurt when her cell had blared to life.

"This is Hannah," she'd answered absently, pushing aside fancy jars of preservatives and Cesar's expensive blocks of cheese.

Sixteen years had passed since she'd heard Sam's voice, but she'd known it was him in an instant. There was no mistaking that deep rumble. Plus, he was the only person on the planet who called her Hurricane Hannah.

She'd been high-key shocked by his request, which had been for her to remotely disengage the security system to a Panamanian telecom guru's compound. But when he'd said it was a matter of life and death, she'd done as he'd requested.

She'd then spent the next sixteen hours refreshing all her news tabs. And wouldn't you know it? Reports had begun popping up about an "unknown group of men" rescuing the DEA agent who'd been held hostage.

Coincidence? she remembered wondering. *I think not.*

Sam had joined the Marines the day after graduating high school. But no matter how hard she'd looked. And she'd lifted every online rock and peeked around every cyber corner, she'd been unable to determine what, exactly, he'd been up to since he left the military with a chest full of medals and a file full of commendations.

In the days following the hack, she'd called his number a dozen times. To her frustration, her attempts to reach him had gone straight to voicemail. And all her text messages demanding an explanation had been left unanswered.

Then, a dozen white roses had arrived at her door. The card attached to them had read: You're a lifesaver, Hurricane Hannah. And that was the last she'd heard from him.

Until now…

"Think about what?" Cesar waved emphatically at the phone that was still blaring with Lizzo's unbeatable voice. "It's Sam! The wonderful, witty, sexy, Southside Sam. The one you haven't stopped talking about for the last six months. No. Scratch that." He shook his head. "You haven't stopped talking about him since I've known you. *Answer it!*"

Blowing out a shaky breath, she thumbed on the device and held it to her ear.

"Sam?" It sounded like someone had shoved a fist full of loose keyboard keys down her gullet. She had to clear her throat before going on. "To what do I owe the pleasure?"

"Hurricane Hannah." His deep, rich voice slid down her spine like melted chocolate. "I find myself in need of your services again. You free?"

For you? she thought giddily. *I'm always free.*

Of course, aloud she said only, "I could probably find a few hours. But I should warn you, they come with conditions this time."

CHAPTER 8

Black Knights Inc.

"Thanks for loaning me the clothes," Grace told Eliza as she pulled her freshly combed hair into a low ponytail.

She would've been perfectly happy staying in her muddy suit, but Eliza had *insisted* she'd be more comfortable on the long motorcycle ride ahead if she was wearing something clean and, quote, *"More likely not to leave you with a fatal case of road rash should you get into an accident."*

When Eliza put it *that* way, who was Grace to argue? And truly, she felt better in fresh duds, even though the jeans were a little tight around her ass, and even though the arms of the jacket were too long.

Eliza Meadows was one of those lovely, lithe women with an athletic figure that Grace couldn't hope to achieve even if she spent hours in the gym.

She knew this because she'd *spent* hours in the gym trying to whittle away her curves. Including the first six months after her divorce when she'd hoped to get "revenge hot" as her little sister had termed it.

Alas, there were parts of her that refused to budge unless she wanted to employ the mad skills of a plastic surgeon. And since she had a natural aversion to needles—blame that on the time her older brother spilled her mother's sewing kit on the floor and she ended up with three push pins stuck in the bottom of her bare foot—she'd just decided to let Mother Nature have her way.

Thankfully, Kimmie K brought booty back.

Eliza gestured toward the canvas jacket. "That jacket has always attracted everything but men and money for me." As if to prove her point, she pulled a piece of lint off the sleeve. "Maybe it'll bring better luck to you."

"I've been doing without men since my divorce, so there's no real loss there." Grace pulled the front of the borrowed T-shirt away from her body. The thing fit like a second skin. She did up the buttons on the jacket because no amount of yanking seemed to help loosen the top. "But I wouldn't say no to a little money," she added.

Of course, her next thought was she might not live long enough to spend any sort of windfall. Had anyone survived Orpheus? If so, she'd never heard of them.

It'd taken ten minutes of convincing, but eventually she'd agreed to go with Hunter to his hidden cabin while letting Sam and his mysterious associate do the dirty work of forwarding her investigation.

To say the plan grated was an understatement. It made her jaw and her hands clench. But what choice did she have? All her resources were tied into the bureau. And *she* didn't have the know-how to hack into Morgan's accounts on her own.

With her father's voice ringing in her head—*"It takes courage to ask for help, Gracie girl"*—she'd bitten her tongue and given in to the plan to let loose of the reigns of the investigation and go squirrel herself away.

Her thoughts must've registered on her face because Eliza's expression turned sympathetic. "Don't worry." She squeezed Grace's forearm and gestured to Sam and Hunter who were conversing quietly by the base of the stairs. "They're two of the best. They'll find a way to get you out of this mess."

She tilted her head. "Two of the best *what*? What aren't you guys telling me about this place?" They were standing beside the row of fantastic motorcycles and she gestured around the soaring space.

"Not every private defense firm works out of a sprawling complex of offices with firing ranges and O-courses," Eliza told her. "Smaller ones, like ours, share space with civilian companies. It's a win/win. They get the rent we pay for the space. And we get a credible cover for our covert activities."

"Hmm." Grace narrowed her eyes. "And if it walks like a duck and talks like a duck, sometimes it turns out to be a houseplant. I mean, what's with the ten-foot brick wall topped by razor wire? What's with the guy at the gatehouse?"

Eliza chuckled. "I bet you're very good at your job. You're like a dog with a bone." She pointed toward the front of the building. "The guy at the gate keeps crazy motorcycle aficionados from waltzing in through the front door. A quick Google search will show you BKI is famous in the world of custom bikes. This place has more than its fair share of overzealous fans. Also, in case you didn't notice, this isn't the nicest part of town. And there are *millions* of dollars' worth of tools, equipment, and motorcycles stored here."

Before Grace could respond, a series of chimes and jingles echoed around the room. She blinked as cell phones were dragged from hip pockets. But it was Hunter who caught her eye after he checked his screen. "Rafer texted to say the FBI is here."

"Shit." She swallowed convulsively when a knot tightened her throat. "I thought they'd take longer to hack my phone. I really thought I'd have—"

"I'll go stall 'em," Sam interrupted as he headed toward the front door.

"Why put off the inevitable?" She dragged in a steadying breath, regretting the minutes she'd wasted changing clothes while Hunter had made some calls. "They beat us. They got here before I could leave. Let them take me. You all won't get in trouble if you let them take me. I'll tell them you had no idea what you were doing when I called you to come get me."

Hunter's hazel eyes nailed her in place as he stalked across the room. A muscle ticked in his wide jaw. And his hands were clenched into fists when he stopped beside her. "I'll say this only once. The FBI is coming in here and taking you over my dead body."

Seeing him so fierce in his conviction to help her had a kaleidoscope of butterflies hatching in her belly. They fluttered around until she felt sick.

Or maybe she was excited.

It was hard to tell the difference.

"Unless you have a secret way out of here"—she frowned as she watched him hand his cell phone to Eliza and then pocket a cheap-looking flip phone—"I don't see how you'll be able to stop them."

"As it happens"—Eliza walked over to large rolling toolchest—"we *do* have a secret way out."

When she shoved the toolchest aside, a big red button was revealed. She smashed it with her palm and Grace felt her jaw unhinge.

Beetlejuice was her first thought.

Her second thought was *no flippin' way.*

But as the cracks in the grout lines between the bricks opened wider, revealing a door built into the wall, she was forced to admit her vision wasn't playing tricks on her.

Unlike the *Beetlejuice* door, BKI's secret door—*please don't let it lead to the realm of the Recently Deceased*—didn't swing open. It popped forward about a foot before sliding to the left on some sort of rail system.

She was hit in the face with a waft of cool air that smelled dank and fishy, like one of her dad's old minnow buckets. And she wasn't sure what she expected to jump out of the dark void. A colony of screeching bats? Freddy Kruger? Pennywise the Clown?

I mean, any and all horrors would be par for the course given my recent run of bad luck.

But the only thing that met her eyes was an inky-black tunnel not much wider than an SUV. Its paved floor quickly disappeared below the level of the shop. And the hollow sound of dripping water echoed out of the dark cavity.

"Seriously." She blinked. "Who *are* you people?"

Instead of answering, Hunter handed her a helmet. "Saddle up."

She *couldn't* ask more questions after that. He'd already swung his leg over the fantastical green motorcycle and cranked over its engine. The shop was filled with the bike's throaty roar.

"Thank you," she said, or rather *mouthed*, to Eliza who, along with Sam, had taken on the herculean task of not only trying to help her clear her name, but also help her escape the clutches of Moscow's favorite executioner.

No matter how things ended up, she would be eternally grateful to these people. And she hoped to express that by pressing a hand to her heart and making sure her gratitude shined in her eyes. Then she did the only thing she could. She flung a leg over the motorcycle's seat and hoped she didn't bust the seam in the ass of her borrowed jeans while doing it.

When Hunter motored them to the mouth of the tunnel, she pulled the list Eliza had asked for from her jacket pocket and handed it over. It contained everything she could think of that might help Sam and his hacker friend: her email address, her phone number, all her passwords, the *director's* email address.

Eliza placed the folded sheet in her pocket and offered Grace a reassuring smile. Grace nodded then turned back to the yawning mouth of the dark, dank tunnel and felt her stomach drop down in an attempt to exit her ass.

She made herself focus on the breadth of Hunter's broad back pressed against her breasts and the feel of her thighs cradling his lean hips. It was either than or hop off the motorcycle and run screaming outside and straight into the arms of the FBI.

She'd hated closed-in spaces ever since she was six years old and accidently locked herself inside her grandmother's root cellar for an entire afternoon and—

Oh, lord. Here we go.

The front of the bike dipped over the lip of the tunnel. And just like that they were going down, down, *down.*

She wanted to close her eyes. But she was afraid she might miss the ghosties and ghoolies waiting for her to let down her guard before swooping in to tear out her eyeballs or rip off her helmet to snatch her baldheaded.

When she tightened her arms around Hunter's waist, he gave her a comforting pat with his gloved hand.

So much for showing him I'm a strong, independent woman capable of facing all comers, she thought miserably. *I can't even face an underground tunnel without losing my shit.*

Then again, what person in their right mind *wouldn't* be freaked out by concrete walls oozing water—or maybe *sweating* was the more appropriate verb—like a dank crypt?

The tight tunnel seemed to narrow as they descended farther below the earth's surface until the only light was the one created by the bike's headlight. It was impossible to guess which direction they were going, but something told her they were traveling *under* the river.

Under the damn Chicago River!

She imagined a tiny crack forming in the walls that would quickly become a monster fissure. She imagined water rushing in to fill up the cramped space. She imagined treading water and pressing her cheek to the top of the underground passage as she fought to drag in a final breath of air.

She wasn't sure which was worse. Death by drowning, death by a subterranean soul-sucking phantom, or death by Orpheus?

Just when she was about to have herself a good, old-fashioned panic attack, the slope changed and instead of going down, they were headed up. To her astonishment, they soon popped out of the tunnel and into an empty parking garage.

Scratch that.

It was empty except for a baby-blue Saab parked in a slot at the other end. The car was covered in an inch of dust. Proof it'd been sitting in the same spot for months. Maybe years.

She dragged in a desperate breath of air that, blessedly, no longer smelled of damp concrete and the slimy creatures that called the bottom of the Chicago River home.

Not that the parking garage smelled *great*. There were triple scents of car exhaust, motor oil, and urine. But those were *above ground* smells which she would take any day of the week and twice on Sunday over *underground* smells.

Hunter was quick to hit the gas and, just that easily, they were off. As they took the first curve, she looked back and was astonished to see nothing but a blank wall where there should've been an opening to the tunnel.

She squinted and realized it was an optical illusion.

The wall wasn't one solid structure. It was two walls, one built about eight feet in front of the other. But the concrete blocks had been painted so their horizontal lines matched up and made it look like one wall.

Ingenious, she thought. And then immediately followed that up with, *Who the hell are you really, Hunter Jackson? Double-Oh-Seven?*

CHAPTER 9

"**S**he *was* here, Misters Men in Black," Sam told the three dudes spread out in front of him. Each of them wore a suit and tie and sported the traditional G-Men haircuts. Two of them had donned aviator sunglasses.

Straight outta central casting. He stifled a grin.

"But she's gone now," he added.

"Where to?" The taller of the three Feds demanded. He'd introduced himself as Agent Greenlee. Sam assumed he was the lead agent since he'd been the one asking all the questions.

"Dunno." He shrugged, leaning back against the closed gate. "She said she needs to clear her name. As the Federal Bureau of Investigations, you guys probably know how she'd go about doing that better'n me."

"We'll need to come inside to make sure you're not lying to us." Greenlee placed his hands on his hips. The move pushed back the sides of his suit jacket, revealing the service weapon he kept in a shoulder holster.

An intentional gesture. A wordless threat.

Sam had to bite the inside of his cheek to keep from braying like a donkey.

He'd lost count of the number of times he'd come face-to-face with fuckers fifty times more intimidating than Greenlee. And only about half of those encounters had been in parts of the world racked by war or conflict. The other half had occurred right there on the mean streets of Chicago when Green Bay Packer fans came into town to play against the Bears.

Cheeseheads were scary sonsofbitches. And in a bar brawl, they never fought fair.

"Sure thing." He bobbed his chin. "Problem is, I'm a stickler for protocol. You're gonna need a warrant to get through this gate." As if to put punction to his point, he patted the wrought iron at his back.

Greenlee snapped his fingers at the man standing next to him and the dude immediately reached into his breast pocket to pull out a sheaf of papers. With a flourish, he handed the papers to Sam.

"Wow." Sam chuckled. "You guys are quite the trio. Who does your choreography? Will you break into harmony next? If you're taking requests, I choose Green Day. "American Idiot." Annnnd, go."

A muscle ticked in Greenlee's jaw, but that was the only indication he gave that Sam's jibe had found its mark.

"As you can see"—Greenlee lifted his chin at an arrogant angle—"we have the authority to search this entire area." He waved at the expanse of the BKI compound.

"Not so fast!" called a strident female voice. "Let me see that warrant."

Sam looked up to find a vision stepping off the sidewalk and heading in his direction.

Hurricane Hannah. The snot-nosed kid with the mouthful of metal who'd always hung out with him on the front porch of her parents' house while he waited for her older sister to finish getting ready for one of their dates.

Except, Hannah wasn't a kid anymore. She was...

He searched for the right word. The only thing that came to mind was *spectacular.*

At thirteen, her hair had been long and dark. Her legs had been scrawny and knobby-kneed. And her chest had been flat.

Now her long hair was a jaw-dropping shade of purple. Her figure was that of a full-fledged woman complete with a tucked-in waist and dramatically flaring hips which she'd wrapped in a pair of ripped up jeans that allowed whole sections of her creamy white skin to show through. And then there was her face...

That Bratz doll mug he'd loved to watch tell a story because her expressions were so animated had matured into a beautiful heart shape with high cheekbones and a piquant little chin. Her dark eyes still took up too much space. Her nose still reminded him of a button. And her small, pouty mouth still seemed to form a perpetual moue of disapproval. But now she wore winged eyeliner, her lips were painted a shocking shade of bloodred, and her coltish lope of a walk had been replaced by a graceful—and determined—gait.

He realized with a start he hadn't pictured her as an adult when they'd talked on the phone. And so he'd been expecting her to look like that same thirteen-year-old scamp.

Crazy because she was…what? He had to do the math. Twenty-eight? Twenty-nine? Old enough to be a wife and a mother, although he'd learned from her big sister she was neither.

He'd run into his old high school flame eight months earlier at a local bar. Candy had been there with a group of friends celebrating a birthday, so she hadn't been able to talk for long. But she'd mentioned how Hannah had put all her computer geekiness to good use by taking a job with the Department of Defense.

Professional curiosity had prompted Sam to do a little snooping. Which was how he'd discovered Hannah was a super hacker working in the cybercrimes division. Curiosity satisfied, he hadn't spared her another thought until Panama.

He and his teammates had been poised to make a spectacular forced entry during the guard change at the Central American telecom executive's sprawling residence when a storm knocked out power to BKI headquarters right as Ozzie was due to take down the security system. To make matters worse, BKI's backup generator, a big diesel motherfucker, had refused to start.

Turned out, there'd been a short in its ignition.

Since Sam & Co. had been operating in a very short window, and since intel had shown the captured DEA agent had been scheduled to be executed that night, they hadn't been able to wait around for Ozzie to fix the generator. Sam had taken a chance and called the only other person he'd known who had the skills and the equipment to do what needed doing.

Hannah Bella Blue. AKA Hurricane Hannah.

She'd saved their asses that day. And it'd killed him not to answer her follow-up phone calls or texts. But he hadn't wanted to lie to her about who he was or what he did for a living, so he'd figured it'd been best to let sleeping dogs lie. He'd assumed he'd never have reason to need her know-how again.

But you know what they say about the word assume *and it making an* ass *outta* you *and* me, he thought now as he watched her saunter closer.

Aloud, he said, "Hurricane Hannah." She came to a stop next to him, adjusting the black backpack she had slung over one shoulder. He felt a smile split his face wide open. "You went and grew up on me."

"A person tends to do that after sixteen years." She shrugged, her eyes quickly surveying the compound at his back and widening slightly. People always had that reaction when they first saw BKI's setup. Then, she gathered herself and returned her attention to his face. "Although I don't think I gained an inch since the last time you saw me. Not in height anyway. Candy hogged the tall genes for herself and left me with the hobbit DNA."

Candy Blue... The name alone had been enough to give the high school boys wet dreams. The girl herself? She'd been heaven.

To look at anyway.

Once Sam had stopped being blinded by her dazzling face and amazing body, he'd come to understand Candy had been rather vain. On top of that, she'd lacked any sort of sense of humor. But worst of all? She'd been a Cubs fan.

What Southside girl worth her salt likes the Cubs?

Then again, Candy had always been determined to get out of their Englewood neighborhood and live the high life in the Gold Coast with all the Richie Riches in the Windy City who preferred to keep house north of that great divide known as the Chicago River.

"I want more, Sam," he remembered her saying. *"I want it all."*

Which, of course, had made it easy for him to bid her a fond farewell when graduation rolled around and the Marine Corps came calling. It'd taken everything he had to try to make something of himself *for* himself. Which meant he'd had nothing left over to make a life for someone else too. Especially not a social climber like Candice Blue.

"But I remind myself that it was the small folk who saved Middle Earth in the end," Hannah added with another shrug, dragging his mind back to the present.

"You know what they say," he told her with a wink. "It's not the size of the dog in the fight. It's the size of the fight in the dog. And something tells me you're as scrappy as ever."

"Mmm." She pulled the papers from his hand and glanced over them. "Probably scrappier."

"You still a Tolkien fan?"

He remembered how her copy of *The Lord of the Rings* had been frayed around the edges.

"For life," she said. "Although I've moved on from fantasy."

"To what?" he asked curiously.

She tucked the sheaf of papers under her arm so she could open her backpack and pull out a paperback novel. When she held it up, he felt the threat of a blush burning the tips of his ears.

The cover of the book showed a muscular blue humanoid holding a human woman in his arms. The woman's head was thrown back, and it was clear the illustrator had wanted to create the illusion she'd just been ravished into a near coma by the blue dude.

He ran a hand over his beard. "Um, alien porn?"

A harsh scowl pinched Hannah's eyebrows together. "Have you been talking to Cesar? It's not *alien porn*. It's science fiction erotica. It has intergalactic intrigue, space travel, and, sure, sex. But the sex isn't the sundae. The sex is the cherry on top."

"Who's Cesar?"

"More importantly," Greenlee interrupted. "Who are *you*?" He narrowed his eyes on Hannah's face.

She shoved her book back into her pack. "I'm Hannah Blue."

"What are you doing here, Miss Hannah Blue?" Greenlee pressed. "Are you an attorney or something?"

"Do I look like a lawyer?" She made a face even as she resumed scanning the warrant.

Sam had to bite the inside of his cheek to keep from laughing when he saw indecision enter Greenlee's eyes. He could read Greenlee's mind as Greenlee tried to determine which answer, a *yes* or a *no*, was least likely to offend the prickly little purple-headed imp.

Hannah's impatience was palpable when she rolled her eyes. "Don't break yourself trying to answer. I'll do it for you. No. I'm not an attorney. I'm just here visiting an old friend." She slapped a hand on Sam's shoulder.

For a second, he thought he felt a frisson of awareness. But he chalked it up to the delight he felt at her handling of Greenlee.

Physically she might have metamorphosized. But her droll sense of humor and general disdain for authority didn't seem to have changed.

"And are you aware your *old friend*," Greenlee stressed the two words, "was, or perhaps still *is*, harboring a fugitive? A woman suspected of killing a man just last night?"

Sam hadn't given Hannah many details over the phone. Just that they had a blocked number they needed her to trace and an email account and some phone logs they needed her to hack. So he wasn't surprised when some of the color drained from her face.

Of course, in the next instant, she lifted her chin defiantly. "You know, despite this fair nation of ours having turned into a complete shitshow over the last few years, one of the great things that hasn't been flushed down the ol' poop shoot is that people are still considered innocent until proven guilty. There's a world of difference between a *suspected* murderer and a *convicted* murderer."

She pointed to the papers. "Also, you're wrong about your warrant here. It only covers the factory building. That little house you see behind me." She turned and indicated the tiny foreman's cottage visible through the gates. "Off-limits. So are any outbuildings."

After handing the warrant back to Sam, she looked the trio of Feds up and down. "You're not CPD. Our local boys wouldn't be caught dead in those cheugy suits. So who are you?"

The muscle in Greenlee's jaw had twitched earlier. Now it was positively throbbing.

Sam didn't remember the last time he'd been more tickled by another man's discomfort. And he contented himself with crossing his arms and letting Hannah run the show.

"I'm Agent Greenlee, Federal Bureau of Investigations," Greenlee managed to grit through clenched teeth.

"Mmm." Hannah nodded. "And these guys beside you are Tweedle Mute and Tweedle Muter? Do either of you speak? Or is your job to stand there and look sus in your shades?"

"Agent Newland, ma'am," the guy beside Greenlee said. When he pulled off his sunglasses and nonchalantly deposited them in his breast pocket, Sam worked hard not to throw back his head and laugh.

"No need to ma'am me. I'm not your momma." Hannah turned to the third guy. "And you?"

"Agent Floyd."

"Well, Agents Greenlee, Newland, and Floyd, it's too hot to be standing out here on the curb." She pointed to her snowy complexion. "Even though my main man, Cesar, makes sure I'm slathered in sunscreen, I still try to avoid direct sunlight. I'm nocturnal by nature, you see. Plus, there's the triple threat of wrinkles, freckles, and skin cancer. So why don't you guys come inside, do your search, and then go about your day so we can go about ours?"

Sam experienced the oddest pang at her second mention of Cesar.

Who is this guy? Her boyfriend?

He brushed off his odd reaction as fraternal misgivings. A natural protective reaction toward someone he'd once considered a sort of kid sister.

When Rafer, who had been leaning out the guardhouse window blatantly eavesdropping, caught Sam's eye, Sam gave him a subtle nod.

A second later, the big gates slid open.

"After you," Sam gestured for the agents to precede him. He let them walk a few yards ahead, out of hearing range, before bending down to whisper in Hannah's ear. "Nice catch on the warrant."

"When you work for the DOD, you get really good at reading the fine print," she said from the side of her mouth. "I'm assuming you guys have squirreled away the suspect in question, so me telling these suits to do their search is okay?"

"Mmm." He nodded. "And since you brought up the suits again, what's cheugy?"

The look of disdain she shot him might have driven a lesser man to his knees. "Come on, old-timer, keep up. Cheugy means démondé, untrendy, out-of-fashion."

"Old-timer?" He lifted an eyebrow.

"Well"—she shrugged one shoulder—"you're older than me. Thirty-four, right?" When he nodded, she went on, "Which in our fast-paced world is basically ancient. Have you started receiving pamphlets from AARP? If I were to open your medicine cabinet, would I find it filled with chewable antacids and Bengay?"

"Men in their prime"—he puffed out his chest—"get sore muscles too, you know. And are you telling me you've never had a single bout of indigestion?"

"I'm telling you you're over the hill the moment you no longer understand what the youths on the street are talking about."

"I take it your boyfriend is your age?" He didn't know why he asked that.

Okay, maybe he did. He was curious what kind of man the feisty, ineffable Hannah Blue would choose.

"Boyfriend?" One jet-black eyebrow arched up her forehead.

"Cesar? The one who makes sure you apply SPF?"

"Ha!" She tossed back her head and laughed. His eyes were inexplicably drawn to the creamy length of her throat. "Cesar is my best friend and roommate. He does two shows a night at the Kit Kat Lounge. And this morning he introduced me to his latest conquest, a tall, Viking god who goes by the name of Pete."

When a wave of relief washed over Sam, he told himself it was because he still saw her as that thirteen-year-old kid and thoughts of her with a man felt...icky. "The Kit Kat Lounge? Isn't that a drag club?"

"Mmm." She nodded. "Cesar is a very handsome man. But Cesarine? She's unquestionably *the* most beautiful woman in the whole of Chicago." She tossed her heavy hair over her shoulder and slanted him a look. "You should come to one of her shows. The girls backstage would have a field day with you."

"Meaning what?"

"You ooze heterosexuality, Sam. And that's like catnip to a drag queen."

He narrowed his eyes. "Why do I feel like you're setting me up for an exercise in humility?"

"Probably because you've always had an uncanny sense of self-preservation."

He snorted at her lightning-fast reply. Even as an adolescent, she'd been able to match him word-for-word. "You haven't changed a bit," he told her affectionately.

He'd meant it as a compliment, so he was a little confused when a strange look came over her face. But it was gone before he could study it.

"Well that makes one of us." She pointed to the large scar running along the front of his neck. "Do I even want to know how you got that?"

He grinned and offered his arm as they followed the agents across the grounds of the compound. "Depends. Do you have a death wish? Because if I told you, I'd have to kill you."

His teasing smile faltered when her eyes met and held his. That strange sensation was back.

This time he told himself it was simply his excitement at seeing her again after so many years. A blast from his past.

When the voice in his head answered back with, *Are you sure about that?* he chose to ignore it.

CHAPTER 10

Hannah couldn't get over the sight of Sam.

He was everything she remembered.

And more.

His beefy high school baseball player body had been whittled down to heavy bones and lean muscle. He used to look like he enjoyed the odd cheeseburger and weekend lounging on the sofa. Now he looked like he moved his body all day, every day.

At eighteen, he'd been trying to grow facial hair. But it'd been thin on the sides and a little scraggly under his chin. Now his beard was thick and shiny and a shade darker than the stuff on his head, which reminded her of a rich, dark chocolate.

He still preferred Chicago Black Sox T-shirts and jeans, she noted. But he'd traded in his Vans for chunky biker boots. And he'd gotten a tattoo. A stylized eagle feather peeked from under the sleeve of his T-shirt. It covered the upper part of his muscled arm and ended at his elbow.

He still smells the same though, she thought a little giddily. *Sweet and earthy, like salted caramel and blackberry musk.*

He'd been a boy on the cusp of manhood before. Now he was *all* man.

Unfortunately, he seemed to have missed the part where she'd grown up to be all woman. For the last hour, as they'd sat at the conference table on the second floor of the old factory building that housed the famous Black Knights Inc. custom motorcycle shop, of all things—and while the Feds had been executing their warrant—he'd been telling the woman, whom he'd introduced as Eliza Meadows, stories about Hannah as a kid. And, as if to really drive home their buddy-buddy, pal-pal status, he'd kept punching her in the arm like she was still thirteen. He'd even reached over once to scob her knob.

At that point, she'd been sorely tempted to grab his head and shove it between her boobs. The only thing that'd saved him from a forced motorboating was the fact that she hadn't wanted to scandalize his colleague. At least not on their *first* meeting.

"Well?" he asked the FBI agents who came to a stop beside the table, interrupting her disgruntled musings. "Are you satisfied she's not here?"

"You could still be hiding her in that little house out front." Greenlee frowned. "Or in any of those sheds outside."

"We're *not*," Sam assured the agent. "And we'll be happy to let you take a look to verify that once you come back with another warrant."

"You know, innocent people don't usually run when they find themselves crosswise with the law. And yet Agent Beacham rabbited the first chance she got. And innocent bystanders don't usually require warrants before cooperating with the authorities. And yet here you are doing exactly that."

Sam's shrug was purposefully laconic. "Like I mentioned outside, I'm a stickler for the rules."

The only indication that Greenlee was losing patience was the flare of his nostril as he pulled a notebook from the inside breast pocket of his suit jacket. "What time did you say she left?" He checked his notes.

"Right before you arrived. She said she was gonna try to clear up this misunderstanding you boys seem to be operating under with regards to the death of her partner."

"The *murder* of her partner," Greenlee emphasized.

Sam cocked his head and Hannah watched his ice-blue eyes narrow. She'd drowned in those eyes the first time she'd met him.

It was safe to say, she'd never fully recovered from the experience.

"If you were able to break into her phone records to see who she called last, then surely you *also* saw the text message she received from a blocked number warning her some dude named Orpheus is out to get her." Sam frowned at the agents. "Why aren't you guys looking into *that*?"

"We're looking into *everything*," Greenlee said with a sniff. "But if you ask me, that text was a red herring. Agent Beacham probably sent it to herself. Or had one of her friends send it for her." He glared at Sam meaningfully. "As far as the bureau's concerned, Orpheus is a myth."

"Well, that's convenient." A line appeared between Sam's eyebrows. "Is that how the FBI usually does things? Ignores any clues that don't fit their narrative?"

Hannah had to suck in the sides of her cheeks to keep from grinning.

Physically, Sam had changed from the boy she'd known. But he was still as acerbic as ever.

His quick mind and even quicker wit had always left her laughing. Which was why she'd found his relationship with her sister so surprising.

Candy was the *opposite* of quick-witted. In fact, Hannah was pretty sure her big sis had been absent from class the day they were handing out senses of humor.

But what Candy lacked in personality, she more than made up for with beauty. Five feet ten inches of perfect face and killer bod that'd cast a spell over eighteen-year-old Sam.

Greenlee's lips tightened. "If Agent Beacham was worried about someone hunting her, the last thing she should've done was run. She'd be far safer in custody. So you can understand my skepticism. Now…" He glanced around the room. "Where is the cell phone Agent Beacham called?"

Eliza pulled a black smartphone from her pocket and placed it on the table without saying a word.

"Are *you* the one she asked for help?" Greenlee asked as he marched toward the table. When he reached for the device, Eliza slapped her hand on top of it.

"This isn't part of your warrant." Her tone was cordial but there was a warning in her eyes. Hannah decided then and there that Eliza Meadows was a badass.

Greenlee pulled back his hand and regarded the dark-haired woman closely. "How do you know Agent Beacham, exactly?"

Eliza shook her head. "Never met her until today."

Greenlee frowned. "So why did she call you?"

"She didn't."

For a second, Greenlee looked nonplussed. Then understanding dawned. "I take it that's not your phone?"

"You don't have to answer any of these questions without a lawyer present," Hannah intervened. She jerked her chin back when Greenlee swung on her with a look so slicing she wouldn't have been surprised to feel a cut open up on her face.

"You watch too much *Law & Order*," he snarled.

"*Hawaii Five-O.* The original show. Not the new one," she corrected and then shrugged. "What can I say? I'm a night owl. I catch a lot of reruns."

"It's okay," Eliza told her. "We don't have anything to hide." To Greenlee she added, "Agent Beacham called one of our mechanics, Hunter Jackson. This is his work phone, which is why I'm sure you saw the number was registered to Black Knights Inc."

Greenlee scribbled in his notebook. "And where is Hunter Jackson now?"

Eliza shrugged. "He knew you guys would be coming to look for Agent Beacham, and he didn't want the rest of us to be dragged into any legal entanglements. Which means he didn't apprise us of his itinerary or destination. Just left his phone and hauled ass for parts unknown."

"How did you say Agent Beacham and Mr. Jackson knew each other?" Greenlee inquired.

"She didn't." Sam's tone was flat, his expression even more so.

When Greenlee glanced at Sam, it was clear his patience was wearing thin. The muscle under his left eye ticked in time with the one working in his jaw. "Then would you mind telling us how Agent Beacham and Mr. Jackson knew each other?" The words were snarled from between his clenched teeth.

"Sure." Sam shrugged. "But it's *Major* Jackson. Hunter spent a decade as a Green Beret. Let's give the man the respect he's due, huh?"

Hannah watched, fascinated, as *both* sides of Greenlee's jaw started twitching along with his eye. He was seconds away from losing his shit, and honestly? She'd kind of like to see it.

"How did *Major* Jackson and Agent Beacham meet?" Greenlee asked, nostrils flaring.

"A few years back, Agent Beacham needed an *in*"—Sam made air quotes—"with the Michigan Militia. Hunter is a born and bred

Michigander. He has a cousin who's part of the group."

Greenlee narrowed his eyes. "And who knew about Agent Beacham's need and connected her to Major Jackson?"

Sam shrugged. "Beats me. You'd have to ask him." He seemed to revel in stating the obvious. "Unfortunately, he's not here."

Greenlee glanced around the large space at the equipment. "You all sure have a lot of computing power for a simple motorcycle shop."

The woman who'd introduced herself to Hannah as Becky Knight had stayed downstairs to work on one of the fantastical bikes. Her voice echoed up to them now. "There is nothing *simple* about this shop! My motorcycles are state of the art, and I need state-of-the-art computer aided design programs to make them that way!"

Hannah's backpack sat on the table in front of her. She dropped her gaze to the zipper and fiddled with it. Cesar always said she had a terrible poker face, and she didn't want Greenlee to see the truth in her eyes.

Becky was lying.

As a bona fide computer nerd, Hannah could say with some authority that Black Knights Inc.'s wall of hardware wasn't just for designing custom Harleys.

She could see LAN Turtles sticking out of various USB ports, giving the Black Knights stealth remote access to the web and the ability to gather network intelligence without anyone being the wiser. Stuffed into a space between two monitors was a Raspberry Pi, a minicomputer that was the cornerstone of any hacker's tool kit. And situated around the room were various Wi-Fi Pineapples used as rogue access points. They allowed the Knights to employ targeted man-in-the-middle attacks.

In fact, the stuff along the back wall made the hardware she'd brought with her in her backpack look like child's play.

"Welp"—Sam slapped the top of the conference table—"since you've seen what you came to see, and since we don't have the answers to your questions, I'd say it's time for you boys to make like a scrotum and haul balls. This is a place of business, and we've all got work to do."

Eliza took that as her cue. She pushed up from the table and extended her hand toward the metal stairway. "After you, agents," she told the G-Men, her smile cordial although it didn't reach her eyes.

Greenlee hesitated, looking like he wanted to say something more. But it was beyond obvious he'd gotten all the cooperation he was going to get. He was left with no recourse but to jerk his chin toward the two junior agents and head down the stairs.

Hannah pushed up from the table and walked over to the railing to watch the agents cross the lower-level shop floor and exit out the front door. After Eliza followed them outside, undoubtedly to make sure they didn't stumble into the little cottage by accident—*whoopsie*—she swung on Sam.

"Okay. Before I get started hacking that email account, I need you to go back to the beginning and tell me what in the world is going on here. Who's Orpheus? Why does the FBI suspect one of their own is a murderer? And why the *hell* did you call me in when it's obvious you guys can do any and all the hacking and tracking you need?" She waved her arm in a circle at the bank of computers.

"We need you 'cause the guy who usually runs all this"—he mimicked her motion toward the back wall—"is vacationing in Spain with his wife. Orpheus is an infamous Russian assassin who, as I'm sure you picked up on, is so mysterious and clandestine that most people don't believe he actually exists. As for why the FBI thinks Agent Beacham killed her partner? That's 'cause her Swiss Army knife was the murder weapon."

Hannah wasn't a newb when it came to intrigue. But in her line of work, the enemy was lines of code, assassins came in the form of black hat hackers who could steal a person's identity or a company's private information, and the only things that got murdered were Trojan horses, malware, and viruses.

She wasn't surprised she sounded breathless—she *was* breathless—when she said, "As they say, the sauce thickens."

"We're asking a lot." Sam's tone was sympathetic. "And if we had another option, we'd use it. But right now you're our best bet."

She swallowed. "If I ask a question, can you promise I'll get a straight answer?"

His eyes narrowed slightly. "Anything you ask, I'll *try* to answer."

"What is this place?" She once more gestured around the state-of-the-art computer room. "There's more going on here than the building of custom motorcycles. I mean, motorcycle mechanics don't need someone to take down a Panamanian's security system hours before news stories about a rescued DEA agent start circulating. And they *certainly* don't have this much hacking equipment. So before I can agree to help you, I have to know. Are you the good guys or the bad guys?"

"I like to think we're the good guys," he said quickly and simply. "But sometimes the line between good and bad depends on who's drawing it."

She wanted to believe him, but she needed more. "Who do you work for, Sam?"

"Same entity you work for, Hannah." His blue eyes held hers fast. "The good ol' USofA."

"In what capacity?"

"In whatever capacity we see fit. Black Knights Inc. is an independent government defense firm."

Her stomach sank. "Like Academi?"

Back when Academi had been named Blackwater, it'd employed men who were little better than mercs. Soldiers for hire who'd proved frivolous with human life. They'd gotten away with mass murder in Iraq and Afghanistan and had covered it up with the banner of war.

"Academi is a huge company. They employ thousands of contractors to go into active war zones and engage in combat," Sam said. "They're a hammer. And like most hammers, they sometimes miss the mark and leave things broken and battered."

"If they're a hammer, what are you?" Her voice sounded hoarse.

"We're a needle. Our mission isn't war. Our mission is pinpoint operations too delicate or too important to be left to the heavy hand of traditional forces or groups like Academi. We target individual bad guys and bring them to justice. We go in and take out strategic supply lines so our enemies have trouble supporting their adversarial endeavors. We risk our necks rescuing Americans who've been captured and tortured or who've been left behind by our government 'cause Uncle Sam refuses to negotiate with terrorists."

Her hesitation must've shown on her face. He quickly added, "I never woulda dragged you into this if I thought it'd impinge on your honor or your code of ethics, Hannah. I know you might not believe that. You don't really know me anymore."

"You haven't changed that much," she admitted softly. "You might look like you got in a fight with a weed eater and lost." She gestured toward his neck. "But I get the impression that where it counts, you're still the same Samuel Harwood who brought me bags of Garrett's popcorn so we could watch *Raising Arizona* and *Intolerable Cruelty* on my portable TV while Candy did her hair."

"Your sister always did take forever to get ready."

"Still does."

"So…" His eyes roamed over her face. She would swear she could feel their movement like a physical touch. "You in?"

The reasonable, rational part of her brain told her she should shoulder her backpack and adios herself right out the front door. It was clear Sam and his friends, or coworkers, or super-soldier-spy-buddies—or whatever the hell one was supposed to call government defense contractors—were in *real* trouble. The kind that involved Feds and assassins and might very well end in gunfire. Which she'd managed to avoid her entire life and would like to continue the trend, *thank you very much*.

But the part of her brain that was stuck on Sam? The part that was beyond happy just to breathe the same air as him? *That* part had her admitting, "I'm in. But you're going to owe me a steak dinner at Gibson's when this is all over."

His teeth blazed white against the inky darkness of his beard. "Deal." He pushed up from his laid-back lounge in the rolling chair and walked over to the railing where she was standing. He thrust out his big hand so they could shake on it.

The instant she slipped her fingers into his, she was struck. *Seriously.* It felt as if she'd been hit by a bolt of lightning from the clear blue sky.

His palm was warm and rough. His fingers were long and callused. She would swear the air around them crackled.

If she looked down, would she see the hairs on her arm standing up?

Sam had to feel it too.

I mean, this can't be all one-sided, can it?

Apparently it could. When she searched his eyes, all she saw was the same friendly affection he'd shown her when she was thirteen.

Cockwaffle!

CHAPTER 11

Flour Power Bagel Shop,
Goose Island, Chicago, Illinois

"The FBI has exited the compound." Pavel held his cell close to his ear as he watched the changing of the guard in the gatehouse at the same time the three federal agents pulled their standard-issue black sedan away from the curb. Had he not been there to witness the exchange of the guards, he would not have known the original man had been replaced. As far as he could tell, the one who took over sentry duty was the first man's clone. "They don't have Agent Beacham with them."

"Damnit," Bishop snapped. "It would've been easier just to have her rot in jail. Now you'll have to kill her. But make it look like a suicide, if you can. A rogue agent who offed herself after going crazy and murdering her partner."

"Consider it done." Pavel lifted the paper cup of coffee to his lips and absently fiddled with the pack of cigarettes lying atop the bistro table. Even though he was sitting outside the bagel shop located kitty-corner from the custom motorcycle factory, the owner of the place had informed him there was no smoking allowed.

Americans, he thought with disdain. *They don't let a man enjoy a vice, even outside.*

"Second hand smoke kills, you know," the twat had said, gesturing to the man sitting two tables over from Pavel.

Just one more reason the entire country should rot. It was full of self-righteous assholes who believed everyone should care about the person sitting next to them.

Pavel might have lit up anyway. Truly, what would the scrawny bagel man have done if he had? But, regrettably, he was keeping a low profile. So all he'd done was nod and shove his lighter back inside his pocket.

He missed the America of the Cold War. The America that was all about radical individualism, rampant capitalism, and a desire to keep a boot on the neck of the world.

That America had been an enemy to reckon with.

Although, at thirty-four years old, he only knew of that America from the stories told to him by his father and grandfathers. He'd been drawing breath for only four months when the Berlin Wall fell, and only three years when the Soviet hammer and sickle lowered for the last time over the Kremlin and the Russian tricolor was raised in its stead.

He had high hopes things were changing for the better, though. His countrymen were nostalgic for the glory days of the U.S.S.R. And many of Russia's leaders were looking to reconstitute the old block.

Pavel's motherland was on the rise once again. And with his help, and the help of those like Bishop, it would fly even higher with America's demise.

Drumming his fingers on the table, he raised an impressed eyebrow at the compound laid out in front of him. "These motorcycle men have tight security. There's a guard at the gate, the whole place is surrounded by a three-meter brick wall topped by razor wire. The only weakness I see are their cameras. They have light sensitive chips. If I hit one or two of them with a laser, I can overload the chips and slip in before—"

"No," Bishop interrupted. "That isn't a simple custom motorcycle shop. And the men inside aren't simple mechanics."

Pavel straightened in the chair; his interest piqued. "What do you mean?"

"I mean Black Knights Inc. is a front for a covert government defense firm."

"Ah." He took another sip of coffee and relaxed back into his seat. "So *that* is why you sounded worried before."

"Yes. These motherfuckers were picked by the president herself. They're the best of the best. You *don't* want to enter that compound alone. Believe me."

"Well, well, well." Pavel shook his head. "Imagine that. America's illustrious leader employing her very own goon squad. I bet the rest of the world would *love* to get their hands on this information."

"They will. In time." Bishop's tone had changed, grown avid and passionate, that of a zealot.

It happened anytime they discussed the downfall of the president. Not for the first time, Pavel wondered if Bishop had a personal ax to grind with the woman who sat at the big desk in the Oval Office.

"I don't think they'll keep Agent Beacham onsite," Bishop continued. "They've got too much to hide and having her there will inevitably bring in more law enforcement who'll ask more questions and do more poking around."

"Unless they spirited her away before the FBI arrived, she has not exited the compound. I would know. I've been watching."

"There's a back way out that very few people know about."

Pavel lifted an eyebrow. "But you know."

Bishop laughed. The voice changer gave it an odd, tinny sound. "Don't you get it? I know *everything*." Before Pavel could respond, Bishop added, "If they went out the back way, they'll have been caught on CCTV cameras leaving the city. Hang tight. Let me dig through some footage. I'll call you back."

When the line went dead, Pavel pushed up from the table. He needed a cigarette.

Whistling as he pulled his lighter from his pocket, he turned when the only other outdoor patron stopped him with, "The Fugees. Nice. Been a while since I heard that one."

The fresh-faced American apparently knew little of music.

The Fugees? Please, Pavel silently scoffed.

"The song was written and originally recorded by Lori Lieberman," he said disdainfully. "And later made a hit by Roberta Flack. You should investigate either version. They're far superior."

He didn't wait for the young man to respond. Instead, he lit his cigarette and stepped off the curb, whistling "Killing Me Softly" between drags on his cancer stick.

A soft death was a nice thought. But impossible in practice.

Death could be slow or quick. It could be messy or clean. But soft? *Never.*

CHAPTER 12

State Highway 140,
north of Benton Harbor, Michigan

Hunter nearly dropped the hose to the gas pump. Watching Grace walk out of the station in those painted-on jeans made his hands go numb. Made his *whole* body go numb if he was being honest.

Uh, except one part.

There was one very specific part of him that was experiencing *all* the feels.

Not counting the night of the cocktail dress, it was the first time he'd seen her out of her FBI agent attire. And now he understood why she insisted on wearing those formless suits when she was on the job.

She wanted people to pay attention when she spoke, and a figure like hers was a *major* distraction.

He hoped she didn't notice how he missed the slot with the gas nozzle when he tried to return it to the pump. And he wished he had an excuse to continue staring sightlessly at the numbers glowing on the readout, but he wasn't waiting on a receipt.

Rule number one when going off-grid was to pay for everything in cash. He'd already given the clerk inside the station two twenty-spots.

There was no reason for him not to swing back around to face her immediately. No reason other than he had to take a deep breath and gather himself or, as observant as she was, she'd see the unbridled *lust* on his face.

He wanted to blame his fierce desire for her on three years of fantasies. Three years of imagining peeling that slinky cocktail dress off her body. Three years of daydreaming about all the parts of her he'd explore with his hands and tongue.

The truth was, however, he'd been drawn to her—had *wanted* her—from the first moment they'd met. More than that, he'd wanted to protect her. Reassure her. *Know* her.

She'd been so… He wasn't sure what the correct word was. *Sad* wasn't right, because she'd still been quick to smile and fast with a joke even though he'd been able to tell it'd taken more effort than she was used to.

Maybe *defeated* was the word he was looking for.

He'd only had to probe a little before she'd offered up the story of her then-recent divorce. She'd explained how her ex-husband had been the traditional sort who'd become unhappy at sharing his work life with his wife.

Traditional had been the word Grace had used. In Hunter's opinion, the more appropriate term for a guy like that was *Neanderthal*.

She'd gone on to tell him that her ex had grown envious when she'd risen through the ranks of the FBI more quickly than he had. And then she'd revealed that her prick-of-an-ex had taken out his frustration and jealousy by having an affair with a woman from the human resources department.

"As much as his betrayal stings," he remembered her saying one night after they'd kicked off the clock and gone to the local pub to share a drink. Or, rather, Grace had ordered a beer. Being a firm believer in the science that said alcoholism was hereditary, he stayed away from the stuff. *"It's my family's disappointment that really bothers me."*

"Your family is disappointed in you because your husband cheated?" He'd tried to keep his tone neutral, but he'd known his expression had been incredulous.

"No. They're disappointed for *me. All of them have sparkling marriages. None of them will say it to my face, but I know they think I failed in my choice of husband. That I let a handsome face and a slick tongue blind me to Tim's—that's my ex—less desirable qualities."*

"Sounds like one of those less desirable qualities is an outsized ego that's easily bruised," he'd observed. *"Not to mention a lack of honor."*

Cheating was SOP—standard operating procedure—in the military. A lot of guys and gals excused their infidelity with the "it's the long-distance thing" or "when death lurks around every corner, a person needs to be reminded they're still alive." Hunter had heard it all over the years. But none of it had ever held any water with him.

He could forgive many human weaknesses.

He couldn't forgive infidelity.

In his opinion, if a person was unhappy in a relationship, they should leave it. Cheating was the coward's way out. Plain and simple.

"I can't argue with you there." She'd taken a long pull on her beer before continuing, *"And really, what does that say about me? That I chose him?"* She'd shaken her head and he'd noticed how it caused her soft bob to brush against her cheeks.

Before he'd been able to respond, she'd added, *"The truth of it is, I think I picked Tim less for him and more for me. Because, with him by my side, I felt beautiful."*

She'd scrunched up her nose. *"I was always the wallflower at the school dances. The bridesmaid who was never the bride. When the handsomest, most charismatic guy at the academy wanted me? Me? I was charmed. Or maybe grateful is a better description."* She'd leaned down and pressed her forehead against the bar, and he'd tried to imagine her as a wallflower and failed.

Grace wasn't the Best Supporting Actress type. She was a leading lady.

"Lord, I'm a cliché. Gloria Steinem would be so disappointed," she'd finished miserably.

He'd wanted to drag her off that barstool and show her just how beautiful he thought she was. He'd wanted to kiss her wide mouth and caress her decadent body until she'd understood just how *sexy* she was. But most of all, he'd wanted to wipe the look of defeat off her face and replace it with a gasp of passion.

He *still* wanted that.

Maybe more than ever.

When he finally turned around, he made sure to focus on screwing in the gas cap…just in case he hadn't managed to wrangle the hunger in his gaze.

"Didn't you tell me you were raised somewhere around here?" She handed him a bottle of water and blinked at the long stretch of lonely road unfurling to the north. He'd been keeping them off the major highways, hoping to avoid as many traffic cams as possible. It was going to be nothing but country lanes all the way to Traverse City. "Benton Heights, was it?" she asked.

He shook his head and twisted the cap off the cold water. He took a long pull, hoping it would help cool his ardor. "Benton *Harbor*. We passed the exit about thirty minutes ago. But believe me, we didn't miss anything by not stopping."

She frowned. "I just realized I don't know anything about you. Do you still have family there? Parents? Brothers and sisters?"

Okay, and now he needed no help cooling his ardor. Talk of Bert and Susan was like a bucket of ice water dumped on his libido.

"I'm an only child. And my DNA suppliers have been gone for years now. Cirrhosis of the liver took Bert when I was seventeen. Three years later, Susan followed him to the grave. I'd already split town by then, but her neighbors told me she passed out in the snow while stumbling home from the bar. She wasn't discovered until the next morning and by then it was too late."

"Dear god," Grace rasped, her dark eyes huge.

"God never wanted anything to do with Bert and Susan Jackson. I can guarantee you that."

"I'm so sorry, Hunter. I can't..." She stopped and shook her head. "I can't imagine how difficult that must've been for you."

That was always the way people reacted. But to him, Bert's and Susan's deaths made sense. They'd been grim and grisly endings to two grim and grisly lives.

"My entire childhood I was nothing but a passing thought to them." He twisted his lips. "A nuisance, a mouth to feed when they would've rather blown their dough on booze. I was *removed from the home*"—he made air quotes—"when I was fourteen. I never looked back. So save your condolences. I don't need them."

He realized he'd sounded harsh and was quick to add, "Not that I don't appreciate your sympathy. It's just that it's misplaced. The people who created me weren't parents. Not in any sense of the word other than, after a night of a few too many, they forgot to use a condom. So I don't mourn them the way most people would."

Even though he wanted to avoid her eyes—Grace always saw too much—he made himself hold her stare when she searched his face. "Hunter, I—"

The instant he saw pity enter her expression, he stopped her with a raised hand.

He *hated* being pitied. He'd been pitied his entire childhood.

In elementary school he'd been the ragamuffin from the wrong side of the tracks who sat alone at a table in the cafeteria because the other kids said he smelled bad. In middle school, he'd been the kid with holes in the soles of his shoes and clothes that'd come from the charity box at the local church. And in high school, he'd been the guy whose parents stumbled around town in drunken stupors.

"Don't feel bad for me, Grace. There are others who had it way worse."

"But it's so…" She shook her head. "*Unfair.* You were just a baby. You should've been coddled and cherished and made to feel safe and loved. And instead you were—"

"Life's not fair," he interrupted. "Those of us who get bad starts have a choice to make. We can look at our pasts as a life sentence and let that define us. Or we can look at our pasts as lessons and learn from them. I chose the latter. At least, I *hope* I did."

The smile she gave him was so damn sweet, it made his heart swell. "I've known a lot of men in my life and—" Her smile fell into a frown. "Uh, that didn't come out right. Makes me sound like I've *known* a lot of men in my life. Which, I haven't. Well, I guess that depends on your definition of *a lot.* I mean, it's not like I'm a virgin or anything." She coughed into her hand. "As I'm sure you surmised since you know I was married. But I wasn't one to really spread myself around before *or* after the marriage."

She blinked rapidly and he watched, mesmerized, as pink flooded her cheeks. "Not that I have any issue with women…er…*people* who sleep around," she quickly added. "I'm all for everyone being free to do what they want with their own bodies. As long as all parties involved give full consent, then 'good for them' I say and—"

"Grace," he interjected, trying and failing to contain the grin that twitched at his lips. "Is this sudden onset of verbal diarrhea the result of some medical condition I should know about?"

He saw her fighting not to laugh. Then she stopped fighting.

The sound of her humor was like champagne bubbles that popped and fizzed in his ear. It was intoxicating.

She was intoxicating.

She swiped at his shoulder, her dark eyes sparkling. "I thought if I kept talking, I'd be able to dig myself out."

"I'm not sure there's a shovel on the planet big enough to handle all the stuff you were unearthing."

"It's your fault."

His chin pulled back. "How do you figure?"

"You got me all flustered." As if to demonstrate, she fluttered her hands. "But what I was *trying* to say is that having grown up with brothers, and having been around all their friends, and having worked in a profession dominated by the opposite sex, I've gotten to know my fair share of men. And you? You're one of the steadiest, most accomplished, and most capable I've ever met. Please don't take this the wrong way, or feel like I'm being condescending, but I'd say you *definitely* haven't let your past define you. In fact, considering your start in life, ya done good, kiddo."

She winked and gave him a friendly nudge to keep the mood light. But the weight of her words, the sincerity of her compliment, had spaces inside him he hadn't known were empty filling up with… Well, he couldn't say *what* they were filling up with.

Something warm and wonderful.

Instead of telling her as much, he crossed his arms and cocked his head. "How did I get you all flustered?"

"Please." She rolled her eyes. "When you stand there looking like *that*"—she motioned up and down his length—"I'd challenge any woman not to get flustered."

He lifted an eyebrow. "And what do I look like?"

"Six feet two inches of twisted steel and sex appeal."

He had to clear his throat because her candor caught him off guard.

Although, he shouldn't be surprised. From the very beginning, he'd been struck by her directness.

Grace Beacham didn't play games. She wasn't coy or cagey. She was what his drill sergeant had called *a square-shooter*.

"Not to brag or anything." He leaned forward and was gratified when her gaze fell to his mouth. "But I'm six three."

He saw her pulse flutter beneath the skin of her neck. And he would swear the air around them began to flutter too. To throb with excitement. *Expectation.*

"Grace?" Her name tasted so good in his mouth, he wanted to say it over and over again.

"Mmm?" Her breathing had picked up the pace right along with her heart.

"I like that the truth just falls out of you whether you want it to or not."

Her smile turned rueful. "I think that's a product of me having zero, and I mean *zero*, game."

"I disagree. I think your game is that you have zero game. It's…" He leaned forward again, until there were only a few inches separating them and he could see how her brown eyes had flecks of gold near her pupils. "Very attractive."

Her swallow was audible. Her voice on the other hand? That had become a bare whisper. "It is?"

If she was as aware of him as he was of her—and he was beginning to think she was—then *why* hadn't she used his number before now? If she'd felt *half* of what he'd felt when they'd kissed, *how* could she have stayed away?

"Why did you wait three years to call me?" He'd dropped his own voice to a low rumble.

Something that looked like embarrassment came over her face. She confirmed it when she said, "I know you only gave me your number because you felt sorry for me. Because I was such a wreck back then. I didn't like the thought of you pitying me."

"I never pitied you."

"Of course you did. I was *pathetic.*" She made a face and took a step back. He wanted to growl at the extra inches it put between them. "You saw how I froze when Tim came up to me at that stupid fundraiser. He insulted me, accused you of being a gigolo, and all I could do was stand there with my mouth opening and closing like a fish out of water."

Ah, yes. He straightened. *That night at the Waldorf Astoria.*

He'd never been much for crowds, or a suit and tie. But he'd been happy to suffer both because it'd meant he got to walk around with Grace on his arm.

They'd been at the bar when Tim had made his presence known. Hunter's mind drifted back to replay the entire scene…

"Grace. I didn't think you'd be here."

Hunter stopped talking to the bartender when he heard Grace's name. And even had her hand not clenched around his arm, he would've known the tall, blond dude who stood on the other side of her was her ex-husband by the way her jaw tightened.

He didn't know what possessed him, but he dropped his hand to the small of her back and took a step closer to her. So close his hip pressed against the curve of her ass. Then he slowly, deliberately slid his hand around until he gripped her hip.

It was a subtle move of possession. But her ex didn't miss it. Hunter watched Tim's lips thin into a straight line and felt a little burst of satisfaction.

Grace had said Tim was a handsome man. Hunter supposed there was truth in that. But, in his opinion, Tim suffered from a rather weak chin.

And that hairline is fading fast, he thought spitefully.

"Why would you think I wouldn't come? The whole bureau is here." Grace's low, sweet voice had turned raspy. "Last I checked, I'm part of the bureau."

"I know I'm not your favorite person right now." Tim rubbed a hand over the back of his neck and gave her a sheepish grin. Hunter thought the expression looked practiced. "But please, Grace, there's no need for sarcasm. Let's act like adults."

Hunter had been poised to dislike the bastard on sight for breaking Grace's heart. But the condescension in the man's tone turned dislike into white-hot loathing.

The asshole was baiting her. Trying to make her look like the bad guy.

"You've always thought sarcasm was juvenile." Grace shook her head.

"Oscar Wilde said it was the lowest form of wit."

"See? That's the thing. You leave off the backend of that quote. He said, 'Sarcasm is the lowest form of wit, but the highest form of intelligence.'"

Tim sighed. "We all know you're the smartest person in the room, Grace. Thanks for reminding us. Again."

"That's not what I—"

Before she could continue, Tim interrupted, "Are you going to introduce me to your…uh…" *Tim left his sentence dangling as he gave Hunter the once-over.*

Hunter could only smirk. He'd lost any sense of self-consciousness in the army. Or rather, it'd been beaten out of him through rigorous training and the trial-by-fire that was active combat.

The suit he wore wasn't a Brioni. But it'd been tailored to within an inch of its life to emphasize the breadth of his shoulders and the trimness of his waist. It was the kind of suit that didn't make a statement because it didn't have to. It left the statement-making to the man who wore it.

And in the name of making statements, he thrust out his hand. "Name's Hunter Jackson. You must be the ex…um…Ted, is it?"

"Tim." *The man's mouth thinned further.*

"Right. Sorry." *Hunter might have squeezed Tim's hand just a* little *harder than was strictly necessary.*

Tim went from looking annoyed to looking smug when a redheaded woman sidled up beside him. The infamous human resources rep, no doubt, *Hunter thought. After throwing an arm around the woman's shoulders, Tim dropped a lingering kiss on her temple.*

It was patently obvious the move was for Grace's benefit. And Hunter had a nearly overwhelming urge to punch the assclown straight in the dick. Instead, he smiled and said, "I'm really glad we bumped into you, Ted."

"It's Tim," *Tim corrected again.* "And why are you glad?"

"I've been wanting to thank you personally for tossing this amazing woman"—*he pulled Grace back against him, noting the way the globes of her plump ass cradled the length of his cock*—"back into the sea for a…" *He stopped and glanced down at Grace.* "Is it okay if I use the word you used?"

She blinked at him in question but swallowed and nodded for him to continue.

"For a" bigger *fish to snatch up," he finished.*

The human resources rep's mouth slung open at his not-so-subtle inference that Tim wasn't all he should be below decks. From the corner of his eye, he saw Grace stick her tongue in her cheek to keep from laughing.

Tim, on the other hand, curled his top lip into a cruel sneer. "Jesus, Grace." *He shook his head.* "What corner of the internet did you find this guy in. Dumb Jocks for Hire? Wherever it was, I hope it was a bargain site. Because we both know you need to be saving your money to pay off your divorce attorney."

Grace made a little sound of shock that had Hunter glancing down at her.

He was fully prepared for her to shake off her dismay and come back at her ex with something that would cut him down to size. But all she did was gape and swallow and gape again.

He had to step in.

"If you think a woman as beautiful, smart, and funny as Grace would need to pay a man to stand by her side, then you're even more of a fool than I thought, Ted. And that's saying a lot. Because ever since I met Grace and heard you threw her over, I've thought you were the biggest idiot on two legs."

He didn't wait for Tim to respond. Instead, he turned Grace in his arms and framed her pretty face.

"I've been wanting to do this all night," he whispered. And then slowly, ever so slowly so she had a chance to refuse his advance should she want to, he lowered his lips toward hers.

Tim wasn't the only one capable of putting on a show.

Grace's breath was warm and smelled sweetly of the strawberry cheesecake tartlet she'd snagged off the tray of a passing waiter before Tim's arrival. When his mouth finally touched hers, it felt like a victory. Or maybe a gift.

At first, the kiss was delicate. Hesitant. Just a gentle press of firm lips. But all too soon the chemistry that bubbled between them erupted into a cauldron of roiling wantonness.

They were no longer putting on an act for the benefit of Tim the Turd. In fact, Hunter forgot anyone was watching.

His tentative invasion of her mouth became ravenous. The hands she'd placed on his shoulders traveled up to tangle in his hair. It'd turned into the hottest kiss he'd ever shared. Explosive and carnal and exciting.

By the time they pulled apart, they were both breathing heavily. Panting, really. And he could see by the surprise and wonder in her eyes that she was just as shaken as he was.

"Your ex's nasty response was my fault," he told her now, having to adjust his stance because the memory of that kiss always had his blood running hot. "No matter how condescending he was, I shouldn't have antagonized him. And I definitely shouldn't have gone all fourteen-year-old boy on him and cast aspersions on the size of his dick. That was rude. I apologize."

"Please don't," she implored. "Tim deserved it. But more than that, my self-esteem and dignity were at all-time lows, and with a well-timed speech and one very impressive kiss, you helped me regain both. It was the nicest thing anyone's ever done for me."

"I wasn't doing it to be nice, Grace."

"Then why *did* you do it?"

He lowered his chin and stared at her from beneath his brows. "Because I meant every word. Every. Single. One."

Her mouth fell open.

An invitation?

Damn, he hoped so.

Lifting a hand, he was poised to wrap it around her neck and haul her into his arms. But his arm fell against his side when she blurted, "Shit."

"Uh…" He scratched his chin. "Not exactly the response I was hoping—"

"No," she cut him off. "We have company." She hitched her chin over his shoulder.

Casually, he turned and watched a sheriff's cruiser pull into the gas station's parking lot.

"I didn't think they'd put out an APB on me so soon," she whispered, her cheeks going pale. "The FBI usually likes to keep things like this in-house for as long as possible. Rogue agents aren't something they enjoy advertising."

"Put your helmet on." He tossed his empty water bottle into the trash can before grabbing his own dome from where he'd hung it on Canteen Green's handlebars. "Act natural. If they were here for us, they would've come in lights on and sirens wailing."

"I hope you're right."

Less than fifteen seconds later, they pulled onto the deserted road and headed north. As soon as it became clear the sheriff's cruiser wasn't following them, he felt Grace slump against his back.

The move rubbed her breasts down either side of his spine and he was reminded of the times he'd fantasized about those sweet breasts hanging down in his face as she straddled his raging cock and rode him to completion.

It was going to be a long ride to Traverse City.

CHAPTER 13

Majestic Ridge Road,
Traverse City, Michigan

By the time Hunter pulled off the little country lane onto a narrow gravel drive, Grace was seconds away from admitting defeat and raising the white flag.

Who knew riding on the back of a motorcycle could be such a workout?

After six hours of stop and go that required her to tighten her arms around his waist whenever they took a curve and clenching her legs around his hips to keep from falling off the back of the bike when they went uphill, every muscle in her body ached.

She was also hot, dusty, thirsty, and in desperate need of sustenance. She regretted not *snapping into a Slim Jim* when they'd stopped at the gas station.

To take her mind off her various maladies, she forced herself to focus on the conversation they'd had beside the gas pump. Or maybe *re*focus was a more accurate word since she'd thought about little else since.

"Because I meant every word. Every. Single. One."

Despite the sweat that plastered the borrowed T-shirt to her spine and was surely giving her swamp-ass, she had to suppress a shiver. If he'd been telling the truth, it meant he really *did* think she was beautiful and smart and funny. It meant he really *had* wanted to kiss her the night of the fundraiser.

No accounting for taste, I guess.

As soon as she had the thought, she heard her little sister's voice in her head. *"You've got to get over your whole ugly duckling syndrome, Grace."*

Last 4th of July, she and Felicity had been sitting on the front steps of their parents' house, watching the fireworks spark over the tops of the trees and passing a Cherry Bounce back and forth between them—the unofficial cocktail of North Carolina consisted of cherries, sugar, and whatever clear alcohol a person happened to have in their cupboard—when Grace had made some self-deprecating remark about her appearance.

Her kid sister had sent her a disparaging look. *"You know I love you like family, right?"*

"I'm your sister!" Grace had shot back.

Ignoring her, Felicity had pressed ahead. *"But there are some hard truths I think you should hear. You ready?"*

"No." Grace had shaken her chin even though she'd known it wouldn't stop her kid sister.

"Were you chubby as a child? Sure. Did you go through a phase where your ears and feet were too big for your body? Unfortunately. Were your teeth a horror show before Mom and Dad put you in braces? No doubt."

"Need a good ego stroking? Just find yourself a baby sister," Grace had countered sarcastically.

"But you grew up, Grace," Felicity had insisted. *"My friends say you're what would happen if Christina Hendricks and Scarlett Johansson made a baby. And the fact that you can't see that, the fact that you still look in the mirror and see the girl with the rolls and buck teeth and the Dumbo ears, is why you fell for that butthole Tim. Wake up!"*

Felicity had whacked her on the back of the head, and Grace had been tempted to devolve into one of the slap fests they'd gotten into as kids. Instead, she'd simply sighed and assured Felicity, *"I'll try."*

Since she prided herself on being a woman of her word, she silently coached herself now, *You're smart and funny and Hunter Jackson wants you. You. Grace Beacham. So get out of your head, get out of your own way, and let him have you.*

The thought of spending the next who-knew-how-long alone with him in a cabin in the woods had excited her from the start. But now? Oh, now she was breathless with anticipation.

The pesky, rational side of her brain reminded her their little trysting spot would probably be *way* more romantic if she wasn't accused of murder and wasn't the target of an infamous Russian assassin. And you know, hadn't witnessed her partners awful, untimely death. *Poor Stewart!* But she told that side of her brain to screw off because...*beggars can't be choosers.*

And what better way to get over the trauma of the last day and her fear of what her future might hold than getting under Hunter Jackson?

"Almost there!" He yelled above the engine noise. "One more mile!"

She nodded her understanding and, for the first time since turning down the gravel road, looked around.

Evergreen trees grew close to the edge of the drive until their lowest branches were nearly close enough to brush the top of her helmet. The forest floor beneath the trees was covered in pine needles, pinecones, and the few solitary white flowers that'd managed to eke out an existence in the shafts of sunlight filtering down through the canopy.

The air smelled of tree sap and fresh dirt. The bay was somewhere close by because she could just make out the fishy-fresh zest of a big body of water.

And then, like curtains pulling back to reveal actors on a stage, the trees gave way to a small clearing. She leaned around Hunter's shoulder to get a better look, and the scene that met her eyes was a fairy tale.

A tidy log cabin sat in the middle of a little meadow. Someone had positioned a bright red rain barrel to the left of the porch and arranged two rocking chairs separated by a little metal table to the right of the door. Green moss covered the cedar shingle roof. Wisteria wound its way up a trellis on the one side of the cabin, and even though the growing season was nearly over, a few dense purple flowers remained.

Grace wouldn't have been surprised to see a fairy flutter out the front door on iridescent wings.

This quaint little cabin in the middle of nowhere is Hunter's hideaway, she thought. And then she immediately wondered what he was hiding *from* when he came here.

His past? That wouldn't surprise her. It sounded like his formative years had been loveless and filled with enough trauma that her tender heart broke for poor, baby Hunter. His present too, maybe? As a defense contractor, his life was no doubt chock-a-block full of danger and intrigue. Perhaps this was where he came to get away from it all.

Or maybe he wasn't hiding at all.

She'd seen the third floor of the factory building on Goose Island. Eliza had taken her there to let her freshen up. And as she'd changed out of her suit, dropping it straight into the trash because there wasn't a dry cleaner on the planet who could have saved it, Eliza had explained how Hunter and the rest of the Black Knights not only worked onsite but lived onsite too. Which made the old factory building a sort of dormitory—minus the communal bathrooms and plus one fat, overly friendly kitty.

So perhaps the cabin was Hunter's idea of a bachelor pad. A home away from home where he could seduce women in private.

By the sound of it, I'll be his next conquest.

The notion filled her with excitement and displeasure in equal measure.

The excitement she understood. *I mean, come on. Duh.* But why the displeasure?

The answer formed inside her head with crystalline clarity. *I don't want to be just another notch on his bedpost. I want—*

Before she could finish the thought, he cut the engine and she was immediately struck by the silence surrounding them.

It was deep. Profound. Highlighting just how far off the beaten path they were. Of course, as soon as she removed the helmet, she realized it wasn't that quiet after all. There was the buzz of insects, the chirp of a songbird, and the soft *hiss* of the pine trees when the warm breeze tickled their branches.

"I called ahead to the guy who takes care of the property for me." Hunter pulled off his own helmet. His sweat-damp hair was matted to his forehead. "I had him bring by provisions. We should be good to go for a few days."

It occurred to her then… "I haven't thanked you for riding to my rescue in the middle of the night. Or for convincing your friends…er…is associates a better word? Coworkers?"

He shrugged. "Take your pick."

"For convincing them to help me clear my name. Or for bringing me here where I'm safe from the FBI and Orpheus."

He didn't dismiss her thanks like so many people might have done. Instead, he swung his leg over the handlebars and pushed to a stand. All six three of him cast a soft shadow over her face when he said simply, *sincerely*, "You're welcome, Grace."

She couldn't help thinking how much her father would like him. Unlike Tim, Hunter didn't fawn or flatter. He didn't equivocate or exaggerate. He said what he meant, and he meant what he said.

Of course, in the next breath she reminded herself that just because Hunter had made it clear he found her desirable, that didn't mean he'd ever meet her family.

A guy like him, one so obviously in love with his perilous job and fly-by-the-seat-of-his-pants lifestyle, wasn't looking for the ties that bind. And meeting someone's family? That was a tie.

A thick one made of reinforced nylon.

"You ready to get off that bike and go inside where it's cool?" He held his gloved hand out to her, palm up.

"Lord, yes."

She tried to mimic his smooth dismount, but her legs mutinied. Had he not stepped forward at the last minute, she might have ended up ass-planted in the dirt.

There's no way that wouldn't have blown out the butt of these jeans!

Instead of keister kissing ground, she found herself back in his arms. Her legs intertwined with his muscled thighs. Her face a mere inch from his so that his warm breath fanned her heated cheeks.

She was suddenly aware of the weight of her breasts, the tightening of her nipples, the warmth unfurling low in her belly.

She wanted him.

She was pretty sure she'd never wanted anyone more.

"I feel like I've just run a marathon." She made a face, chagrined by her clumsiness.

"It'll take it out of you if you're not used to riding. You want me to carry you in?"

A laugh burst out of her at the absurdity of the idea. She sobered when she realized he was serious. "My inner Hallmark Channel heroine is screaming yes. But the part of me who prides herself on being a tough, resilient, independent woman won't allow it."

"Even tough, resilient, independent women need help sometimes, Grace."

Grace. How was it he made her name sound like music?

She slid out of his embrace. It was either that, or she was going to climb him like a tree, straddle his face, and insist he wear her around like a face mask.

"Stop being so wonderful, would you?" She grinned so he'd know she was teasing.

"Why?" He cocked his head, looking genuinely perplexed.

Because if you don't, I'm going to fall in love with you!

The thought zipped through her head so quickly it nearly gave her whiplash. It was followed by the sinking of her stomach and another thought. *Oh, hell.*

CHAPTER 14

3 Majestic Ridge Road

H unter had been concerned he wasn't going to like having anyone in his sanctuary. Partly because it *was* his safe space and introducing someone new came with inherent risks. But mostly because he loved the little cabin tucked back in the woods, and he wasn't sure how he'd handle anyone lifting a nose at the second-hand leather sofa he'd snagged from a yard sale or the multicolored afghan blanket that'd been knitted by the wife of the man he paid to look after the place.

He should've known better than to worry about Grace, though. The moment he opened the door, she clasped her hands in front of her and breathed, "Oh, my god! It's like something from a storybook."

Stepping inside, she immediately began making her way around the main space. Her eyes taking in everything. Her lower lip caught between her teeth in concentration. And, not for the first time, he noted she was a tactile person.

As she drifted past his bookshelves, her soft fingertips brushed over the spines of his novels. The basket of shells he'd collected from the nearby beach sat on the mantel above the fireplace. She picked up two of the shells and rubbed her thumbs against their smooth, pearlescent centers. The bits of sea glass he kept in a shallow candy dish on the coffee table got the benefit of her attention as she grabbed a handful of the sparkling pebbles and let them run through her fingers like colorful sand.

She picked up the afghan and rubbed a corner against her cheek, pinched the leaves of the succulents he kept in the windowsill, and by the time she'd skimmed a hand over the glazed handle of an earthenware mug hanging from a mug tree on the kitchen island, he was holding his breath.

It was as if she'd spent five minutes exploring him. Touching *him*. Learning all his surfaces and textures.

Stepping behind the kitchen island so she couldn't see what her innocent ministrations had done to him, he asked, "So? Will this do?"

"It's perfect, Hunter. So comfy and cozy." His heart swelled with pride. "But I pegged you for one of those guys who'd have shelves filled with titles like Sun Tzu's *The Art of War* or *A Farewell to Arms*. Turns out, you like novels about family dynamics."

She kept it to herself if she noticed his voice had gone a little raspy when he told her, "When you grow up like I did, reading about fictional families fighting together to overcome trials and tribulations feels almost as fantastical as anything Hemingway could've written."

"Makes sense." She nodded, then gestured to the heavy-hued watercolor hanging above the armchair. "Did you do that?"

"I wish." He shook his head. "But I don't have an artistic bone in my body. That's one of Dale's. He's the caretaker. The one who filled the fridge for us."

"He has a way of making the sky look…" She trailed off, searching for the right description.

"Like a dream," he supplied, and she nodded.

"Exactly. Makes me feel lonely and nostalgic for a place I've never seen."

Warmth spread through his chest when he thought of how much Dale would love that description. "I'll be sure to tell him. And I'll be sure to take you there." The words were out of his mouth before he realized he'd formed the thought. Before he realized how *much* he wanted her to see one of his favorite spots.

"That's a real place?" She pointed to the painting again.

"About a mile from here." He nodded.

"How magical," she enthused, and then indicated the black-and-white photos sitting on the mantel. "Will you tell me about those?"

The instant the request left her mouth, his gut tightened into a fist.

Vulnerability wasn't something he was good at. Probably because he'd learned early on that people either looked down on the vulnerable or, worse, took advantage of them. It was unnerving to think about ripping open his chest and showing Grace his heart. Because that's what those pictures represented. The soft, beating center of him.

Then again, for the first time ever he wanted to be *known*.

It suddenly felt as if he'd been waiting his entire life for someone like Grace, someone kind and brave and brilliant and *good*, to come along and know him.

"The one on the left is of me and Sergeant Cooper." He pointed to the framed photograph. "He was my drill sergeant."

"Aha!" She pointed to his nose. "I *knew* you were military. So what? Ranger? Night Stalker?"

"Green Beret," he admitted.

She offered him a soft, flirty smile. "I bet you looked amazing in uniform."

He chuckled and relaxed a little. Flirting was an area he was comfortable with. Flirting was something he was good at. "I looked even better out of it. Still do, as a matter of fact. Want me to prove it?"

"Hunter Jackson!" Her tone was scandalized, but her eyelids lowered seductively. "Are you flirting with me?"

"Woman, I've been flirting with you since the moment I met you. I was just trying to be subtle about it. I've since decided subtle doesn't work with you."

She laughed and there was that effervescent sound again. "Blame it on my raising by no-nonsense tar heels. I'm terrible at reading between the lines. I'm more of a hit-me-over-the-head-with-it kind of gal."

"In that case, I want to make love to you, Grace," he told her boldly. "I've been fantasizing about making love to you ever since we met."

The humor in her dark eyes was instantly replaced by something that looked like a combination of embarrassment and excitement.

The embarrassment he understood. She probably wasn't used to men coming right out and telling her such things. Although, he had no doubt every hot-blooded, hetero guy she met *thought* them. And the excitement? Well, the excitement gave him hope she felt the same way he did.

"Lord, you make me nervous," she admitted shakily.

His burgeoning hope withered on the vine. "That's the second time you've said something like that. I don't know if it's a good thing or a bad thing. But…" He added the next part cautiously, "I'm getting the impression, at the very least, it's a no to the lovemaking?"

She shook her head and hope once more bloomed into brilliant life inside him.

"Then, is it a yes?"

"Tell me more about Sergeant Cooper." She avoided his question. But her voice had gone husky.

As much as he wanted to pin her down—literally and figuratively—he took pity on her. "What do you want to know?"

She pointed again to the photo of Hunter with his arm slung around the giant shoulders of a man with a shiny, bald head and skin the color of polished mahogany. "I want to know why he looks like he wants to eat you."

Laughter rumbled out of him at her apt description. His fresh-faced, eighteen-year-old self wore a thin-lipped smile in the photo, but Trayvon Cooper? Well, Coop wore his patented I-eat-Johnny-Raws-like-you-for-breakfast frown.

He sobered when he saw Grace blinking at him myopically. "What?" he asked. "Why are you looking at me like I suddenly sprouted a third ear from my forehead?"

"That's the first time I've heard you laugh."

"That can't be right." He dismissed her observation with a wave of his hand.

"It is." Her nod was insistent. "I've heard you chuckle once or twice. And you've snorted with amusement on occasion. But I've never heard you laugh. Not like that."

His teammates accused him of being a sourpuss, but he'd assumed that was because he didn't participate in their asshattery as often as they'd like. Now he was forced to admit maybe he *did* brood too much.

"Coop always looks like he suffers from a bad case of asshole-itis. But he's the furthest thing you'll find." He had to swallow before admitting this next part. "He took me under his wing the first day I set foot in basic training. I'm not sure why. Maybe because, as a dad to five rug rats, he knew when he was looking at a kid in desperate need of a father figure."

He absently turned the knob on his watch, thinking back with a sense of horror and happiness on the hell that'd been basic under Coop's eagle eye and exacting standards. "Which isn't to say he wasn't tough on me," he was quick to tell her. "By the time bootcamp was over, I didn't know whether I loved Coop or hated him. But he saw something special in me. He's the one who encouraged me to pursue a career in spec-ops."

"You loved him," she said matter-of-factly.

"Yeah," he admitted a little sheepishly, rubbing his hand over the back of his neck. "I guess so."

"Do you keep in touch?"

"Mmm." He nodded. "We call each other on the major holidays. And I try to get out to see him in California a couple times a year. He's retired now. Spends most of his time fixing up the old Victorian he and his wife bought."

"Sounds nice," she murmured.

"*Is* nice," he assured her.

"And her?" She pointed to the middle photo of a dark-eyed woman wearing a hijab.

Looking at the picture always made his stomach tighten. But he couldn't bring himself to take the photo down.

Jah deserved better than that. She deserved for him to be reminded of her courage and care, her dry sense of humor and her unassailable sense of right and wrong.

"She's very beautiful," Grace mused. "Who is she?"

"Jah." His voice came out rusty sounding. "Jahedah, actually. She was part translator and part den-mother to my unit during my third tour in Afghanistan. She would bring in lavash and ashak dumplings. She made sure we all washed our uniforms and oiled our gear. She was the first one in the field when we needed to speak to the village women, and the last one to leave the base at night, always waiting until the soldiers she considered her adopted sons were back inside the wire."

Tears burned the back of his eyes as he stared at Jah's pretty face. "I fought tooth and nail to have her and her family brought here before the U.S. pulled out. But my phone calls, emails, and letters to every ranking official I knew fell on deaf ears."

The anguish in Grace's eyes matched the grief in his heart. "She didn't make it out before the country fell to the Taliban?"

He shook his head.

For a while after that, neither of them spoke. They both knew how things had gone down after the American withdrawal. The video footage of people desperately clinging to the last planes leaving Kabul Airport and then falling to their deaths was burned into the collective psyches of anyone who'd watched the humanitarian crisis unfold.

Hunter had certainly been watching.

He'd scoured news footage for hours searching for a glimpse of Jahedah. Futilely hoping to see her boarding a plane for the U.S. or being escorted into a Humvee and driven to a refugee camp.

But there'd been nothing. And in the weeks and months that'd followed, all his inquiries into her whereabouts had been met with shrugs and a litany of *we don't knows.*

There was little hope Jahedah was still alive. The Taliban had gone door-to-door torturing and killing anyone who'd helped the NATO forces during the occupation. And it was a damned travesty more hadn't been done to safeguard the Afghans who'd done so much to forward America's cause in their country.

It meant Hunter had a complicated relationship with his job working directly for the head of the government that'd left those good people to their fate. Granted, it hadn't been Madam President's decision alone and there was no way she could have known the Afghan security forces would buckle so easily under the Taliban's advance. *I mean, for fuck's sake, the last flights hadn't even left the airport before the Afghanis were throwing down their weapons and surrendering.* And granted, the withdrawal had been negotiated by the previous administration against the recommendations of the former president's military advisors. But even despite *all* of that, Hunter's boss, the one who oversaw his missions and cut his paychecks, was indirectly responsible for Jah's fate.

It was something he continued to struggle with.

Something he would *always* struggle with.

His only comfort was knowing that, before he and his teammates swore their oaths to the president, she'd assured them she would never give them orders or send them on an assignment that would mar their honor or test their morals.

At BKI he wasn't bound by orders. He had the power to do good without having to live with the collateral damage that was inevitable during any sort of major military operation. At BKI he had the opportunity for redemption.

He'd failed Jah.

He wouldn't fail others.

After a while, Grace pointed to the last photo. It showed Sam and his five BKI teammates astride their custom Harleys. "I recognize you and Sam," she said, her voice quiet in deference to the weighty subject matter they'd left behind. "Who are the others?"

Black Knights Inc. 2.0 was comprised of men he both admired and respected, all in different ways because each man was as unique and as complicated as the bike he rode.

In the years since the six of them had banded together as Knights, they'd become more than coworkers and colleagues. They'd become friends. They'd seen each other at their worst and were always there to cheer each other on when they were at their best. They had each other's backs when things went all *Lord of the Flies*. Which happened *a lot* in their line of work. But they'd also never hesitated to hold each other accountable when one of their number was being an idiot or an asshole. Which *also* happened quite a lot.

In short, the Black Knights were the kind of friends who came around once in a lifetime. If a guy was really, *really* lucky.

"The sandy-haired dude next to Sam, the one with the goofy grin, is Fisher Wakefield," he told Grace. "Fisher's a Louisiana boy through and through. I've never seen anyone eat so many crawfish in one sitting." He'd also never seen a man so dedicated to the seduction of women, but he left that part out.

"On the other side of Fisher is Graham Colburn," he continued. "Graham can make a bomb out of a toothpick, table salt, and chewing gum." Graham also knew a dozen ways to kill a man and make it look like natural causes. But, again, Hunter didn't think that was the kind of information Grace was looking for.

"Then there's Britt Rollins and Hewitt Burch," he finished. "Britt is an adrenaline junkie. Whether it's rock climbing or hang gliding or street racing, Britt's in. The more likely a hobby is to kill him, the more excited he is to do it. By contrast, Hewitt is a total bookworm. His idea of a good time is a quiet corner, a comfortable chair, and a classic novel."

"I guess if I were to ask where the others are, why I didn't get to meet them back at the factory, I'd get nothing but prevarication from you?" She slid him a sly glance.

"Prevarication makes it sound like I'd lie to you. I might sidestep your question. But I'd never lie," he told her sincerely.

"Lord"—she shook her head—"my father would absolutely *adore* you."

Her words had everything inside him going still.

He wasn't sure what he was feeling. Whatever it was, it must've been written across his face and made her think she'd made a blunder because she quickly returned them to their original subject. "So…" She eyed each of the framed photos closely. "Your family."

"Hmm?" He frowned, still trying to figure out what that strange sensation was that had balled up in the center of his chest when she'd mentioned her father. "What do you mean?"

She pointed to the picture of Coop. "Your dad." Her finger drifted to Jahedah. "Your mom." Her fingernail made a clicking sound on the glass of the last photo. "And your brothers."

"I *wish* that were true. I wish I could claim all of them as family." He tried to throw a little levity into the conversation by adding, "Unfortunately, the only blood relation I have is Chuck. Whom you've met. And whom I suspect you probably hope to never meet again."

She eyed him curiously. "Family isn't always the ones we're born to, Hunter. Sometimes they're the ones we choose. The ones who choose *us*."

The idea had a lump forming in his throat. He'd never been chosen before. Not by his parents. Not by any of the foster families he'd lived with. Not even by the women who, over the years, had come in and out of his life.

Then again, the president had chosen him to be part of Black Knights Inc. Coop had chosen to mentor him despite his cocky, teenage attitude and tendency to take on too many challenges at once. And Jahedah? Well, she'd chosen to love and care for him in a place where loving and caring for a loud-mouthed American was dangerous enough to get her killed. A place where it very likely *had* gotten her killed.

Maybe Grace was right. Maybe the photos on his mantel showed more than his friends and colleagues. Maybe they were portraits of his family.

He cleared his throat and changed the subject. It was either that or break down in a full-on snot-nosed, tear-stained bawl-a-thon. "You hungry?" He moved to the refrigerator and hoped she couldn't hear the roughness of his voice. "You barely touched your quiche. And it was a long ride to get here."

"I take it the tour is over?" She arched an eyebrow.

"You've seen it all. Except for the bedroom." Crossing his arms, he lowered his chin so he could stare at her provocatively. *Sex.* It was a subject he was *far* more comfortable with. Unlike family, it was a subject he knew something about. "Do you want a tour of the bedroom, Grace? All you have to do is ask. I would be *more* than happy to oblige."

A delightful wash of pink tinged her cheeks. "I think you enjoy shocking me with your directness when it comes to this subject matter." She blew out a windy breath and shook her head. "But you know what I could really use?"

Please say a kiss followed by a make out sesh followed by a good, old-fashioned roll in the hay to make you forget this day. "What's that?"

"A shower." She made a face. "I'm hot and sticky and even though Eliza was kind enough to lend me some clothes, I've been wearing this same underwear for..." She scrunched up her nose, thinking. Then she shuddered. "Almost two days now."

He was tempted to ask if she wanted company in the shower. But he'd already made his intentions crystal clear. The ball was in her court. He had to be patient and see what she'd do with it.

"Through that door." He pointed. "Bathroom is on your left. There are clean boxer briefs and T-shirts in the dresser. But if you really feel like doing me a solid, you'll put those jeans back on once you're out of the shower. I really, *really* enjoy the sight of you in those jeans."

"I might not have a choice." She curled her lip. "I think my sweat and the dust from the road have formed a paste. They could be permanently affixed." She scrunched up her nose and widened her eyes. "Has anyone ever died from being stuck inside a pair of jeans?"

"Oh, I could help you peel them off. Believe me."

"You're relentless," she accused.

"When I see something I want?" He nodded. "Absolutely."

She slanted him a look from beneath her lashes. "Sam said you don't let anyone in here."

He narrowed his eyes at the swift change of subject. "It's not a hard and fast rule. It's more of a loose guideline."

"Well, I'm honored you brought me here."

"It's not a big deal." As soon as the words were out of his mouth, he wanted to suck them back in. It was the first—and *only*—lie he'd ever told her.

"It is to me," she insisted. "How long have you had the cabin?"

"Almost three years. I bought not too long after I signed on with Black Knights Inc." When he read curiosity in her expression, he asked, "What?"

She looked a little sheepish, but that didn't stop her from asking, "Am I your first house guest?"

"Are you asking if I've had other women here?"

"Have you?"

"No, Grace. Besides Dale's wife, Sissy, you're the only woman to step through that door since the day I bought it."

"Good." She grinned and turned toward the bedroom. She stopped in the doorway and tossed back over her shoulder, "I like the thought of being the one to help you christen it."

Before he could stop himself, he'd taken a predatory step in her direction.

"Ah!" She lifted a finger. "I didn't mean right now!"

"When?" Was that his voice? It sounded more like the growl of an animal.

"After I get cleaned up. And after you make me a sandwich. Because you're right. I *am* hungry. And if the look on your face is anything to go by"—she pointed to what he knew must be an expression of pure, unfiltered lust—"I'm going to need my strength."

"Or you could just lie back and let me do all the work."

"Where's the fun in that?"

He took another step in her direction. "Let me show you."

She squealed and slammed the bedroom door behind her. "Shower first. Sandwich second. Sex third!" she called through the solid wood. "That's the order of operations!"

Unbeknownst to him, his legs had carried him across the room. He placed his palm flat on the door so he wouldn't wrench it open and show her exactly what he thought of her order of operations.

If he forced his way into the bedroom, she'd succumb to his charms. He knew she would. The fire in her eyes when she'd talked of christening his cabin told him all he needed to know.

But good things come to those who wait, he reminded himself. *I've already waited three years. What's thirty more minutes?*

It took some effort, and a metric shit-ton of self-control, but he managed to call through the door, "Do you want mayonnaise or mustard on your sandwich?"

Her words were muffled, but he could hear how she deliberately deepened her Southern accent. "Sugar, where I was raised, it's not a sandwich unless it has mayonnaise."

Sugar. She'd said it to be funny. Even still, the endearment hit his ears like a tongue, swirled around in his chest like tickling fingers, and then settled directly behind his fly.

He could quite clearly imagine her whispering in his ear, *"Harder. Deeper. I want to feel all of you inside me, sugar."*

Hard as a damn rock. That's what he was. And he had to adjust himself or risk injury.

When he heard the shower switch on, he forced himself to head back to the kitchen. But as he began building their sandwiches, he imagined her in the shower. In *his* shower.

Imagined the hot water sluicing over her pale skin and pooling in her belly button. Fantasized about the crystalline droplets clinging to her stiff nipples. Could see quite clearly in his mind's eye the way her hand rubbed his bar of soap over the length of her body.

Would her fingers find the place between her legs?

Would she tease herself?

Ready herself for him?

"Shit." In his daydreaming and distraction, he'd spread half the jar of mayonnaise on one slice of bread.

CHAPTER 15

Black Knights Inc.

"**W**hat's the verdict?"

Hannah stood in front of BKI's bank of computers watching lines of code scroll across multiple screens. But she looked up at the sound of Sam's voice.

And nearly fell off her legs.

He was naked.

Okay, not really.

He had on jeans and his biker boots. But his wide chest was bare. Or, at least it *had been* for a split second before he pulled a clean T-shirt over his head.

That split second had been enough for her to get an eyeball full of heavy pectoral muscles, flat, brown nipples, and a smattering of dark, crinkly chest hair, though. And from her body's reaction, he may as well have been fully nude.

H-h-holy hell, he's h-a-w-t. Straight fire.

A handful of minutes earlier, Peanut, the fat, notch-eared tomcat who'd introduced himself to her by jumping into her lap and licking her chin with his sandpaper tongue, had done as cats were known to do. Which was create mayhem and mischief. He'd batted a full mug of coffee off one of the computer tables and directly into Sam's lap.

Luckily, it'd been Hannah's cup. The coffee at BKI was strong enough to wake the dead and she'd added enough cold cream to the concoction so that the liquid had only been lukewarm instead of scalding hot. Otherwise, Sam might've gotten a second-degree burn on his nether regions.

And wouldn't that *have been a crying shame? Especially because, rumor has it, his nether region is a rather fine specimen.*

After leaping up and cursing the cat—Peanut had only slow-blinked at Sam before lifting a leg to meticulously bathe his balls—Sam had disappeared upstairs to change. Apparently, he hadn't felt the need to complete the task before tromping back down to the second floor though.

Now Hannah had a dry mouth, a flip-flopping belly, and a flaming hot pair of panties to contend with.

"Hannah?" His heavy brow was drawn down when he stopped beside her.

"Hmm?" She blinked up at him dreamily.

"I asked if you've had any luck?"

"Don't know." She shook her head. "Can't think."

"Why?" His bearded chin pulled back. "What's wrong?"

"I'm dumbstruck by the sight of your six-pack abs and sexy smile."

"Cut it out." He waved a hand.

"What? You don't think your smile is sexy?"

"It's not that. It's—"

"So you *do* think your smile is sexy?" She tsked. "Sam, really. How conceited."

"What I *meant* was cut out the flirting." He gave her a censorious look she thought was meant to be intimidating. Instead, it just made her want to use his ears as handles as she kissed the glower right off his mouth.

"Why?" she asked. "Is it inappropriate? Are you seeing someone?"

"What?" He shook his head vigorously. "No." She felt a rush of relief. "I don't have time for—" He shook his head again. "What I meant is, you shouldn't be flirting because it's like…incestuous or something."

Okay. Now she wanted to kiss him *and* strangle him.

"Incestuous? Last I checked, we're not related."

"But I dated your sister. Which sorta makes me like a brother. Or a brother-in-law, at the very least."

That did it. She was ready to forgo the kiss altogether and get straight to the strangling. The man was an idiot.

"In what world?" she demanded.

Instead of answering, he asked, "How is Candy, by the way? When we ran into each other in the pub all those months ago, we didn't really get the chance to catch up. We talked about you and what you've been up to since graduating, and then her friends dragged her off to dinner before I could ask how life has been treating her."

All Hannah's indignation leaked out of her. It was replaced by defeat, because...

Candy.

Her entire existence things always came back to Candy.

Candy the beautiful.

Candy the glamorous.

Candy the golden girl.

She'd assumed Sam had looked her up and *that's* how he'd known what she did for a living. She'd assumed he'd been home alone one night and thought to himself, *I wonder whatever happened to little Hurricane Hannah?* And she'd felt giddy knowing that, even after all the intervening years, she'd still crossed his mind.

But of course it'd been Candy who'd mentioned her and reminded him that once upon a time he'd sat on a porch swing with an awkward thirteen-year-old girl.

Her shoulders slumped and her tone was less than enthusiastic when she told him, "She's married to a commodities broker and living in the Gold Coast. She wears Prada, carries Birkin bags, and spends most of her time with her trainer or at the spa getting beauty treatments. In short, she's living her dream."

Sam nodded. "Yeah. She looked pretty fancy when I saw her. The rock on her left hand probably cost more than I make in a year. She always said she was getting out of Englewood by hook or by crook."

"She chose the first way. She took one look at Jared...he's my *real* brother-in-law, by the way," she added with a pointed stare, "and sank her hooks into him so fast and so deep he had no hope of escape."

Canting her head, she reconsidered her words. "Or, maybe it's more accurate to say she took one look at his Ivy League degree and nearly seven-figure salary and decided he was her meal ticket out of the Southside."

"You make her sound predatory." Sam frowned. "I never thought of her that way."

"Not predatory. Just…" She wrinkled her nose as she tried to think of the right word to describe her big sister. "Determined. And more than ready to use the assets she was born with to get exactly what she wanted."

When a distracted look crossed Sam's face, she thought he was thinking about Candy's assets and her hands curled into claws. Then he crossed his arms and his expression turned contemplative. "Is that jealousy I hear in your voice?"

"More like exasperation." She pursed her lips. "Jared reads books like *A People's History of the United States* and Candy reads *Allure*. He watches documentaries about the melting of the polar ice caps and she can't be bothered to tune in to anything more intense than TikTok. He's a rabid fan of NPR and she listens to Fat Mascara."

"Fat Mascara?" Sam raised an eyebrow.

"It's this beauty podcast. Which is actually sort of interesting, if you're into those kinds of things. But that's beside the point." She shook her head. "The point is, Jared and Candy have nothing in common. Nothing to talk about at the end of the day. And so you know what happens? He calls *me* to discuss politics and the latest *National Geographic* article."

"That bothers you?"

"No." Her chin pulled back. "I love Jared like a brother. But I can't help thinking men are like magpies when it comes to beautiful woman. They get distracted chasing after shiny shit and don't pay any attention to any of the stuff that really matters."

"And what really matters?"

"Cooperation. Communication. Compatibility." She ticked off the list on her fingers.

"Ah, yes. The three C's. So very romantic."

If it were possible to light someone's hair on fire with a look, Sam would've gone up like a Roman candle. "It *is* romantic, you big ape. But you're like most guys and don't care about anything other than a pretty face."

"I think I take offense at being judged by my gender and lumped into the *all men* category."

"Well, I didn't mean it as a compliment."

He fisted his hands on his hips. There was a look on his face she couldn't read. Which annoyed her further.

"*What?*" she demanded.

"I don't know how to say this," he said cautiously.

"Succinctly usually works best, I've found."

"You sound…*bitter*. Like someone broke your heart. Who was it?" The teasing light was back in his eyes. "I'll kill him."

That would mean you'd have to commit suicide, she thought grumpily.

On second thought, it wasn't fair to say Sam had broken her heart. It was more like…after he left Englewood, her world kept spinning, her life moved on, but her heart was an ancient flower stuck in amber. Frozen in time and form. Unchanged.

Unable to change.

"No one broke my heart," she told him breezily. "Although I did date a guy for two years in college who ended up cheating on me with a Kappa Alpha Theta."

Sam narrowed his eyes in mock menace. "Do you want me to kill *him*? Where does he live? What's his name?"

"Brian Gibson. And last I heard he's hocking sports equipment in Arlington Heights. But you don't have to kill him. Or even maim him. I decided back then that revenge is best served with a side of strange dick. So after we broke up, I started sleeping with his roommate."

Sam coughed into his fist. "Jesus, Hannah."

"What? I'm a firm believer in letting Karma slap a bastard in the face so I don't have to. But back to my point…"

His smile was chagrined as he shook his head. "I gotta admit, I've lost the thread. What were we talking about?"

"The fact that so many of your"—she gestured up and down his length—"particular persuasion—"

"You mean cis-gendered, straight men?"

She placed a fingertip on the side of her nose. "Precisely. So many of your persuasion choose partners based solely on looks. But beauty is only skin-deep. And once the novelty of sleeping with a pretty woman wears off, what's left?"

"You tell me. You seem to be the expert."

"I detect a hint of sarcasm in your tone." She narrowed her eyes. "But I'm going to ignore it and answer you anyway. I'm gracious like that."

When he opened his mouth to make what she suspected was a snide remark, she lifted her hand and plowed ahead, "In my experience, what's left are phone calls to the kid sister-in-law because, despite Jared having a beautiful wife sitting on the sofa beside him, he has to reach out to me for mental stimulation. And while I think he enjoys our conversations as much as I do, I can't help wondering if he'd enjoy them *more* were he able to have them with Candy. Were he able to have it *all* with Candy."

Sam grinned broadly and, for a split second, he looked eighteen again. "Don't sell yourself or your conversational prowess short," he told her. "I bet, if you asked him, Jared would say he's content with things the way they are."

"You mean separating intellectual intimacy and physical intimacy?" She frowned at the idea.

"Sure." He shrugged. "The two don't have to be connected. I've had great sex with women I didn't even particularly *like* and *certainly* couldn't have had deep, philosophical conversations with."

"Ugh." She curled her upper lip. "Like I was saying, you're such a guy. Hashtag all men!"

"Are you telling me you've had intellectual compatibility with *every* man you've ever slept with? Including the ex's roommate?"

"Well, no. Are *you* telling *me* you've never fantasized about getting back at someone who's shit all over you? Come on." She scoffed. "It's the ultimate shit on fantasy."

His beard twitched. "I feel like we should workshop that title."

She rolled her eyes. "The thing is, I wasn't planning to spend the rest of my life with Chad. For one thing, his name was *Chad*. I mean, who does that to a kid? For another thing, all I wanted out of the relationship was a few weeks wherein we'd both have some fun at the expense of Brian the Buttmunch. But when it comes to looking for forever? When it comes to finding someone to grow old with? *Then* I want a man who is as stimulated by my brain as he is by my boobs."

Was it her imagination or did Sam's gaze flicker to her chest?

She decided it was her imagination when he shook his head and chuckled. "Hannah Blue, are you saying the girl who swore boys were only good for being video game opponents or D&D groupmates is actually on the hunt for Mr. Right?"

"Aren't we all searching for our very own happily ever after?"

"Dunno." He shrugged. "I think most of us are more concerned with happy-for-now. But even if we *are* all in the pursuit of life-long happiness, who says that has to be wrapped up in one person?" His eyes held hers in a hard blue grip. "Maybe there's no such thing as a soulmate. Maybe we'd all be better off if we admitted it's impossible to have all our needs met by a single individual."

No such thing as soulmates? No such thing as *soulmates*?

Was he serious?

One look in his eyes proved he was.

"Your vision is very reasonable and pragmatic and unexciting." Her tone sounded as crushed as her spirit. "And I hope beyond hope you're wrong."

"I never woulda pegged you as a romantic, Hurricane Hannah." He canted his head as he regarded her. "An idealist? Sure. But not a romantic."

"Why? Because I wasn't boy-crazy at thirteen?"

"Well, that and 'cause you're too smart to believe in the bullshit the rom-coms and love stories about sparkly vampires would have you believe. The idea of finding your one true love is a myth. But if it makes you feel any better, I don't think the idea of finding a perfect, lifelong relationship is."

"No?" She was tentatively heartened by the glimmer of hope he was offering.

"A perfect, life-long relationship requires exactly two things." He held up two fingers. "Two imperfect people who refuse to give up on each other when times get tough."

She eyed him consideringly as warmth spread through her chest. It might not be as neat and tidy as *soulmates*, but it was just as poignant. Maybe more so. Because it left less up to fate and more up to the people involved and the work they were willing to do together.

"Now who's the idealist?" Her smile was teasing.

"I prefer the term *pragmatist*." When something that looked very near sadness flickered in his eyes, her smile turned upside down. If she wasn't mistaken, a ghost of a memory drifted across his face and brought with it pain and suffering.

"Why do you suddenly look like someone firebombed your entire Minecraft world?" she asked.

He blinked. "You realize I don't have the first clue what that means."

"Doesn't matter." She waved away her explanation as a thought occurred. "Sixteen years is a long time to be out of touch. A lot can happen. Did you ever get married? Do you have any kids?"

Silently she added, *Is that sorrow I see as the result of some idiotic woman who gave up on you when times got tough?*

Before he could respond, the speakers attached to one of the monster-sized monitors dinged. Her eyes shot to the screen.

Yippee! A breakthrough. *And grr.* At the worst possible time. Just when they were getting into the meat of a really juicy conversation.

"What is it?" he asked.

"I think I finally might have something. But it can wait."

"No." He shook his head. "It can't. A woman's reputation, not to mention her *life*, is on the line."

Double grr.

After taking a seat in a chair, she scooted it in front of one of the monitors. She punched in a couple of keystrokes on the Bluetooth keyboard and a ten-digit number flashed on the screen.

"There." She pointed. "That's the number that sent the text to Grace. Hot *damn*, I'm good!"

"Yes, yes." Sam leaned over her shoulder to get a better look. "You're very smart and resourceful and crafty."

She pursed her lips. "Funny. Your words say one thing, but your tone says another."

Instead of answering her, he stood to his full height and crossed his arms. "I thought you were gonna start with the director of the FBI? *He's* the one who either has to be the double agent or who has to be sharing his information with the person who is."

Before the cat/coffee incident, he'd filled her in on all the details regarding Agent Beacham's investigation into the troll farm, her partner's death, her flight from the Russian assassin, and her suspected frame-up by someone in a position of power who was acting as a double agent.

"I am." She pointed to the screen on her right, which continued to flash lines of code. "I'm running a program that covertly tests for weak spots in the FBI's internal database. But stealth takes time. And while I was waiting, I used Grace's phone number to hack into her cellular log. After a bit of cyber magic, I was able to pinpoint where the blocked number originated." She gestured toward the screen. "Voila!"

He leaned over her shoulder again to look at the number. "Where's area code 896?"

God, he smells good, she thought longingly. She wanted to bury her nose in his warm, tan neck and pull his scent into her lungs. Take a part of him inside herself.

"Hannah?" He turned his head to look at her and she realized she'd been holding her breath when it wheezed out of her.

The temptation to close the short distance between them and catch his lips in a kiss was intense. In fact, she'd never been more tempted by anything in her life.

Except for maybe that 3D printer I saw at last year's tech conference.

Unfortunately, at ten G's, it'd been out of her price range.

No, no. On second thought, I want Sam more.

He was *so* close. All it'd take was three, maybe four inches, and she'd have him lip-locked. Maybe she could fake a rolling chair malfunction that just, *oopsie,* happened to have her mouth landing on his and—

"Hannah." He snapped his fingers in front of her face and she blinked. "Where'd you go?"

"Sorry." She shook her head. "What was the question?"

A concerned frowned drew his eyebrows together. "The area code?"

"Oh, right." She keyed in a quick Google inquiry, then sat back and covertly slipped a watermelon Jolly Rancher into his hip pocket.

It was a trick she'd been doing since she was a kid and first learned he loved them.

Once the webpage she was after opened, she nodded. "Yeah. I'm not surprised. This"—she pointed at the monitor—"says 896 is an unassigned area code."

"Meaning what? The number you found isn't right?"

"No. It's right. It was simply fabricated out of thin air by someone with a little know-how. Probably so they could use it just that once and then discard it."

When Sam straightened, taking his tempting lips with him, she didn't know whether to sigh with relief or cry out in disappointment.

"So, what? We're screwed?" He ran a hand over his beard and she enjoyed a brief fantasy of what it might feel like to have that beard brushing against her neck, over her nipples, between her thighs.

"Not necessarily." She had to force herself not to shift uncomfortably because her brief daydream had made parts of her southern hemisphere heat up. "Whoever made up the number probably sent the text via their PC as opposed to their cell phone. It's possible if we try to…" She trailed off as her fingers flew over the keyboard.

For a good five minutes, she worked her magic until… "There." She pointed at the glowing curser as it blinked on the screen. "If they're monitoring anyone trying to communicate with that number, and if they'll deign to answer, we should see a response come in here."

It felt like an eternity as they both waited, watching the blinking cursor as if it held the answers to the meaning of life. And maybe for Agent Grace Beacham, it did. Then…

Who are you?

When those three words appeared on the screen, Hannah shot a hand of victory in the air.

"Hurricane Hannah!" Sam spun her around in the chair, then pulled her to her feet and into a bear hug. "I knew you could do it!"

Her self-congratulations were forgotten because there wasn't an inch between them. They were chest to chest, thigh to thigh. Even the outsides of her feet touched the insides of his.

To say her skin was electrified was an understatement. It felt like every nerve was singed raw. And she was *very* aware of just how big he was against her. How wide his chest was. How powerful his thighs were. How *solid* and warm he felt.

She would've taken a moment to revel in the embrace. But he pushed her away so quickly, she nearly got a crick in her neck.

The fanciful part of her hoped the move was a result of him being shocked by the feel of her in his arms and the subsequent awareness that she was a grown-ass woman. But the practical part of her knew that was fantasy. He proved it when he said, "Go, go! Answer! Hurry!"

Suppressing a sigh, she retook her seat and paused with her fingers over the keyboard. "What should I say?"

"Holy fucknuts, Hannah." His gaze was diamond-hard. "What's going on? Why do you look like you've seen a ghost?" He jerked his chin toward the words glowing on the monitor. "Who's Kerberos?"

Her voice was little more than a rasp. "According to Greek legend, Kerberos was the three-headed dog who guarded the gates of the Underworld to keep the dead from leaving."

When he only stared at her in confusion, she added, "But in hacker circles and on Reddit threads, Kerberos is like Anonymous on crack. They're geniuses who do what no one else can. I assumed they were a myth conjured up by nerds who daydreamed about superhero hacktivists the way most kids dream about Iron Man. But"—she had to swallow—"looks like they're real."

He shoved to a stand. "First a Russian assassin named Orpheus who most people don't believe exists, and now a group of souped-up computer geeks who—"

"They're more than souped-up computer geeks," she cut him off. "*I* am a souped-up computer geek. *These* people?" She gestured toward the monitor. "They were able to figure out where we are in three minutes when it should've taken them three hours. They aren't just good. They aren't even just great. They're *scary* great. No cap."

When his dark eyebrows pulled into a deep V, she waved off his scowl. "No cap means no lie. Sheesh. Do you ever open social media?"

"Sorry I'm not hip to the lingo you kids are using nowadays." He rolled his eyes and she wanted to poke them out. How many times since she'd arrived onsite had he called her *kid*? "I've been busy for the last decade and a half." She gave him a dirty look and he was quick to add, "Not that your degrees and your job haven't kept you busy. I wasn't saying that."

She crossed her arms and harumphed. "I forgive you. This time. And only because our emotions are running high because this…" She gestured toward Kerberos's glowing words. "This is big. No. On second thought, it's *huge* if Kerberos is involved. You think Agent Beacham has a clue what she's stumbled into?"

"I think she started to suspect right around the time she was warned the Kremlin's very own version of John Wick was on her tail."

She frowned. "At least John Wick abides by a code of ethics. From everything I've read about this Orpheus character"—she pointed to another monitor showing what she'd found in the dregs of the dark web regarding the assassin—"he has no problem killing innocents if the price is right."

"Orpheus. Kerberos. Why does every shadowy, underworld figure turn to Greek mythology to pick their code name?" His glower might've looked frightening to anyone who didn't know that his center was soft and squishy.

"Probably because Greek mythology has influenced society in just about every way over the millennia. From culture to traditions to politics, it has shaped the way we think. Hell, most of the lessons we're taught as children about what it means to be a good person and the possible repercussions of being a bad person can be traced back to a specific Greek myth. So… in the fight between good and evil, it makes sense the people involved are attracted to the source material."

Sam just blinked at her.

"What?" she scowled. "You asked."

"Ever heard of a rhetorical question?"

"The whole point of a rhetorical question is not to respond because the person who asked it already knows the answer. I didn't get the impression you *did* know the answer."

His frown melted into a grin. "God, I've missed you." And then he crushed the joy that sentence brought by tacking on a "kid" at the end.

She almost lifted her shirt to flash him her boobs and prove, once and for all, just how much of a "kid" she *wasn't*. Instead she asked, "What do you want me to type next?"

If he noticed she'd gritted the question from between her teeth, he didn't let on. "Ask 'em why they stepped in to help Agent Beacham."

The man has zero clue how close he came to a drive-by boobing, she thought as she typed in the question. Once again, the response was almost immediate.

She's an innocent in the game.

"Guess she was telling the truth when she said she didn't kill her partner," Hannah muttered.

"Ask 'em who *isn't* an innocent in the game," he prompted, and she enthused, "Oh, that's a good one."

Many that we know of. One we don't.

His chin jerked back. "The fuck is that supposed to mean? Do all hackers imagine they're some version of The Riddler?"

It was becoming clear Kerberos wasn't going to offer up evidence on a silver platter. And what answers they did give were going to be cryptic.

"I think we should ask how they found out about Orpheus," she offered. "The FBI is a threat to Grace's freedom. But the assassin is a threat to her life."

Sam gave a staunch dip of his whiskered chin. "Agreed."

You will find the answers you seek once you follow the director's emails was the reply from Kerberos after she keyed in the question.

"Aha!" Sam drew her attention over her shoulder when he snapped his fingers. "We were *right*." Then he frowned. "Whoa. What's that?"

"What's what?"

He pointed to the monitor where letters, numbers, and symbols assembled in tight groups scrolled across the screen. To the layman, they would look like gibberish. Even to the casual hacker they would be confusing as hell. But to Hannah? They were clear and concise and absolutely beautiful.

Whomever had written the code was a master artist. The Michelangelo of the computing world. And her eyes were drawn to the screen like most people were drawn to the painting of the *Mona Lisa*.

"Good god," she wheezed, leaning forward until her face glowed in the light from the monitor. "It's a secret backdoor into the FBI's servers."

CHAPTER 16

650 West Chicago Avenue,
Chicago, Illinois

W hen Pavel's cell phone vibrated in his pocket, he was sitting on the bank of the river outside the building where they printed the *Chicago Tribune*. He'd wiled away the hours watching tourists lean over the rails of their tour boats. Their noses all sunburned. Their faces all sweaty. But they always smiled as they snapped pictures of the skyscrapers growing in the near distance like limbless metal trees.

When was the last time he himself had taken a vacation? He couldn't remember. And the last assignment he'd had in Aruba, taking out the former Japanese prime minister, certainly didn't count. He'd been on and off the little island in less than twenty-four hours.

His phone buzzed again, but he didn't immediately answer it. Instead, he listened to the end of this most recent tour guide's tale of how the gangster, Al Capone, had once held the city in his thrall with bootleg booze, tommy guns, and men in three-piece suits riding around in bulletproof Cadillacs.

He felt a certain kinship to Mr. Capone. Like Pavel, Al had lived hard. Lived fast. And answered to no one.

There was honor in that. Greatness even.

When the guide finished his spiel, Pavel thumbed on his phone. "*Da?* Yes?"

"Took you long enough," was Bishop's opening salvo.

Impatient, as always.

Refusing to rise to the bait, he asked, "Have you found Agent Beacham?"

"I was able to pull CCTV footage showing she exited the city on the back of the same motorcycle that rode to her rescue earlier. A traffic camera caught her traveling through Gary, Indiana. And then security footage from a gas station had them heading north in Michigan on Highway 140."

Pavel pushed up from the embankment and rubbed the loose grass from the seat of his jeans. Play time was over. He had to get back to work.

Lighting a cigarette, he headed toward the public parking garage where he'd stowed his rented car.

"Do you know their final destination?" he asked.

"Not yet. But I do know *who* she was riding behind. Man's name is Hunter Jackson. Before he became part of the president's *goon squad*, as you so accurately called them, he was a decorated Green Beret. I won't bore you with the details of all his medals and commendations, but he's not your everyday, average army grunt. Keep that in mind when you confront him."

"*Nyet.* There will be no confrontation," Pavel shook his head even though Bishop couldn't see him. "There will only be death. Do you still want me to make it look like she committed suicide?"

"That'd be best. But at this point, I think she just needs to die. If her death leads to more inquiries into what she was investigating, I'll deal with them as they arise."

"Very good." Pavel nodded, his options for terminating the lady agent expanding exponentially. "I'll see that it's done once you get me her location."

"Working on it," Bishop assured him. "Now that I know who she's with, I can start sifting through the man's life until I find out where he's most likely to take her. Initial inquiries haven't revealed any properties he owns in the state, but he does have one cousin there. I'm lifting every rock to see what comes crawling out from under it. In the meantime, get out of Chicago. Get to Michigan. And start heading north. I'll call you when I know more."

"Very good," Pavel repeated and then shoved the phone in his pocket when Bishop abruptly ended the call.

There was a lightness to his step as he crossed the street, ignoring the blaring horn of a disgruntled taxi driver who took exception to his jaywalking. When he started whistling his favorite tune, the notes sounded sweeter. Truer. Brighter.

It had been years since one of his targets had made him work for it. He had forgotten how much he enjoyed the chase. And how much sweeter it made the eventual catch and kill.

CHAPTER 17

3 Majestic Ridge Road

Hunter decided the level of enjoyment he got from watching Grace eat bordered on a kink.

Every morsel she shoved between her sweet, upside-down lips had saliva gathering in his mouth. Each time she used the tip of her tongue to swipe at a crumb, his stomach tightened into a painful fist. And when she sucked mayonnaise from her fingers?

Fuck a duck. His dick actually jumped behind his fly.

She'd emerged from the bedroom *not* in the painted-on jeans, but in a pair of his boxer briefs and one of his T-shirts. The jeans had been sexy as hell, but nothing had prepared him for how he'd feel seeing her in *his* clothes. To know a shirt *he'd* worn a hundred times was draped across her breasts. Underwear *he'd* lounged around in cupped her sweet, heart-shaped ass.

Her blond hair was damp and falling around her shoulders. Her pretty face was scrubbed free of the dust from the road. And her long legs were bent so her bare feet perched on the lowest rung of the barstool as she sat at the kitchen island.

It was all so domestic and sweet and…romantic. Although, he'd never really associated the first two with the last one until going to work at BKI. Now, he couldn't untangle the trio. They went together. *Belonged* together.

Grace had been focusing on her sandwich. When she finished the last bite, she finally looked up, smiled her appreciation, and gave him a thumbs-up. "That was really good. Didn't realize how hungry I was."

He did. Realize how hungry *he* was. And not for a sandwich. It could've been a piece of cardboard for all he tasted of his own final bite. His whole attention, his entire *being* was pinned on Grace.

"Tell me about growing up in Asheville," he asked suddenly.

He stood across the island from her because he hadn't trusted himself to snag the barstool beside her. He hadn't been sure, with her so close, that he could've kept from grabbing her and dragging her off to the bedroom caveman-style before she got the chance to finish her sandwich. And now he needed to give her time to finish her lemonade. And *himself* time to recover from the unconsciously erotic show she'd put on while eating.

"What do you want to know?" She cocked her head, causing a lock of damp hair to fall over her shoulder. The end curled atop the gentle slope of her right breast, and he found himself unreasonably jealous of every single one of those golden filaments.

Is she not wearing a bra?

He was afraid to look and find out. If she wasn't, then he'd *really* be incapable of staying on his side of the kitchen island.

"What was it like to be a kid in the mountains? What are your siblings like? Are your parents the type to bicker? Or are they the lovey-dovey sort to slow dance in the garage?"

He'd seen Becky and Boss do that last thing back in the shop on those nights when a deadline forced Becky to work late. Boss would put their girls to sleep in the portable cribs he kept in his office, and then he'd wander down to the first floor where Becky would inevitably grab his hand and say, *"Dance with me."*

And Boss would.

Not well, mind you. The big oaf had two left feet.

Becky never seemed to mind, though. In fact, the way she stared up at Boss with such love shining in her eyes always made Hunter clear his throat and leave the room.

"Whew." Grace grinned now. "That's a lot of ground to cover."

"You don't have to answer any of it if you don't want to," he said, even though he hoped she would.

She'd come into his cabin, and by doing so, she'd gotten to know him. The *real* him. Not the stoic, tough military man he showed the world. But the side of him that liked handmade blankets and locally sourced pottery and the bits and bobs of colorful glass that washed up on the beach.

He was desperate to learn about her. All the elements of her life that had coalesced and culminated into making Grace Beacham the smart, witty, wonderful woman she was.

"I don't mind answering." She shrugged, and he felt a little jolt of anticipation. "It's just…" She tapped her lips. "Where to start?"

Her eyes went a little dreamy then. And he thought, if he concentrated, he could see reflections of rolling green mountains and skies the color of a robin's egg in her eyes.

"In the summer, the mountain laurels bloom and the whole place is vibrant with shades of pink," she began, her voice filled with affection. "There are waterfalls and hiking trails and swimming holes fed by high elevation streams that stay chilly even in the middle of July."

She took a sip of her lemonade before explaining, "The Appalachians aren't like the Rockies. Winters aren't harsh. But we still get snow a couple times a year, and it's so clean and fluffy. The rolling terrain makes for some of the best sledding on the planet. Although you have to be careful."

She pulled up the sleeve of her borrowed T-shirt and pointed to a small, crescent-shaped scar on her shoulder. "I got this when I was twelve. I was trying to impress Ricky Hollingsworth by taking my sled down the *big* hill, the one that was off-limits. I swear I was going forty miles-per-hour when I hit that hidden stump and got launched into a tree."

The face she made was so self-deprecating, he fought a smile.

"Needless to say, Ricky was not impressed. Most especially because he had to cut his own sledding short so he could run home and have his momma call my momma to come get me and take me to the hospital for stitches."

"So what you're saying is you've always been daring. From sledding down the *big* hill straight to becoming an FBI agent." He reached across the island and ran a finger over the scar, thrilled at how soft her skin was and beyond gratified when his touch caused goose bumps to erupt up the length of her arm. When he pulled back and she dropped the sleeve of the T-shirt, he noted her pupils had dilated.

He'd experienced the strange alchemy that was physical chemistry plenty of times. But there was something different about Grace. Touching her set him on fire and, at the same time, brought him comfort.

It was the damndest thing. That strange dichotomy. He couldn't quite figure it out.

"Daring?" she countered with a wry twist of her lips. "Or dumb? Ever notice how it's hard to tell the difference between the two? I mean, look at me, accused of murder and hiding from a hired killer. Not sure anyone would congratulate me right now on being the brightest star in the sky."

It was easy to forget what'd brought them to the cabin when she was sitting across from him looking so fresh and sweet—and with the promise of what was to come hanging in the air between them. But her words brought reality crashing back in.

"We're going to get you through this," he assured her.

Her expression turned rueful. "I feel a little like Princess Leia." When he only frowned, she quoted, "'Help me, Obi Wan Kenobi. You're my only hope.'" Her rueful expression turned sour. "I hate being thrust into the role of damsel in distress. I hate that I can't be the one to solve this thing and save my own ass. And I *really* hate that I dragged you and your friends into this. If I'd known—"

"I don't hate it," he cut her off. "If you hadn't dragged me into this, we wouldn't be here now, sitting across from each other while you tell me more about Asheville."

Her delightful mouth pursed into a perfect oval. "Suave. Very suave how you got us back on topic."

"I'm more than just a pretty face."

"True." She lifted a finger and he imagined her running it down the center of his back the same way she'd run it over the spines of his books. "Although, if I'm being honest, your pretty face was one of the first things I liked about you."

"And here I thought it was my effervescent personality and my introducing you to my gem of a cousin, Chuck."

That made her laugh. For whatever reason, maybe because he'd never been accused of being a comedian, he felt unreasonably pleased with himself.

"How is Chuck by the way?" She lifted an eyebrow.

"Plotting to overthrow the government. But what else is new?"

All the humor died in her eyes. "Maybe our government *needs* to be overthrown. Or parts of it, at least."

He hated the worry he saw on her face. Hated more that it was accompanied by fear.

Since there was nothing he could do to assuage either, the next best weapon he had in his arsenal was distraction.

"So...Asheville?" he encouraged.

Her expression relaxed. "It's this old hippy town. Tons of music festivals, farmer's markets, and colorful murals painted on the sides of the buildings. It ranks as one of the most LGBTQIA-friendly cities in the US. Which means you can walk around downtown feeling accepted and loved and included no matter who you are or who you love or what you look like. It wasn't until I moved away for college that I realized the whole world isn't like that."

The way she talked about her birthplace made it seem magical. Hunter couldn't imagine loving the place you're from. From the time he'd been old enough to realize leaving was an option, he'd counted down the seconds until he could put Benton Heights in his rearview mirror.

"In the springtime, we would load up the station wagon and leave the bustling metropolis behind for the high country." The look on her face told him Asheville was a far cry from a bustling metropolis. "That's where my daddy was raised and where my grandmother lived until the day she died. Granny Pearl always had cornbread in the oven and a hound on her front porch. She taught us kids how to color Easter eggs with dye made from berries and how to cook collard greens so we didn't poison ourselves."

Her childhood sounded better than any books he'd read or any movies he'd watched. True happiness really existed for the lucky few. And that made the work he did, the struggle to make the world a better place, feel like it was worth it.

"What about your brothers and sister?" he prompted when she fell silent.

Her expression turned a little peevish, but there was humor in her eyes. "My oldest brother, Merit, is the family comedian. Or so he thinks. Really he just loves practical jokes. He once filled the mayonnaise jar with Greek yogurt, and you've never seen a house full of madder Southerners. He's lucky he survived. My momma spent thirty minutes chasing him around with a wooden spoon."

"Did she catch him?"

She nodded. "Merit was fast, but Momma had stamina. Eventually she wore him down. By that point, though, she'd run all the mad out of herself. Instead of giving him a good wallop, all she did was hand him the spoon and tell him he had to finish the entire mayonnaise jar full of yogurt before he could have anything else to eat." Her grin turned evil. "It took him two days, and he *still* turns green at the sight of Greek yogurt."

"Your accent gets thicker when you talk about them." His ears hummed with the roundness of her vowels and the softness of her consonants.

"Lord, you don't know the half of it." She chuckled. "You should hear how country I get when I'm back there. It's like the instant I step off the plane and breathe in that moist mountain air, the singsong sounds of Appalachia take over."

"It hits the ear like a lullaby," he told her.

She regarded him curiously. "You know, you might not talk much. But when you do, you really have a way with words."

He wasn't sure he agreed, so all he did was shrug. "And your other siblings?" he prompted. "What are they like?"

"Noble is only a year younger than Merit, but they couldn't be more different. He's quiet and reserved." She slid him a considering look. "Reminds me of someone else I know. My daddy always says Noble took the words *give every man thy ear, but few thy voice* to heart. And I think since Noble hasn't spent his life flapping his lips, he's been able to concentrate on the why and the how of things. He has a rare gift for seeing the big picture. It's what makes him such a good detective. And what makes him such a good father too, I reckon."

She patted her hips as if looking for something in a pocket. And then made a rueful face. "If I had my phone, I'd show you pictures of Jessie and Jemma." She let out a sad little sigh for her lost device. "Noble was the first of us to have kids. Which means he holds a special place in Momma's heart. I'm pretty sure her goal in life has always been to become a grandma."

The first of us to have kids...

It was such a casual remark, but it revealed so much.

A hard stone settled in the pit of his stomach. He ignored it to ask, "And your sister?"

She laughed. "We were fire and gasoline when we were younger.

But that's because she was wolverine mean." Her smile went soft. "She's mellowed with age. Still fierce, but she's less likely to poke me in the eye or pull my hair if I make her mad."

"What's her name?"

"Felicity."

He crossed his arms. "Merit, Noble, Grace, and Felicity. That's quite the quartet."

"I think my folks thought if they named us after a virtue then maybe we'd take on the quality of our namesakes."

"And have you?"

She chewed on her lower lip in consideration. He barely refrained from jumping over the island to help her with the task.

"Hard to say," she finally admitted. "I'm too close to the subject matter to be unbiased. Plus, my opinion of them is tainted because I know just what shits they all were between the ages of eight and eighteen."

"Yourself included?" He cocked an eyebrow.

Her nod was immediate. "Of course. I was the annoying kid sister to my older brothers and the vicious big sister to Felicity."

"You?" He regarded her from the corner of his eye. "Vicious? I don't believe it."

"You *should*. Big sisters are notoriously heinous. It comes with the job title. Although I'll admit Felicity deserved everything I ever dished. Wolverine mean, remember? But there was one time I took things too far."

When he said nothing, simply waited for her to continue, she sighed. "Felicity was *terrified* of spiders, you see. And to get back at her for freezing my training bras, I spent an entire afternoon catching every grandaddy long legs I could find. And I found *a lot*."

"Oh, no." He fought a smile, imagining pubescent Grace scheming up an act of diabolical revenge. "What did you do with them?"

"Put them in her bed."

A shocked chuckle shot out of him. "You didn't."

"I did." She nodded again, and her mouth twisted with regret. "Felicity had *no* idea they were there until she'd snuggled under the covers and they started crawling over her face."

She closed her eyes and shivered. "If pure, undiluted terror has a sound, it's Felicity's scream that night. The memory of it still haunts me."

She opened her eyes. "She was afraid to sleep in her own bed for *months* afterward. And she *still* refuses to climb into bed if she hasn't pulled back the covers and checked for spiders."

"I bet she never froze your bras again," he said with a chuckle.

"Be glad you were an only child." She made a face. "Siblings are one of the main sources of trauma."

"But you wouldn't trade them for the world." It was a statement, not a question.

"No." Her expression turned rueful. "I wouldn't. The love we share now outweighs the damage we did to each other back then."

Envy spiked through his heart. Or maybe it was wistfulness, a longing for something he never had and had no hope of *ever* having. Family that was bound by blood and shared history.

"My parents were high school sweethearts," she continued and he was glad for the interruption to his melancholy thoughts. "Fell in love at fifteen and haven't spent more than a day or two apart ever since. Daddy's a sheriff and Momma's a librarian. Their favorite things to do together are garden and read. They don't dance in the garage much, but they're always the first to get out on the floor at weddings. They can two-step like nobody's business. And every day of my life they've made me feel loved."

There were so many thoughts and feelings swirling around inside his head. All of them were too big to articulate. So he simply said, "Sounds nice."

"*Is* nice." She parroted his words from earlier. "And they'd love you."

Once again, everything inside him stilled. And once again, his expression had her quickly forging ahead, "Not that I think you'll ever meet them. I just mean that hypothetically if you *were* to meet them, they'd love you."

"Why?" He hoped she couldn't hear just how desperate he was for her answer.

"Because you're honest and trustworthy and selfless enough to come running when yours truly"—she pointed to herself—"calls you up in dire straits."

"It wasn't selflessness, Grace. I wanted to see you again."

The teasing dimmed in her eyes. For the count of several heartbeats, neither of them spoke. Finally, she shivered. "Lord, there you go again. Looking at me like that."

"Like what?"

"Like you're thinking about swallowing me whole."

Warmth unfurled in his gut. And lower. "I've found most really delicious things taste better if you savor them."

He watched, mesmerized, as two things happened simultaneously. One, her breathing picked up. And two, her nipples hardened into tight points beneath the T-shirt.

She *wasn't* wearing a bra.

Just as he'd known would happen, his feet took him around the island before he'd made the conscious decision to move. Spinning her barstool until she faced him, he placed his hands on the counter's edge on either side of her and leaned close.

Close enough to see the golden flecks sprinkled through the brown of her irises. Close enough to feel warmth bathe his hungry mouth when she blew out a shaky breath.

She smelled like his soap and shampoo. But underneath was...Grace. The hint of Dove deodorant and Downy dryer sheets—so wholesome and pure.

Which just made him want to do really *unwholesome* and *impure* things to her.

"You've showered and finished your sandwich, Grace." His voice sounded less like his voice and more like Canteen Green's rumbling engine. "If I recall, according to your order of operations it's time to..." He trailed off and let his eyes drift down to her mouth. A muscle twitched in his jaw when her tongue darted out to wet her lips in an unconscious invitation. "How did you put it?"

"Christen the cabin?" she ventured breathlessly.

Cupping her cheek in his palm, he gently rubbed the pad of his thumb first over her bottom lip and then over the top one. He remembered being tempted by her lips the first time he'd seen them. He was even *more* tempted now because he knew how soft they were. How eager they could be when she met him lick for lick, suck for suck.

"I want to take you to the bedroom, Grace." He'd meant to ask a question. It'd come out a statement.

She swallowed again. And instead of answering, she simply nodded.

The Green Berets had trained him to control his breathing, slow his heart rate, and tamp down his adrenaline. But all it took was that small gesture of acquiescence and he forgot everything he'd learned.

Three years of longing, three years of yearning, three years of dreaming and fantasizing were about to become reality.

When he held out his hand and she slipped her fingers into his, he noted how pale her skin was compared to his. How delicate her fingers looked cradled in his thick, callused palm. The contrast of her feminine softness held tight within his masculine strength had his inner barbarian beating at the gates.

He wanted to pillage. To plunder. To ransack and ravage and claim. But he also wanted to cherish. To treasure. He wanted to wrap her up and hold her close and make all the ugliness and danger that was the world outside disappear.

When he gave her a gentle tug, she came willingly to her feet. He was stopped from dragging her into the bedroom, however, because the move brought her close to him. Close enough so the tips of her breasts brushed his chest.

It was like being hit by the prongs of a stun gun. Electricity sizzled his nerve endings. Crackling heat fired his blood.

The bedroom's too far, he decided.

CHAPTER 18

The instant Hunter's lips claimed her own, Grace realized she'd been lying to herself for three straight years.

The fire she'd felt when he kissed her the night of the fundraiser had nothing to do with her being vulnerable and stinging from her ex's foul accusations. It had everything to do with Hunter himself.

The man was a marvel.

Unlike others, he didn't begin the kiss by shoving his tongue into her mouth. No. His lips were soft and firm. The palms of his hands were callused and gentle as he framed her face and canted her head to the side so he could better fit their mouths together. And his breath was warm and sweet as he nipped and sucked and teased, igniting her desires so *she* was the one who eventually went up on tiptoe, curled her hands into his hair, and dipped her tongue into the waiting wonder that was his hot, delectable mouth.

"Mmm," he hummed with delight. And it was all the encouragement she needed to sample and suck and play.

For long minutes, he let her take the lead and matched her play-by-play. Catching her tongue. Sucking her lips. Eagerly exploring her mouth.

He tasted like lemonade, sugary and tart. And he felt so warm and strong against her, a wall of brute strength that he'd tamed into tenderness.

When she was in the shower, he must've taken the opportunity to wash the road off his face and arms. The twin scents of aftershave and leather oil still clung to his skin, but beneath was the citrusy aroma of fresh soap.

She hooked an ankle behind his knee to better align their bodies and his restraint broke. He no longer followed her lead. Instead, he grabbed her ass—his fingers leaving five perfect divots in each cheek—and bent her backward.

His kisses went from savoring and sweet to ravenous and greedy. And because he'd taken the time to stoke her libido, she welcomed his unbridled passion.

The brawniness of his chest created eye-crossing friction against her nipples. The strength of his thigh against the juncture of her legs had her heedlessly rubbing herself against him, seeking more stimulation. And as she threaded her arms around his neck to pull him even closer, there was no mistaking the hard bulge of his arousal, so thick and insistent and pulsing against the soft curve of her lower belly.

It had been a heady thing to hear Hunter say he wanted her. It was headier still to feel the undisputed evidence of his desire.

"You taste like lemon drops," he said between long, luxurious, breathtaking kisses. "Sugary and tart. I could kiss you forever."

"Who's stopping you?" She caught his bottom lip between her teeth and laved it with her tongue. The man had the most amazing lips. Full and firm and so perfectly made that his cupid's bow looked like it'd been drawn on by an artist's exacting hand.

He groaned his pleasure when she bit his lip—not hard; just a little pressure to test the texture of his flesh—and she tucked that bit of information away. That he liked it when she used her teeth.

She imagined softly catching his nipple between her canines and flicking it with her tongue. Fantasized about kissing her way down his corrugated belly and biting the jut of his hip bones. Envisioned taking his thick, turgid length into her mouth and sucking him to near completion only to stop and back him down by scraping her teeth along his length—an erotic warning that *she* was the one in charge and setting the pace, and that *she* was the one who'd tell him when it was time to finish.

Either he read her mind, or they were thinking the same thing, because his lip popped free of her teeth when he hissed, "Fuck me. I want to go slow with you, Grace. But I don't know if I can. Not this first time."

"Slow is for sloths and glaciers," she countered.

One corner of his mouth twitched and she thought he might gift her with one of his rare smiles. Instead, he bent and scooped her into his arms.

With one hand beneath her knees and the other around her back, he had her across the room, through the bedroom door, and in front of the bed before she could do more than blink at the ease with which he carried her.

She wasn't a small woman. But she felt delicate in his embrace.

The *man* in him called to the *woman* in her. Where he was hard, she was soft. Where he was rough, she was smooth. The more he pushed, the more pliant she became.

The mattress dipped under his knee. And then...

He lowered her until her back rested against the coverlet, and he was stretched out beside her. His weight depressed the mattress and had her sliding toward him until her side was pressed all along his front.

She expected him to keep up the voracious pace. She was a little disappointed when he suddenly slowed everything down by gently nipping the corner of her mouth before pulling back completely.

When she opened her eyes, she found him propped up on one elbow as he studied her. His hazel eyes looked impossibly green in the soft light shining in through the window above the bed. His lashes were so thick and dark, the kind women the world over shelled out the big bucks for. And when he picked up a lock of her damp hair, running it between his fingers, she thought she caught a hint of a smile.

"I like your hair this way." His voice had dropped an octave. She'd heard of bedroom eyes, but a bedroom voice? That was a new one. "It's longer now."

"You have more hair too." She ran a hand over his neatly trimmed facial hair. It was too long to be called stubble but probably too short to qualify as a beard. The devil in her, the one who was always hanging around but was *particularly* feisty when she was panting with lust, had her adding, "I like it. I've always enjoyed a well-upholstered seat."

It took a second for her meaning to sink in. But she saw the instant it did because his nostrils flared with desire at the same time humor glinted in his eyes. Then he did the most amazing thing.

He laughed.

Not a simple snort or even a respectable chuckle. But a full-bodied, full-throated laugh that was low and rumbly and so much more special than it might have been otherwise because the man was too serious by far.

Which, of course, only made her want to give him joy. Make him smile. Pull laughter out of him again and again until that shadowed look she sometimes saw in his eyes disappeared forever.

"I swear, woman," he wheezed when he finally lowered his chin. "I usually know what people are going to say before they say it. But the stuff that comes out of your mouth sometimes catches me off guard."

She wrinkled her nose. "Doing and saying what's expected is boring. Much better to keep folks on their toes."

"You know, I thought you were sexy the first time I saw you. But it was your sense of humor, the utter *sass* of you that kept me fantasizing about you for the last three years." He slid her a seductive glance. "Well, your sass and that red cocktail dress. Do you still have it?"

"Mmm." She nodded, thinking back to the night of the fundraiser when her little sister had FaceTimed her and *demanded* she wear the dress they'd purchased on a recent girls' trip.

Grace had only agreed to buy the shiny red number to shut Felicity up. She'd never intended to actually flounce around in public in the darned thing. After all, who did she think she was? Jessica Rabbit?

But after much arm-twisting and ego-stroking on Felicity's part, she'd squeezed herself into the dress for the charity event. Which had turned out to be the right decision if the look in Hunter's eyes right now was anything to go by.

"I don't have it with me unfortunately," she added a little breathlessly. Seriously, the *look* in his eyes. It was desire made palpable.

"At some point I hope I can convince you to drag it back out of the closet," he said...or rather *rumbled*.

"Big fan of fundraisers, are you?" she asked cheekily.

"Not particularly. I *am* a big fan of Grace Beacham, though. And that cocktail dress leaves little to the imagination." His lashes lowered along with his voice. "Although please don't think I haven't imagined. I have. I've imagined *plenty*."

She shivered at the idea of him fantasizing about her in that dress and touching himself. Stroking himself. Getting himself off while moaning her name.

Using a single finger, he softly traced a path from her forehead, over her nose, and down to her lips. He stopped with the pad of his finger pressed lightly over the seam of her mouth. And when she kissed it, his gaze became so acute she thought she could feel his eyes touching her mouth as surely as she could feel his fingertip.

I could kiss you forever.

His words echoed through her head and settled in her heart.

She desperately wanted to believe him. Believe that forever kisses were possible. But, lord, the way his eyes had gone wide when she'd made that comment about him meeting her family told her everything she needed to know.

Hunter Jackson wanted her for now. Not forever.

So whatever this is, she told herself, *it will begin and end here.*

Left to her own devices, she *would* fall in love with him. She knew it as surely as she knew her name was Grace Lynn Beacham. The man was just too wonderful.

The cabin is the boundary, she decided. The safe zone. *The place where I can pretend, just for a little while, that Hunter Jackson is mine.*

And when it was over, she would let him go, grateful for the time they'd spent together. For the intimacies they'd shared. And for him helping her feel like a desirable woman again and not some dried-up divorcee.

"You have the best mouth," he whispered, his eyes still glued to her lips. "You realize it's upside down, right?"

"Upside down?" Passion made her voice rusty, like the hinges on her granny Pearl's old garden gate.

"Mmm. Your top lip is fuller than your bottom." As if to prove his point, he leaned forward and caught her top lip between his teeth. The tip of his tongue was soft and warm as he leisurely tasted her.

And then tasted her some more.

She had no idea how long he spent making love to her mouth. And that was definitely the best way to describe it. Not kissing. Not making out. But *making love.*

By the time he let her up for air, her toes were curled and she felt her heartbeat hammering at the juncture of her thighs. She thought he might climb atop her then. Thought he might yank down her borrowed boxer briefs, rip open his fly, and thrust inside her before she could catch her breath.

Her hands landed on the button at the top of his jeans before she made the conscious decision to move. She had the button undone and was ripping down his zipper when, in the farthest corner of her mind, she registered the ringing of a telephone.

Surely not. She shook off the distraction and returned her full attention to his recalcitrant zipper. It was stuck halfway.

"Hold that thought." He gripped her busy fingers.

She whimpered and he made a face of regret. Pressing one of her hands flat to his chest so she could feel his thundering heart, he said roughly, "If you make that noise again, I swear to Christ, Grace, I won't be able to answer the damned phone."

"Good." She offered up a seductive grin. "Don't."

His expression went from regretful to pained. "You're killing me, woman. You think it's possible to die from lust?"

"Let's find out." She leaned forward to press a kiss over his pulse point, loving the feel of his strong heart hammering against her tongue. Then, because she wanted to put her theory to the test, she bit the bulging tendon in his tan throat.

"*Fuucckk,*" he breathed and moved her hand from his chest to his crotch.

No hesitation. No bashfulness. Just a man showing her exactly what he wanted.

She was thwarted by the denim of his jeans and the cotton of his boxer briefs. Even still, she could feel how hard he was. How large he was. How much she pleased him because he pulsed and flexed beneath her palm.

When she gave him a squeeze, he hissed. When she lightly raked her nails over his length, he moaned her name. And then, to her annoyance, he pulled her hand away so he could snag the phone from his hip pocket.

"The only people who have this number are the Black Knights." She was pleased to note how rough his voice had become. "If they're calling, it's important."

Blowing out a shuddering breath, she allowed lust to make way for reason and the real world. The shitty, awful, ugly *real* world where someone in the government was a spy for the Russians. Where she was accused of murdering her partner. *Poor Stewart!* And where an assassin sent by the Kremlin was hellbent on seeing her six feet under.

"Okay." She pushed up on her elbows and nodded for him to proceed. "But don't forget where we left off."

He glanced down at his partially undone fly. "Believe me when I tell you that will *never* happen."

She chuckled and followed his gaze. Her laughter died in her throat when she saw his erection was pushed up tight against the hem of his black boxer briefs. Right at the tip of the briefs was a damp circle of fabric.

More proof of what she did to him. Of how badly he wanted her.

The urge to pull his underwear down and lick the salty moisture beading on the head of his cock had blood rushing to her cheeks—and somewhere decidedly *south* of there. She might've said to hell with the call from BKI and launched herself on top of him had she not glanced up to find him smiling at her.

Smiling.

The expression turned him from handsome into drop-dead, butter-my-butt-and-call-me-a-biscuit *gorgeous*. "You should do that more often." She pointed. "You have an amazing smile."

He nodded. "Having you here makes me happy."

Liquid warmth surprised her by gathering behind her eyes. Then, as if he hadn't just given her an unbelievably beautiful gift, he flipped open the phone and answered without preamble, "What do you know?"

The voice on the other end was low and tinny-sounding. She watched his expression go hard before he abruptly interrupted whoever was talking. "Hang on. Grace will want to hear this."

He hit a button on the side of the phone, said, "Okay, you're on speaker. Go," and Sam's Chicago accent filled the room.

"Like I was saying," Sam said, "we found out who sent Grace the text message about Orpheus. It's a group called Kerberos."

Just that easily, her heated blood went ice-cold. The tears that'd gathered behind her eyes dried up like they'd been hit by a desert wind. And she didn't recognize her own voice when she wheezed, "No way."

"Yes way." A sweet-sounding female voice, presumably Sam's DOD contact, came over the airwaves. "Oh, I'm Hannah Blue, by the way. Nice to informally meet you both." Before Hunter or Grace could return her introduction, Hannah pushed ahead, "And I get your incredulity, Agent

Beacham. I live and breathe online conspiracies and chicanery, and even *I* wasn't certain Kerberos was real."

"Wait," Hunter frowned. "I'm missing something. Who's Kerberos?"

As Hannah waxed poetic about the online vigilante/white-hat hacker group, Grace listened with only half an ear. Her mind was numbed by the surreality of the situation she was in.

Thirty-six hours ago, she'd been 50/50 on whether Orpheus was real. Same for Kerberos.

And now look at me! Neck deep in international intrigue complete with shadowy figures and code names that could be the plot of a James Bond novel!

She tuned back into the conversation when Hannah said, "Kerberos gave me a backdoor into the FBI's servers and told me to follow the emails."

"So like us, Kerberos suspects the double agent is the director." Grace felt sick to her stomach at the thought of her boss siccing Orpheus on his own agents. "Or whomever he was sharing his information with."

"It would seem so," Hannah confirmed.

"Have you tried the backdoor?" Hunter asked.

"Working on it now," Hannah said and Grace thought she could hear the *click-clack* of a keyboard in the background. "Not sure how much I'm going to need to sift through. So hold tight. I'll have Sam get you an update in a few hours unless I find something before then."

When Hunter signed off, Grace flopped back onto the mattress, and then immediately regretted the move when it made the muscles in her lower back—muscles unused to spending hours clinging to a man on a motorcycle—spasm.

"Oh!" She rolled onto her side so she could press a hand to the knot that'd formed to the right of her tailbone.

"What is it?" There was worry in Hunter's tone.

"Back spasm," she rasped. The pain was enough to make her toes flex.

"Hang tight. I have just the thing."

He was off the bed and through the bathroom door in an instant. She expected him to reappear with pain killers or muscle relaxers so she was a little confused when he reemerged with a stack of towels and a bottle of massage oil.

Although, she noted the towels and oil as an aside, because he'd *also* kicked off his biker boots and removed his T-shirt. His jeans were still on, still partially undone, and hanging so low on his hips she could clearly see the big veins that snarled beside his well-defined Adonis lines.

If all of that wasn't mouth-watering enough—seriously, she had to swallow for fear a line of drool might slip out the corner of her mouth—there was his chest. Wide and heavily muscled with a smattering of dark, crinkly hair that arrowed down his six-pack abs and finally went the way of his Adonis lines and got lost in the waistband of his boxer briefs.

So much tough, tan skin.

So much raw, restrained power.

So much...*ink*.

She'd seen the eagle feather peeking from the sleeve of his T-shirt. But getting an up close and personal view of the entire thing was awe-inspiring. Whoever the artist had been, they'd certainly dedicated themselves to shading, to meticulously drawing so many fine black lines she thought if she reached out and touched the tattoo, she'd be able to feel the individual shafts of the feather.

And, of course, there were the scars.

A thin line on his flank that looked like it came from a surgery. A puckered circle up near his collarbone that most likely came from a bullet. And an angry red crease beside his belly button that looked fresh, and like it might've been caused by the tip of a blade.

A warrior's body.

A warrior's wounds.

She wanted to soothe each and every one. Wanted to run the tip of her finger over the damaged flesh and then follow it up with a soft kiss to ease any remembered ache.

The phone call and all the things they'd learned—and had yet to learn— leaked out of her head. What took the place of her fear and worries was lust and longing...and the deep desire to show this wonderful warrior exactly how good life could be.

He spread the towels atop the comforter and patted them. "All aboard," he told her.

She didn't immediately obey. She *couldn't*. The sight of him had paralyzed her. The rich, warm smell of all that male skin so tantalizingly close had stunned her. And the thought of him pouring that bottle of oil over himself and letting her use him as her personal Slip 'N Slide made her so weak she was incapable of movement.

"Come on, Grace." He patted the towels again. "This will make you feel better."

"I *already* feel better." She breathed heavily, her back spasm overshadowed by her growling libido. "I could have a missing limb and that"—she gestured up and down his length—"would make me numb to it. I'd be all Monty Python." She whipped out her best English accent. "It's just a flesh wound."

One corner of his mouth twitched, but he stingily refused to let it curve into a smile. "I like what I see too, Grace," he told her lowly. "And I want to see more of it. I want to see *all* of it. But first, I want you totally relaxed. Pain free. So that when I give you pleasure, it's the only thing you feel." He lowered his chin until he was staring down at her from under the ridge of his brow. "And I *am* going to give you pleasure, Grace."

Blowing out a shaky breath, she gathered all her strength and rolled onto the towels. Placing her flaming cheek on her stacked hands, she watched him upend the bottle of massage oil and rub it between his broad palms. The move made his biceps bunch into hard balls and had the veins and the tendons in his forearms standing out in harsh relief.

"The only massage I ever had was in Thailand," she admitted. "I walked away more maimed than when I arrived. The masseuse twisted me like a pretzel."

He chuckled and the warm, rumbling sound bypassed her ears and swirled deep in her belly. "No pain, Grace. Just pleasure. I promise." He fingered the hem of her T-shirt. "May I?"

"I'd let you strip me naked and paint me like one of Leonardo DiCaprio's French girls if that's what you wanted."

His sigh was overly dramatic. "I've never lamented my lack of artistic ability so much in my life."

A laugh shot out of her, making the muscles in her back fist so hard her humor was cut off by a hiss. Then her hiss melted into a moan when Hunter's warm, oiled hands landed on her lower back and began to knead.

He used firm but gentle pressure to work out the knots, alternating between rolling his thumbs over her sore spots and then running the balls of his hands over the entire length of the muscle.

The oil was warm and smelled like coconuts. His hands were wide and hot and calloused, but they slipped over her flesh in long, sensual strokes that had her feeling as loose as a goose in under two minutes.

She was more than ready to flip over and finish what they'd started before the phone rang. But before she could move, he pulled her T-shirt higher and began working the muscles in her midback, and all she could think was…*his hands!*

Lord almighty, they had supernatural powers.

"God, that feels good." She closed her eyes, then gasped when his fingers brushed the sides of her breasts.

Okay. That's it. Time to get naked and nasty, she thought hungrily. But when she tried to roll over, he stopped her with an oil-slicked hand on her flank.

"I'm not finished." Was it desire that deepened his voice? "I'd like to finish, Grace. I'd like to massage every inch of you."

A rush of red-hot lust set her sex on fire.

Her voice was husky when she told him, "I'm not sure I'll be able to stand it. The thought of you rubbing me from tip to tail…" She trailed off at the erotic images that flipped through her heated head. "Oh man, if I say yes will you *please* pay particular attention to my tips and my tail?" she finally finished, gratified by the sound of his chuckle.

"Do you always say exactly what you're thinking?"

"My daddy says we Beachams are blunt instruments. Frankness to the point of artlessness runs in the family."

"Let's not talk about your father right now."

She laughed. "Good idea."

"Want to hear an even better one?" There was a heavy note of suggestion in his voice.

She pressed up on one elbow so she could look at him over her shoulder. Passion had darkened his hazel eyes and set a muscle in his square jaw ticking.

He was sex. Personified. And he was hers.

For now, she reminded herself.

Since she wasn't sure her voice would work, she nodded.

"I think you should let me take off your clothes. This will work better if I'm not fighting fabric."

He must've caught the flicker of hesitation in her eyes because he lowered his chin again. Did he do it on purpose? Because he knew how sexy it was to stare out at her from beneath his eyelashes?

"Now, I know by the way you pull at your shirts and hide yourself away in those straitlaced suits that you might be shy about showing me your body," he said softly.

"Damn your uncanny observational skills," she teased, hoping to disguise how close to the mark his words were. Like, bull's-eye. A direct hit.

He went on as if she hadn't spoken, "But remember I've seen you in that cocktail dress. And I've seen you in those borrowed jeans. And let me assure you, Grace Beacham, you are the *sexiest* woman I've ever laid eyes on." As if he felt he needed to prove his point, he grabbed his dick through his boxer briefs. "Anytime I'm within ten feet of you I'm hard as a fucking rock."

He dropped his hand and leaned forward to catch her mouth with his own. It was a quick kiss. A soft, reassuring kiss. "Let me see you, Grace. Let me see all of you." His words were hot against her lips. "Let me touch you and learn every inch of you with my hands so that when I'm using them to do other things, I'll wish they were still on you."

Lord have mercy!

"Oh," he added with a little smirk, "and I promise to spend a considerable amount of time on your tips and your tail."

CHAPTER 19

Once Grace nodded her consent, Hunter wasn't slow about pulling the T-shirt over her head.

Even though everything in him wanted to flip her onto her back so he could see the glory of her beautiful breasts—were her nipples dark or light? Small or large?—he satisfied himself with drinking in the sight of the pale skin that covered her pretty back. Contented himself with letting his eyes map the sexy way her rib cage dipped in at her waist. Was beyond charmed to note the two little divots at the top of her butt that he promised himself he'd spend long minutes exploring with his lips and tongue.

He was more circumspect when it came to removing the boxer briefs. Those he took down leisurely, loving every inch of skin that was revealed. Enjoying the way the plump hemispheres of her ass bounced softly when the waistband slipped over them. Savoring the sight of the tops of her luscious thighs and knowing he'd put his face between them soon.

Her hands were stacked flat under her cheek. And her eyes were closed. But he didn't need to see her expression to know she was as turned on by her...*unwrapping*...as he was. Goose bumps peppered her flesh. A soft blush stained her pretty profile. And there was a dreamy smile curving her mouth.

Take your time, Hunter, he coached himself even as he slipped the boxer briefs free of her delicately arched feet and tossed them to the floor. *Even though she said slow is for sloths and glaciers*—and truly, could the woman *be* any more adorable?—*take things easy anyway. You'll want to remember every part of this.*

Because there would come a time, probably in the not-too-distant future, when memories would be all he had.

Even if their careers and their lives weren't miles apart, even if she *was* interested in something more than sex for the sake of sex, there was no future for them. She'd made it clear whether she'd intended to or not. She wanted something he'd never be able to provide. Something profound.

A deal-breaker.

And so, he'd make himself savor this moment and all the moments she'd let him steal in the hours or days or weeks to come. Then he'd take them out and relive them when he was forced to let her go so she could move on to a man capable of making all her dreams come true.

When that thought had something fisting hard and fast in his chest, he forced himself to shove worries of the future aside and concentrate on what was in front of him right then.

The massage oil was cool as he upended the bottle and watched the liquid pool into his palm. He rubbed his hands together to warm it before gently gripping her shoulders.

Her skin was velvet beneath his callused fingertips as he thoroughly kneaded her delicate muscles. He watched the way her flesh bounced back beneath his touch. Listened to her breathing for cues about how much pressure she liked. And did his best to tell her with his touch just how much he adored her body.

"Let me have this arm," he said and was gratified when she immediately obeyed.

Her bicep was small yet firm. Her forearm was thin and delicately turned. And when he got to her hand, he slipped his fingers between hers. Noting, once again, the difference in their skin tones. The broadness of his palm compared to the slimness of hers. How delicate her fingers looked next to the thick bluntness of his own.

She did something wonderful then...

She closed her fingers around his until they were holding hands.

It was such a simple thing. Yet it felt profound.

Holding hands wasn't about sex; it was about connection. And until that moment, he hadn't known it was possible to be eye-crossingly horny and emotionally moved all at the same time.

When she released his hand, he blew out a ragged breath. Then held it again when he massaged her other arm and she did the same thing. Only that time, the hand-holding lasted longer. And when she finally let go they *both* let loose with frayed sighs.

"You're so fucking beautiful." He wasn't talking about her body, although he certainly thought she had the most amazing figure he'd seen. He was talking about *all* of her. All the wit and wonder, all the honesty and integrity that made her who she was.

"You make me feel beautiful," she admitted after restacking her hands beneath her cheek.

"I want to make you feel *everything*." He returned his hands to her back because now that he'd touched her, he couldn't stop.

He made sure his strokes were lingering and purposeful. He was careful to smooth every ligament and muscle and tendon. And his cock, which was so hard he thought it a wonder the damn thing hadn't split the skin, throbbed unabashedly when he got to her waist and realized his hands could span the small expanse.

He paid special attention to the little divots at the top of her perfect ass—dear god, he'd avoided looking directly at it because it drove him to distraction and had him wanting to mount her like a stallion scenting a mare. And then he smiled at her groan of impatience when he skipped over her luscious butt and instead moved down to the end of the bed so he could start massaging the soles of her feet.

Of course, her groan of impatience turned into a moan of pleasure when he used his thumbs to work out the tension in her arches. Then he journeyed upward. Reveling in the smoothness of her finely turned calves. Letting his touch turn featherlight on the backs of her knees until she giggled. He increased the pressure and the length of his strokes as he smoothed out the muscles of her kissable, lickable thighs.

By the time he swiped his thumbs beneath the lower curves of her ass, they were both breathing hard. And when he began to knead each plump globe, she arched her back, bringing up her butt in an age-old declaration of submission, of offering.

It was almost more than he could stand.

He felt a drop of passion squeeze from the tip of his raging hard-on when he slid his fingers down the seam of her ass, barely brushing the entrance to her sex.

"Hunter," she gasped, encouraging him by arching higher.

He could feel the heat of her, the exquisite promise of wet female flesh, and he desperately wanted to dip his fingers inside. But he'd promised himself slow.

"Roll over, Grace," he instructed. When she did, all the breath was sucked from his lungs. Her hands fisted the comforter on either side of her flaring hips as her large breasts bounced and settled against her narrow rib cage. "You're even more gorgeous than I imagined."

Her cotton candy-colored nipples had beaded into tight points. Her belly button was a perfect oval that begged for the flick of his tongue. And the strip of hair covering the top of her sweetly swollen mons was two shades darker than that on her head.

She grabbed her breasts, one in each hand, gently tugging at her own nipples, and he couldn't stand it any longer. Shoving his hand into the top of his briefs, he fisted himself in a long, slow tug. Just a little friction to take the edge off.

Her small, secretive smile told him she liked to watch. He tucked that bit of information away for later.

"Where would you like me to start this time?" he asked. Or, rather, *rasped*.

The urge to continue touching himself, to stroke himself to completion with his oily hand while watching her tend to her breasts was intense. But when he came, it would be inside her. And so, with one last squeeze, he released his straining cock.

If the thing had a mouth, it would've cried out its disappointment.

She shook her head. He didn't know if that meant she didn't care where he began or if it meant she'd lost the ability to speak.

Either way, he figured he couldn't go wrong. "Dealer's choice then," he growled approvingly.

The bottle of baby oil was upended one more time. And the moment he had his hands nice and lubricated, he began the process of learning each newly exposed inch of her.

This time he started at her ankles and slowly made his way up her legs. Her muscles were lithe and strong. Her skin was hot and silky. And once he'd worked out all the tension in her thighs, ever-so-close to her sex without ever touching it, he once again skipped over the part of her they *both* wanted him to explore.

She whimpered and the soft, sensual sound made his stomach muscles tighten. When she pumped her hips invitingly, it took every ounce of self-control he had left not to rip down his zipper and free his raging cock.

He felt his blood rushing close to the surface of his skin as he slowly moved his hands from her belly to her rib cage. And when he finally, *finally* cupped her glorious breasts, his hands were shaking from having to hold himself back.

Her pale skin turned shiny with oil as he plumped and kneaded and caressed. Truly, the woman had a rack like a 50's pinup. But he was careful to avoid her nipples and simply tease close by them. Drawing out her pleasure. Building her anticipation. And loving the way her breath caught each time he got close to the pearled peaks before backing away.

"Touch me, Hunter," she eventually begged. "Please. I need to feel your hands on me."

"My hands have been all over you, woman."

"Not in the places I want." Passion had two red flags flying high in her cheeks.

"No?" He quirked a teasing brow. "Which places have I missed?"

He was pushing her. Testing her to see if she'd say the words. And, because she was Grace—*A blunt instrument? Is that what she called herself?*—she didn't disappoint.

"I want you to touch my nipples. I want you to touch my pussy." She lowered her chin. When their gazes collided, his breath caught at the untamed lust burning in her eyes. "I want you to make me cum until I scream your name."

"Fuck me." The words wheezed out of him and her upside-down mouth curved into a vixen's smile.

"Yes." She nodded. "And then I *definitely* want to do that."

CHAPTER 20

Grace couldn't stop her eyes from fluttering shut when Hunter finally, *finally* rubbed the callused pads of his thumbs over her straining nipples.

He'd so thoroughly seduced her with his touch that when he gently flicked the pearled tips, she nearly came. Truly, her inner muscles flexed so hard she was amazed when she *didn't* fly over the edge of ecstasy.

"You have the most amazing breasts." His voice was so low and rumbly she barely heard it. "And I'm going to kiss them and suck on them until you tell me to stop."

What she wanted to say was she was past the point of words. But since she *was* past the point of words, all she could do was nod her head in encouragement.

"Easy," he whispered and she realized he'd leaned down because she felt his hot breath bathe her right nipple. "Just relax and let me..."

He didn't finish. She knew why when his warm, wet mouth closed over her sensitive peak.

He sucked it to the roof of his mouth as he used his thumb to flick her opposite nipple. She was instantly overwhelmed by a symphony of erotic sensation.

Every suck, every tug seemed to echo from her breasts into her aching sex. And had he not spent an eternity driving her wild, the suction of his mouth might've been too intense. Because he *had* worked her into a feverish frenzy, it felt *just right.*

So right that when he flicked the ruched tip with his tongue, she could feel herself hurtling at breakneck speed toward orgasm.

She squeezed her thighs together, clenched her inner muscles hard. But either he was a mind reader, or he was experienced enough to know what she was doing. Because her nipple popped free of his mouth at the same time he stopped stimulating her opposite breast.

She grumbled her displeasure. Then gasped when, a split second later, he had both hands between her knees, pulling them apart.

"Ah, ah, ah," he scolded. "Not so fast. When you cum, it's going to be with my fingers inside you. When your sweet pussy convulses and melts, I want to feel every moment of it."

"Lord have mercy," she breathed.

"You're not the only one capable of saying exactly what you think." His glittering eyes held her desire-drugged gaze in a seductive grip. "I can be a blunt instrument too."

As if to prove his point, he rubbed the edge of his thumb between her swollen folds, quickly finding and pressing on the part of her that screamed the loudest for stimulation.

"That's it." His breath was warm and sweet against her mouth as he bent to flick his tongue across the seam of her lips. "Now relax and let me finish what I started."

She'd lost the power of speech again. The most she could manage was a soft, mewling whimper when he slipped a finger inside her—just a shallow foray to test her readiness—before he retook her mouth in a kiss that was as deep as it was thorough.

He added a second finger to the first and her walls clamped around his intrusion. Not because her body tried to evict him. Because it tried to keep him in. Tried to hold him still as her inner muscles fluttered around him, seeking the satisfaction those wonderfully talented hands had been promising all along.

He groaned against her mouth, "You're so fucking wet, Grace. So damn soft. Like damp silk."

All she could do was hum her pleasure and wiggle her hips in invitation.

He answered by setting up a rhythm that he matched with his tongue.

In and out. Long, slow, delicious strokes that were firm without being harsh. Determined without being demanding.

He fucked her with his fingers. Filled her. Over and over. Again and again until whatever logical, reasoning part of her mind that had remained melted away.

She became sensation. Mindless, heedless, wanton *flesh*.

Setting up a counter-motion with her hips, she met him stroke for stroke. Coaxed him faster. Harder. *Deeper.* Until the tension at her core became a mind-melting pressure.

Just when she thought she couldn't take it a second longer, orgasm burst through her as hard and as fast as a bullet fired from a rifle. It snapped her back clean off the bed. And had her thighs clamping tight around his marauding hand.

"Thatta girl," she thought she heard him say. Although she couldn't be sure of his words because the blood rushing between her ears was an incessant, rhythmic roar.

She had no idea how long she stayed there in that wonderful abyss of orgasm. It could've been seconds or minutes. Time had no meaning when it came to ecstasy.

Eventually, she began to drift down from the heights of release. Feeling the mattress beneath her back. Smelling the warm coconut scent of the massage oil as it mixed with the earthier aroma of sex. Hearing Hunter's ragged breathing as he stood above her.

She was boneless, breathless, nearly *brainless* from release. So it took an immense amount of excursion to crack open her eyes. She was glad she made the effort because…

Dear lord!

He'd shoved the fingers he'd just had inside her body into his mouth. She watched his nostrils flare at the smell of her. Saw his eyelids lower in ecstasy when he tasted her. Heard his deep groan of unsatiated lust as he licked his fingers clean of her desire.

Sex. That's what Hunter was as he stood there with his bare chest heaving. With his partially undone jeans riding low around his trim hips. With his raging erection peeking above the waistband of his boxer briefs.

He was the embodiment of sex, and she was overcome with the urge to give him the kind of pleasure that would make his eyes cross and his toes curl. Make him feel so good he forgot his own name even as he screamed hers.

Her loose muscles made her motions slow and lethargic. Even so, it was only a handful of seconds before she had his jeans unzipped the rest of the way and shoved down to his knees.

"Wow."

The word popped out of her mouth before she realized her vocal cords were working again. And then she grimaced when it occurred to her that "wow" was an asinine thing to say in a moment like that.

But seriously, the little voice that lived in the back of her head reiterated, *wow*.

Hunter was long and thick, heavily veined, his plump head shiny. His testicles were large and round and pulled up tight against the base of his shaft.

She had never been one to request a dick pic. It seemed lewd and puerile. But she wouldn't say no if he ever asked to send her one. Because…*gaht dayum*, the man was hung.

If there was such a thing as a Hall of Fame for Cocks, his would be in a place of pride. With a big sign that said, *"Perfect specimen pictured here."*

She grabbed the bottle of massage oil from the bedside table and tipped it so that one lone dollop of clear, slick fluid dripped from the opening. The instant it hit his swollen head, his cock jerked so hard it went nearly vertical. She watched, fascinated, as his stomach muscles accordioned.

"Fuuuccckkk me," he hissed when she used her palm and fingers to spread the oil all down his throbbing shaft.

"I told you that's the plan." She chuckled, even as she luxuriated in the feel of him.

He was a thick, stony column covered in flesh as soft as velvet. She could feel his heartbeat in the veins sliding beneath her fingertips. See how her ministrations made him grow thicker, longer. And hear how much his restraint cost him by the ragged way he breathed.

Over and over she stroked him, ran her fingers around the sensitive ridge that circled the base of his head. Then, when he was panting and mindless, she changed tactics.

Using her fingernails, she started at his base and slowly, gently—but not *too* gently—scraped up his raging, bucking length.

A low groan rumbled up from deep inside his chest. The next thing she knew she was flat on her back with him looming above her on all fours. The skin over his face was tight and flushed. A drop of sweat beaded at his temple. And his eyes were so bright and piercing, she felt burned by them.

"I have to fuck you now, Grace." He immediately shook his head. "Sorry. That came out wrong. I should've asked but—"

She pressed a finger over his lips. "Sugar, you don't have to ask. I think I've made it clear that's exactly what I want."

"Say it again." A muscle went crazy in his jaw. "Call me *sugar* and tell me you want me to fuck you."

She framed his face with her hands and arched into him so her nipples rasped against his chest hair. "I want you to fuck me, sugar. I've wanted you to fuck me since the moment you knocked on my car window and told me you'd been sent to help me find a way in with the Michigan Militia."

The noise he made then was more beast than man. And when he crashed down on top of her, reclaiming her mouth in a ravenous kiss, his hot, raging cock split her folds.

He wasn't inside her. Not yet. He simply nestled against her. All his heat held snug against her wetness. All his hardness pressed tight against her softness.

They stayed that way for long minutes. Her oiled body making his slick so that when they moved and bumped against each other it was sleek and deliciously sinuous.

But it wasn't enough.

Whatever edge her orgasm had taken off had been re-honed. Her want of him, her *need* of him, was stronger than ever. When she pumped her hips in a wordless appeal, he ripped his mouth from hers and rolled to the side of the bed.

She whimpered because after all his weight and warmth, she felt horribly bereft with him gone. Then she heard him whisper, "Dale, for the love of all that's holy, don't fail me now," and she turned onto her side to run a finger down the groove of his back.

"What are you saying?" She noted how his broad, tan back sported as many scars as his front. She ran a thumb over the puckered circle near his neck. Let her fingertips drift over the angry, raised line of flesh that marred the skin of his flank. And followed the jagged line of the white scar that zigzagged near the base of his spine.

"I told you I've never had a woman here." His voice was guttural. "So I don't keep protection. When I phoned Dale, I asked him to—aha!"

He pulled a long strip of condoms from the bedside table and turned to her with a face like a kid on Christmas morning.

"I don't know whether I should be miffed or mortified that your property manager knows you brought me here intending to seduce me," she teased. Then she lifted what she hoped was a seductive eyebrow. "That *was* your intention, wasn't it?"

"My *intention* was to keep you safe." He used his teeth to rip open a foil packet. "My *hope* was that once you were here you would succumb to my myriad charms."

"I feel like you're splitting hairs, but I'll let it slide." She grinned as she snagged the latex ring from his fingers.

"The devil is in the details." He winked. "And you shouldn't be miffed *or* mortified. Because I know for a fact that Dale and Sissy still do it on the regular despite being well into their seventies. I came up here unannounced one winter and found them canoodling naked on a blanket in front of the fireplace. Sissy blushed to the roots of her curly white hair and told me they just needed a change of scenery. You know, to spice things up."

Grace placed the ring of latex directly over his swollen head. But she didn't slide the condom down his length. Instead, she looked up to find him intently watching her progress. "So we *won't* be the first to christen this place?" she asked.

His gaze jumped to her face. "This cabin is eighty years old. It's had four owners before me. There was no way we were ever going to be the first ones to have sex in it. But if it makes you feel any better, you can christen *me* and—"

He didn't finish his sentence. Instead, he threw his head back and let loose with a long, low hiss as she fisted the condom down his swollen length.

When he dropped his chin, she bit her bottom lip and lifted an eyebrow. "Sugar," she whispered, "the time for talk is over. I need you to—"

He was on her before she could get another word out.

"Mmm," she hummed as, once again, his weight pressed her into the mattress.

And then…

He entered her. Just a little. Just by notching his hips back so that his fat head nosed her entrance.

There was a pause as they each dragged in a ragged breath at that first intimate touch. And then their moans were synchronized when he thrust forward. Only an inch. Maybe two. It was enough to have her pulling him down so she could catch his bottom lip between her teeth.

He was rather large, you see. And even though she was warm and wet and ready—*lord, am I ready*—she needed time to adjust. She needed him to go slow.

The edge of her teeth was a wordless warning. He understood the assignment.

Holding himself on his elbows, he gently pulled his lip free from her so he could frame her face with his wide, warm hands. His hazel eyes held her gaze prisoner as he slowly, *oh so slowly*, pressed into her another inch.

"Hunter," she breathed his name.

"I know." He nodded, a bead of sweat trickling down the side of his face. "Just be still and let me…" His words trailed off as he thrust deeper. Deeper. Deeper still. Smoothing out every wrinkle along the way. Abrading ever screaming nerve ending. Filling her until she felt complete in a way she never had before.

All the while, never dropping her gaze.

By the time she felt his hot, weighty testicles hit the curve of her ass, she was panting.

"Y'okay?" A muscle ticked in his jaw, the only indication he gave that he was struggling to hold himself back when what he really wanted was to hump and rut and *fuck*.

She didn't trust her voice. She simply nodded.

"Good." He hummed his approval. And then, still framing her face, he reclaimed her mouth.

For long moments that's all he did. Held himself still inside her while his lips and teeth and tongue seduced her all over again. It was only when she began to wriggle and writhe in voiceless encouragement that he moved.

His thrusts were slow and shallow at first. His thick shaft barely retreating before sliding back home. But soon his strokes became longer. Faster. Harder. Until eventually he was pumping into her in a strong, steady rhythm that had them both groaning as sensation built and built and *built*.

"You feel so good," she rasped after ripping her mouth away from his to try to catch her breath. To try to slow things down because she was close again. So close. And she didn't want it to end.

But she couldn't stop the inevitable. Mostly because he never broke stride. Never once changed up the rhythm or the angle or the depth. And so there was no escape from the perfect friction he'd created.

"Hunter, I can't hold off. I'm going to—"

"Cum for me, Grace." His eyes were ferocious with desire as he watched her every expression, his nostrils flaring as the first coil of release wound tight inside her and then sprung loose.

She screamed his name.

Literally *screamed* it. Not on purpose. Not because that's what she thought he wanted to hear. But because the pleasure was unlike anything she'd known, so bright and intense and all-encompassing.

She wanted to blame the heightened sensation on the adrenaline that'd been pumping through her system for twenty-four hours. She feared the *truth* was it was Hunter himself.

Hunter who was everything she'd always wanted and never dreamed she could have.

Hunter who, even though she'd never admitted it to anyone—even herself—might have stolen a piece of her heart three years ago.

And never given it back.

CHAPTER 21

The sound of his name being ripped from the back of Grace's throat, the feel of her unraveling around him, was too much for Hunter.

He couldn't hold back.

He wanted to. He wanted to stop time and stay in that moment with her for eternity. But the way her nails dug into his shoulders, the way her heels pressed into his ass, and the way her inner walls clamped and spasmed and sucked at his pistoning cock had his own release bubbling in his balls, hot and ready.

"Grace!"

Her name was a roar that matched the explosiveness of his orgasm as he held himself deep inside her. As he gritted his teeth and growled his pleasure while it spurted from him in long, rapturous eruptions.

He'd had plenty of good orgasms before. And a handful of really great ones. But this?

This defied description.

It was transcendent. Infinite. Unparalleled.

By the time the last vestiges surged through him, he felt like he'd hiked forty miles in full battle rattle with no food and stingy water rations.

He was done for. Drained. His muscles useless and his balls empty.

He hadn't realized he'd collapsed atop her until some of his senses returned and he felt her running a single finger up and down the sweaty groove of his spine. His cock was still held tight inside her hot, silky sheath. And her face was turned into his cheek so she could leave sweet, soft kisses against the side of his jaw.

As erotic as the massage and the sex had been, that's how beautiful and tender the aftermath was.

When a lump formed in his throat, he realized two things. One, he'd never felt as at peace or as at home with anyone as he did with Grace. And two, he was falling in love with her.

Or maybe it was more accurate to say he'd *fallen* in love with her three years ago. But since he'd had no experience with the emotion, he hadn't recognized it for what it was.

He recognized it now.

It was as warm and as wonderful as the poets described. As exhilarating and as liberating as the lyrics in the love songs made it sound. Better than any movie with Kate Hudson and Matthew McComeOnAndWearAShirt.

Oh, and it also scared the ever-loving shit out of him.

He'd stared down the barrel of an enemy AK-47 without batting a lash. Crouched in the corner of a mud hut while mortars fell around him without sweating. Taken a six-inch blade to the flank without freaking out and screaming his head off. But the difference between those experiences and this one was that *those* could be fixed with strategic countermoves and/ or a surgeon's scalpel.

There was no cure for this. No counterattack that could mitigate the misery. No doctor who could mend a broken heart.

And his heart would break.

The moment he had to watch her walk away from him, the damn thing would explode into a million pieces.

He remembered something Dan "The Man" Currington—one of the original Knights—had told him one night when they'd been talking about Dan's first wife, a woman named Patti who'd been killed in crossfire back when the original BKI was in its infancy. Hunter and Dan had been out on the back patio, sipping sparkling waters because neither of them drank. Dan had watched his second wife and their adorable little girl, Cora May, chase each other around the fire pit.

"A heart can heal after it breaks," he'd said in that hard Detroit accent of

his that over-pronounced the R's. *"But the pieces never quite fit together the same. I'm not saying it's better or worse. I'm just saying it's different. And that's okay. Nobody gets out of this thing we call life with all their parts still tuned to their factory settings."*

So Hunter would love Grace in the time he had. And then he'd lose her and his heart would shatter. But eventually, with time, it would reform itself. And if he was to believe Dan, it would be okay.

"Hunter?" she whispered in his ear before placing another sweet kiss on his cheek. "If I had my way, we'd stay like this forever. But I don't want the condom to leak."

He didn't have the heart to tell her a leaky condom wasn't a problem.

"Of course." He pushed up on one elbow so he could grab the rim of latex and hold the condom in place as he slowly pulled out of her beautiful body.

The sight of his semi-rigid dick sliding from the soft, swollen, pinkness of her sex had desire once again stirring low in his gut. But it was impossible to look into her eyes. If he looked into her eyes she might see the love shining in his. And if she saw the love shining in his…

His thoughts skidded to a halt so quickly he figured if he peeled back his skull, he might see skid marks on his brain.

What *would* happen if Grace knew he'd fallen in love with her? What would she do? What would she say?

His heart thundered at the idea that she might say she'd fallen in love with him too. That it'd happened for her like it'd happened for him. Slowly, with that first "you might be a redneck if" joke they'd shared after he introduced her to Chuck. And then more quickly, with those four days of quiet lunches and after-work conversations, two of which had stretched long into the night. And finally ended with the charity event and that kiss. *The* kiss.

The one that'd ruined him for kissing anyone else.

Or maybe she'd be sweet and gracious and thank him for his affection while letting him down easily by telling him that while she *liked* him and certainly *lusted* after him, her feelings began and ended there.

Honestly, he didn't know which would be worse. To be outright rejected? Or to have his feelings returned only to have to tell her it'd never work because he could never give her the children she talked about as if they were a foregone conclusion.

He used the excuse of going to the bathroom to dispose of the condom and give himself the opportunity to gather his thoughts. After he'd dumped the used Trojan in the trash can, he studied his face in the mirror over the sink.

His cheeks were flushed from exertion. The hair at his temples was damp with sweat. And the look in his eyes reminded him of all those times as a teenager when he'd moved into a new foster home with no idea if it was going to be simply terrible or outright torturous.

It was the look of fear that came over a person when they had no clue what the future might bring but were fully prepared for it to bring the worst.

Stop worrying about what's going to happen tomorrow, he scolded himself. *Enjoy the time you have with her now. Soak up every minute and every kiss and every smile.*

"Grace?" He poked his head around the doorjamb. "I'm jumping in the shower to wash off this massage oil. Join me." He chuckled and shook his head. "God *damn*, I meant…join me?"

She turned onto her side so she could prop her head in her hand. The curve of her hip down to her waist was amazing. The way her heavy breasts shifted against her rib cage was the very definition of femininity. And that coquettish look in her eye? Pure seductress.

"Asking for things isn't your strong suit, huh?" she said with a grin.

"Apparently not."

"Why do you suppose that is? Is it your military background? You got so used to giving orders?"

He knew she was teasing him. And any of the other Knights might've been able to go along with her light banter and come up with something appropriately clever. But for the life of him, the only answer he had was the truth.

"I think it's probably more of a throwback to my childhood. If I asked for something, it gave the adults in my life the opportunity to say no. I got used to just stating my needs. That generally got me better results."

Just as he'd known would happen, the teasing light dimmed in her eyes. *Why* couldn't he be more like Sam or Fisher? Quick with a quip? Easy to laugh?

"I know you just got *out* of the shower," he told her. "But unless you want to slip and slide around the cabin like a seal for the rest of the day, you'll need to wash off the oil." He held out his hand. "Will you do me the honor of joining me?"

"Sugar." She deepened her accent, and she might as well have wrapped her lips around the head of his dick the way the sonofabitch perked up. "I would like nothing better than to get wet and soapy with you." She stood and sauntered toward him, her hips swaying so dramatically he nearly went cross-eyed. "Plus, we were so hot and hurried earlier I didn't get the chance to kiss you in all the places I wanted to kiss you."

"Oh, yeah?" He arched an eyebrow. "And where did you want to kiss me?"

"Everywhere. Absolutely everywhere."

He wouldn't have thought it possible, but he was hard again.

"Good." He dragged her into the bathroom. "We can take turns."

For the next forty minutes, until the hot water ran out, that's exactly what they did.

CHAPTER 22

Black Knights Inc.

"**A**ssmonkey!"

Boss and Sam were standing on the second floor near the top of the stairs when Hannah let loose with another colorful curse in what was turning out to be a mile-long string of colorful curses.

Frank "Boss" Knight, who'd come in to work shortly after they'd had the exchange with Kerberos, chuckled and shook his head. Then he returned to his task, which was getting everyone's pizza order because ten minutes earlier, Becky had declared herself "hungry enough to eat the north end of a southbound camel." Which was when Sam had realized it'd been hours since he'd inhaled Eliza's quiche and was fairly famished himself.

He wasn't one to miss a meal. But the day's hubbub, and especially Hurricane Hannah's arrival, had distracted him from the rumblings of his stomach.

In fact, it was safe to say Hannah had distracted him from just about *everything*.

It was so strange to see her sitting in the war room, her vibrant hair twisted up and secured with a pencil, and her red lips pursed in concentration. Because his *eyes* saw a pretty woman, but his heart still looked for that wide-eyed kid.

"So that's a meat lovers for me and Becky," Boss said. "A supreme for Eliza, a pepperoni with extra cheese for our resident computer whiz." He hitched his chin toward Hannah. "And a Hawaiian for you." This last part he said with a curled lip.

"What?" Sam demanded. "I like it. The sweet of the pineapple and the salty of the ham?"

"It's a crime against humanity." Boss gave a sad shake of his buzz-cut head. "Or, at the very least, it's a crime against pizza. And you have the cojones to call yourself a born and bred Chicagoan? You should be ashamed."

"Shitgibbon!" Hannah shook a fist at the monitor.

Boss rolled in his lips to keep from laughing again. "She has a rather remarkable command of profanity. I mean, I've been around plenty of cursing in my time. But I can't remember ever meeting anyone who did it with quite so much…panache."

"She's…uh…" Sam scratched his chin and glanced over at Hannah, "experiencing some frustrations with the emails." When he turned back, Boss had crossed his arms over his chest and was regarding him consideringly. "What?" he demanded.

"You *like* her," Boss declared, and Sam snapped another quick look over his shoulder to make sure Hannah hadn't heard.

"Of course I like her," he muttered. "She's my high school girlfriend's kid sister. I knew her when she had pink rubber bands on her braces and ran around in SpongeBob SquarePants pajama bottoms."

Boss narrowed his eyes. "She's not a kid now though, is she?"

"To me, she'll always be thirteen."

"Bullshit." Boss snorted.

"First you judge me for my Hawaiian pizza and now you're calling me a liar? You know, I've punched men in the dick for less."

"They were lesser men," Boss said without a hint of concern.

That's undoubtedly true, Sam thought, although he wouldn't give Boss the satisfaction of admitting it aloud.

Frank "Boss" Knight was the kind of man that guys like Sam looked up to. Which spoke volumes about just what a *good* man Boss truly was. It was an understatement to say that guys like Sam—guys who knew what it truly was to sacrifice and suffer—had exacting standards.

"Even if I *didn't* look at her and see that thirteen-year-old girl, she's still too young for me," he insisted.

"How old is she?" Boss leaned around him so he could study Hannah more closely. "Cockwaffle!" she yelled at the screen.

"Dunno for sure." Sam shrugged. "Twenty-eight. Twenty-nine. Somewhere in there."

"And how old are you?"

"Thirty-four."

The look that came over Boss's face did a better job of calling Sam an idiot than words ever could. "You know my wife is more than a dozen years younger than I am, right?"

Sam swallowed. He *hadn't* known.

Well, that wasn't exactly true. He'd known there was an age gap there. But Boss had one of those craggy, Russel Crowe-type faces that made him appear timeless.

"But you didn't know Becky when she was a kid, right? *That's* the difference."

"Mmm." Boss canted his head. "Again, I call bullshit."

Sam flattened his mouth into a straight line. "I don't care what you call it, it's the truth."

"If that's the truth, then you've either lost your ever-lovin' mind, or you're lying to yourself."

"I *have* lost my mind." Sam grinned. "A long time ago. Now I just use the package it came in."

Boss chuckled. "Given your abysmal taste in pizza toppings, I'm prone to believe that."

Before Sam could come back with something appropriately pithy, Boss turned and clomped down the metal stairs. The *thud* of his gigantic footfalls nearly, but not quite, drowned out the sound of Hannah muttering, "dick breath" as she continued to type like a mad woman.

Time to offer some help, Sam decided.

Although he wasn't sure how much help he could be. He could email and surf the web and handle most of the products in Microsoft Office. But beyond that? Useless.

At least I can lend some moral support, he decided as he headed in her direction.

He was halfway across the room when Boss's words came back to him.

"She's not a kid now though, is she?" And suddenly the ground didn't feel entirely firm beneath his biker boots.

She *wasn't* a kid. That was true. She was a beautiful woman with amazing purple hair and arms full of bangle bracelets. And if he'd met her on the street? Sure. He'd have tried to snag her digits.

But he'd met her before she grew boobs. So to look at her now with an eye toward romance?

Absurd.

He stopped beside her only to stumble back a step when she glanced up at him with her dark eyes slitted in menace. "If you've come to ask about my progress, I swear to god, I might kill you."

"Sorry to disappoint, but others have already tried that and failed." He pointed to the scar on his neck.

The menace in her eyes turned to concern. "What happened?"

"Too much to condense down into a five-minute convo." He hitched his chin toward the screen. "So how's your progress?" He *almost* managed to finish the question without cracking a smile.

Despite her earlier threat, she didn't attempt to end his life. Instead, she turned back to the computer screen with a scowl. "If you must know, it's like when Keanu kept seeing the black cat."

He blinked, not getting the reference.

She fluttered impatient fingers. "There's a glitch in the matrix."

"Ah." He nodded. "What kind of glitch?"

"If I knew that, it wouldn't be a glitch," she stated flatly.

"Are you always this grouchy when things don't go your way? Or are you suffering from a low blood sugar situation?"

"Can't it be both?"

He took another step back. "So I guess that means I should keep my distance 'til you figure out what's wrong with the matrix or the pizza arrives."

"No. No." She kicked out the rolling chair next to her and gestured for him to sit. "Maybe what I need is a second set of eyes."

He made a show of tiptoeing toward her and then gingerly settling into the seat.

She rolled her eyes. "I may be hungry, but a promise I won't bite." And then she sent him a lascivious grin. "Unless you want me to."

"Cut it out."

She'd always flirted. And he'd always chalked it up to her testing out her burgeoning pubescent skills on a boy she'd known was safe. Back then, he'd thought it was cute.

Now? Well, her flirting, and *particularly* the look in her eyes, had his body reacting in ways it had no business reacting. Since he sure as shit didn't want her to see, he shoved his hands deep in the pocket of his jeans and felt something in the left pocket that didn't belong.

He knew what it was the instant he wrapped his fingers around it.

Pulling out the candy brought back a million memories of a time long gone. "Talk about a blast from the past." He unwrapped the treat and popped it into his mouth. "I remember how your sister would sneak one of these into my pocket on our dates. I never knew when or how she did it. It would just suddenly be there." He snapped his fingers.

His eyes rolled back in his head as the sugary sweet flavor exploded on his tongue. It tasted like youth and sexual awaking and that breathless feeling of teetering on the cusp of manhood. "Did Candy teach you her trick with the watermelon Jolly Ranchers?"

Something strange passed over Hannah's face, and her pouty Bratz Doll lips formed a perfect bow. Before she could answer, however, a snippet of information on the screen snagged her attention.

"There." She pointed. "There's another one."

"Another what?" He turned to the monitor but couldn't see anything other than an email exchange.

"They don't make any sense. Here." She grabbed the arm of his rolling chair and pulled him next to her.

She smelled good. Not like bubble gum and Noxzema, as she had when she'd been thirteen. But like orange blossoms and vanilla. Warm and citrusy, reminding him of sugar cookies topped with sherbet.

"See this?"

He followed her point to where her bright blue fingernail tapped the screen. "Read this exchange between Agent Beacham and Director Morgan."

Sam was keenly aware that her fingers were still on his armrest and touching his forearm. The coolness of her skin against his heated flesh caused the hairs there to stand on end. Also, was his heart beating faster? Was his breath shallower?

182   JULIE ANN WALKER

Damn you, Boss!

He now found himself fixating on things he wouldn't have thought twice about fifteen minutes earlier. Fixating on *Hannah*.

"So?" she prodded. "What do you think?"

His glance was startled. "About what?"

A line formed between her eyebrows. "About the email exchange." She turned her head to the side. "Are you okay? Maybe *you're* the one suffering from low blood sugar."

"I'm fine," he brushed her off, glad his expression hadn't given away his thoughts. For a second there, he thought it had. "I'm just a slower reader than you." *Liar, liar, pants on fire.* "Gimme a sec."

She opened her mouth to say something, then snapped it shut when Lizzo's voice suddenly blared to life. Pulling her phone from her pocket, she frowned and then pointed to the monitor. "After you're done reading those emails, scroll down and read the others. I need to take this."

"Boyfriend?" When that familiar pang zapped through him, he convinced himself, once again, that it was simply fraternal misgivings.

Of course, when she said, "It's Cesar," he didn't look too closely at why he was relieved. "Should I tell him you'll be at the next show?"

"N—"

That's all he got out before she thumbed on the phone and cried, "Bestie! You'll never guess what Sam just told me. He'd *love* to come to your next gig. And if you could arrange it, he'd be honored to come backstage and meet the rest of the girls."

When Sam caught her eye, he ran a thumb across his throat in a slashing motion. In response, she winked and blew him a kiss. Then she hopped from the chair, pressed a hand to her ear to drown out the sound of Becky working the grinder down in the shop, and ambled toward the stairs to have some privacy for her conversation.

He didn't watch the sway of her hips as she walked away.

No. Nope. Negative. He most certainly did *not*.

CHAPTER 23

"How's it going?" Cesar whispered. "Tell me everything. Is he as yummy as you remember?"

Hannah glanced over her shoulder to find Sam studying the computer monitor. He had one of those profiles that screamed masculinity, so hard-planed and angular and...*hairy*. And the way his mouth pursed as he sucked on the Jolly Rancher was suggestive.

Correction. *Everything* about Sam was suggestive, from his loose-hipped walk to his broad-palmed hands.

"He's yummier," she admitted grumpily.

"Take a photo. I need to see."

"You *have* seen. I showed you my sister's yearbook. Take that image and imagine him leaner, meaner, and with a full beard."

"I have a terrible imagination. I need actual, factual footage."

"I can't do it," she hissed. "He's only fifteen feet away. He'll know what I'm doing the minute I take the phone away from my ear and hold it up."

"You don't have to be *obvious* about it. Just act like you're checking email or something and snap a sneaky pic."

She was tempted. If for no other reason than to prove to Cesar *why* she'd been hung up on Sam since...well...since *forever*. As good as he'd looked in his high school baseball uniform, with that patented Samuel Harwood grin? Well, multiply that by about a hundred, and *that's* what she—and her horny, horny hormones—were dealing with now.

"I'll see if I get the opportunity later," she promised.

"Fine." Cesar pouted. She couldn't see him, but she could tell by his tone he was pouting. "Can you at least tell me what he does? Were you right? Is he a spy? Or…ooh! He's like a real-life Jack Reacher, isn't he? But is he, like, the Tom Cruise Jack Reacher or the Alan Ritchson Jack Reacher? Please say Alan Ritchson. That man is…"

"The spitting image of Pete. Except maybe a little beefier."

"Oh my god. You're right. Why didn't I see it before?"

"I'm thinking you were too busy ogling all Pete's bronzed muscles and didn't pay too much attention to his face. Which is a shame. It's a damn good face."

"It is, isn't it?" His sigh sounded dreamy. Then he returned them to the subject. "So…Sam? Spy? Former special operations guy gone rogue and out to save the world one mission at a time?"

"Sort of all of the above, I think. I'll fill you in on all the deets when I come home."

"Fine." Cesar pouted again. "But at least tell me you've kissed him. You've been dreaming of kissing him for sixteen years."

"I hate to disappoint you, but no. Although…" She grinned devilishly. "I *have* been tempted to flash him my boobs a time or two. Or, you know, grab his head and smash his face into my cleavage."

Cesar was quiet for a while after that. Then, "I mean, it's not as classy as a kiss. But it'll certainly get his attention."

"Are you saying my boobs aren't classy?" She huffed in mock affront. "I'll have you know they are posh AF. If there was ever an award for swankiest tatas, mine would win."

"You realize that right there is why men ghost you."

"What's that supposed to mean?" She frowned.

"It means you're too quick. To witty with a comeback. It's intimidating."

"Are *you* intimidated?"

"Of course not, darling. But I'm gay. Snappy clapbacks come with the territory. Also, I've seen you on Saturday mornings with two-day-old makeup and crunchy hair while wolfing down a popcorn-sized bowl of

Froot Loops in your SpongeBob SquarePants pajamas. After that, I could *never* find you intimidating."

"We can't all be as well-groomed as Cesar or as glamorous as Cesarine," she countered. "Besides, Saturdays are made for bad hygiene and poor breakfast choices. You'd know that if you'd get off that whole nine-step-skin-routine and Keto ride and join me in the land of drugstore bar soap and carbs."

"And there you go again with the rapid-fire comebacks." His sigh was dramatic. "Try tittering at Sam. Bat your lashes a little. See if that works before you assault him with your high-class titties."

"I would rather eat a handful of CPU's than titter or bat my lashes."

"I don't know what a CPU is." She opened her mouth to explain. He must've sensed it because he rushed ahead. "And *please* don't tell me. I'm sure the explanation is boring and dorky and I don't have the time or the patience. Pete is taking me out to dinner at Maple & Ash. Can you believe it? He knows one of the sous chefs and was able to squeeze a reservation out of her. I just wanted to call and check up on you before we head out."

She let loose with a theatrical sigh. "Bed-shaking sex with a golden god followed by a romantic dinner? I'm glad *one* of us is enjoying a satisfying love life." She glanced furtively at Sam. "Sam's treating me like I'm still thirteen."

"Which explains your impulse to flash him your boobs," Cesar correctly surmised. "Well, that's better than wrapping your legs around his head and rubbing your cooter in his face, I suppose."

"No one uses the word *cooter* except for guys named Jim Bob or Billy Joe."

"I don't have much experience with that particular body part. So what's the preferred nomenclature?"

"Vulva," she told him. "Or vagina. Of course, if you're a fan of brevity, you can shorten that to vag. Pussy is also acceptable if you'd rather err on the side of slang."

"Pussy sounds so sexual. And vagina and vulva sound so scientific. Isn't there something in the middle?"

"I'm sorry, you have a problem with a body part used for sex sounding sexual?"

"You've gotten us off topic."

"Right." She realized. "What was the topic?"

"You finding a way to show Sam you're no longer thirteen without resorting to shoving your boobs or girly bits in his face. If I may be so bold as to offer some advice?"

"Depends." She curled her upper lip. "If it's more tittering and lash batting then save it."

"Kiss him." Her mind blanked at the very notion. "Nothing too long or too kinky. Something simple. Something quick. If The Everly Brothers are right, he won't know what he's been missing until you kiss him."

"I have *got* to expand your record collection," she said about the twenty albums he spun pretty much nonstop back at the apartment. He'd inherited the records from his grandfather, a man who'd been a big fan of that country/rock style popularized in the 50's and 60's. "You think *my* references about CPU's are bad? At least most people our age have heard of central processing units. No one younger than the age of fifty remembers The Everly Brothers."

Instead of getting bent out of shape, he ignored her and repeated, "Kiss him."

"Easier said than done."

"Kiss him."

"Okay, bestie, but how do you suggest I go about it?"

"You've always had a wonderful imagination. Use it."

"You're no help," she grumbled unhappily.

"That's because I'm walking out the door as we speak." He blew her raspberries over the phone. "Later tater."

"Another saying no one uses anymore!" she hissed, but he'd already hung up.

Kiss Sam? Ha! What a joke! she thought. *He barely lets me touch him.*

Her steps were slow, weighed down her own defeat, as she walked back to the bank of computers. Sam had scooted his rolling chair directly in front of the monitor she'd been using, but her rolling chair was still next to his.

She purposefully brushed her hip against his shoulder when she went to sit down. And, sure enough, he pulled away from her as if she were made of battery acid.

Kiss him? I'd have better luck getting close to a crocodile.

"Everything okay with your roommate?" he asked absently, his eyes continuing to scan the emails.

"Fine. Pete, the golden god, is taking him to dinner at a swanky restaurant over in the Gold Coast. Cesar wanted to rub it in that he's being wined and dined and I'm here staring at a bunch of emails that don't make sense."

"You're being dined." Sam shot her a quick glance. "I have a pepperoni pizza with extra cheese on its way as we speak. And if you want some wine, I'm sure Eliza has a few bottles down in the kitchen I could bring up."

"You're being purposefully obtuse."

His grin was so wide and white, she almost went blind. "It's one of my rare talents."

"Pfft." She rolled her eyes. "Says the baseball star who became a Marine hero who became a wildly enigmatic private defense contractor. When it comes to your talents, *rare* isn't a word I'd use."

"I'm no hero." His tone had gone flat right along with his expression.

"Come on, Sam. Save the humble act for someone who hasn't seen your military file." She ticked items off on her fingers. "Two purple hearts, two bronze stars, and one silver star. You are, quite *literally*, a hero. You have the medals to prove it."

"I'm no more or less heroic than any of the men I served with. I just happened to be in the right place at the right time." He seemed to think about his answer and then rephrased. "The right place at the right time for the bronze and silver stars. I was certainly in the wrong place at the wrong time when it comes to the purple hearts."

She pointed to the gruesome scar slashing across his throat. "Would that be one of them?"

"How did we get off topic?" He waved a dismissive hand and then pointed to the monitor. "I see what you mean 'bout the emails not making sense."

"Right?" She nodded. "It's almost like their messages are coded or something. I understand Agent Beacham's reports to Director Morgan. And I understand Director Morgan's responses back to Agent Beacham. But it's like…"

She trailed off, not knowing how to describe the disparity.

"It's like two completely separate conversations that've been jammed together," Sam finished for her. "It's like there's a ghost in the machine or something."

She blinked when his words gave her an idea. "Scootch," she told him, using her rolling chair like a bumper car to nudge him away from the keyboard.

"Whatcha thinking?" he asked.

"Don't know yet. But it's possible…" She trailed off as she concentrated on the task at hand. When her hunch was confirmed a few minutes later, she shot a fist in the air and yelled, "Jackpot!"

Grabbing Sam's shoulders, she dragged him forward and planted one right on his mouth, careful to make it nothing more than a quick, friendly peck. Just like Cesar had said. Even still, she thrilled at the firmness of his lips, the heat of his watermelon candy-tinged breath, the titillating rasp of his beard against her chin.

When she released him, she found him wide-eyed and blinking. "You beautiful, brilliant man." She smiled warmly. "You've cracked the case."

Was it her imagination, or was his voice a little squeaky when he asked, "I have?"

"Yes. There *is* a ghost in the machine. Look." She pointed to the screen where a second set of emails now showed alongside the first set. "Someone cloned Agent Beacham's email account and Director Morgan's email account. They're playing the middleman between the two."

"I don't understand." He shook his head, looking a little dazed.

Or maybe that's just wishful thinking on my part.

"Whenever Agent Beacham sends an email to Morgan, it ends up in the mystery person's inbox first. And the same when Morgan sends an email to Agent Beacham. Whoever this person is, they're fudging the communications. Tampering with Agent Beacham's messages before they get to the director and vice versa."

"Right." Sam shook his head like he was trying to gather his thoughts after her sneak attack. Then he gestured toward the mouse. "May I?"

"Be my guest."

For long minutes he scrolled through the email exchanges. She alternated between reading them with him and trying not to jump into his lap and kiss him again.

Only this time it wouldn't be a peck. It'd be a long, slow, deep, *wet* kiss that left no room for misinterpretation. The kind of kiss that said, *I want you.* The kind of kiss that said, *I'm a grown-ass woman.* See *me!*

"Director Morgan has no idea Grace and her partner uncovered the truth about the people working for the troll farm," Sam muttered. "He still thinks the employees there are oblivious to being hired by the Kremlin. And the stuff related to the account cutting their paychecks and the rejected subpoenas? The middleman never passed that bit of information on to him."

"Which means the mole isn't the director *or* whomever he's been sharing his information with," she surmised. "The mole is whoever cloned these accounts."

When Sam turned to her, she felt herself being sucked into the blue whirlpools of his irises. "Can you find out who it is?"

"I can try." She nodded. "It might take me a while."

"Anything I can do to help?"

She arched a flirty eyebrow. "What did you have in mind?"

She expected him to brush her off as he'd being doing all along. Instead, his expression hardened. "Please stop, Hannah."

"Stop what?" Nervousness made her voice catch. She didn't like that look in his eye. And she *definitely* didn't like the muscle ticking in his jaw.

"You *know* what. The flirting. It was cute when you were thirteen. But it makes me uncomfortable now that you're twenty-eight."

"Twenty-nine."

"Okay." He shrugged as if the difference was inconsequential.

Swallowing convulsively, she ventured, "I know you said it's like incest, but we're *not* related. So how could it possibly make you uncomfortable?"

His answer was immediate. "I don't like having to reject you."

Now it was her turn to say, "Okay."

"I'm sorry, Hannah."

"No." She lifted a hand and shook her head, regretting that damned kiss. Obviously it hadn't had the impact she'd wanted. Quite the opposite, it'd been a bridge too far. "There's nothing to be sorry about. *I'm* sorry for making you feel uncomfortable."

His expression cleared. Softened. And when he chucked her on the chin and said, "No worries. We're still friends, right?" it took everything she had not to dissolve into a puddle of tears.

In her twenty-nine years, she'd had to give up plenty of childhood dreams. Her dream of inventing reusable rockets for one. SpaceX had beaten her to that. Her dream of being the first woman to sit behind the desk in the Oval Office for another. The current Madam President had snagged that honor. And finally, her dream of winning *Jeopardy* with Alex Trebek. *Fuck cancer.* But the disappointment she felt knowing she'd never reach any of those objectives didn't hold a candle to the disappointment she felt having to admit her dream of making Sam fall head over heels for her was just that.

A dream.

A *pipe* dream.

If he heard how hoarse her voice was when she said, "Still friends," he didn't mention it.

Instead, he simply smiled. "Good. I'm glad we got that settled."

"Right," she managed around the monster-sized lump in her throat.

The *beep* and the *buzz* of the front door had him glancing toward the second-floor railing. She used his distraction to covertly wipe away a mutinous tear from the corner of her eye.

"That's Boss back with the pizza. You wanna come downstairs and—"

"Mind bringing mine up here?" she cut him off. After grabbing the mouse, she pretended to scroll through the emails one more time. But her eyes were blind to anything on the screen. "I can eat and hack at the same time."

"Gotcha." He gave her shoulder a friendly pat—emphasis on the *friendly*—as he pushed up from the chair. "Back in a sec with bread and pepperoni and enough cheese to constipate an elephant."

She knew he expected her to laugh. But all she could manage was a weak smile. Then she waited until she heard his biker boots clomping down the metal stairs before she allowed her shoulders to collapse in defeat.

"Sonofa—" She grunted when Peanut hopped into her lap. Seeing the cat's round, furry face had more tears burning the back of her nose.

She buried her face in his neck and told herself to *get it together*.

Sam had asked her earlier if someone had broken her heart. The answer had been *no*. Now, thanks to him, she wasn't sure that was still the case.

CHAPTER 24

State Highway 37,
Mesick, Michigan

"The man's name is Dale Carlson," Bishop said. "I'm texting you his address now."

"And what makes you think Major Jackson and Agent Beacham are with him?"

"If they aren't with him, I've no doubt he knows where to find them. The FBI got a subpoena for Jackson's phone records, and there's only one number in Michigan he calls with any frequency."

"Dale Carlson," Pavel said, not for the first time wondering just exactly who Bishop was. Someone in Congress? Someone who worked for the Department of Justice? Maybe even a rogue FBI agent? Whoever he was, he had no trouble accessing classified information.

"Bingo," Bishop said. "And I don't believe in coincidence."

Pavel's cellular phone dinged with the text from Bishop. He clicked on the address and it opened in Google Maps.

"I can be there in approximately forty minutes."

"Good." Even with the voice-changer, there was no mistaking the relief in Bishop's tone. "The Feds in Chicago have tapped the local office there in Michigan to send agents up to question Carlson. But they're coming from

Lansing. So they're at least two hours behind you."

"Two hours behind? You might as well have said two days. I'll be long gone before they arrive," he boasted.

"That's exactly what I wanted to hear. I'm ready to finish this. It's gone on for too long now."

"Do you have any instructions on how you would like me to deal with Major Jackson and this Carson fellow once I arrive?"

"There can be no witnesses."

"Obviously."

After Pavel disconnected the call, he caught his reflection in the rearview mirror. The small smile on his face was one of anticipation. And the car filled with the sound of his high, clear whistle as he pressed his foot on the gas pedal and watched Dale Carlson's house draw nearer on the map displayed on his phone screen.

CHAPTER 25

3 Majestic Ridge Road

"I feel like we should slap high fives," Hunter said huskily while giving Grace's luscious hips a squeeze. The way her flesh filled his hands would've made his dick hard had she not just finished riding him—and herself—to completion.

She'd collapsed on top of him after coming down from the throes of another orgasm, but his words had her pushing up on her hands so she could grin down at him.

Her long, blond hair hung around them like a curtain. Her warm, brown eyes were soft with spent passion. And the skin around her pretty mouth was pink from beard-burn.

"You mean because teamwork makes the dream work?" she asked. The quickly setting sun beaming in through the windows gave the light inside the room a sweet, rosy tinge. He felt like he was looking at everything through rose-colored glasses.

And maybe he was. Because he was in bed with the most amazing woman he'd ever known. And for this small moment in time, she belonged with him. Belonged *to* him in a way no one ever had before.

"Well, sure, that." He grinned. "But I'd say, considering how exhausting the last twenty-four hours have been, we've put on quite a performance today. How many was that for you? Four?"

"Five, but who's counting?" Her eyes twinkled.

"Apparently you are."

"Two pre-shower. Two in the shower. And now this most recent one."

"Two in the shower?" He arched an eyebrow. "I remember the one with my mouth."

Holy *shit*, did he remember. She'd been standing with her back against the tile wall and he'd gone down on his knees in front of her. After draping one of her lovely legs over his shoulder, he'd spent a mind-melting few minutes tasting her, teasing her soft, swollen flesh, and filling his nose with the smell of a warm, healthy woman who was ripe with passion.

"When was the other?" he asked.

"When I was down on my knees sucking you, I was...um..." Her little blush was the most delightful thing. "I was also taking care of myself."

"God, yes," he breathed. "I remember that too."

The way her succulent mouth had wrapped around his straining dick while one of her hands was busy with her own flesh was seared into his brain like the most erotic brand. Even though he wouldn't have thought it possible, he felt his dick pulse inside her with renewed interest.

In response, her velvety walls clamped around him.

"But I didn't know you came." He gave her hips another squeeze as he thrust into her slightly. The friction was gentle. And the easy way she moved with him made it seem like they'd been doing this forever.

"That's because you were too busy having your own orgasm," she teased.

He sighed happily. "Don't know if you've been told, but you have a very talented mouth. And, as delighted as I was, and still am, by that orgasm, I'm very sorry I missed yours."

"Speaking of keeping track." She went down on her elbows. It smashed her amazing breasts into his chest, and he couldn't stop his fingers from drifting up her sides to lightly brush the soft, pillowing edges. "That's five for me but only three for you. That seems unfair. Whatever shall we do to even the score?"

"Considering women are the ones who have to suffer periods, pregnancy, and childbirth, I think it's only right Mother Nature gave you guys the upper hand when it comes to orgasms."

"Well..." She pressed a kiss to his lips. He growled when she darted her little tongue out to taste him. "When you put it that way, who am I to argue?"

Before he could open his mouth, her expression changed. In an instant, it went from soft and lazy to troubled. "What is it?" He frowned.

"I think…"

She pushed into a seated position, and he had just a moment to enjoy the view. The flare of her hips as she straddled him. The teardrop shape of her pretty breasts. The sight of their joined sexes. Then she gingerly disengaged their bodies.

He watched avidly as his semi-erect cock slipped from her, all shiny and slick. And it was then he understood what'd caused the change in her demeanor.

The condom was broken.

The latex ring was still secured around his base. But the body of the condom, attached to the ring by a tiny strip, lay wrinkled and useless against his thigh.

"Oh, lord," she breathed, crawling off him to sit cross-legged. She pressed a hand to her forehead and a worried frown puckered her kiss-swollen lips.

"It's okay," he assured her. "I'm clean. I was tested three weeks ago, and I haven't been with anyone since. And didn't you say in the shower I'm the first man you've been with since your divorce? I'm sure you don't have anything to worry about. I'm sure you're—"

"It's not that." She cut him off and pressed her hands over her eyes. "Damnit! I wish I had my phone."

He was confused. "Why?"

"So I could check my app. The one that keeps track of my cycle." She started counting on her fingers, her lips moving silently.

It hit him then what she was worried about, and his stomach tied itself into a hard knot. "You're not pregnant," he assured her.

She shook her head. "I'm not on birth control. What would be the point since I wasn't getting any until…" She flapped her hand back and forth between them. "Never mind. Is there a pharmacy close? We should grab a Plan B. Because if I'm remembering correctly, I'm pretty sure we're in the danger zone here."

"We're not." He got up from the bed to walk into the bathroom and dispose of the broken condom. When he returned, he found her lying on her side, her breasts doing that lovely slide-and-hang that drove him wild.

"What do you mean we're not?" A little line had formed between her eyebrows.

"I can't get you pregnant." Never in his life had those five words sounded so foul. But saying them to Grace had them dripping from his tongue like poison.

Her frown deepened and he waited for understanding to dawn. He saw the moment it did because her eyes widened. "Did you…" She paused and started again. "I know a lot of guys who went in for vasectomies after Roe v. Wade was overturned. They didn't want to put their partners at risk."

"I didn't get a vasectomy, Grace."

The line between her eyebrows deepened. "Then…I'm not sure what we're talking about here then. Are you…" She cocked her head. "Are you sterile?"

And there it was. Out there with such clinical accuracy.

"Yes." That single syllable growled out of the back of his throat, sounding like tank tracks crunching over gravel.

He wasn't sure what he expected her response to be. Confusion, maybe? Or his arch nemesis…pity? He should've known better, though. It was Grace he was talking to, after all. Good, tender, kindhearted Grace.

Her pretty face filled with compassion. "What happened?" She jerked back her chin and waved a hand. "No. That's such a personal question. You don't have to answer if—"

"Considering what we've just been up to, I'm not sure there's anything you could ask me that's too personal."

She searched his eyes and quietly asked again, "So what happened?"

"Testicular torsion."

The two words didn't sound so very awful. Maybe it was the alliteration. But despite their poetic cadence, the truth of them was devastating.

"I'm assuming that's exactly what it sounds like?" She made a face of sympathetic pain. "Your testicles got twisted?"

"Not so much the testicles themselves, but the big blood vessels that attach them to my body."

"How?"

"Wish I knew." He shrugged.

How many times had he gone over it in his head? How many times had he thought back on the days before it happened, looking for some inciting incident? Like an injury or a strenuous bout of exercise. But…nothing. As hard as he'd racked his brain, he'd come up with a big ol' handful of nada. And every medical professional he'd spoken with since assured him testicular torsion was a medical mystery, seeming to have no discernible cause other than bad fucking luck.

"I simply woke up one morning with a stomachache like nothing I'd ever experienced before," he explained.

"How old were you?"

"Twelve."

Her compassionate expression turned into one of worry. "So you were still living with your parents? What…what did they do?"

In his mind's eye, he could see the derision and anger on his father's face when he shook him awake from his drunken stupor. Any hope he'd had that the man who'd supplied half his genetic material had actually *loved* him—or even just cared for him a *little*—had died that day. Right along with his ability to father children of his own.

"Bert told me it was just the flu. Wacked me on the back of the head and said I needed to suck it up and stop crying like a baby."

"Dear sweet lord." Wetness gathered in her eyes.

"I laid on my little mattress on the floor in my room for eighteen hours trying to be as still as possible. Even breathing made me feel like I was dying." He sat on the edge of the mattress and closed his eyes at the remembered agony. He'd taken a bullet and been sliced by blades that didn't hurt half as much. "It wasn't until I reached down and felt my tiny twelve-year-old balls the size of grapefruits that I finally thought *to hell with my parents* and called 9-1-1."

She pulled him down until he was stretched out beside her. When she framed his face with her palms, her fingers were wonderfully cool against his hot cheeks. "I'm so sorry, Hunter. I can't imagine." This time, the pity in her eyes didn't sting. In fact, it felt sort of nice. Like a balm to his bruised and battered heart. "You were just a child. And should've been able to rely on the adults in your life to take care of you."

"I was lucky actually." He hitched a shoulder. "After that much time, it's not unusual for the testicles to die and need to be removed. Miraculously, I was able to keep mine. And so far…" He rapped his knuckles on the wooden headboard. "The injury hasn't affected my ability to perform sexually."

"It just robbed you of any chance of becoming a father."

"Yes." He nodded. "It did do that."

The tears that'd pooled in her eyes slipped over her lower lids to trace down her soft cheeks.

"Don't cry, Grace." He used his knuckle to wipe away the warm wetness. "What's done is done. And I've learned the shortest route to unhappiness is not accepting the things we can't change."

She shook her head. "I don't even know if you *want* kids, but to be denied the ability because your parents were too drunk or selfish or whatever…" She trailed off, anger on his behalf making her face burn red. "It's unconscionable."

"It wasn't like I was the only one they failed and neglected," he said philosophically. He'd grown very philosophical about his folks over the years. "They failed and neglected themselves too. Over and over again. Because they didn't know how to be different. Bert and Susan were products of their own raising, you see."

When she shook her head, he explained. "My grandparents on both sides were horror shows." He hooked a thumb toward his chest. "You're looking at a classic case of how abuse and addiction travel along the branches of family trees. How poverty and ignorance and suffering perpetuate themselves generation after generation. You'd have to go all the way back to my great-grandfather, Walter Jackson, before you'd find anyone in my family who wasn't the human equivalent of a raging dumpster fire."

He told her about his great-grandfather's WWII exploits. Showed her the watch he wore with pride. And explained about the name of his motorcycle.

"You're wrong," she declared once he'd finished. "You aren't a prime example of how poverty, abuse, addiction and neglect can travel along the branches of family trees." Her voice was as tremulous as her smile. "You're a prime example of the exception to the rule. The one who refused to perpetuate the cycle. The one who beat all the odds."

"I don't know about that." He'd never been good at receiving accolades. Probably why his medals were stored in the bottom drawer of his nightstand back in his room at BKI instead of displayed on a shelf somewhere, like Dale did with his Vietnam memorabilia. "I just know I saw an alternative and I took it. Or more like I grabbed onto it with both hands and never looked b—"

He was cut off by the sound of his burner phone ringing. Grace's eyes pinged over to the device on the bedside table, and he watched her expression harden.

For a few hours they'd been able to pretend this day was nothing more than a romantic getaway. They'd gotten so lost in each other that the world outside had disappeared. Now, reality called.

Literally.

"Chin up." He gave the underside of her soft little chin a bump with his knuckle. "Hopefully this means we're one step closer to figuring this whole mess out."

She nodded shakily and he snagged the phone off the nightstand. "What do you know?" he asked without preamble after flipping it open.

The tone of Sam's voice had the hairs on the back of his neck lifting. "The FBI knows about your property manager."

Hunter's mind blanked, the words not making sense. But his body seemed to understand because bile burned up the back of his throat. "Wait. What? How?"

"They found CCTV footage of you and Grace driving north on I-140. They know you're in Michigan. They also subpoenaed your phone records and Hannah was able to see they flagged a man named Dale Carlson. Dollars to doughnuts they're headed there now to question him. Which means they'll know where you and Grace are soon enough."

"It's worse than that." Hannah's voice came through the receiver, although it sounded far away, as if she were across the room from Sam. "If the double agent has access to the same information, it means they've passed that information along to the assassin."

"Oh, fuck." Sam hissed at the same time Hunter's heart grew legs and jumped into his throat. "I hadn't considered that part." His voice was diamond hard when he added, "Call your guy, bruh. Tell him to get the hell outta Dodge. And then you and Grace find somewhere else to hide until I call you and tell you it's safe to come out."

Click. The line went dead.

Apparently, his face during the call had told Grace all she'd needed to know. She'd already run to the bathroom to yank open the door to his all-in-one washer and dryer. "What is it? What did he say?" she asked while hastily pulling out her clean clothes.

"He says the FBI knows about Dale and Sissy." Hunter didn't bother with his own clothes as he bolted toward the kitchen. "Which means Orpheus knows about Dale and Sissy."

Why the fuck didn't I think to plug Dale's number into the burner? He berated himself, while hoping he still had Dale's business card in the junk drawer.

"Tell me what to do to help." He barely looked up from his scrounge through loose batteries, paperclips, and tape. But his brief glance was enough to show Grace standing in the doorway to the bedroom and stepping into her panties.

Any other time, he would've stopped to enjoy the show. Why was the sight of a woman slipping into her underwear and putting on a bra so sexy? As it stood, he sent a silent prayer of thanks out into the universe when he located the wrinkled, stained business card.

"Finish getting dressed," he told her even as he punched in Dale's number. "We need to be on the road before—" He cut himself off. "It's ringing."

The thundering of his heart made it hard to hear the jangle on the other end. The first ring had him holding his breath. The second had him muttering, "Come on, Dale." Apprehension tightened his shoulders on the third ring. And by the fourth and the fifth, he felt like someone was taking a carving knife to his stomach.

"Fuck!" he snarled when the call clicked over to voicemail. He waited for the recorded message to finish before yelling into the receiver. "Dale! I hope you're just taking a shower or something, man. If you get this message, get Sissy and get out of the house. Once you're hell and gone, *call* me on this number. I'll explain everything." He hung up and immediately tried the call again.

"Do you know where he lives?" Grace asked as the line rang and rang. She'd already slipped back into her borrowed T-shirt and jeans and was in the process of pulling on socks.

"Yeah." He nodded, slamming shut the burner when the call to Dale clicked over to voicemail again. "But it's possible the Feds beat Orpheus there. And then what? If we show up and it's the FBI questioning Dale and Sissy and not the Russian, do we just turn you over to them?"

"Yes." She nodded. "Because the alternative is that Orpheus has beaten my colleagues there and your friends are sitting ducks. We can't take that chance. We can't risk them. So, how far is it?"

He wasn't surprised she was willing to throw away her own freedom and safety for two people she'd never met. But that didn't make it any easier to say, "We can be there in five minutes."

CHAPTER 26

56 Crimson Valley Ave,
Traverse City, Michigan

In interrogation, there was an old saying. *Violence perceived is violence achieved.*

While Pavel appreciated the sentiment, he *far* preferred *actual* violence to the perception of it. It was so incredibly satisfying to look into a man's eyes—or a woman's—and watch pain squeeze their pupils down to pinpoints.

Such a visceral experience. Primal even.

Nothing else compared.

Perhaps sex, he thought. *If it's with the right woman. One who understands pleasure and pain are two sides of the same coin.*

But I digress…

Turned out Dale Carlson was married. A boon since the old goat had been tough-as-nails so far, unwilling to give up Major Jackson and Agent Beacham's whereabouts even though Pavel had broken his nose, busted his lip, and clipped him in the eye hard enough to open up a gash near his eyebrow.

If pain doesn't make the grizzled old bastard talk, he thought as he walked toward the opposite end of the kitchen table, *then I'll have to find another way.*

The phone lying atop the table jangled with life once again. And the sound had Mrs. Carlson grunting and screaming against the duct tape Pavel had slapped over her mouth. Tears trekked down her reddened face. And the wooden dining chair he'd tied her to scraped against the tile floor as she rocked forward in a bid to bring her useless mouth closer to the ringing phone.

What did she think? That the person on the other end of the call would hear her pig-like squeals?

Funny how people lost the ability to reason when they were desperate. When the life of the person they loved best was on the line. And he had no doubt Mrs. Carlson loved her husband best. The way she'd wailed against the duct tape every time he'd cracked his fist into Mr. Carlson's wrinkled face told him everything he needed to know about the married couple.

Of course, there was *also* that sepia-toned picture hanging in the hallway. The one showing the two of them in their wedding attire, so fresh-faced and dewy looking. He'd guess they'd been little more than teenagers when they'd tied the knot and had since spent their entire lives together.

Now they will die together. It's poetic when you stop to think about it.

Whistling, he made a show of flipping the knife he'd taken from the block on the counter and then neatly catching it by the tip of the blade. Over and over he tossed it and caught it. Tossed it and caught it. Watching the yellow glow of the overhead light glint menacingly against the metal. And smiling at Mr. Carlson who, bound as tightly as his wife to a chair, sat stoically, his bloodshot eyes taking in every revolution even as blood from the cut on his brow dripped from his stubby eyelashes.

Stopping behind Mrs. Carlson's chair, Pavel grabbed her forehead and wrenched back her head. Her weepy eyes were cornflower blue and filled with terror when she stared up at him. Her whimper sounded like a kitten being kicked when he pressed the blade to her throat.

"No!" Dale roared that one word so loudly it reminded Pavel of a canon shot. The old man struggled against his restraints until he made his chair hop. "Don't you touch her, you sorry sonofabitch!"

"Ah." Pavel chuckled. "So you *do* possess vocal cords. That's good." He pressed the knife tighter against Mrs. Carlson's wrinkled throat and watched, fascinated, as a line of bright red blood oozed from her flesh onto the blade.

His phone buzzed in his pocket. Bishop, of course, probably looking for an update. *Always so impatient.* He ignored the call and kept his tone conversational as he cocked his head at Dale. "You will tell me where I can find Hunter Jackson. And you will do that because you honor your wife more than you honor your own life. Or the life of Major Jackson."

Dale's ruined face crumpled as tears joined the blood on his cheeks. "Yes." He nodded vehemently, his thin, white hair fluttering. "I'll tell you whatever you want to know. Just...let Sissy go."

"Give me the address of where I will find the major," Pavel countered. "And I promise to remove the knife from your wife's delicate throat."

Dale rattled off an address. Pavel easily committed it to memory. "It's very close," Dale added. "South of here."

"Good." Pavel nodded. "Thank you. Now, for my end of the bargain."

With a little pressure and a hard jerk of his arm, he removed the knife from Mrs. Carlson's throat. Of course, he laid that same throat wide open in the process.

Crimson blood sprayed across the table. Dale howled his wife's name, his face a picture of horror and shock. And Pavel went back to whistling as he watched Dale rock so hard in his chair it tipped over and crashed onto its side.

The old man howled again. But this bellow wasn't one of horror and grief. It was one of pain. Pavel would guess the fall had broken the old man's shoulder. Or perhaps his collarbone.

When he released Mrs. Carlson's forehead, it had her crumpling forward in her chair. Blood poured from the wound on her neck to stain her flowery blouse. And her bound hands fluttered and twitched behind the chair as her bare feet scrabbled uselessly against the tile floor.

Barely three heartbeats later, she fell still. Silent.

The only sounds in the room were the high notes of his whistle and the wet, soggy cries that burbled up from the depths of Dale's chest as he tried inchworming his way across the floor toward his wife.

Pavel carefully stowed the blade in his back pocket, then pulled out his handgun and silencer. After screwing the attachment to the end of the barrel, he checked to make sure it was secure. And then aimed at the blubbering old man.

"Shhh," he whispered, shaking his head. "Quiet now. You were doing so well. You want to meet your death with dignity, *da*?"

Dale stopped crying long enough to lift his head and stare daggers at Pavel. There was rage in the old man's eyes. But there was also relief. As if he were happy to hear he would not have to remain attached to his mortal coil now that his beloved wife had been cut from hers.

"Very good," Pavel smiled. "Keep looking at me just like that and it will be a good death. Not a soft one, as the song says. But a good one."

Curling his finger around the cool trigger, he started whistling again. But just as the muscles in his hands tightened, the roar of a motorcycle engine sounded outside. It was followed by the strobe effect as a headlight briefly beamed in through the kitchen window.

Craning his head, he caught a glimpse of the two riders as they motored past and then quickly disappeared. Their helmets made their identities indiscernible. But he'd bet his last ruble it was Major Jackson and Agent Beacham come to join the party.

Like moths to the flame. How convenient.

Dale screamed for help and Pavel shook his head, disappointed in the old man. Which made it that much easier to the pull the trigger.

Poom!

The silencer deadened the sound of the muzzle blast. But it didn't deaden the impact of the bullet. Dale's head snapped back and then rebounded on his neck so that, once again, he stared at Pavel. Only now, his eyes were sightless.

A deep, red hole in the center of Dale's forehead oozed a single line of blood. So innocuous looking if one was to ignore what the back of his head looked like. Pieces of Dale's skull and globs of gray matter had splattered across the tiles behind him.

Now, for Major Jackson and Agent Beacham, Pavel thought with anticipation as he headed out of the kitchen to the den and the sliding glass door that led to the backyard.

When his phone buzzed again, he rolled his eyes at Bishop's relentlessness. With an annoyed press of a button, he turned off the device. He couldn't have it alerting his prey to his presence.

CHAPTER 27

Grace was off the back of the motorcycle the instant Hunter cut the engine. But he beat her to the front door, his long legs eating up the distance.

"Dale! Sissy!" He slammed the side of his big fist into the solid wood and then smashed the doorbell with his thumb. "Open up! It's Hunter!"

Night had fallen, and the lights were on inside. Two cars were parked in the drive—neither of them sporting government plates, which meant her colleagues had yet to arrive. But only silence met Hunter's appeal.

Silence, the gentle buzz of night insects in the grass, and the soft hiss of the breeze blowing through the trees.

Dale and Sissy Carlson lived in a little cottage down a long country lane. It was an idyllic setting. More shabby chic country chalet than cabin, all cozy and quaint with the porch light burning and the moon shining down on the tin roof. And yet…something felt off.

The air felt heavy. The quiet felt grim. The stillness felt wrong.

No, not wrong, she thought. *Sinister.*

She wasn't big on the paranormal, but she'd been to enough crime scenes to know recent violence and new death had an otherworldly way of hanging in the atmosphere. Of befouling the air so anyone who entered the space could feel the ominous effects of it.

Guilt had swirled in her stomach the entire ride from Hunter's cabin to the Carlson's little cottage. Now that guilt mixed with dread.

Had she brought trouble to the doorstep of Hunter's friends? Would he find something horrible on the other side of that door and blame her for whatever had happened there?

Not that she didn't *deserve* the blame. She did.

Her only excuse was that, when she'd made the phone call to Hunter, she'd never in a million years dreamed the repercussions of her predicament would fall on anyone's head but her own.

More fool me, she thought, fighting the urge to bend over the porch railing and hurl the turkey sandwich Hunter had fed her directly into the Carlson's front flower bed.

"Dale! Sissy!" He gave the doorknob a frantic rattle. "Locked," he muttered, yanking his pistol from the back of his pants. "Stand back."

She scurried down the front steps and turned back in time to see him pull his trigger. *Bam!* The muzzle blast flashed orange in the darkness.

After her ears stopped ringing, she noticed how the savage roar of the weapon had silenced the insects. Had even seemed to silence the wind. It was as if the entire world held its breath, waiting for that door to open and reveal—

He planted his steel-toed biker boot next to the knob. *Crash!* The ruined lock gave way and the door swung wildly on its hinges, smacking into the wall behind it with so much force the doorknob embedded itself into the drywall.

Biting her lip hard enough she was surprised she didn't draw blood, she peeked around him into the lit room beyond. She'd been so certain they'd find carnage on the other side of the door. But all she saw was a comfy-looking flowered sofa, a dark mahogany coffee table, and two overstuffed armchairs illuminated by the glow of floor lamps.

The wall behind the sofa was decorated with a gun rack and shadow boxes that held military medals, pictures of men in uniform, and was that…

She was pretty sure the little green-gray ball in the farthest shadow box was a grenade.

Hunter ran through the front door, his weapon out and at the ready as he yelled again, "Dale! Sissy!"

Clutching her service pistol firmly in her hand, she followed him inside and took up a position at his six. Her training had her sectioning off the room with her weapon, left, right, and center.

"Dale! Sissy! Answer me, goddamnit! It's Hunter!" Again, he was met with only the hum of the appliances in the kitchen and soft *whap, whap, whap* of the ceiling fan as it stirred the air.

"Check the bedrooms." She hitched her chin toward the darkened hallway. "I'll check the den and kitchen."

Part of her expected him to argue. To insist they stick together because he was a big, bad soldier, after all. And she was just a little lady who played at being an investigator for the federal government.

But all he did was give her a curt nod and a "Copy that" before turning to stealthily make his way toward the hall, his weapon leading the way.

He'd given her plenty of compliments in the time they'd known each other. But his confidence in her ability as a professional was the highest praise he could've offered.

Let's hope I'm worthy of it.

Unlike him, she didn't do this sort of thing for a living. Despite what Hollywood would have people believe, the life of an FBI agent rarely, if ever, involved high speed car chases or shootouts in back alleys.

In fact, most of an agent's time was spent on monotonous interviews followed by piles of paperwork. She hadn't had to "clear a room" since her DFE—Deadly Force Encounter—training back at Quantico.

After he disappeared down the long hall, she pressed her back against the doorway leading to the den and realized two things in short order. One, that *was* a grenade. And two, Dale Carlson had been part of the 5th Special Forces Group (Airborne) in Vietnam. The greenish-gray beret with the iconic patch worn by the row of men in the pictures told her that much.

And it gave her hope.

Hope that even *if* Orpheus had made it to the little cottage that Dale had had the wherewithal to recognize the danger the assassin posed and spirit his wife away to safety.

Or maybe they're out on an evening walk, she told herself. *Maybe that sinister vibe I picked up on outside was just my imagination running away with me.*

She wasn't as quick as Hunter. Or as quiet. But she liked to think her instructors at the academy would be proud of the way she turkey-peeked into the den, sidearm up and aimed. After quickly sectioning the room, she found the space blessedly empty.

Stepping through the doorway, she noted how cozy the room was. The afghan draped over the back of the sofa looked almost identical to the one Hunter kept in his own living room. There were photos stacked on every horizontal surface. And an easel was set up in the corner with a half-done watercolor that had the same dreamy feel as the painting in Hunter's cabin.

Even though she'd never met Dale or Sissy, she felt like she knew them from the photos alone. The warm light from the lamps bracketing the sofa showed a picture of them in Hawaii and another of them at the Grand Canyon. One large, glossy 8x10 showcased the couple looking young and fresh and standing in front of the little cottage Grace found herself in now with a "sold" sign held between them. And still more featured the couple at holiday celebrations spanning the years.

Please let them be alive. Please, please *let them be alive.* She sent the silent prayer out into the ether even though she wasn't sure anyone was listening.

"Guest bedroom clear!" Hunter called and she felt a jolt of relief before immediately responding, "Den is clear!"

Which left only the kitchen.

Her stomach crawled into her throat as she carefully, quietly made her way across the carpeted floor, past the sliding glass door with only inky blackness showing beyond, toward the doorway leading to the kitchen. Her heart joined her stomach when she stepped through the threshold and was confronted with a reality too grizzly to fully grasp.

Orpheus *had* beaten them to the Carlson's house.

And he'd done his worst.

"Sweet lord almighty." The words wheezed from her as the shock of the carnage stole her breath. Tears burned her eyes and cold dread singed her veins until her entire body felt poised for flight.

She *so* much wanted to run away and hide. To turn her face away from the truth of the horror staring back at her, but…

"Beachams don't run, Grace," her father's voice sounded in her head. *"Beachams stand and face the consequences of their actions."*

Squaring her shoulders, she rubbed the back of her hand over the hot tears that'd trekked down her cheeks. And then she did what had to be done.

"*Hunter!*" The scream tore from the back of her throat with enough force to scrape the tender flesh raw.

She didn't remember stowing her weapon. She didn't remember taking the three steps that brought her to the table. But suddenly she was down on her knees beside Dale's body, carefully pressing two fingers to the old man's carotid.

It was a useless endeavor, she knew. The neat hole between Dale's sightless eyes, not to mention the horror that was the back of the man's head, told her all she needed to know. But her training prompted her to check. To be sure.

The iron-rich smell of blood crawled inside her nose like slimy vermin and stuck there until she had to fight not to gag. Memories of finding Stewart, of trying so desperately to save him while knowing it was impossible, flashed through her head.

So much blood. So much violence. So much needless death.

She'd been so busy running and hiding and fighting to get her life and good name back, she hadn't had time to truly process her partner's murder. But now, looking at the brutality around her, she knew processing would be nearly impossible. The barbarism of the last day was permanently imprinted on her psyche and the unfathomable *unfairness* of it all, of lives cut short by the hand of someone in her own government—because even though the Russian was the bullet, someone else had held the gun—had tears clogging the back of her throat.

"Oh god!" Hunter skidded to a stop in the doorway, his face draining of blood. "Oh god, *no*! Sissy!"

He dropped to his knees beside the old woman's chair. Like Grace, he tried to find Sissy's pulse. But it was clear from the amount of blood still running in rivulets down the woman's chest that she was dead.

"That goddamn sonofabitch. That goddamn sonofa*bitch*!" The last word was barely a wheeze by the time he finished. And his anguish had the tears standing in Grace's eyes spilling over her bottom lids.

Her own voice was tight. "I—I'm so sorry, Hunter. I never should've involved you. I should've just—"

He jumped to his feet. "We have to get back to the cabin."

"What?" She blinked and ran the back of her hand under her runny nose.

"He obviously tortured our location out of Dale and Sissy." His voice cracked on the couple's names, and that sound alone was enough to crush her heart to dust.

"Right." She nodded, pushing shakily to her feet. "But he hasn't been gone long. Dale and Sissy are still…" She couldn't bring herself to say *warm and bleeding*. So instead she rephrased. "They haven't been dead for long. We need to—"

"I'm going to kill that motherfucker."

Anyone listening would've said his tone was conversational, almost cool. But she'd been around him enough to know he was anything but. His nostrils flared. His big chest worked over each heavy breath. And murderous rage filled his hazel eyes.

She understood his urge to end Orpheus. Hell, she *shared* it. The Russian needed to die before he had the chance to murder more innocents. But the assassin was nothing if not wily. And the last thing she wanted, the last thing she could live with, was for Hunter to go off half-cocked and get himself killed.

She needed time to think. Time to *plan* so that no more blood ended up on her hands.

"Hunter, we need to take a minute to—"

"Grab the afghan off the back of the sofa. There's another one folded up by the fireplace. We need to cover them up." His jaw was clenched so hard she could see the individual muscle fibers reaching up into his cheeks. "I know it's stupid, but I want to drape their bodies in Sissy's blankets before we leave."

When his voice broke again, she swallowed down all her objections. "It's not stupid." She turned for the door, biting back her own tears because it seemed self-indulgent to give into her sorrow when he was fighting so hard to hold onto his. "It's thoughtful," she finished.

After grabbing the soft blanket from the back of the couch in the den, she bent to snag the folded blanket from the hearth. The material was well-worn and soft, cool to the touch and smelling of dryer sheets.

How many hours had Sissy worked on these? How many cold winter nights had she and Dale snuggled beneath them for warmth? And now, because of Grace, these soft, bright blankets would be the couple's death shrouds.

She was so consumed by guilt, so preoccupied by the horrible pain she'd seen in Hunter's eyes, she didn't hear the sliding glass door slip open behind her. In fact, the first indication she had she wasn't alone was the warm barrel of a weapon as it kissed her temple.

Warm because it'd been recently fired.

"Here you are, little rabbit." The Russian's breath was hot in her ear and stinking of stale cigarette smoke. His accent made the words sound that much more malevolent. "Did you doubt I would find you?"

Her heart hammered so hard it made her ribs ache. Still, she shook her head, ever so slightly, wincing when the move rubbed the barrel of the pistol against the skin of her temple.

She *hadn't* doubted Orpheus would find her. She'd just hoped by the time he did, her name would be cleared, they'd have found the double agent inside the government, and she'd have the entire Federal Bureau of Investigations backing her up to bring him down.

"Good girl." He reached into her shoulder holster and pulled out her weapon.

Any other time, her jaw would've clenched at the condescension in his tone. As it was, she couldn't bring herself to care about anything other than getting out of the house. Getting *Orpheus* out of the house.

"I'll go with you," she whispered frantically. "I won't fight. Just…please leave Hunter alone."

"Sorry." That one word hit her ears like a death knell. "My instructions were clear. No witnesses."

She closed her eyes, her mind spinning in a million different directions, searching for the path that would allow Hunter to live. But each route led to a dead end, emphasis on the *dead*.

Except for maybe…one.

There was one thing she could think to do that might give Hunter a fighting chance.

When she opened her eyes, she saw the framed photo of Dale and Sissy sitting atop the credenza. It was a picture of them with their arms thrown around Hunter on their fiftieth-fifth wedding anniversary. She knew it was their fiftieth-fifth because of the banner behind their heads, and the couple looked so happy and *alive* and glad to have Hunter there with them.

She hadn't been able to save Dale and Sissy. She hadn't been able to save Stewart. Maybe she could save Hunter.

Calm washed over her as she drew in a steadying breath. The instant she opened her mouth, Orpheus would send a bullet straight through her brain, but she didn't care.

All she cared about was warning Hunter and, hopefully, giving him the upper hand against the assassin. Hunter, who was so good and brave and loyal and strong. Hunter, who hadn't thought twice before entangling himself in the messy web that'd become her life.

Hunter, the man she loved.

There was no longer any reason to deny it.

She'd fallen for him three years ago. And this past day had shown her exactly why all her feelings were justified.

"Run Hunter!" she screamed so loudly her voice frayed. "He's h—"

That's all she managed before her head exploded and she knew no more.

CHAPTER 28

Hunter had been scared plenty of times in his life.

He'd been six years old the first time his parents had gone on a bender for five days, leaving him alone with only a jar of pickles and a sleeve of saltines. He'd been twenty-six the time in Afghanistan when he'd been well outside the wire, cut off from his unit and listening to the boots of his enemies crunch around in the gravel barely two feet from where he'd hidden himself in a crevice. And he'd been thirty-one the time Sam had been bleeding out in his arms and their damn extraction team had been late arriving at the LZ.

But nothing had ever chilled him to the bone like the horror in Grace's scream. Nothing had ever made his blood run cold like the sound of her little cry of pain and then…silence.

He appeared in the doorway to the den in time to see her go limp in a stranger's arms. A thick trickle of blood slid from her temple down her pale cheek to drip from her chin.

The only thing that kept him from flying across the room, propelled by mindless rage, was the certainty she wasn't dead. There'd been no report from the silencer held tight against her temple.

Plus, had she been dead, the Russian would've dropped her. Instead he held her tight to him, using her as a human shield. Which had undoubtedly been the point. Incapacitate her and use her as cover while taking out Hunter.

Enough! he roared in his head as his grip on his pistol tightened. Too much innocent blood had already been spilled in this house, and he'd had enough.

He was going to end that sorry sonofabitch. He knew it as surely as he knew the sun rose in the east and set in the west. As surely as he'd known he'd do anything Grace asked when he'd first heard her voice on the phone. And as surely as he knew he was ass over teakettle in love with her.

"What is it you Americans like to say?" The assassin's smile pulled his thin lips wide. "Glad you could join the party?"

He wasn't sure what he'd expected the infamous hired gun to look like, but it wasn't this nondescript, middle-aged white dude. The Russian had thinning blond hair, a totally forgettable face, and he wore a polo shirt tucked into a pair of jeans like a suburban dad at a soccer game.

"Drop the woman." Hunter's voice was so guttural he didn't recognize it as his own. His senses sharpened until he could see every tick of the bastard's steady pulse in the side of his neck. Until he could smell the faint hint of cigarette smoke wafting in the air.

"Not a chance." Orpheus shook his head.

"I could put one between your eyes right now," Hunter growled, seeing quite clearly the spot where his bullet would enter.

"Perhaps you could." Orpheus shrugged and the move made Grace's head bounce on the end of her neck. More blood had run down her pale face to stain the front of her borrowed T-shirt, and he had to remind himself head wounds always bled like a stuck pig. If he didn't, desperation might take over. And a standoff called for one thing and one thing only: calm calculation. "But could you be sure your bullet would end me before I blew Agent Beacham's brains out the side of her skull?" the Russian added.

The thought had the bottom dropping out of Hunter's stomach. "Then we're at an impasse here, aren't we?"

"Not necessarily." There was a cruel gleam in Orpheus's eye that told him everything he needed to know about the man.

The shitstain *enjoyed* this stuff. *Liked* torturing and killing people.

"You could drop your weapon and let me kill you," the assassin said casually. "I promise to make it quick. And then you will not have to witness Agent Beacham's death. She cares for you, *da*? She was willing to sacrifice herself trying to warn you. And something tells me you feel the same about her."

When Hunter didn't agree or disagree, Orpheus shrugged again. "You don't have to admit it. I can tell by the look on your face. Which means the last thing you want is to watch the moment the final drop of life leaves her body. Knowing the one you love met their end in such a brutal way is not a good or easy death. Just ask your friend, Dale." He hitched his chin toward the doorway to the kitchen. Then he smirked. "Oh, right. You can't."

The thirst for violence that rushed through Hunter then was swift and icy cold. It raised the fine hairs all over his body.

A man with less training might've let himself be led by that feeling. Might've taken a chance and pulled his trigger. But years of experience told him the Russian was right. He couldn't be sure killing the assassin wouldn't result in the motherfucker having an involuntary muscle spasm that ended Grace too.

So he simply held his ground. And held his sight square between the bastard's beady eyes.

"Drop your weapon," Orpheus said again. Then he began to whistle and Hunter immediately recognized the tune. "And I promise I will kill you as softly as I can. One shot." The assassin made a clicking sound with his tongue. "You won't feel a thing."

Hunter ground his jaw so hard, he was surprised his molars didn't turn to dust. His mind worked through all the scenarios, all his options, and settled on the reality that none of them were good. None of them assured him with one-hundred percent certainty that Grace would come out the other side of this thing alive.

Just when he was about to open his mouth to stall or negotiate, he saw her eyelids flutter. Her lips pursed like she'd tasted something sour. Then her eyes popped open and her dark gaze was clear and…*direct*.

She was trying to communicate something to him, but he couldn't determine what. Then, it hit him that she hadn't moved. Hadn't lifted her head. Hadn't so much as suffered a hitch in her breathing.

She was playing possum. Making Orpheus think she was still unconscious. And *that* was going to be his opening.

He dipped his chin ever-so-subtly. To the Russian, it probably looked like he was still considering his options and calculating his odds. To Grace, it was a signal he was ready for whatever she had planned.

"Let me make it easy for you." Orpheus sneered. "Either you let me kill you quickly and easily. Or you try to be a hero and I kill you anyway. Only, I promise you it will not be quick *or* easy. I would love for you to watch as I show Agent Beacham what true pain is. I would love for you to—"

That's all he managed before Grace stood to her full height and threw back her head. *Whack!* She clocked the assassin square in the nose.

Hunter heard the crunch of cartilage a split second before he roared, "Down!"

She didn't hesitate, letting all her weight drop against the Russian's grip, catching him by surprise. She slipped through his grasping arms like a wet noodle slipping through a slotted spoon.

Boom!

The sound of Hunter's Glock in the enclosed space was deafening. He prided himself on being a quick shot. Unfortunately, Orpheus was quicker. The assassin had already turned to dive through the sliding door and Hunter's bullet missed the bastard's head by a fraction of an inch, hitting the glass instead and creating a neat hole that immediately expanded into a spiderweb of cracks.

He fired again and watched his shot graze the assassin's left flank.

Poom! Poom! Poom!

The Russian was quick to return fire, forcing Hunter to dive for cover as one round slammed into the wall above his shoulder. Another clipped the wooden frame on the doorway. And the final one sliced through the meaty part of his shoulder before he hit the carpet behind the sofa.

He felt the burn of the bullet, but that was it. Just that quick, stinging pain. And then…nothing.

Adrenaline was a wonder drug at stopping agony dead in its tracks.

"Get to cover!" he bellowed, rolling to a crouch and shoving his pistol around the side of the sofa.

He squeezed off round after round, laying down cover fire to give Grace time to crawl away. He had no doubt the assassin would aim for her at his first opening, and it was up to Hunter to make sure the bastard never got that chance.

"Clear!" She cried out barely two seconds later.

Peeking around the edge of the couch, he saw three things in an instant. One, the glass in the sliding door had shattered and fallen from the frame. It lay all over the ground in shards that glittered in the starlight and the lamplight shining out into the backyard. Two, there was a dark sedan parked nearby, and it was only the cover of night that'd kept him from seeing it before. And three, Orpheus was nowhere to be found.

Grace's breathless voice came from somewhere near the fireplace. "I...I think he's trying for his c-car."

"You okay?"

"Still alive."

He grunted his approval. "Stay that way, will you?"

"That's the plan."

Squinting against the darkness outside, he saw the driver's side door on the sedan slip open.

"I got you, you sorry sonofabitch." He sighted down his barrel and waited for Orpheus to poke his balding blond head above the doorframe.

Unfortunately, the assassin remained in a crouch. Which meant Hunter had to go for the next best thing.

Aiming at the center of the open door, he plugged it with two rounds.

Thunk! Thunk! The shots buried themselves deep, but he never heard an accompanying yowl of agony or grunt of pain. Which meant the metal was enough to stop the bullets.

Fuck!

Lowering his aim, he focused hard on the ground beneath the open door, wished he had a larger target and more light to work with, and then reminded himself when it came to shitting in one hand and wishing in the other, the hand with shit was always going to fill up faster.

He took his shot.

"Fuck!" This time he cursed out loud when his bullet ranged too low and hit the dirt an inch from his intended target.

An immediate adjustment and *that* time his aim was true. He heard Orpheus yip in pain. And then, when he immediately squeezed off another round, he heard the sound no operator ever wanted to hear.

The dreaded *click* of an empty magazine.

He was up and running around the couch just as the Russian wrenched the car door shut and cranked over the engine. By the time his feet hit the rug in the middle of the room, the assassin had laid on the gas and was spinning his tires in the wet grass.

"Weapon!" he bellowed to Grace, who was tucked into the corner between the brick hearth and an armchair.

"No." Her hand was pressed to the wound on her head. "He…he took it."

Her words barely registered because he'd gotten close enough to see how much blood stained her shirt. How pale the skin over her face had grown. How her gaze, so bright and sure just moments earlier, looked unfocused.

His desperation to stop Orpheus was instantly eclipsed by his concern for her. A second later, he was down on his knees, gently tugging at her wrist. "Let me see."

She didn't comply. Instead, her fuzzy gaze focused on his fresh wound and the blood that leaked over his elbow and forearm. "You're hit!" she gasped.

"No." He lifted his shirtsleeve and tilted his shoulder forward so she could see the shallow groove the bullet had left behind. "Just a graze."

Hot tears welled in her eyes. "I'm so s-sorry, Hunter." She hiccupped on a sob. "I'm so sorry I dragged you into this. I'm so s-sorry I—"

"Grace." He gently tugged on her wrist again. "Let me see your head."

Instead of lowering her hand, she shook her head. There was desperation in her watery eyes. "What if he goes after your friends in Chicago next? He's already killed my partner. And now he's k-killed your—"

"Let me see your head, Grace."

"He has to be s-stopped, Hunter."

"I know. I'll stop him." It wasn't arrogance that made him think he would be the one to end Orpheus. It was experience. Once he decided to do a thing, he didn't quit until it was done. "If I have to hunt him to the ends of the Earth," he swore lowly, "I'll stop him."

Another sob escaped her. "I can't lose you t-too." The way her voice cracked on the last word was like a dagger to the heart.

"You won't lose me," he promised and wanted to add, *You'll never lose me. I'm yours for as long as you want me.* But instead he said again, "Show me your head." His tone brooked no argument this time.

Her fingers were coated with thick, sticky blood when she pulled her hand away. He gently pushed back her hair and then swore when he saw the three-inch gash through her scalp. It was so deep, he thought he saw bone.

"We need to get you to the hospital."

"No." She grabbed his arm, her grip frantic. "I'll be fine. And if we're going to go after Orpheus, *now* is the time. Before he has a chance to hide and lick his wounds. Before he has a chance to regroup."

She was right, of course. But…

"I'm out of ammo. Even if—"

"The gun rack in the living room," she cut him off and he stilled, his mind's eye recalling the two shotguns Dale kept next to his Vietnam memorabilia. Dale had become an avid duck hunter after returning from the war.

"Figured I could use the skills the government taught me for good, ya know?" Dale had once said. *"To put food on the table instead of puttin' men in the ground."*

Thoughts of his friend had tears burning the backs of Hunter's eyes, but he had no time to let them fall.

"Let's go." There was a determined cant to Grace's chin. "I'm not as bad as—" She tried to stand, wobbled, and then fell back onto her butt in defeat.

His heart hurt for the guilt and self-recrimination he saw in her eyes. None of this was her fault, but that didn't matter. Knowing her, she'd blame herself for everything anyway.

"You stay here," he told her. "I'll go finish this." Because even though it *killed* him to leave her, she was right. *Now* was the time to stop the assassin. While the bastard was bleeding and hurting and desperate.

Her voice was little more than a wheeze as she shook his arm. "You stay alive, or I swear I'll never forgive you."

It was then he realized there were two things he didn't have in him to deny. One was that he loved her more than he loved life itself. The other was that no matter what she asked, if it was within his power to give it to her, he would.

CHAPTER 29

Black Knights Inc.

"Nice to see you again, Agent Greenlee," Sam said to the disgruntled-looking FBI agent who stood at the top of the second-story stairs. The hours that'd passed since Eliza had escorted Greenlee out of the building were evident in the slight rumpling of the agent's suit, the little grease spot staining his tie, and the tired look in the man's eyes.

"Yo." Sam lifted his chin to include the junior agents who were, as always, lined up behind Greenlee. "How's it hangin'?"

Hannah rolled her eyes as she pushed past him and approached the Feds. "No one uses 'how's it hangin' anymore, Sam. Sheesh. Why am I surrounded by men who refuse to keep up with the times?"

"Huh?" He quirked an eyebrow, wondering which *other* men in her life were using outdated language.

Instead of answering, she shook the agents' hands and motioned them toward the conference table. "Thank you for coming back, gentlemen. I know it's late and you've got a case you're working. But if you'll bear with us for a little while longer, I think you'll see why it was important for us to call you back here."

Greenlee narrowed his eyes, grabbing a seat at the table while his dutiful junior agents snagged the chairs on either side of him. "If this is some sort of distraction, I hate to be the one to tell you, you're too late. We have a lead on Agent Beacham." He looked at his watch. "Very soon now, I expect to be hearing from our colleagues in Michigan that they have the fugitive in custody."

"I very much doubt that." Hannah shook her head. "But on the off chance you're right, they'll be able to tell her we know where her investigation in Indiana went sideways."

Greenlee lifted a questioning eyebrow at Sam, as if asking for corroboration.

Sam shook and then hitched his chin toward Hannah. "This is her show."

She hurriedly arranged laptops around the conference table. One for the agents to share. One for Eliza who, ever the gracious hostess, topped the stairs with a tray full of assorted beverages. He'd taken a seat across from the Feds, so she sat the last one in front of him.

Greenlee waved away Eliza's offer of something cool to drink, but Agent Newland took a soda and Agent Floyd happily accepted a…juice pouch, of all things.

"You're sure your contact will be able to get our guest of honor to show up for this?" Hannah asked Eliza, anxious anticipation coloring her voice.

Eliza nodded. "We're good to go. I'm just waiting on the code to the conferencing system. He's supposed to text it to me in a couple minutes."

Once Hannah had pinpointed the double agent, Sam and Eliza had discussed with Boss the best way to disseminate the culprit's identity.

Even though, technically, Frank "Boss" Knight was no longer on the government's payroll, he *had* been for decades. And in that time, he'd accrued the wisdom and the prudence necessary to hammer out the best course of action in such situations.

"The FBI director has to be informed, of course," he'd said while rubbing a considering finger under his big, square chin. *"And I'd bring back the G-Men from this morning. They were manipulated by the double agent's lie, and they need to be made aware of that subterfuge. If you can let both those parties in on the information at the same time, all the better. Less room for confusion and/or chaos."*

And so, that's what they'd done. Eliza had informed Hannah she had a contact on staff in the White House who would be able to get Director

Morgan onboard. But, of course, Eliza had kept it secret that her "contact" was her father, and that he wasn't simply *on staff* at the White House; he was the freaking *chief* of staff. Then Sam had phoned the local FBI office, requesting Greenlee et al come back to the factory building. And Hannah had set up everything so their guests would find out the identity of the double agent together.

Bada bing, bada boom. Neat as you please.

Hostessing duties complete, Eliza gracefully pulled out the rolling chair at the head of the table and nimbly lowered herself into it. Hannah, on the other hand, plopped into the chair next to Sam with enough force to make the springs squeak.

He rolled in his lips to keep from laughing. Even though she was a pipsqueak of a woman, she threw what little weight she had around like a bull in a china shop. Which appeared to go hand in hand with her in-your-face, no-bullshit way of approaching just about *everything*.

After thumbing on the laptop, she frowned over at him. "What?"

"What?" he came back innocently.

"What are you smiling about?"

"Can't a guy just be happy this whole dog and pony show is 'bout to come to a close?"

Her scowl telegraphed her disbelief in his explanation, but she didn't push the subject. Instead, she turned to Agent Floyd and said, "Capri Sun lover, huh? I thought I was the only one still drinking that stuff."

Floyd shrugged. "Got addicted when I was a kid. Never was able to break the habit."

"Same." She nodded and Sam watched Floyd's gaze linger on her face. Then he watched it linger some more and felt the muscle in his jaw contract.

"I looked you up, you know," the junior agent announced. When Hannah quirked an eyebrow, he added sheepishly, "Consider it a hazard of the job, but I always google people after I've met them. Your social media paints you as…" When Floyd trailed off so he could grin broadly, Sam was forced to admit the bastard was handsome and *also* that the urge to punch him square in the nose was growing stronger with each passing second. "A pretty interesting person. You like drag shows, alien romance novels, Dungeons and Dragons, and *Schitt's Creek*."

"Just call me a renaissance woman." Hannah winked.

That was it. Sam had had enough. He did his best to scowl Agent Floyd into the ground, but it was a wasted effort because the sonofabitch wasn't looking at him. Floyd was too busy making googly eyes at Hannah.

A split second later, when it occurred to Sam that Hurricane Hannah would absolutely *eat* Agent Floyd's lunch—seriously, she was *far* too cool and smart and trendy for the straitlaced agent—he satisfied himself with settling back in his chair and waiting for the fun with the Feds to begin.

The shop was oddly quiet since Boss and Becky had left for the day. No phones rang. Eliza wasn't banging pots and pans in the kitchen. And with the rest of the Black Knights still out on assignment, there was no *crack* of pool balls from the third floor. No hum of music drifting under someone's bedroom door. No gleeful insults being shouted across the room.

When the silence stretched on, Agent Newland shifted uncomfortably in his chair, Eliza took to studying her manicure, and Floyd—the *tenacious* sonofagun—went back to drooling over Hannah.

Thankfully, before Sam could do something sophomoric like snarl at the bastard, *Take a picture; it'll last longer*, Eliza's phone chimed.

He sat up straighter and watched her nod at Hannah.

"Okay." Hannah cracked her knuckles. "If you'll all click on the red buttons at the top of your screens, you should see a text terminal open. Once you have that, type in the following code."

She inclined her chin toward Eliza who quickly rattled off ten digits that included letters, numbers, and two special characters. Hannah's lithe fingers made short work of typing in the code and Sam watched the screen change from the text terminal to a video conference chat format.

Sure as shit, there was Director Morgan in the upper left square. Next to him, in the upper right square were the FBI agents' faces. Eliza showed up in the bottom right square, with Sam and Hannah in the lower left square respectively.

Greenlee adjusted his tie at the same time Agent Floyd's eyebrows tried to disappear into his hairline. As for Agent Newland? His chin jerked so far back it was impossible to distinguish where his neck ended and his face began.

"Director Morgan." Greenlee's tone had gone from tired and annoyed to military-grade-professional. "Good evening, sir."

"Good evening." Morgan's resonant voice reminded Sam of James Earl Jones. "To whom do I have the pleasure of speaking?"

"It's Agent Greenlee, sir. We spoke via email last night. I'm the one assigned to Agent Beacham's case."

"I know Agent Beacham. And I've heard what she's been accused of. But I haven't communicated with anyone on her case, last night or any other time."

All three Feds frowned, and Hannah jumped in. "I know where the confusion lies, Director Morgan. If you'll bear with me for a few minutes, I'd like to fill you and the agents here"—she inclined her head to include the Feds sitting opposite them—"in on what's been going on."

"And who are you?" Morgan arched one steel-gray eyebrow.

"My name is Hannah Blue. I work in the cybercrimes division of the D.O.D. My friend Sam brought me in to do some…um…online snooping in an effort to clear Agent Beacham's name."

Sam felt the director's dark eyes focus on his image on the screen. "And Sam, you are…?"

It was clear the director's patience was running thin, so Sam didn't prevaricate. "I'm Sergeant Samuel Haywood, director. I work for a small, independent defense firm here in Chicago. And one of my teammates, Hunter Jackson, was partnered with Agent Beacham a few years back on an unrelated case. When she found herself in a whole lotta trouble a couple hours outside of town, Major Jackson was the first person she called to help her out of the jam."

"I *knew* this place was more than a custom motorcycle shop." Greenlee pointed a finger at Sam and then waved his hand to indicate the entirety of the factory building.

"Yes, yes." Sam rolled his eyes. "Your powers of observation are very keen."

Greenlee opened his mouth to come back with something acerbic. But Eliza jumped in before he could get a word out. "And my name is Eliza Meadows, sir. I work with Sam here at Black Knights Incorporated as support staff."

"Meadows?" The director's forehead formed half a dozen wrinkles, making him even more dour-looking. "Are you related to—"

"Yes, sir. I am," Eliza was quick to cut him off, not wanting the others to know her connection to the chief of staff because that would put the Black Knights just a *smidge* too close to the president when it came to the game of seven degrees of separation. "And I hope that reassures you the information Miss Blue is about to reveal can be trusted."

When Morgan pursed his mouth and nodded his acquiescence, Hannah took that as her cue to begin explaining the series of events as she knew them, starting with Grace Beacham's investigation into the Indiana troll farm and ending with Grace's problem securing subpoenas and her suspicion that someone above her paygrade was working as a double agent and throwing up roadblocks in her and her partner's path.

"Wait a minute." Morgan lifted a wide-palmed hand. "Her reports to me mentioned nothing about subpoenas."

"I know." Sam nodded. "If you'll hang with us a little longer, sir, we'll tell you why that is."

Hannah went on to explain how Grace had found her partner dead from a wound inflicted by her own blade, and how she'd received the mysterious text warning her that Orpheus was on her six. And then she dropped her first bomb. "I was able to make contact with the sender of that text."

"We've had techs trying to trace that number all day," Greenlee grumbled. "How is it *you* were able to find Agent's Beacham's mysterious guardian angel so quickly?"

"Skills." Hannah pretended to buff her fingernails on her shirt. Then she grew serious. "But honestly, there was a little bit of luck involved too." She waved a hand, suddenly looking annoyed that she'd been led off track. "The point is, *Kerberos* is the group that warned Agent Beacham." The name rolled off her tongue like a prayer, all hushed and reverent.

"Is that supposed to mean something to me?" The director raised an imperious eyebrow.

She was quick to school the gathered group on Kerberos and their self-assigned role as the internet's watchdogs-slash-vigilantes.

"Right." Agent Greenlee nodded. "I've heard of them. But what are they doing tangled up in this?"

"Not sure." Hannah shook her head. "But it's a good thing this situation caught their attention. Because not only did they warn Agent Beacham in time to escape the assassin, but they helped point me in the right direction to unmask the double agent."

Her hands jumped to the keyboard and Sam watched her bring up a program in a second window. He had just enough time to recognize the email exchanges between Grace and the director paired side by side with the *second* set of emails that'd been fudged by the double agent before she hit send.

He could tell when the rest of the group had access to the emails by the way everyone's eyes started moving side to side as they read their screens.

Hannah gave them about thirty seconds to get a feel for the information before she said, "As you can see, Agent Beacham's reports weren't making it to you, Director Morgan. At least not in their entirety. Additionally, the responses she thought she was getting from you weren't from you at all. There's been a middleman manipulating your correspondence, sir."

"Who?" Director Morgan's expression had gone rock-hard. "Wait. Before you answer that, how the *hell* did you get your hands on these emails?"

Hannah had the grace to look chagrined. "Kerberos gave me a back door into the FBI's servers."

"Jesus tapdancing Christ, those sonsofbitches are a menace," Greenlee snarled. Then he winced. "Sorry for the language, Director Morgan."

"I've heard far worse, Agent." The director turned his attention back to Hannah. "Okay, Miss Blue. So who is it? Who's the damned dirty double agent pretending to be me?"

"Felix Graves." Hannah spat out the name like it was poison. And Sam supposed it was. Especially to the director. "Your personal assistant."

Morgan was too stunned to speak, so she went on to explain more about what Graves had been up to. "He's been manipulating pretty much everything. Not to mention, Agent Greenlee, he's been closely watching your progress in tracking Agent Beacham down. Acting as the director, he's been in contact with your supervisor. He knew as soon as you reported it that you'd used CCTV footage to find out Agent Beacham and Major Jackson were headed north in Michigan. He also knew you'd subpoenaed Major Jackson's phone records."

"So he knows we have local agents headed out to question Dale Carlson even as we speak."

For the first time, Agent Newland spoke up. "Which means he's probably passed the information along to the Russian."

Greenlee pulled his cell phone from his breast pocket. "We need to warn the agents in route. We need to warn Dale Carlson. We need to warn—"

"So *now* you believe he's real?" Sam's mouth flattened. "When it's your Michigan counterparts in danger and an innocent citizen? But when it was Agent Beacham's neck on the line, you—"

Hannah squeezed his arm to cut him off. And he realized there were more important points to make.

"We've already alerted Major Jackson to the situation," she said. "And I'm sure he's called his friend to let him know to get in his car and start driving. But it'd be good to inform whoever you've got going up there to be on the lookout for any suspicious persons prowling around the Carlson residence."

Greenlee nodded and pushed up from the table to walk to the edge of the room and make his call.

"Sounds like I've got some house-cleaning to do," the director grumbled.

"I'm afraid it gets worse, sir." Hannah grimaced. "Those subpoenas I mentioned? They were for a set of financial records that likely would've proved two things. One, that Felix Graves was funneling money from Russia to pay the trolls. And two, that the trolls knew where their paychecks originated, making them all conspirators and traitors."

"How many?" Floyd asked, his expression grave. "How many Americans are knowingly working for the Kremlin?"

"Two hundred."

"Fuck me. Uh…" He grimaced. "Sorry, Director."

"Again"—Morgan waved a hand—"I've heard worse."

Greenlee returned to the table. "The Michigan agents are still thirty minutes out from the Carlson residence. But I've updated them on the situation."

"Very good." Morgan nodded. "Be ready to start getting warrants for the traitors in Indiana just as soon as I give you the say so."

Greenlee blinked. "What did I miss?"

"I'll fill you in later," Floyd promised.

"Now…" The director took a deep breath. "We need to get Major Jackson, Agent Beacham, and the Carlsons to safety until we can arrest Graves and cut off the information he's feeding the assassin. Give me fifteen minutes to find an appropriate safe house. I'll call you with the location"—his gaze was pinned on Sam's face—"and then you can pass that information along to Major Jackson."

"You think once Graves has been arrested, Orpheus will give up the hunt?" Hannah asked.

"That's my hope." The director's tone was grim. "And once we have Graves in custody, maybe we'll be able to get the assassin's true identity out of him."

Sam clenched his jaw, reading between the lines. Morgan was already considering cutting some kind of deal with traitor. A lesser sentence if Graves gave up information.

He shouldn't be surprised. He'd worked for the government long enough to know that just about everything came down to quid pro quo.

"Okay." Morgan sighed heavily and slapped the top of the desk he sat at. "I think everyone has their assignments. Thank you all for your service to our country this day. Let's throw everything we have at this thing and expose the rot within, yeah?"

Hannah waited until everyone had nodded or voiced their affirmatives before the square she shared with Sam on the screen went black. Director Morgan's face disappeared barely two seconds later. The three FBI agents were third to go and Eliza was the last to cut her connection.

Five minutes later, Sam escorted the Feds to the front gate. He nodded at Toran Connelly, and the big redhead hit the button that had the wrought iron sides sliding open with a well-oiled *whir* and a little *clang* at the end.

"Hey," Sam said to the agents before they could pile into the sedan parked by the curb. It was black, utilitarian, and screamed *government vehicle* even before he noticed the government plates. "You boys mind keeping what you now know about this place to yourselves? I mean, me and my partners' jobs kinda rely on secrecy, ya know?"

The overhead streetlight highlighted Greenlee's unfriendly expression. For a second, Sam thought the lead agent might try to give him shit. Then Greenlee shrugged. "Sure. I mean, we're all working for the same team, right?"

"Right." Sam dipped his chin and then watched the agents head toward their car.

Toran was quick to hit the button that sent the two halves of the gate swinging shut. But when they began to close, Sam heard Hannah call, "Wait! I'm leaving too!"

He turned to see her beating feet across the pavement, backpack slung over her shoulder and bouncing right along with the ends of her hair. When she skidded to a stop next to him, her face flushed prettily, he frowned. "You're taking off already?"

"I need to get home and get the scoop on Cesar's romantic dinner. Besides, my work here is done, right?"

Right. So why did her leaving feel so wrong?

"I guess so." He shrugged, trying to figure out why he wanted her to stay so badly.

Maybe so they could reminisce? Maybe because she reminded him of his youth or a simpler time? Maybe because—and he hadn't realized it until that very moment—he'd *missed* her?

"Alrighty then." She used her elbow to nudge his arm. "Keep it one hundred."

He snorted. "Which means?"

"It means keep it real." She rolled her eyes.

She turned to walk away, but he stopped her with, "Hey, Hurricane Hannah?" She swung around and he noticed how the streetlight sparkled in her dark eyes, making them look mysterious. And uncomfortably grown-up. "Thank you. You really came in clutch today. Well..." He rubbed a hand through his hair. "And three months ago, too, I guess. I owe you for both." He remembered their morning phone conversation and felt a little jolt of happiness. "A steak dinner, right? When you wanna cash in on that?"

"Eh." She lifted a shoulder. "How about I text you the next time I'm feeling carnivorous?"

His little jolt of happiness fizzled. "Deal."

She canted her head, her gaze steady on his face. "It was good seeing you again, Sam."

"It was good seeing you too, Hannah. I'm proud of you. You've really made something of yourself, kid."

Something moved behind her eyes. But it was gone before he could determine what it was. "Take care of yourself, okay, Sam?" Her voice was low. "It's a dangerous world out there."

He felt his brow wrinkle. Why did that sound like a goodbye? Like, goodbye *forever*.

Before he could question her, Agent Floyd called from the sedan's open window, "Hey Miss Blue? Can we give you a ride?"

"Absolutely!" Her voice brightened and she skipped off toward the waiting vehicle. "You just saved me a thirty-dollar Uber bill!"

Floyd hopped from the backseat to hold the door wide. He placed a proprietary hand on the small of her back as he helped her inside.

When a muscle in Sam's jaw twitched at seeing the agent's big mitt sprawled across her narrow waist, he chalked it up to being low on potassium and decided he needed to go inside and eat a banana.

CHAPTER 30

56 Crimson Valley Ave.

Pavel gritted his teeth against the blistering pain in his ankle when his rental car bounced from the soft earth of the Carlson's backyard onto the narrow road that led past their property into a night-darkened pine forest.

For the first time in his career, he had not succeeded in eliminating his target. It grated. More than grated, it was embarrassing. Which was why he hated the thought of what he had to do next.

But needs must…

Blowing out a steadying breath, and sweating with the effort of controlling his pain, he carefully pulled his cellular phone from his jeans. After turning it back on, he realized he'd missed ten calls from Bishop.

The dread he felt at telling the man he'd failed was compounded by the certainty that something bad had happened on Bishop's end. No way the man would've tried phoning that many times unless things had gone sideways.

Hitting auto-dial, he wasn't surprised when Bishop answered immediately. "I've been trying to get ahold of you for the last twenty minutes."

"Had my hands full." Pavel gritted because his jaw was clenched down tight in an effort not to scream when he hit a particularly bad bump. His side hurt. But the bullet had only grazed him. The *real* agony radiated from his ankle, throbbing horribly with every beat of his heart and gnawing with teeth like a rabid dog anytime he bumped against it.

"Well?" Bishop demanded. "Is it done?"

"The Carlsons are dead." A muscle worked in his jaw. "But Major Jackson and Agent Beacham still live. I'm injured and fleeing the scene."

A few seconds of silence sounded on the other end of the call. Finally, Bishop said, "You, uh, you need to do more than flee the scene. You need to get out of the country. There's a shitstorm coming and I'm going to have to retreat and retrench. The last thing I need is you getting caught."

Bishop didn't need to add *and making a deal or handing over intel that might potentially lead to me.* Pavel could read between the lines.

"What sort of shitstorm?" he asked.

"The kind where the FBI and BKI know where I've been getting my information. The kind I was helpless to mitigate. So now I have to play defense. You're close to Canada, right? Cross the border and disappear."

"Did you hear me say I'm injured?" Pavel was usually a patient man. But agony had a way of shriveling up his composure like salt on a slug.

"Is it fatal?" Bishop's tone lacked even a hint of sympathy.

Not that Pavel expected any. Not only did their working relationship preclude such sentiments, but their shared goal meant there was no time for it. Sympathy was a luxury afforded to those who were not trying to rearrange the world order.

"I'll live."

He'd live. But would he ever work again? He could feel the squish of the blood that filled his shoe. If the bullet had hit bone, if he was crippled for life, his stint as the world's most prolific assassin was finished.

His job required grace. Agility.

"Good." Bishop's voice had lowered, and that one word was even more clipped than usual. If Pavel had to guess, Bishop was worried about being caught on the call. "Call me when you've found a place to lay low. Once you're there, I'll help you in any way I can."

Click. The line went dead.

Pavel placed the phone in the cupholder, glad it was too dark to see the floorboard. He highly suspected it held a puddle of blood. And when he glanced back up, his heart skipped a beat.

A single headlight rounded the bend behind him and reflected in the rearview mirror. Below the *hum* of the rental's tires, he could hear the louder, throatier rumble of a big engine.

Major Jackson.

The man had no quit in him.

CHAPTER 31

Sandhill Crane Rd,
six miles east of the Carlson residence

Shock and awe were simply layman's terms for what the military liked to call *rapid dominance.*

When governments did it, they used a big ol' bunch of bombs. When spec-ops guys did it, it required three things: stealth, surprise, and lightning-fast action.

Luckily, the twisty, turny country road had afforded Hunter the first two. It'd concealed Canteen Green's headlight from Orpheus until he was right up on the murderous sonofabitch. Similarly, the denseness of the forest and the proximity of the trees to the road had muffled the roar of the motorcycle's V-twin.

Which left that final piece of the puzzle.

Lightning-fast action.

He pulled the pin on the grenade and lobbed it with all his might.

There were two ways to turn a car into a fireball. One, put a block of explosives on the battery and wire it to the ignition. Or two, blow up the gas tank.

Option two was his intent while simultaneously hoping the grenade still worked. After all, it was fifty years old, and—

BOOM!

Yup! Works!

The explosion took out the rear driver's side tire and was enough to lift the entire backend of the vehicle off the road. Unfortunately, it wasn't enough to ignite the gas tank.

Plan B, he thought as the nondescript sedan fishtailed. The bare rim, now bent and glowing with heat, sparked against the asphalt. Despite the blown tire, Orpheus kept the car on the road.

Hunter had shoved one of Dale's shotguns down the back of his shirt, the barrel secured through his belt. It took concentration and more than a little coordination, but he one-handed the handlebars so he could grab the scatter gun by its stock. Gritting his teeth with the effort of keeping Canteen Green on the road and in line with the sedan, he pulled the weapon up and out of his T-shirt with more ease than he would've thought possible when he'd stowed it there.

What *wasn't* easy was aiming one-handed after positioning the shotgun against his shoulder. The flash from the grenade's explosion had fucked up his night vision. And even the bright beam of Canteen Green's headlight wasn't enough to make the sedan's remaining rear tire come into focus. Not to mention, the three-wheeled sedan was kicking up an absurd amount of sparks.

Dale's Remington semi-auto was a 4 + 1, meaning it held four rounds in the magazine plus one loaded in the chamber. And while five shots might sound like plenty to some people, Hunter had put enough rounds downrange to know five was next to nothing.

There was no point-and-squeeze and pray his shot was close. Then, if it wasn't, adjust next time. He had to make sure each round counted.

The sound of the sedan's rim scraping across the pavement was loud enough to hear over Canteen Green's roar and irritating enough to make his back teeth itch. Even still, he automatically fell back on his training.

Three shallow breaths in. One long breath out.

When his lungs were nearly empty and the sedan's back tire came into momentary view, he pulled the trigger.

Crack! The muzzle blast flashed orange.

Since the duck gun doubled as a tactical weapon, it had one hell of a kick. Hard enough to have him swerving and struggling to keep the motorcycle on the road.

He didn't see the moment the scatter shot tore into the sedan's single remaining rear tire. Or the moment that tire shredded and flew off its rim. So he was caught off guard when it bounced across the pavement toward him, headed right for Canteen Green's front spokes.

Gritting his teeth, he tried to make an adjustment to avoid the flying debris. But it was too late. The shredded rubber slammed into his motorcycle's front wheel.

Fuck a duck! was all he had time to think as the bike's front end locked up. It took every ounce of strength he possessed not to go flying over the handlebars. Instead, he was able to throw his weight to the side, kicking away from Canteen Green before the bike could hit the ground and crush his leg beneath it.

The only reason he didn't lose all the skin on his left side was because the blown tire had already slowed the sedan's momentum and, subsequently, Canteen Green's momentum. He'd guess he'd only been going about thirty miles per hour when he abandoned the motorcycle.

Even still, it hurt like a sonofabitch when he slammed into the rough ground, bounced, slammed again, and then skidded a good ten feet before coming to rest in the ditch.

He didn't have time to take a physical inventory of the damage done to his body before he heard the sound of the sedan careening through the brush on the side of the road. Flipping onto his stomach, he saw the instant the assassin lost control.

The bare back rims dug into the soft shoulder and immediately sent the vehicle onto its side. It rolled once. Twice. The sound of breaking glass and bending metal loud in the silence of the forest. Dirt and broken tree limbs flew everywhere as the sedan tumbled into the trees. Until, finally, it slammed into a huge pine and came to a smoking, creaking, engine-whining stop.

The harsh breath that whooshed out of Hunter as he flopped onto his back sounded obscenely loud in the sudden silence following the crash. For a moment, he lay there, staring up at the stars twinkling through the reaching branches of the trees, his heart thudding, his lungs heaving, his mind blanked by the surreality of it all.

Once he'd caught his breath, he rolled onto his stomach and managed to get his knees under him. With a grunt, he pushed to a stand.

The shotgun.

Where the hell was the shotgun?

His eyes scanned the darkened road behind him. Canteen Green was over her side in the ditch, her headlight still on, her back wheel still spinning, her hot engine clicking as it cooled. But he couldn't see the Remington.

He thought back on his fall and whether he still had the scatter gun in his hand when he went down. But it was all a little hazy.

Breaking into a trot—*ow!* He'd definitely twisted his left ankle—he made his way down the narrow country lane, guided by instinct and starlight. Just when he thought he *had* to have run past the spot where he'd dropped the weapon, he found it. It'd come to rest next to a shallow pothole.

Bending—*ow!* His left hip hurt too. It'd taken the brunt of the fall—he grabbed the weapon, checked the bolt action, and slowly stood, feeling every strain of muscle, every creak of bone.

"Drop it."

The hairs on the back of his neck lifted.

"I said *drop it*, motherfucker."

He should've felt the heated surge of fresh adrenaline. But, instead, a cool calmness washed over him.

He didn't drop the shotgun. But neither did he brandish it as he slowly, *slowly* turned until he faced the Russian.

His first thought was, *This is one tough bastard.* His second thought was, *He looks like hammered dog shit.*

The crash had left Orpheus with a deep gash above his right eye. It leaked thick rivulets of blood that mixed in with the blood still trickling from his nose thanks to Grace's well-timed headbutt. The way he held his left arm told Hunter the appendage was broken. And the fact the assassin limped forward heavily on one foot broadcasted that the bullet wound in the opposite ankle had made that limb nearly useless.

Why hasn't he shot me?

Then he knew. Orpheus's gun hand shook violently from shock and pain and blood loss. The Russian *needed* to close the distance between them to make sure his shot actually hit his target before Hunter had time to lift the scatter gun and fill the assassin's chest with buckshot.

"Drop it. I will not ask again," Orpheus snarled, limping ever closer so that the starlight blinked dully against the matte black finish on the end of the silencer. "Kick it toward me," he added harshly.

Lifting the hand not holding the shotgun, Hunter slowly bent and deposited the big Remington on the ground. After straightening, he used his booted toe on the butt of the weapon to send it zinging across the road. It made a terrible rattling sound as it skimmed the asphalt and then came to rest two feet behind the Russian.

It was at that moment the world around him faded to black. His entire existence condensed down to the assassin and the few feet separating them.

Come on. Come on, you sonofabitch. Do it. Do it!

Orpheus did it.

The Russian turned his chin to see where the shotgun landed and it was the opening Hunter had been waiting for.

With a roar, he launched himself at the man. The minute his booted feet left the ground, time stood still. Or, at least, it seemed to slow to a snail's pace.

He saw Orpheus turn back, eyes wide with shock. Saw the instant the man understood his mistake. And then saw the Russian squeeze the trigger.

Poom!

The round flew by Hunter's cheek, displacing the air at the same time he heard the report. But not only was the shot wide. It was too late.

He hit the Russian with all of his two-hundred-and-five pounds. And, for a brief moment, they were airborne.

With time slowed, he was able to think through how things would go next. Which meant when they hit the ground, Orpheus's back smashing into the pavement and cushioning Hunter's landing, he was fully prepared to take advantage of the assassin's shock.

He wrestled the pistol and its attached silencer out of the man's stunned hand and shoved it beneath the bastard's chin before the Russian even had time to catch the breath the fall had knocked out of him.

"No—" was all Orpheus managed before Hunter pulled the trigger and blew the top of the fucker's head off.

"That was for Dale and Sissy," he snarled as he watched the life fade from the assassin's blue eyes. After he shoved to his feet, he gave in to the urge to spit on the corpse. "And I hope your death was anything but soft, you weird, whistling, murderous prick."

CHAPTER 32

56 Crimson Valley Ave.

Something was wrong.

Grace's eyes wouldn't focus. Her tongue felt too big for her mouth. And after she'd stumbled from the den to the front door to await Hunter's return, she'd been too weak to keep standing.

Blood loss? she wondered. The wound over her scalp continued to seep despite using a tea towel to apply continual pressure.

She sat half-in/half-out of the front door, leaning heavily against the jamb, staring numbly at the darkness engulfing the acreage beyond the house. The night insects buzzed as they called to their mates. And somewhere off in the distance, the lonely cry of a whippoorwill echoed through the trees.

I used to love the night, she thought groggily. Love the dark and the quiet and the cool. But after the past two nights, she was beginning to loathe the idea of the sun setting.

Bad things happened under the stars.

The distant rumble of a big engine didn't immediately catch her attention. And when the low, throaty sound *did* filter through her sluggishly working gray matter, she thought maybe she was hallucinating. Hunter hadn't been gone long enough to finish off the assassin.

Had he?

In truth, she couldn't be sure. Her gray matter was mush, unable to hold on to thoughts much less measure time.

Maybe it's my colleagues.

Weren't they supposed to be headed to the Carlsons? Hadn't Hunter said as much? She blinked and tried to recall the conversation they'd had after Sam's last call and couldn't grab on to more than bits and pieces.

Then she saw a single headlight coming down the long drive and her heart leapt so high she was surprised it didn't lift her out of the doorway.

Hunter!

She didn't realize tears were pouring down her cheeks until she saw them plop onto the wooden porch slats in front of her. The drops had mixed with the blood on her cheeks to turn a strange pinkish hue.

She tried to push to a stand, but her legs refused to cooperate. Instead, she simply pasted on the biggest grin she could muster as Hunter—big, beautiful, brave Hunter—came to a stop in the drive. He cut Canteen Green's growling engine, toed out his kickstand, and swung his leg over the bike's leather seat.

Even in her cloudy state, she noted how the front fender was bent up at an odd angle and how the sparkling green paint along the side was scratched down to the primer. It was clear there'd been a wreck. But, thankfully, it hadn't been bad enough to keep him from walking away from it.

Her relief was so intense, she felt dizzy.

Or maybe that's the head wound.

"Hunter…" His name was a whispered prayer as she watched him walk up the front porch steps.

No. Not walk. *Limp.* Was there something wrong with his leg? And where was all that blood on his arm coming from? Had he been shot?

She thought maybe she remembered—

"Grace." He was down on one knee in front of her, his big, warm hand gently cupping her cheek.

He had the best face. So serious. So concerned. So very dear to her.

She lifted a hand to cup *his* dusty cheek, loving the scratchy feel of his beard against her palm.

We must look the pair. Both dirty and bloody and the worse for wear.

"You came back." She hadn't realized there'd been a sob perched at the back of her throat until it erupted out of her mouth.

It *hurt* to cry. Made the steel spike in her head twist. But she couldn't stop the tears any more than she could stop loving the man kneeling in front of her.

"Of course I came back. Did you doubt it?"

She didn't want to admit it, but the Russian had terrified her. He'd attained nearly godlike status in her imagination.

Instead of answering, she asked, "Is it done?"

"Orpheus is dead." The words were full of meaning and menace.

The hand that cupped his cheek shook with the enormity of the relief that crashed over her. "Thank the lord. No." She shook her head when she realized her mistake. "No. Thank *you*, Hunter."

Words of appreciation seemed so trite compared to what he'd actually done. To the danger he'd been in because of her. To the risks he'd taken to put an end to the nightmare that'd become her life. And so she did the only thing she could to show him how grateful she was.

She pulled him into a hug.

Another sob burst from her tight throat when he didn't hesitate to wrap his big, warm arms around her. And even in her muddled state she realized holding him felt like more than a show of gratitude or an act of comfort.

It felt like coming home.

Which brought to mind something her father had said once when she'd caught him staring at her mother as if June Beacham was the most beautiful thing he'd ever seen. Her mother hadn't been wearing makeup or a flattering dress. She'd been in a pair of paint-splattered overalls, and a big wicker sunhat had been plopped atop her head as she dug in the flowerbed with a trowel.

"How do you do it?" Grace had asked her father.

"Do what?" he'd countered, filling a watering pot from the spigot.

"Keep yearning for each other even after thirty-five years?"

He'd pushed up the sweat-stained baseball cap he wore when he wasn't on the job. And for a few seconds he'd considered his answer. Eventually he'd said, *"Sometimes your heart makes its home in someone else. And it doesn't matter how many years pass or how far you travel or even how long you're apart from that person, your heart always yearns to return home. My heart yearns for your momma, even when she's just twenty feet away."*

It'd been a beautiful sentiment. But it wasn't until this very moment, here with Hunter, that she truly understood it.

Her heart had made its home in him.

And even though she knew he couldn't possibly feel the same, even though she knew what they'd shared would likely be *all* they would ever share, she wanted him to know how she felt.

Honesty was always the best policy, wasn't it?

Besides, it's never wrong to let someone know they're loved.

"Hunter?" She pushed back and frowned when his handsome features swum in front of eyes.

"Yes, Grace?"

"I want you to know I—"

That's as far as she got before her world faded to black.

CHAPTER 33

Northwestern Memorial Hospital,
Chicago, Illinois
Eight days later…

H unter stepped inside Grace's hospital room in time to hear her little
sister, Felicity, say, "The automatic paper towel dispenser in the
bathroom refuses to recognize me as human. It just ignores me as I
stand there in front of it, gesticulatin' like an idiot."

"Maybe it's mistakin' you for a blimp." Merit smirked. "Ow!" he added
when his wife, Rachel, who sat next to him on the uncomfortable love seat,
wacked him on the back of the head. "What was that for, Rache?"

"What have I told you are the two things you're not allowed to joke
about?"

Merit's expression was that of a scolded child. "Death and pregnancy."

"Exactly." Rachel nodded.

Hunter thought Grace's younger sister looked less like a blimp and more
like she'd swallowed a ripe watermelon. He was glad they were already in a
hospital because the youngest Beacham sibling appeared as if she might go
into labor at any minute, despite her having assured him she still had six
weeks before her due date.

When Rachel punched Merit on the shoulder, giving him a look, he threw his arms in the air. "*Now* what did I do? I was just sittin' here!"

"Exactly." Rachel nodded. "While your heavily pregnant sister whose ankles swell the minute she hops out of bed in the mornin' is standin'."

"If you're waiting for me to care," he said with a sniff, "better pack a lunch. It's goin' to be a while."

Rachel punched him again.

"Fine!" He grumpily pushed to a stand. "But I want it put on the record that even though I'm not an astronomer, I'm pretty sure the Earth revolves around the sun and not Felicity. Besides, why are we all feeling sorry for her? She did that to herself." He gestured toward Felicity's round belly as she waddled by him, headed for the seat he'd vacated.

"I like to think *I* had a little somethin' to do with it," Brandon, Felicity's husband, leaned against the doorjamb. He wore a self-satisfied grin and a T-shirt that read: *the man behind the bump.*

"Yes, yes." Felicity rolled her eyes, awkwardly lowering herself into the love seat. "You did an excellent job, honey. And thanks to that"—she pointed to his T-shirt—"the world knows it." She turned from her husband to her brother. "Hey, Merit? Mind kickin' that stool over?"

With a put-upon sigh, Merit moved the rolling stool the doctors used when they came in to examine Grace toward Felicity. She propped her pudgy ankles through the rungs, moaning with relief.

"Happy now, sister dearest?" Merit asked sweetly.

"As a pig in shit, big brother." Felicity's smile was saccharin.

Their Appalachian accents had Hunter missing the sound of Grace's voice. Even though she'd lost the deep drawl the members of her family shared, it still crept in from time to time. Like when she was excited or mad.

Or when she's in the throes of passion.

The entire Beacham clan had arrived barely a day after Grace had passed out in Hunter's arms. But a lot had happened in those first twenty-four hours.

Hour one had seen him loading her into the backseat of the FBI's SUV—two agents from the Lansing field office had arrived on the scene seconds after she'd gone limp. Then they'd flown down the little country road because everyone had agreed they could get her to the local emergency room quicker than the ambulance could arrive. And the entire drive into town, Hunter had held her head in his lap, staring down at her pretty face and praying to a god he didn't even believe in to please, *please* let her live.

The next hour he'd sat in the waiting room of the tiny, rural hospital, alternating between nearly shitting himself with fear—she'd been so still and pale when he'd carried her into the ER—and coordinating with Sam and Eliza back at BKI to find the contact information for her parents.

The next twenty-two hours had mostly been a blur punctuated by points of crystalline clarity. Like the smalltown doctor's face when he'd come out after examining Grace. His voice had been grave as he'd explained how Life Flight had been called because he didn't have the tools or the knowhow to drain the epidural hematoma that'd developed inside her skull. Like the six-hour motorcycle ride through the night that Hunter had managed to whittle down to four and a half because the helicopter crew had refused to let him go with her on the flight to Chicago. Like arriving at Northwestern Memorial Hospital in time to talk to the surgeon who'd drilled a burr hole into her skull to relieve the blood and pressure. And like meeting her entire family in the waiting room when they arrived en masse.

Seven days had come and gone since those first twenty-four hours. Seven days of Grace being so pale and unresponsive in that hospital bed. Seven days of taking turns going to see her in the ICU until, finally, the evening before, she'd been moved into a private room and taken off the propofol that'd kept her unconscious. Seven days of being surrounded by the Beacham clan and understanding why Grace loved them so—they were a loveable bunch, full of wit and sarcasm and good-natured ribbing. Seven days of shared meals, coffee runs, board games in the waiting room, and being pulled into the bosom of her family as if he'd always been a member.

Now, they were waiting for her to wake up.

And the waiting was even more agonizing than the thought that he had a plane to catch soon. That he had to leave her here. That he might not get to see her beautiful, dark eyes open for the first time.

The only thing that gave him a measure of comfort was knowing she didn't need him. She had her whole family to wrap her up and hold her close the minute she started showing signs of consciousness.

Plus, there was that voice in his head that kept asking, *Will she even want to see me?* Or was she going to want to forget the horrible set of circumstances that'd brought them together? Was she going to want to put behind her all the chaos, trauma, and death of her last assignment, him included?

He turned to stare at her, looking so fragile and still. Gauze wrapped her head until nothing was visible from her eyebrows up. There were dark circles beneath her eyes. And her full, soft lips were dry and cracked.

Without hesitating, or considering his audience, he walked over to the side table where the nurses had left a tube of petroleum jelly. After squeezing until a dollop of jelly formed on the rounded tip, he dipped a cotton swab into the cool mixture and then lightly applied a hydrating film to Grace's lips, wishing with everything inside him he could see them pulled into a wide smile or caught between her teeth like she did when she was concentrating or nervous.

After tossing the used cotton swab in the trash, he screwed the cap back on the Vaseline tube. But his fingers fumbled it when…

"H-Hunter?"

His eyes jumped back to the bed to find Grace staring at him. Her expression was a little groggy and confused, but her eyes were clear and bright.

A sob caught in the back of his throat.

"Where am—"

When she tried to sit up, he caught her shoulders and gently pushed her back into the bed. "Shhh. You're in the hospital. You're okay."

You're okay. Such simple words and yet they meant the world. Hearing them aloud, and knowing the truth of them, nearly had him losing his shit.

She's okay. She's really going to be okay.

Despite the doctor assuring him when they took her off the propofol that she was out of the woods and that they had every reason to expect a full recovery, it was the first time he'd let himself truly believe it.

Fortunately for him, with the first sound out of her mouth, Merit had run into the hallway yelling, "Nurse!" so now he was saved from making a fool of himself by dissolving into a six foot, three inch column of tears and snot because two nurses ran into the room to examine her.

He stepped aside, staying out of the way while one nurse flashed a penlight in her eyes and the other peppered her with questions.

The surgeon who'd drilled the hole in her skull walked briskly into the room and spent five minutes examining her reflexes, asking her more questions, and repeating the penlight-in-the-eye maneuver. Then, with a satisfied nod, he declared Grace, *"Lucky"* and *"Well on the road to being released from the hospital"* before the medical staff exited the room and left her to be swarmed by her family.

With his back pressed against the wall, Hunter watched her bask in the hugs and kisses and amiable insults that seemed to be the Beacham's main love language. And just when he thought she'd forgotten him, she turned and held out her hand.

"Hunter."

Had anyone ever said his name the way she did? So it sounded like music in her mouth?

He couldn't say if his feet even touched the tile as he flew to her side, threading his fingers through hers. He basked in the feel on her hand sheltered within his own.

"My memory's all fuzzy." She pressed two fingers to the thick bandage wrapping her head. Her voice was hoarse from the days she'd spent on the ventilator. But miraculously, and to his eternal delight, all the things that made her *her* were still there in her words. "I feel like my brains got scrambled."

"More like they were stuffed inside a pressure cooker." He loved the way that brought a soft smile to her face.

"What happened after we found Dale and Sissy? The last thing I remember was going into the den to get the blankets and then…" She drifted off and a deep line appeared between her eyebrows. Her eyes flew wide as a piece of her memory snapped into place. *"Orpheus."*

She tried to sit up again. For the second time, he had to gently push her back onto the narrow mattress. "It's okay. He's dead."

"You got him?" There was such fear in her eyes. But behind it was hope.

"I got him." He nodded, then frowned. "And it almost cost you your life. I never should've left you to—"

"No," she cut him off. "You did what had to be done. He had to be stopped. Oh, Hunter, *thank you!*"

She tugged on his hand and he didn't hesitate to let her pull him into a hug.

It was a bit of déjà vu, since they'd gone through this exact routine in the doorway of Dale and Sissy's house. But he'd have been happy to repeat the process on a loop for the rest of his life if it meant he got to keep holding her in his arms.

The urge to bury his nose into the crook of her neck and suck in that sweet, clean smell that was uniquely Grace was strong. But he satisfied himself by simply catching the lock of hair that poked from the bottom of her headwrap and rubbing it between his fingers. Her soft cheek was so warm and alive next to his.

When she pulled back, he saw another line appear between her eyebrows. "What about the troll farm? Did Sam and Hannah find the double agent?" Her gaze snagged on his upper arm. "Wait. Weren't you shot? Didn't you—"

"It was just a graze." He rolled up the sleeve of his T-shirt to show her the large bandage covering the healing gouge through his flesh. He was black and blue from the crash. And his knee and hip still got sore by the end of the day. But he was alive, Orpheus was dead, and Grace was safe. So all was right with the world. "And if you promise me you'll lie back and relax, I'll fill you in on everything you've missed."

"We're goin' to get the others while you two catch up," Merit said from the end of the bed.

Grace's parents, Calvin and June, had gone to the cafeteria with Grace's other brother, Noble, and his wife and children. It'd been decided the group would eat lunch in shifts to ensure there were friendly faces surrounding Grace the moment she woke up.

"Are Momma and Daddy here?" Her gaze was hopeful when it landed on her brother.

Merit made a face. "Where else would they be, silly goose?" Shaking his head at the ridiculousness of her question, he herded the others out the door.

Hunter was left alone then to tell Grace how they'd discovered it'd been the FBI director's personal secretary who'd been the mole inside the government. How the troll farm had been raided and its employees arrested. How Orpheus's real name had turned out to be Pavel Siderov, and how, despite being trained by the FSB, Russia was denying all association with the man.

"It's been the top story for days," he finished. "Luckily, Director Morgan has been able to keep your name away from the press. But I don't suspect that'll last long. Prepare to be a celebrity. The FBI agent who exposed two-hundred traitors working as Russian agents while pretending to be patriots is going to be hailed as a hero."

She blew out a windy breath. "The last thing I want is fame."

He understood the sentiment. His idea of hell was to live a life in the public eye.

Then her face crumpled. "And I certainly don't deserve it. At least not all of it. Stewart might've been a serious pain in the ass. But he was there with me every step of the investigation."

"I suspect when the press sniffs you out, they'll sniff out your partner's name as well. He'll go down in the history books as a paragon of American exceptionalism. There's comfort in that."

"Is there?" Her expression was full of heartache. Just as he'd known it would be. He'd had eight days to mourn the loss of his friends, to allow the edge of his sorrow to dull ever-so-slightly. But her wounds were still fresh. "Is there ever any comfort to be found after that much senseless violence and death?"

"Yes," he assured her, knowing it was the truth. The human condition was amazingly resilient. She would have a period of mourning her losses and second-guessing herself and lamenting that things couldn't have been different. But, eventually, she would move into acceptance. And then her true healing would begin. "And with the help of friends and family and probably a good therapist," he added, "you'll find it even quicker."

Her sad eyes searched his. "You speak from experience."

He nodded. "And plenty of it."

"I'm sorry," she whispered.

"So am I," he assured her. "Sorry the world isn't a kinder or fairer place. Sorry bad people are allowed to hurt good ones and there's no way for me to stop all of them. But I'll never stop trying to do exactly that. And you won't either, Grace. You'll take some time to heal your body and your soul, but then you'll hop right back in the saddle and continue to do your part to bring just a little more peace and justice to this blue marble hurtling through space."

She swallowed convulsively. He could see how much she wanted to believe him.

In due time, she would.

Blowing out a windy breath, she wrinkled her nose and said, "Felix

Graves, huh? I figured it had to be someone above his pay grade."

"Sometimes the smallest mouse does the most damage."

She nodded, her expression remaining troubled and sad-looking. "I guess so. And I guess I should be relieved right? Comforted the corruption didn't go any higher?"

"It went plenty high enough." He thought of the lives that'd been lost thanks to Graves's access to classified information and his association with Siderov.

"You're right." She sighed heavily. Then, she shook her head in wonder. "It's over, isn't it? It's really over?"

"It is. Thanks to you."

"To you too," she was quick to add. And before he could downplay his role, she cursed and squeezed his fingers. "How's your motorcycle? Don't I remember it being—"

"It'll be fine. Becky's been working to fix her."

"I know how much you love that thing."

Not as much as I love you, he thought hopelessly. He loved her and yet, if the past week had proved anything, it was that he was *not* the man for her.

She needed someone who not only knew how to navigate being part of a big, boisterous family, but who also would give her the babies she seemed to think were a foregone conclusion. Someone who could make all her dreams come true and then help her make even bigger, better ones.

His gaze strayed to the only thing he possessed that had any sort of sentimental value. As if he needed another reminder of how *different* they were, he realized she probably had dozens, maybe *hundreds*, of such items. All passed down through the generations of a family that had loved and laughed and made more Beachams year after year.

"That's the second time you've glanced at your watch." She canted her bandaged head. "Do you have to be somewhere?"

"I have a flight to catch. Dale and Sissy's funeral is today."

"Oh my god." Her hand jumped to her mouth. Her eyes instantly filled with tears. "I'm so sorry, Hunter. I didn't…" Her voice trailed off. "If I could go back and undo—"

"None of what happened is your fault, Grace," he assured her, his heart hurting for the blame written all over her face.

"But if I hadn't—"

"Don't." The word came out gruffer than he'd intended. This was the part of her waking up he'd dreaded. The guilt. The self-recrimination. "Don't do that to yourself." He softened his tone. "The kind of work we do comes with consequences beyond our control. If we bear the burden of those consequences, we'll never be able to get out of bed in the morning."

He grabbed her hand and gave her fingers a squeeze. "You need to get out of bed in the morning, Grace. You need to keep thwarting the Michigan Militia and exposing traitors. You need to remind yourself that the *good* you do outweighs any of the bad that's happened."

Her nostrils flared wide as tears streaked down her face. Her voice was barely a whisper when she said, "Is that what you do?"

"It's what I *endeavor* to do." He gave her his truth. "I don't always succeed."

She wiped the wetness from her cheeks with the back of her hand. "I wish I could go with you today. I didn't know Sissy and Dale, but I feel like I did after being in their house. After seeing all their pictures. They looked so happy together."

They'd *been* happy together. Just like the former Black Knights were happy with their partners. Just like the members of Grace's family were happy with their spouses.

In the last three and a half years, he'd been shown just what true, imperfect, *lasting* love looked like. And now that he knew what he'd been missing, there was a part of him that never stopped aching.

"They were the best." A lump formed in his own throat when he thought of the couple, how gracious they'd always been to him, how generous. "Their lawyer called to say I should be there for the reading of the will. I think maybe they left me something."

"Of *course* they did. I think they considered you an honorary grandson. I saw the photo of you with them at their fiftieth-fifth anniversary." Her smile was so sweet. "See, Hunter? More family for you. No matter where you go, family to find you. And do you know why?" When he shook his head, her smile grew wider. "Because you're one of the good ones. Because it's impossible to know you and not love you."

He'd always thought it was simply a phrase. But now he knew it was possible for a heart to actually skip a beat. And the lump in his throat pulled a total Grinch move and grew three sizes.

Could she mean—

Before he could finish the thought, Calvin Beacham's big, booming bass called his daughter's name.

Grace's gaze shifted past Hunter to the open door. The instant she saw her father, her face crumpled. "Daddy, I'm sorry I worried you and Momma. I'm sorry I made y'all leave home and—"

"Oh, pumpkin." Calvin was across the room and gathering his daughter in his arms in an instant.

Grace let loose of Hunter's fingers so she could return her father's hug, and he scooted back against the wall to make room for her mother to take his place beside the bed.

His fingers felt bereft without her touch. In fact, his whole *body* felt bereft by the few feet now separating them.

The few feet and the ticking clock.

As if on cue, his phone buzzed in his pocket. It was the alarm he'd set. Once again, he glanced down at his great-grandfather's watch.

Merit clapped a hand on his shoulder. "You need to head out?" he asked as little Jessie and Jemma, Noble's kids, tried to crawl onto Grace's hospital bed and were scolded to *"git down"* by Noble's wife.

"Yes." Hunter nodded regretfully. "But I'll be back tomorrow evening."

Merit dipped his chin. "Good. We'll see you then."

Hunter started to say goodbye to Grace, but she was busy accepting a hug from Noble while simultaneously listening to little Jemma prattle excitedly about the vending machine in the hall that had gummy bears. He decided it was best to sneak out. To let her bask in the light and love of her family.

He was nearly to the door when Felicity stopped him with a hand on his arm. Grace's little sister shared some of Grace's features. Same dark eyes and blond hair. Same upside-down mouth. But where Grace's face was soft and round, Felicity's cheekbones were high, her jaw square.

"Thank you for all you've done for our Grace, Hunter." Her smile was sincere. "We owe you everything."

"You owe me nothing." He shook his head. "Grace is…" Felicity canted her head, speculation filling her eyes as she waited for him to finish. "Well…" He rubbed a hand over his beard stubble. "She's worth every sacrifice, isn't she? She's simply the best."

The speculation in Felicity's eyes grew more intense. "We think so."

He swallowed when he realized he'd probably revealed too much. "I have a plane to catch. But tell Grace I'll be back tomorrow."

Except fate conspired against him. He wasn't back the next day. Or even the day after that.

By the time he *did* make it back to Chicago, Grace was gone.

CHAPTER 34

Beacham Residence,
Blue Ridge Parkway, Asheville, North Carolina
One month later…

O*ne of the most terrible feelings is crying silently because you don't want anyone to know how broken you are,* Grace thought as she sat on the porch swing at her parents' house.

Since she'd left the hospital, her body had healed—the hole in her skull had knitted and all her various bumps and bruises had faded—but her heart? Her heart refused to mend.

Three people were dead. Her partner. Hunter's honorary grandparents. And it was so senseless. So unnecessary. So…*heartbreaking.*

But perhaps most heartbreaking of all—or, at least it was the thing that kept her awake and aching at night—was that she'd lost Hunter.

Not that she'd ever really had him.

Except, for one beautiful day, it'd *felt* like she had. For a short twenty-four hours, she'd been given a glimpse of the joy and connection that was possible when, like her father had said, her heart found its home in another.

Whoever coined the phrase 'tis better to have loved and lost than never love at all was a slack-jawed idiot.

She thought she'd known pain when Tim left her. Now she knew what she'd felt had mostly been disappointment, a sense of failure and hurt pride. *Now* she truly understood what it was to lose someone she loved deeply, profoundly...*completely.*

She didn't want her family to know just how miserable she was, however. She'd caused them enough worry and inconvenience. So every day she came out to her parents' porch to sit on the swing, look out at the rolling hills that were brightening with the colors of fall, and silently cry.

Cry for Stewart, who'd deserved a chance to grow out of his misogyny and become a man worthy of the title and the badge. Cry for Sissy and Dale, who'd deserved to finish out their days together watching sunsets from the wooden rockers on their porch. And cry for herself, because she felt so aimless and purposeless and *broken* by the whole ordeal, and by the love she'd experienced and then immediately lost.

To be fair to Hunter, he hadn't left her at the hospital without so much as a goodbye. He'd called her brother each day to ask about her progress, but he'd had to stay in Michigan for far longer than planned. Turned out, the Carlsons had left everything to him. He'd had to stick around to get the ball rolling with probate lawyers and estate planners.

He'd sent flowers the first week she'd been home. A dozen yellow roses. And the card attached had simply read: *Wishing you all the best.*

She'd spent a full two hours trying to determine the meaning behind the flower choice. Asking herself, *Is this his way of saying he just wants to be friends?* She'd worked herself into such a tizzy that by the time she'd gotten up the courage to call him to thank him for the roses, their conversation had been stilted and awkward.

Looking back, she wasn't sure if it'd been her fault or his. Or maybe it'd been the both of them not knowing how to behave because she'd been tempted to blurt her love for him, and he'd probably been wanting to thank her for a good time and wish her a fond farewell.

Instead of either of those things, however, he'd simply assured her again that he didn't blame her for what'd happened to the Carlsons, and she'd simply thanked him again for all he'd done for her during the most harrowing time of her life. Then the silence had stretched so tight between them that eventually she hadn't been able to stand it. She'd said she needed to help her mother clean the kitchen. And after she'd gotten off the phone, she'd actually gone to the kitchen to mop the floor because she hadn't been able to bear the thought of having lied to him.

And that'd been it.

It'd now been three weeks, and she'd heard nothing from him but crickets and—

"You could call him, you know."

She looked up to find her father standing beside the porch swing. He had a glass of tea in hand and passed it to her as he sat next to her. She thanked him at the same time he used a toe to push off on the worn, wooden boards of the porch, setting the swing in motion.

The evening wind blew across her shoulder. She turned her face into it, hoping it would dry the tears pricking behind her eyes.

When she thought she could look at her father without blubbering, she asked, "Call who?" all innocent-like.

Her daddy had spent too many years as a lawman to fall for her ruse. He told her as much by giving her a look. *The* look. The one that said, *Don't piss in my boots and tell me it rained.*

She gnawed on her lip and unconsciously tugged her sweatshirt away from her body before relenting. "I tried that, Daddy. I called him after he sent the flowers. But I don't think he really wanted to talk to me."

"No?" A frown pulled at the corners of his mouth. "I can't countenance that. The whole time you were in the coma, he never left the hospital except to go home to shower. A man who's itchin' to bid a woman adieu doesn't act that way."

She'd considered that very thing and was pretty sure she'd come up with the answer. "I think he felt responsible and was sticking around to make sure I woke up. He felt guilty for leaving me when I was hurt to go after Orpheus."

"Mmm." Her father's frown deepened. "But I coulda sworn..." He trailed off.

"What?" she prompted.

Instead of answering, he blurted, "Are you in love with him?"

And there they were, the words spoken right out loud.

Her throat closed up. But she managed to nod and admit hoarsely, "I reckon so, Daddy." Being in the Blue Ridge had brought her accent back with full force. "I mean, what's not to love? He's brave and honorable and loyal and honest. All the things you taught me to look for in a man. And he has this way of listening with his whole body. Makes a woman feel like she's the only person in the whole wide world. But he's got a great big life that doesn't include me. And he's had a month to reach out if he wanted."

She took a drink of tea and stared at the robin that alighted briefly on the porch railing before flittering off. The breeze smelled of fresh rain. And the sky overhead was full of unicorn colors as the sun sank behind the mountains to the west.

It'd been nice to recover at home. Nice to squirrel away in her parents' house because Hunter had been right when he'd said the press would get her name and try to hound her. Luckily, after four weeks of going up against her daddy and the shotgun he whipped out anytime a reporter tried to come on the property, she no longer had to worry about strangers showing up to pepper her with questions she didn't want to answer.

Which meant the quiet and the slow pace of life in the mountains were sinking in. Both afforded her too much time to think. Too much time to wonder *what if?* Too much time to mourn all she'd lost.

Hence, the daily visits to the porch swing.

"Have you heard it said that every hello is just a goodbye waiting to happen?" she mused quietly.

"Lord." Her father made a rude noise. "That's the most depressin' thing I've ever heard."

"But it's true, isn't it? I mean, sometimes it's hours or days before we say our goodbyes to someone who's come into our life. Sometimes it's decades. But there's always a goodbye waiting at the end."

He grabbed the tea glass out of her hand. "Come on, pumpkin. You need something stronger than this. And if we're about to get into the philosophical conversation I think we're about to get into, so do I. Let's put on a pot of whiskey."

She chuckled. Or maybe she choked on her unshed tears. It was impossible to tell the difference.

As she followed her father into the house, her love for Hunter—and the devastating loss of him—felt like a bloodcurdling scream that was trapped inside her soul.

CHAPTER 35

Black Knights Inc.

Hunter adjusted his duffel bag on his shoulder and looked around the shop at all the activity. Becky was busy grinding down the joint on a new frame. Boss was chasing his oldest daughter around and her giggle echoed through the yawning space. Bon Jovi crooned from the second floor, proof Ozzie had returned from vacation. And the sound of pots and pans clattering in the kitchen meant Eliza was hard at work whipping up something delicious.

Coming back to Chicago and the BKI compound after a harrowing mission—*and fuck a duck, this last one was an absolute asshole tightener*—was usually something he looked forward to. The old menthol cigarette factory was the closest thing he'd ever had to a true home. But for whatever reason, this time he didn't experience his familiar sense of relief when he walked through the door.

Instead, all he felt was a sense of urgency.

The rest of the Knights sauntered in behind him, and the big front door shut with an airtight *hiss* followed by a *beep*. His team was quick to disperse. Fisher flung his duffel aside and joined Boss in the chase—much to the delight of little Hazel. Sam sauntered over to chat with Becky. Graham and Britt both headed upstairs to stow their gear. And Hewitt lumbered over to check on his ride because Becky had promised she'd install a new transmission on the fantastical bike while they were away.

As for Hunter? He turned toward the kitchen, intent on talking to Eliza.

He'd barely taken two steps when she appeared at the mouth of the hallway, wiping her hands on the crisp, white apron tied around her waist and smiling her welcome.

"Have you heard from Grace?" His feet had brought him next to her of their own volition.

"Well, hello to you too." She made a face. "Good to see you after nearly three weeks. How was Africa?"

"Hot," he grumbled. "But we were able to prove the intel that came across the president's desk was correct. The Rwandans *are* backing the M23 rebels in the Congo. Shit is about to hit the fan."

"Yeah." She nodded, her expression full of disgust. "That's what I figured."

"Have you heard from Grace?"

He wasn't surprised when she shook her head. The last phone call he'd had with Grace before he'd had to hop a military transport to Africa had been...*awkward*. Although, he *was* surprised when Eliza added, "But her father called this morning."

"Her *father*?" His blood ran like ice water.

"Grace is fine," she assured him after seeing his alarm.

"So why is her father calling me?" He frowned.

"Beats me. But I wrote his number on a Post-it and stuck it to your bedroom door."

She'd hardly stopped talking before he was beating feet. He flew up the metal stairs to the second floor, sparing Ozzie—who was playing air drums—a two-fingered wave. He took the steps up to the third floor two at a time. And by the time he skidded to a stop in front of his bedroom door, he was out of breath.

The pink Post-it Note with the ten-digit number seemed to glow. He couldn't decide if it was a good omen or a bad one. What he *did* know was Calvin Beacham wouldn't have called unless it was important.

After ripping the note off the door, he tossed his duffel onto his bed and had his cell phone out and Calvin's number dialed before he'd fully caught his breath.

"This is Calvin," Grace's father answered after the second ring.

"Hello, Mr. Beacham. This is Hunter Jackson. Eliza said you called. Is Grace okay?" All four sentences came out as one giant stream of speech.

"Depends on what your definition of okay is," Calvin came back and Hunter was suddenly so dizzy, he had to sit down.

Collapsing onto the edge of the bed, he pressed a hand to his forehead. "What's wrong?"

"It's her heart."

For a second, the words didn't compute. Then, they did, and his *own* heart stopped beating. Had the days on the ventilator weakened her cardiovascular system? Had some of the medications affected her heart muscle? "What's wrong with her heart?"

"You broke it."

He blinked. "Excuse me?"

"I will not." Calvin huffed. "But I'd like an explanation as to why you don't think my baby girl is good enough for you."

What the hell is happening? Hunter felt like he'd been dropped into an alternate universe where everyone spoke English, but none of the words made any sense.

"Wh—" He had to stop and clear his throat. "I'm sorry, sir, but I don't know what you're talking about. Grace is *too* good for me. She's smart and funny and brave and beautiful. She's the most wonderful woman I've ever been lucky enough to know. And she deserves the world. Which, unfortunately, I can't give her." He shook his head. "Wait. Did she tell you I broke her heart?"

Hope expanded in his chest as he remembered that thing she'd said in the hospital about it being impossible to know him and not love him.

Had she included herself in that statement?

His hope deflated, however, when Calvin said, "Not in so many words. But I got eyes in my head. Now, what'd'ya mean you can't give her the world? Do you love my daughter or not?"

Hunter flopped back on the mattress. Every single one of his muscles ached from thirty-six hours of travel. Closing his eyes, he thought about how he should respond.

He must've thought for too long because the man's big, booming voice sounded over the line. "You still with me, son? Did I lose you?"

"I'm still here," he replied quietly. "I'm just trying to figure out how best to explain."

"To my way of thinkin', a man can never go wrong with the truth."

He smiled, thinking how much Grace's father reminded him of Grace herself. Calvin Beacham had passed down his no-bullshit, in-your-face honesty to his children. "I don't know if Grace told you anything about how I grew up."

"She said you got a rocky start. So poor you didn't have a pot to piss in and a coupla deadbeat parents who preferred booze to their own boy."

"Mmm." Hunter nodded even though Calvin couldn't see him. "So here's the thing. My whole life I felt like I was living in a dark room. Which was fine. I'm comfortable in the dark since it's the only thing I've ever known. But even still, I was always feeling along the walls for the light switch. And then as the years went by, I started to think maybe there wasn't one. Maybe I didn't *have* a light switch." He swallowed because his voice had gone hoarse. "And then I met Grace and she's the brightest light I've ever seen."

For long seconds, silence echoed from the other end of the call. When Calvin finally spoke, his voice was hoarse too. "So what the hell are you still doin' in Chicago, son? Why the hell aren't you here tellin' Grace what you just told me?"

"Because she deserves so much more than I can give her. I owe it to her to step aside so she can find a man who..." He trailed off and tried again. "A *better* man. A man who's whole."

"I reckon the only thing you owe Grace is the right to choose her own path."

"I can't have children, Calvin," he blurted since Grace's father didn't seem to be picking up what he was laying down. "I'm sterile."

Once again, there was nothing but silence coming from the other end of the call. But eventually Calvin cleared his throat. "Sterile don't mean impotent though, right?"

A startled snort shot out of Hunter. "No, sir. It doesn't."

"So I don't see the problem, then. There's artificial insemination or adoption. Hell, plenty of kids in the foster care system need good homes. And—" Grace's father cut himself off. "Wait. Has Grace ever even said she *wants* kids?"

"Well, no," Hunter admitted, thinking how surreal it was to be having this conversation. "But she's said a few things that make me assume she—"

"Never assume, son," Calvin interrupted, his tone heavy with censure. "You know what they say about it."

"Yes, but—"

"No buts. Get your ass to North Carolina and tell my baby girl all that stuff about being stuck in the dark."

Click.

Hunter was left to stare at his phone.

CHAPTER 36

Beacham Residence
Two days later…

Grace sat on her parents' porch swing, watching the clouds play hide-and-seek with the mountain peaks.

It was one of those days that felt like fall in every way. The sky was overcast. The temperature was cool without being cold. And the smell of damp earth filled the air.

Soon the Appalachians would be burning with color instead of just hinting at reds and oranges and yellows. And she couldn't help but feel a sense of melancholy. The changing of the seasons seemed to put a period on her relationship with Hunter.

They'd been summer lovers.

Now, summer was over.

A low rumble of thunder echoed through the hills and she squinted at the clouds. They didn't seem the type to hold electricity. They weren't the kind that heralded the angry, black, billowing tempests that would sweep across the Blue Ridge, taking down trees and sparking forest fires. They were the low, heavy, *wet* clouds that moved over the peaks like a fog, leaving the air moist without leaving it wet.

Then she realized it *wasn't* thunder when the rumble only grew louder.

Her broken heart was crushed anew.

How long will I equate the sound of a motorcycle with Hunter? she wondered. *Two years? Ten? The rest of my life?*

Would she be eighty years old, wrinkled and working in her garden, hear the sound of a big engine and think... *Once upon a time, I had me a motorcycle man?* And would the same sense of melancholy and loss wash over her then like it did now? Or would she have healed enough to remember the time they'd spent together with only fondness and joy?

She hoped it'd be the latter. She hoped she'd be able to—

Her thoughts screeched to a halt when the motorcycle sounded like it was turning up her parents' drive.

That can't be right, she thought. *Mom and Dad don't know anyone who rides a motorcycle and—*

The cup of tea slipped from her hands when Canteen Green rounded the bend, its big wheels eagerly crunching across the gravel.

Hunter sat astride the detailed machine looking as good as ever in a thick motorcycle jacket and well-worn jeans. The visor was down on his helmet, obscuring his face, but she could feel the moment his eyes found her on the porch swing. What little breath she'd managed to suck into her struggling lungs strangled in her throat and all the fine hairs on the back of her neck lifted as if in warning of a lightning strike.

She couldn't move as he came to a stop near the base of the porch steps and toed out the kickstand. Time seemed to slow to a snail's pace as she watched him pull off his helmet, hang it over one handlebar, and then easily swing his leg over the big bike's leather seat.

He's so beautiful, she thought, her eyes raking over his chiseled jaw, up past his high cheekbones, to lock onto his hazel eyes. Eyes she couldn't read even though she desperately tried to.

Why is he here?

She couldn't think of a reason.

Okay, she *could.* But she didn't want to get her hopes up.

Maybe he hadn't even come to see her. Her family had grown fond of him during the week she'd been unconscious. Maybe he'd come to see them.

The clunking of his biker boots up the worn wooden boards of the front porch matched the hard *thud* of her heart. She wasn't sure what she expected him to do or say, so she simply gaped at him as he squatted to pick up her dropped teacup—thankfully it hadn't shattered or her momma would've killed her—and placed it gently on the wrought iron table next to the swing.

"Mind if I take a seat?" His deep voice was music to her ears as he gestured to the empty space beside her.

She'd lost the ability to speak. The best she could manage was a quick shake of her head.

The chains on the porch swing creaked as he lowered himself next to her. Then he sent them rocking with a gentle shove of his booted toe.

He smelled exactly as she remembered, aftershave and leather oil and the open road. But he didn't look at her. Not immediately. Instead, he gazed out at the view. At the rolling mountains that stretched as far as the eye could see, the tallest ones disappearing into the low river of clouds flowing overhead. At the tips of the trees dancing in the cool breeze. And at the hawk that circled the nearest peak.

When he finally spoke, his voice was low and soft. "It's even more beautiful than I imagined. I understand why you love it here."

Since she wasn't certain she'd regained the use of her voice, she simply stared at him. Waiting for him to continue.

He did. Gesturing to the spot where a thin scar cut through her scalp. "How's your head?"

The hair the surgeon had cut away was growing back. And if she parted her hair down the middle, no one could tell she'd had a hole drilled into her skull.

"It's good," she said hoarsely and had to swallow to continue. "I-I hardly notice it anymore."

"That's wonderful news, Grace." He dipped his whiskered chin and she remembered what it was to have those whiskers tickling her cheeks, her nipples…the insides of her thighs.

The silence resumed as he returned his attention to the expansive view. She studied his profile, appreciated how the helmet had exacerbated his cowlick and tried to be patient as a million questions buzzed through her brain.

Questions like… *Why was that last phone call so strange? What are you doing here now? Do you feel for me even a tenth of what I feel for you?*

The way he wound his watch told her, despite his seemingly relaxed sprawl, he was nervous. But nervous of who? *Her?* Nervous of what? *Did he come with bad news?*

She bit back her questions because she got the impression it wouldn't take much to have him scrambling up and leaving. And the silence stretched on for so long that when the screen door opened, she jumped at the squeak of the hinges.

"Ah." Her father nodded when he saw Hunter. "There you are. Took you long enough."

"Yeah." Hunter dipped his chin. "The ride from Chicago isn't short."

"Hunter?" Grace's mother pushed past Grace's father, who remained standing at the front door. "I made you a cup of tea and put a drop of milk in it, just like you like it."

Grace blinked at the idea that her mother knew how Hunter liked his tea. Then again, her family had officially spent more time with him during her week of unconsciousness than she ever had.

What an odd thought.

"Thank you." He took the teacup and gifted her mother with one of his elusive grins. "You look good, Mrs. Beacham."

"Stop that flirtin' with my wife," Grace's father grumbled. "You got other business to attend to here."

With that, her parents disappeared back inside and she was left to blink after them in confounded astonishment. She turned to Hunter. "Why do I get the impression they knew you were coming?"

"Probably because your dad didn't really give me a choice." He chuckled and the sound poured over her heart like warm chocolate, so sweet and wonderful. He took a sip of tea before setting the cup aside. "I think his exact words to me when we talked on the phone were, 'Get your ass to North Carolina.'"

"You talked to Dad on the phone? Why?"

"Because he wanted to ream my ass for not talking to you for three weeks."

Her stomach sank. As a sheriff, Calvin Beacham had grown comfortable with knowing everyone's business. Which meant he sometimes forgot to keep his nose out of places it didn't belong.

Like my love life.

"I'm sorry." She shook her head, embarrassed and disappointed and so damn heartbroken that he'd come out of a sense of obligation or guilt that it took every ounce of her self-possession not to start bawling. "My father can be—"

"Don't be sorry," he interrupted. "It was just the kick in the pants I needed. In my defense, I was out on assignment and international phone calls weren't really an option. But, still…" He shrugged.

"I hate that you came all this way just because he—" He lifted a hand and the words died in her throat.

"I came all this way to find out for myself if what he said is true."

She was almost afraid to ask, but… "What did he say?"

"That I broke your heart."

She groaned and let her face fall into her hand. "Dear lord."

He tugged on her wrist until she was forced to look at him. The warmth of his fingers sank into her skin and reminded her of how it'd been to lie naked in his strong arms, every inch of her stretched next to every inch of him.

"Did I?" There was so much kindness in his eyes, so much sincerity, she wanted to die.

Why can't the porch boards open up and swallow me whole?

"No." She shook her head, struggling to keep her voice even. "I think it's probably safer to say I broke my own heart. I mean, you never promised me anything. And I knew what we shared in your cabin couldn't last forever. I knew falling in love with you wasn't something—"

"You fell in love with me?"

She screwed up her face. "Duh. Remember what I said? It's impossible to know you and *not* love you. But that's not your fault," she was quick to add. "You don't owe me anything, least of all love. Because love isn't something that's ever owed. If it isn't freely given, it's not love. And I don't—"

"I love you too, Grace."

Her breath shuddered out of her at the same time her heart stopped beating. She *wanted* to believe she'd heard the most glorious words in all the English language fall from his lips. But she didn't trust her own ears.

"From the moment I saw you, there was no past. There was only now and the future I dared to dream of. A future with you in it. You're the air I breathe, Grace. But I can't give you the children you—"

"Wait." She lifted a hand, her brain going in a dozen different directions. There was one thing she was able to grab onto, however. "You *love* me?"

"With all my heart." His handsome, dear face looked like it was ready to crumble. "Like I've never loved anyone in my whole life. But—"

She was across the bench and into his lap before he finished speaking. She had her mouth on his before she even realized what she'd intended to do.

At first his kiss was hesitant. Unsure. Then, he did a little half moan/half hiccup thing that damn near rebroke the heart that'd instantly knitted itself together when he confessed his love, and suddenly his arms were around her. His mouth crushed hers. He kissed her as if his life depended on it.

She had no idea how long they stayed that way, letting their mouths and tongues and teeth communicate all the things there were no words for. Or, at least, no words *big* enough. She only pulled away when she tasted the salt from her tears.

Or maybe those were *his* tears on her lips. His gorgeous eyes were overly bright and tell-tale tracks had left wetness on his tanned cheeks.

Cupping his whiskered jaw in her hands, she assured him, "I don't care if we ever have kids. Having you is enough. But…" She had to swallow because the lump in her throat made it difficult to talk. "But if *you* want kids, if you want to build a family, I'd love to adopt, or foster, or whatever you—"

His mouth was on hers before she could finish. That time, their kiss went from an expression of love and adoration to an expression of lust and longing. She felt him grow hard against her at the same time a rush of wetness slicked her center.

"This is a logistical nightmare," he said when they took a breather. It was either stop what they were doing, or in the next fifteen seconds they'd be ripping at each other's clothes. She really didn't want her daddy to get out his shotgun. "I mean, there are things about Black Knights Inc. I'll need to tell you. But I can't until I get clearance. And since we're on the subject, my job is in Chicago. Your job—"

"Could be in Chicago, too," she told him before he could finish. "There's a field office there. I could put in for a transfer."

His eyes held such hope. "You'd do that for me?"

"Hunter." She framed his face again and thought how good his name felt in her mouth. It was going to feel good there for the rest of her life. How amazing was that? Almost too amazing to believe. And yet…the look in his eyes told her it was true. "I know, because of your background, you're not used to anyone putting you first. But when it comes to me, you need to know, I'll do anything for you."

There it was. That elusive smile. It was so bright and pure and true. And the thought of getting to see it every day until her dying day had her heart expanding so far, so fast she thought her ribs might not be able to contain it.

"I'll only ask one thing in return," she told him, feigning seriousness.

"What's that?" His warm breath feathered her lips, smelling faintly of the mint tea her mother had made him.

"That you promise to love me forever."

He caught her chin between his thumb and forefinger. His expression turned serious. Sincere. "Grace Beacham, I promise to love you for as long as my heart keeps time."

EPILOGUE

Washington D.C.

An assassin was like a mechanic or a dentist. The good ones were hard to find.

Bishop knew there'd never be another like Pavel Siderov. The man had been a machine. Calculating. Cunning. *Meticulous.*

But he wasn't a match for Black Knights Inc.

Not that many were. When Madam President had gone looking for the best of the best, she'd found them.

Sitting back in his desk chair, he steepled his fingers under his chin and looked out the window at the sky roiling above the city. The angry, dark clouds matched his mood.

It was a terrible cut to be down a hitman. But it was salt in the wound to have lost his contact within the FBI.

Felix Graves had been more than an asset. He'd been a compatriot. A true believer in their goal to light a match to the whole damn system and watch it burn. Now, he was dead.

Or he will be soon enough.

Any moment, Bishop expected to hear news the FBI traitor had been found hung by his bedsheets from the light fixture in his cell.

And, sure, there would be raised eyebrows. Anytime a political prisoner died, suspicion surrounded the circumstances. But Bishop had been assured by the guard who'd taken his payoff that all the evidence would point to suicide. And so…one more loose end tied up.

Literally, Bishop thought with a humorless snort.

Which left only…the account.

He'd been careful when he'd opened the account that funded the troll farm. But maybe not careful enough. A good forensic accountant could probably trace the money trail from Russia to him, and so he'd been forced to do something he'd never wanted to do in order to cover his tracks. He'd had to pull a few strings he'd never wanted to pull. Now he owed someone he'd never wanted to owe.

But the end justifies the means, he reminded himself.

As if on cue, the television across the way brightened as the screen was filled with a banner reading: Breaking News! He took a deep breath when the anchor—a pretty blond with fake tits and a too-white smile—announced that Felix Graves, the Russian double agent inside the FBI—had been found dead in his cell.

AUTHOR'S NOTE

As time and society progress, we become aware certain words and phrases that are part of our everyday lexicon actually have problematic origins or can be used to further marginalize already vulnerable readers.

As a writer and a lover of language, I strive every day to educate myself on out-dated, offensive terms and stereotypes, and work to eliminate them from my novels. (We're not talking swear words here, people.) But I'm still learning. And if I screw up, I'd love to be educated and allowed the opportunity to correct any mistakes. Because I truly believe the pen is mightier than the sword.

Or, in simpler terms, *words matter*.

ACKNOWLEDGMENTS

Major thanks to "The Asheville Crew" for keeping me hiking, laughing, and karaokeing. You all save me from atrophying behind the keyboard by forcing me (sometimes unwillingly) out of my pajamas and into the real world. Glad to be on this part of the journey with all of you.

Big hugs to Joyce Lamb for slogging through my first draft. This one nearly killed us when it came to editing and rewriting. But between the two of us, I think we cobbled together a story we can be proud of.

As always, props to the people who do the unsung work of getting a book into readers' hands: Marlene Roberts, proofer extraordinaire, Jennifer Johnson, formatter for the stars, and Erin-Dameron Hill for the beautiful cover.

And last but certainly not least, thank YOU, dear readers, for coming back for more Black Knights Inc. I hope you all had as much fun jumping back into the world of motorcycles and mayhem as I did.

OTHER BOOKS BY JULIE ANN WALKER

BLACK KNIGHTS INC.

Hell on Wheels
In Rides Trouble
Rev It Up
Thrill Ride
Born Wild
Hell for Leather
Full Throttle
Too Hard to Handle
Wild Ride
Fuel for Fire
Hot Pursuit
Built to Last

DEEP SIX

Hell or High Water
Devil and the Deep
Ride the Tide
Deeper than the Ocean
Shot Across the Bow
Dead in the Water

IN MOONLIGHT AND MEMORIES

In Moonlight and Memories: Volume One
In Moonlight and Memories: Volume Two
In Moonlight and Memories: Volume Three

Made in the USA
Columbia, SC
30 June 2024

37925572R00157